Broken Lock

FELICITY RADCLIFFE

DEDICATION

To Peter Hagen, who always encouraged me. You will never be forgotten.

CONTENTS

DAWN

THE OTHER SIDE

EPILOGUE

ACKNOWLEDGMENTS

So many people helped me write this book. Thank you all so much.

I'm grateful that Val Littlewood agreed to design another cover for me. You are so talented, Val. Thanks to you, I'm developing a unique house style!

As with Union Clues, some of my friends make cameo appearances in the story. A few even agreed to appear a second time! Thank you, Chris and Ian Harriman, Esther and Jeremy Crook and the inimitable Jim Packer.

I am lucky to have a fantastic, eagle-eyed group of readers who worked hard to help me improve on the original manuscript. Some brave souls even read it twice! Thank you, Julia Pearson, Mike Hall, Helen Findley, Sally Runham, Hannah Marsh, Val Newman, Joanne Lewis, Chris and Ian Harriman, Fiona Ritchie and Kate. Any errors are all my own work!

My fellow writers in Huntingdon Writers' Group are always an inspiration. Thanks, in particular, to Georgia Rose, Sally Runham and John Sissons.

My book club friends have kept me smiling through a tough year of writing. Maggie Tebbit, Jackie Digby, Ellie McKenzie, Rosalind Southgate, Julia Pearson, Sue Tebbit, Eileen Swanson, Janice Harding, Katy Smith, Emma Penniall and Sarah Fussell – I couldn't have written this without you.

Huge thanks to my wonderful colleagues and fellow scriptwriters at HCR104fm - in particular Sue Rodwell-Smith, Jean Fairbairn, Helen Kewley, Tim Latham and Alice Goulding.

Thank you to everyone who has read Union Clues, especially those of you who have been in touch and given me feedback. I hope you enjoy catching up with old friends in Broken Lock – and making new ones.

Lastly, thanks to my husband Ian. As you're so fond of saying, we didn't kill each other during lockdown – but there's still time...

NATHAN

1 NEVER AGAIN

It's lucky my story starts on Day Zero. I could never have written it inside. Anyone who's been in jail knows the noise is intense. No one's delighted to be detained at Her Majesty's pleasure and many inmates like to make their feelings known, even though the rest of us wish they wouldn't. It doesn't help that there's nothing to absorb this constant din. There are no shag pile carpets in here. Every surface is rock hard, so each anguished scream reverberates, blending with all the other sounds to form a debilitating cacophony. Earplugs are essential if you want to get any sleep, especially if your cellmate snores as loudly as mine does. You might choose to keep them in during the day as well, to stop the noise from messing with your mind. Even so, if you wanted to write a book, I wouldn't fancy your chances.

So Day Zero is my long-awaited release day. Like many others in my position, I calculated the length of my sentence in days when I first arrived here, then divided it by two. I had learned from experience by then and planned to keep my head down and get released on licence halfway through my term, so I patiently ticked off each day and stayed out of trouble while the number reduced at an unbelievably slow rate. It started out in four figures, which eventually became three, then two, and finally single digits. Now, here we are at Day Zero. The waiting is finally over and I'm terrified. That's the polite way of putting it. I promised I would keep it clean and I'm going to do my best. You're probably a nice person and I don't want to upset you more than is necessary. Also, I need to keep you on side. I'm relying on you to make sure I never end up back in here.

Ray and I don't talk much on the morning of Day Zero. Everything has been said. After all, we've had plenty of time to converse. More importantly, we have a morning routine, honed over many months, which dictates that we remain silent until we've topped up our caffeine and nicotine levels. Neither of us sees any reason to change this, just because I'm leaving, and I'd like to give Ray one more ordered, peaceful morning – apart from the constant soundtrack I already mentioned – before he gets a new cellmate, who might not be as co-operative as me. Obviously, if he's not, Ray will lick him into shape, but that will take some effort. So, for one last time, I put the kettle on, make a black coffee in each of our two stained, battle-scarred mugs, then roll my first fag. Ray has two to my one; the first is smoked in a couple of drags before he uses the toilet, and the second in a more leisurely fashion afterwards. I'll draw a veil over the toilet arrangements. You don't need to hear about that. All I'll say is you really get to know someone when you share a cell toilet with them. You're forced to put aside the conventions and niceties which people like yourself take for granted. I wouldn't recommend it as a way of making friends but, if you're lucky enough to share with the right person, you can become close, even if you don't have a lot in common. That's what it has been like, for me and Ray. Now I'm about to leave, it suddenly hits me how much I'll miss him.

While I drink my coffee, I have a quick wash at the sink and dress in my usual T-shirt and tracksuit bottoms. I've had Enhanced status for a long time, so thankfully prison-issue clothing, with its vile stains that never wash out, is a distant memory. Then I check my modest bag of worldly goods for what seems like the thousandth time, although it wouldn't make much difference if I did forget something. Nothing in there is of value to me, either financial or emotional. The only thing I really care about is right at the bottom, wrapped carefully in a pair of cotton boxer shorts. It's a wooden carving of a narrowboat, decorated in bright colours. I carved and painted it myself and made sure it was exactly to scale. I've managed to keep it intact, despite everything that has happened over the past few years. It would be tragic if I left it behind now.

It's nearly time to go. Ray and I both know the exact time at which we'll get the knock on our cell door. Departing prisoners are always collected before those staying behind are released from their cells to begin their day. Ray isn't going anywhere for a long time. If the powers that be knew the full extent of his crimes, as opposed to what he has actually been convicted of, he'd never see the outside world again, but as it is, he still has many days to tick off before he reaches his own personal Day Zero. He can live with it, though. Prisons can't contain men like Ray or constrain their activities to any great extent.

Just before the allotted time, Ray pulls me in for a hug. At this point you might be imagining we have some cosy, banter-filled relationship, like Fletch and Godber in Porridge, or maybe even something more intimate. Neither is true. Real prison isn't like Porridge, and Ray is a dangerous man who doesn't do cosy, as some of his closest allies have found to their cost, when they dared step out of line. He's fiercely loyal to his wife and daughters and, to my knowledge, has never felt the need to seek comfort with a fellow prisoner, while I can't imagine having a relationship with anyone ever again, either in here or on the outside. What I'm saying is - we're close, but I'm always on my guard. You have to be.

Having said that, Ray is keen to remind me, before I leave, about which of his people to contact if I get into trouble. He knows I want to go straight, and he respects my decision, but he also wants to make sure I've got options, just in case things don't go according to plan. As I say goodbye to him for the final time, I cross my fingers and hope I never have to call on them.

I don't recognise the prison officer who accompanies me to reception. Staff turnover is rapid in here, just like in all other prisons. The screws have about as much incentive to stay here as we have but, unlike us, they have a choice, so most of them don't stick around for long, although there are exceptions. Mike, the officer on reception, is one of them. He has been here for many years and is renowned as a fanatical follower of rules, whether or not they make sense. That's why I'm not surprised when he insists on a strip search. Really? What would I want to steal from here? I'm unlikely to be hiding a load of plastic canteen cutlery where the sun doesn't shine. Still, I have no choice, so I submit without protest, and it's not as bad as you imagine. Despite the name, you don't have to take all your clothes off at once; at least, not if the officers are following the correct procedure, which they are, in my case. I say a silent 'thank you' to Mike for being a stickler for protocol as I remove my clothes from the top half of my body, get searched, replace them and then do the same with the bottom half. That's it – nothing more intrusive, I'm relieved to report. You know what I'm talking about. All that now stands between me and the scary chaos of the outside world is a small amount of admin.

To bring back happy memories of my arrival in this place, I'm presented with the clothes I was wearing on the day I was sentenced. I cringe when I open the bag – from the smell as much as the recollection of my despair and humiliation at being sent down a second time. It's not all bad, though. The overcoat will come in handy – it's autumn out there and by the time I've got around to having it dry cleaned, it'll probably be chilly enough to wear it. The suit I wore in court should be useful too, with any luck. I cross my fingers and hope I'll need it for job interviews. At the bottom of the bag I find the silver St Christopher given me by my parents, many years ago. As I pop him in my pocket, I reflect that he hasn't done a particularly good job of keeping me safe; not recently, at least. I guess I have to take responsibility, though, if I'm going to put all this behind me. I must stop blaming other people, including Mum and Dad. It wasn't their fault. They did their best.

As part of the release process, the screws show their caring side by weighing me and taking my blood pressure. No doubt they're keen to make sure I'm going out into the world in a hale and hearty state. I'm positive they have nothing to worry about; I must be a model of health and fitness, after all that wholesome prison food. As they finish up, they point out that my blood pressure is on the high side. What do they expect, for Christ's sake? I'm about to be launched into an uncertain future and I'm shit scared. Sorry - I know I promised not to swear. Anyway, I'm sure my BP will stabilise once I receive the generous allowance I need to regain my foothold in the outside world.

There we go. My discharge grant, all forty-six pounds and fifty pence of it. I tell Mike I'll be careful not to spend it all at once. I won't tell you what he says in response as he hands me the travel warrant which will give me safe passage back to Leicester. I'm lucky I saved as much money as possible this time round, from my various prison jobs, and squirrelled it away in the credit union, otherwise I wouldn't have a chance out there. Right, I just need to sign a couple of forms, then we'll be off.

You probably don't know this, but they make you sign the Firearms Act before they release you from prison. It makes sense, I suppose; I can see why they wouldn't want a load of gun-toting ex-cons rampaging around our towns and cities. However, in addition to guns and other such weapons, you're forbidden from buying or handling fireworks. That's my Bonfire Night ruined, for a start. I sign away my right to light up the sky, then they hand me a final piece of paper with my name on it. It's my release form. My hand trembles a little as I take the piece of paper, carefully sign my name on the dotted line and give it back to Mike. He doesn't even look at me as he puts both forms to one side, ready for filing. As far as he's concerned, I've been processed. Job done.

I know the officer who shows me to the door. His name's Reg and he's one of the good guys. He's no pushover, but he has earned a reputation for being fair and decent. By some minor miracle, he has stuck it out here for quite a few years and hasn't lost his humanity in the process. He has avoided burning out or turning into a cyborg, like Mike. As I'm about to leave, he shakes my hand.

'Good luck, Nathan. Don't make it third time unlucky, will you?'

Then I walk through the wardrobe into Narnia.

You know how it goes in the movies? The prisoner emerges from the jail, blinking at the sudden onslaught of sunlight, and gazes up at the heavens, the expression on his face a mixture of joy and relief. Then the camera tracks across the road, which is miraculously free of traffic, and zooms in on the person waiting patiently opposite the jail door. Maybe it's a mate, sitting in the driver's seat and drumming his fingers impatiently on the steering wheel. Or perhaps it's a beautiful woman, standing tall like a totem, with tears in her eyes as she watches her beloved being released. Anyway, scrub all those pictures from your mind. There's no one here to meet or greet me, which is exactly what I expected. This isn't 'The Blues Brothers'. The sky is grey, and the drizzle soon soaks my tracksuit bottoms, so they cling to my legs as I trudge off towards the bus stop, where a digital display board informs me I have thirteen minutes to wait for the bus which will take me to the train station. The bin is overflowing with fast food wrappers. I sit down and wait patiently. You get very good at waiting, in jail. It's one skill I doubt I'll ever lose.

As I travel on the bus, and afterwards on the train, I try to make myself feel something, anything – but I'm just numb. I watch the flatlands of middle England drift by, the fields sodden and patched with puddles formed by the persistent rain. I see cars queuing at level crossings, their drivers impatient at being held up by my train, and crows circling above the tarmac in search of roadkill. The sight of these birds reminds me I need to eat, and I seize upon that feeling of hunger. It reminds me I'm alive and it's a need I can easily satisfy, with the help of my forty-six quid from the taxpayer. Few of my other needs will be met so easily, and I figure it's a way of greeting the world by doing something normal, which everyone else takes for granted. That's why, when I get off the train at Leicester, I head straight for the station buffet.

It's not a great choice. The food doesn't look much better than prison food, but nevertheless I pick up the topmost in a pile of greasy trays and am about to order a full English, when I spot the cutlery dispenser and peer into its grey plastic troughs. The smallest one, presumably intended for teaspoons, is empty, apart from a few stray breadcrumbs. The other three are crammed with knives, forks and dessert spoons, all made of stainless steel. It's my first encounter with anything other than plastic cutlery in a long time, and for some reason the sight makes the world close in around me. I watch, as through a fish-eye lens, while the man in front of me grabs a knife and drops it onto his tray with a clatter. The sound echoes through my head, more intrusive than the prison racket I'm used to. All of a sudden I feel dizzy; I can't breathe properly. I need some air. I put down my tray and rush through the door, desperate to be out of the station. Once outside, I lean against the wall and wait until the panic subsides. Then I make my way towards the city centre.

I have a couple of hours to kill before my meeting with my probation officer, so when I see the entrance to a shopping centre looming up ahead of me I allow myself to be drawn in. I wander in a daze past the flashy shop façades. Not once am I tempted to go in, or even window-shop, despite the comparative drabness of the prison I've just left – or perhaps because of it. It's all too much, somehow. Too glitzy and abundant. In the central atrium,

I look around at the stalls, which I suppose are meant to lend a market-type vibe to the place, although nothing that's on sale would have appeared on the market stalls I knew as a kid. Home fragrance kits, dried cranberries, chia seeds, goji berries, gourmet ice creams, fancy picture frames and so-called essential oils. They're not essential to me. Who needs this stuff? Plenty of people, it seems. They're milling around everywhere, with glazed, greedy looks on their faces. Queuing placidly to get their eyebrows threaded, whatever that means, or buy three fake pashminas for a tenner, in the hope that this latest bargain will make their miserable lives more bearable for a while. I spot a Burger King near the entrance, remember they don't have knives and forks in there, and escape.

This time I manage not to freak out completely. I'm starving by this point, so I order a towering concoction of burgers, bacon and cheese, with fries and a Coca-Cola. Then I sit down in the corner and almost dislocate my jaw trying to wedge the mega-burger into my face. The explosion of flavours is so intense, after years of bland prison meals, that for a few minutes I just gobble away, until my stomach registers the tsunami of calories and calls time. I sit back, poleaxed, like someone released from a trance by one of those TV hypnotists, and see I've only eaten about a third of it. How does anyone consume a whole one of these meals? I guess it takes practice; I'll have to persevere.

It's time to head off for my meeting. I mustn't be late; that wouldn't be a good start. I have allowed loads of time to find the office, though, and it's easy to locate, so I arrive with twenty minutes to spare. There's a branch of WH Smith next door, so I duck in there and buy a pile of cheap writing pads and a bunch of Bic biros. I'm going to need them, to write the rest of this story. I only had one grubby old pad with me when I left prison and I've nearly filled it up already, before I've even started. It's great to be surrounded by useful stuff – books, stationery, newspapers and the like. I feel calmer than I have all day. In a way, it's the ideal preparation for my first encounter with my new probation officer.

Gemma seems like a decent type. She offers me a cup of tea and chats away while she fusses around with the kettle, teabags and assorted mugs that litter the small table in the corner of her office. I learn she has just returned from maternity leave and hates leaving her son with his grandma every morning, even though she knows he's happy there. Carefully she places my tea mug on a coaster, then opens the biscuit tin and offers me first choice. She shouldn't really, she says, as she has yet to regain her pre-pregnancy figure, but she does. The chocolate Hobnob wins out in the end. Then she sits down opposite me, puts her glasses on, and there's an abrupt mood shift. Suddenly Gemma is all business as she reminds me of my obligations whilst on probation and the consequences if I fail to meet them. I reassure her I'll tow the line and the friendly smile returns as she points out how lucky I am. I agree and the biscuit tin opens for the second time. After the Burger King colossus and these slightly stale biscuits, I probably won't need to bother with dinner once I reach my final destination.

This is what Gemma was talking about when she said I was lucky. Towards the end of my sentence I was assigned a resettlement officer. Everyone's supposed to get an RO, but not everyone does, and few prisoners are fortunate enough to land someone like Martin, who's prepared to fight their corner. He took on the council and tried his best to get me into a B&B, like last time, but it was always going to be a long shot. When you have reoffended, like I did, you are way down the list of priorities, which is understandable, I guess. It would have been a miracle if Martin had succeeded, but he did manage to get me temporary accommodation in a hostel while I sort out my benefits and try to get myself a job. Trust me, that's more than most people in my position usually get. Even so, I'm not looking forward to being in the hostel. I've heard about these places and I'm not expecting room service and a monsoon shower.

As it turns out, my expectations should have been even lower. The place is almost as noisy as prison and the room is about the same size as my cell, with two narrow single beds placed much closer to each other than I'd like. One of the beds is strewn with various grubby items of clothing, so clearly I have a roommate, but there's no sign of him. The walls are paper thin and the threadbare, stained carpets don't absorb any of the racket. Just before bedtime, I venture down the corridor to the shower room with my washbag but end up rushing back to retrieve my flip-flops. Holiday footwear like this is essential when taking a shower in prison. You don't want to know what lurks in the shower trays, and it's no different here in the hostel. Afterwards, I root around in my bag and find my ear plugs, before curling up in a foetal position on my rock-hard mattress, under a flimsy duvet, and praying for a few hours of oblivion. As I lie there, I try not to think back to the years when I would be happy to stay awake in bed at night, listening to the velvet silence of the countryside, broken only by an owl hooting or by the high-pitched, staccato barks of a fox. When I would sometimes be woken by the insistent tapping of a swan's beak on the hull of the boat, imperiously demanding bread. I beg my mind to stop remembering and give me a break by going blank.

Tomorrow I'm off to the job centre first thing, then I'll be heading to the library, armed with one of my brand-new pads. I'm going to write my story for you, just like they asked me to. Thanks in advance for reading it. I know I haven't exactly been a ray of sunshine so far, but I'll try my best to change that. In return, I pray you'll do your bit, stick with me and help give me another chance at life. Goodnight and God bless.

2 PARADISE ADRIFT

My childhood was the kind kids dream about. There was no school, and I lived a new adventure every day. I should explain that I grew up on a commercial narrowboat. We were constantly on the move, delivering cargo all around the country at four miles an hour – on a good day. Our antique boat was always breaking down and its once colourful paintwork was faded and peeling. We were ahead of the game; doing shabby chic long before those trendy designers thought of it. We didn't have much choice, as money was in short supply, but the boat was our home and we loved it. I wanted to spend my whole life on the canals, and I never imagined I'd leave them behind. Things didn't work out that way, but more of that later.

My dad was a lot of fun. During the day he was constantly on the go, steering the boat, working the locks and doing running repairs, but at night he'd often build a fire on the towpath and we'd sit around it, listening to him tell his stories while he carved little wooden toys to keep his hands occupied. He'd tell the same old tales countless times, but on each occasion there was a slight variation. Names and locations were never the same twice; even our family heritage varied according to his mood. On some days, he was proud of our supposed Romany ancestry; on others, we were allegedly descended from a long line of Irish travellers. We didn't care either way; we just loved to hear him talk. Sometimes he'd sing - he had a rare pair of lungs on him - and play either his battered guitar, his rusty old harmonica or even a ukulele he picked up from God knows where.

On some nights, though, we didn't get any stories or music, especially if we happened to moor up near a pub. It was a different kind of evening then. As soon as we had finished dinner, off he'd go, and that would be the last we saw of him until well after closing time, when he'd come weaving back down the towpath singing. If he was off key we always knew he'd had a particularly heavy night. Often he'd be carrying some food he'd traded for a pint of beer; usually something which was of lesser value or impossible to cook in the boat's tiny oven. I recall a large goose – un-plucked and un-gutted – on one occasion. He always expected Mum to be delighted with these dubious gifts and was genuinely surprised at her annoyance. She was particularly unimpressed when he brought back some nefarious character for a nightcap, which happened often, as he easily made instant, lifelong friends when he was in his cups. The poor bloke would be given short shrift and sent packing, and Dad would stay away from the pub for the next few days, until the next time. There was always a next time.

As you've probably gathered, Mum was the sensible one. She taught us to read and write at an age where most kids are still playing in the sandpit at pre-school, and it was the same with maths. She was especially good with numbers, which was just as well, as we were always skint and Dad didn't have a clue, so someone needed to balance the books. My sister took after her; she loved doing her sums, but words were always my thing. As soon as I could write, I started filling notebooks with poems and stories in an attempt to describe the world I saw around me on the canals. Mum bought me a dictionary from a second-hand book shop in Warwick and I tried to use as many different words as I could. I didn't always deploy them correctly, or even put them in the right order, as someone once said, but I loved experimenting. I would spend hours trying to describe the sunflower seed eye of a mallard, the neon flash of a kingfisher or the frenzied powder puff that is a moorhen chick. I've never yet found an activity which absorbs, frustrates and devours time like writing does. I still feel as though I'm in the foothills of my writing Everest, and I might never get far beyond base camp, but the climb's the point, somehow. The summit is irrelevant. I still often get it wrong, as you've probably noticed, but apart from Mum's help, I'm an autodidact. That's my excuse. Anyway, back to the story.

I didn't spend all my time writing, back then. I wasn't allowed to; I had jobs to do. Dad taught me how a diesel engine works and how to repair it, so I was often called upon to help him fix our boat or earn money by helping others who had broken down. I also learned wood carving from him and began making scale models of narrowboats that I painted myself. When we moored up in popular tourist spots I sold them and made myself some pocket money. One time, when we were delayed for a few days in Stoke Bruerne, one of the most popular destinations on the network, we met a boater named Terence who was impressed by my model narrowboats and taught me how to paint roses and castles. If you've never heard of this form of painting, just search for it on Google Images and you'll see what I mean. It's a form of folk art which has adorned narrowboats since the nineteenth century, and which is reproduced on all sorts of everyday items that boaters and tourists love to buy. Once I had learned this new skill from Terence, I quickly put it to good use by restoring and painting any old junk

I could get my hands on. Watering cans, wooden spoons, jam jars, planters, boxes of all descriptions; all got the roses and castles treatment. I'd lay out my wares on the towpath, smile sweetly at the tourists and make a killing on sunny summer weekends and bank holidays. They couldn't believe a young boy could paint so well. Mum helped by embroidering some of my better, shorter poems on pieces of material, surrounding them with flowers and framing them. Although a bit kitsch, they also sold well. Without really meaning to, I'd built myself a modest canal art business which kept me in notebooks, pens and paints, which was all I needed when I was barely into double figures. Sometimes I'd buy a little something for Mum as well. A fancy bar of soap or some chocolates. She deserved it; bringing up a family on the canals isn't easy, particularly when you're married to a wild card like my dad.

As I got older, I began to notice that some of the girls who stopped by my stall were more interested in me than my hand-painted gifts. While this wasn't good for business, it did wonders for my ego. On more than one occasion I was likened to a young David Essex and I began to play up to it. I started dressing in a baggy white shirt, dark waistcoat and red scarf, like the Seventies pop star and your archetypal boaters from a bygone age. I grew my hair, so it was floppy like David's – or like David's used to be – and I pierced one of my ears with my Mum's darning needle, then shoved a cheap silver earring through the hole. It took a few days for the infection to subside but, once it did, I was pleased with the overall effect. Obviously this look wouldn't have got me into a trendy nightclub in Manchester or London but, here on the canals, it was a hit with the pretty girls who were out for a day trip or on holiday with their families. I don't doubt that the novelty of the canal Casanova would soon have worn off, for most of them, but luckily our boat always moved on before that could happen. Throughout my teens, our itinerant lifestyle allowed me to flirt and fool around with any girl who was up for it, secure in the knowledge that I could soon make my escape. Sailors with a girl in every port had nothing on me. Occasionally a girl would show up my youthful arrogance for the sham it was, and my heart would temporarily be broken, but I always bounced right back. In truth, girls were a side issue for me. My main concern was how I could someday acquire my own boat and strike out on my own, but however many wooden spoons and watering cans I sold, I couldn't see how I would ever raise enough money. Nevertheless, I was constantly trying to think of ways to achieve the independence I craved. Much as I loved my family, with each year that passed I grew more desperate to escape the cramped boatman's cabin I shared with them and forge my own destiny on the canals.

My big break, or so it seemed at the time, came when I was twenty. Our narrowboat was moored up in Birmingham for the summer. Mum had secured temporary jobs for her and Dad, as money was especially tight after a hard winter and spring. I started doing odd jobs for the old boys who ran cargo boats out of Gas Street Basin, and quickly made a name for myself as the eager young dude who'd do the work no one else wanted, or which their ageing limbs were unable to manage. One old guy, Jeremiah, became a particular friend. We'd sit together on the towpath every morning, smoking roll-ups and watching office workers scurry past on their way to the glitzy high-rise buildings which had sprung up behind the old sorting office. To them, I'm sure we looked like vagrants, people who were losing at life; but I wouldn't have traded places with them. I thought it was us who were the winners, right up until I walked down the towpath one morning to find Jeremiah gone.

It was a stroke, the others said. Lucky that Jake dropped in on him for a nightcap or he'd never have survived. So I rushed up to the Queen Elizabeth and began the first of many long vigils at his bedside, notebook in hand. I'd listen intently to the sounds Jeremiah made, write down what I thought he was saying and show him the page in my notebook, to see if I'd written down correctly what he was trying to convey. At first I was rewarded only by an impatient shake of the head, but eventually I started to tune in to him and got a few words right. The first time this happened, he grasped my arm with his left hand, while his right lay on the blanket, inert and useless, and his eyes filled with tears. Encouraged, I pressed on, doing what the nurses didn't have time for and desperate to help my friend regain as much speech and movement as possible. Every evening I reported back to Jake and the others on his progress, and sometimes one or other of them would accompany me, but I was there every day. I had become fond of my old mate and it was my first encounter with serious illness. With the arrogance of youth, I thought I had the power to make it all better, as long as I put in the effort and the hours.

After a couple of weeks, they let me push Jeremiah around the corridors in a wheelchair and, once I had written 'sun' in my notebook for the third time, I realised he was longing to go outside. For an old man who'd spent his life at the tiller of a narrowboat, being confined to a hospital ward was clearly intolerable, so I got permission to take him into the hospital garden, and it was there that he asked the question. The three words took ages to form and there was a long gap between each one, but there was no mistaking their meaning.

Take

My

Boat?

I looked up from my notebook. My friend stared intently into my eyes as his own watered with the effort of conveying this vital information. He needed help, so I obliged with a few questions he could answer easily, with a nod or shake of the head.

'Are you saying you want me to look after your boat?'

Jeremiah nodded.

'Have you got any jobs lined up?'

Another nod and finally a new word in the notebook – 'Jake'.

'You mean Jake'll tell me what to do?'

A nod and a smile of relief.

'So, let's make sure I've got this straight. You want me to take care of your boat and run your jobs - just until you're better and can get back to it?'

Jeremiah shrugged and grabbed my hand. I saw the 'thank you' in his eyes and did my best to reassure him.

'Don't you worry. I'll run your jobs for you, and I'll keep your boat in great nick. I promise. I won't be able to come and see you when I'm out on the cut, but every time I'm back I'll come straight up here and let you know how things are going. In the meantime, Jake and the rest of the lads will visit you – I'll make sure of that.'

OK. I can't put it off any longer. Before I head off on Jeremiah's boat, I need to tell you what was happening with my sister while I was hanging out with the Birmingham old boys. I should have brought her into my story earlier, to be honest, but at least I'm doing better than she did. I gather she hardly mentioned me when she had the chance to write her story. So, like the responsible older brother I used to be, I'm going to lead by example and tell you about me and Nancy.

She was born in London, two years after me, so I can't remember a time when she wasn't around. People who said we were chalk and cheese didn't get us; we were more like two halves of the same person. The things I loved, she mainly hated, and vice versa. I was obsessed by books; she only ever opened a book under duress. I'm amazed she ever managed to write her story for you. From the moment she could pick up a guitar, she spent every spare moment playing and singing, whereas I was always strictly an audience member and couldn't sing a note. She loved numbers, did Nancy, and she's good with money, whereas cash has always slipped through my fingers. While we both felt completely at home on the canals, I never had her down as a lifer, like me. It always seemed she was destined to leave them behind. She was never fascinated by everything canal-related, like I was. I loved the changing landscapes and wildlife, while she couldn't tell a mallard from a coot. We did have some things in common, though. She could strip down and repair a diesel engine as efficiently as I could and, when we became old enough to drink, we both acquired a taste for it, which didn't always enhance our lives, as you'll find out.

Like you would expect from two young kids cooped up together in a tiny boatman's cabin, we fought constantly, but if anyone outside the family had a go at us, we'd instantly defend each other. Usually it was me who was called upon to fight Nancy's corner, rather than the other way round. From the moment she learned to talk she had a right gob on her, which frequently landed her in trouble, and I would always bail her out. I was the classic protective older brother, particularly when we were teenagers and guys started hitting on her. I should mention that, while my sister didn't fuss about her appearance like most teenage girls, she was gorgeous. Still is. She has always been very matter of fact about it, so she probably didn't mention it much in her story, but her beauty did mean I spent a lot of my adolescence fighting off a bunch of creepy canal boaters. Sometimes I was overzealous and drove away dudes she liked, which inevitably caused a few arguments, but she always forgave me in the end. Back then, I was her sensible older brother, and she was my wild little sister. While I was eager to get away from my father and lead an independent life, I always knew I'd miss Nancy. However, I trusted in the strength of our relationship and was confident we'd stay in touch after I left. I thought I'd be the one to leave first, but I was wrong. She beat me to it.

Here's how it happened. Nancy had got herself a 'girl and guitar' gig in one of the canal side pubs, performing under her alter ego The Baroness. I told her it was a daft name, but she took no notice of me, and she was right not to listen. One night, she was discovered by a record company guy, who had called in at the pub on his way to cover a gig at the National Indoor Arena, and that was it. She was spirited away to London and her brilliant career began. I admit I was scared for her, at first; terrified the ravenous music industry would consume her and the Nancy I knew would be changed for ever. I should have had more faith. My sister remained the feisty girl I had grown up with and fought her corner perfectly well without me. Before long The Baroness was loved and admired by millions of fans, but offstage she was still the same Nancy. After I left Birmingham to begin my adventures on Jeremiah's boat, she bombarded me with texts, phone calls and photos charting her new life. Whenever I travelled through London and she was in town, we'd meet up, and I'd go to her gigs. I even dropped in on the recording studio a couple of times and tried to be cool if I saw someone famous in the corridor or the canteen. Everything had changed for both of us, but our relationship was still as strong as ever.

So I toured the country on Jeremiah's boat. At first I just picked up his jobs, but when Jake phoned and gently told me that my old friend would never be discharged from hospital, I started looking for my own customers. I didn't make a fortune from transporting cargo, but I supplemented my income by selling my canal art, so I made ends meet, even if a lot of my cash disappeared over the bars of various canal side pubs. It was in one of these establishments, a few months later, that I met Ruth. She was drowning her sorrows as she had lost her job, and I was doing similar as I had just received the news that Jeremiah had died the previous night, leaving me his boat. I had no jobs coming up, so I stuck around for a while, carving my miniature narrowboats, painting my watering cans and waiting to see if our instant, alcohol-fuelled hook-up would turn into something more - and it did. It wasn't a 'love at first sight' kind of thing; it just felt right, somehow. Ruth was the opposite of my sister – blonde, curvy, calm and gentle. The sort of person with whom you could easily coexist on a narrowboat. After a few weeks I persuaded her to leave her rented flat and join me on the canals. She hadn't found another job and was running out of money, so looking back, I guess it wasn't a difficult decision for her to make.

Ruth quickly learned to work the locks and adapted easily to life on the waterways. True, I had to make frequent stops at marinas with shower facilities, and every few weeks she insisted we moor up near a town so she could go shopping and get her roots done, but this was a small price to pay. For the first time in my life, I felt secure and serene. My feisty sister, wayward father and stern mother had never made me feel this way, and I discovered I liked the cosiness that Ruth brought into my life. On a practical level, she transformed my existence. She cleaned up Jeremiah's boat and made it far more habitable, then took over the books, managing our money effectively so it went a lot further, despite our drinking habits. Gradually we discovered a shared sense of humour and developed a repertoire of private jokes. She'd listen as I read out my new poems and she came to love the view from the canals as much as I did. We delighted in seeking out wildlife along the way – kingfishers, herons and occasionally a water vole or a family of otters. Often we'd sit together on the towpath in the evenings, watching the bats flutter through the gathering darkness and holding hands in silence. Our love wasn't the thunderbolt kind. It was the type of love that just creeps up on you.

The following year, the Fates supplied their own thunderbolt. Ruth discovered she was pregnant. It wasn't planned, but we didn't care; we were both overjoyed. The only downside for me was that Nancy wasn't pleased for us. She had never liked Ruth from the start. I remember the conversation we had after the two of them had met for the first time. It was getting late, and Ruth had gone to bed, tactfully leaving us to catch up. We were sitting on the towpath at the side of Regent's Canal, working our way through a bottle of JD which Nancy had brought with her from the flat in Stoke Newington where she was living at the time. In true Nancy style, she didn't hold back when I asked what she thought of my first ever long-term girlfriend.

'She's not for you, bro. She's way too nice. Too soft.'

15

'What d'you mean?'

'She's got no courage. No loyalty. If there's ever a choice to make, she'll go with whatever's easiest for her. She might seem really sweet, but she'll never stand up and fight your corner.'

'And you know this – how?'

'I've met a lot of girls like her, in the music business. They're fine when everything's going well, but when your luck changes, they're gone.'

'So what kind of girl d'you think I need? A carbon copy of you; someone I'd fight with every day of my life? I can't believe you've got such a downer on Ruth. I mean, she was so nice to you earlier…'

'Exactly. I'd rather you were with a mean little cow who hated me, but loved you, than some bland person who's terribly polite to me but doesn't really care…'

'Are you saying Ruth doesn't love me?'

'Not from what I've seen.'

'You're wrong about that.'

'I hope so, bro. Anyway, whatever. It's your life. Doesn't change anything between you and me.'

But it did, of course. Although we stayed in touch just like before, something had been lost, and it was my fault. Much as I loved my straight-talking sister, I struggled to cope when she was candid with me about Ruth and I deluded myself that her warnings were motivated by jealousy, as she could never hold down a relationship of her own. Looking back, I can't believe I expected our baby news to make things any better. I mean, if you've read Nancy's story, you'll know kids really aren't her thing, but I thought she'd feel differently about my child. She didn't, of course; she just thought I had dug myself in even deeper. Her attitude hurt, so I ignored her, stopped returning her calls and focused my attention on the mother of my child.

After we left Nancy and London behind, we headed back to Birmingham. We moored up in Gas Street Basin, my old stomping ground, and had no jobs coming up, so we agreed to take some time out and decide whether we could bring up a baby on the canals or whether we should leave the boat behind. At one time I could never have imagined doing such a thing, but I obviously knew how hard it was growing up on a narrowboat and wondered whether it was what I wanted for my own child. Ruth and I spent two days talking it to death, without reaching a decision. In between I hung out with my old mates in GSB. I asked myself whether I wanted to be like them, when I was their age, and concluded I didn't. It looked as though it was time to say goodbye to the waterways.

On the morning when our fortunes changed, Ruth had gone shopping. I resolved to tell her, as soon as she returned, that we should jack it all in. I was sitting on the roof of our boat, smoking a roll-up and drinking a mug of tea, when I spotted a man walking towards me. He wasn't the type of bloke you normally saw around the Basin; his jeans were too clean and his polo shirt and padded gilet way too smart. He stopped beside the boat and rested one hand on the guardrail.

'Good morning. I must say, you bring down the average age around here by about thirty years. My name's Giles Fernsby.'

'Nathan Parkinson.'

'Is this your own boat?'

'Yes; I inherited it from an old friend.'

'It looks like a fine working boat. You don't see many of them on the network, these days.'

'It's in better nick than it used to be, now my girlfriend and I have cleaned it up.'

'Very impressive. So, do you and your girlfriend run it as a working narrowboat, or is it just a hobby boat?'

'No – it's very much a working boat. We're between jobs at the moment but normally we travel all over the network, delivering cargo to our clients.'

'Perfect.'

'How d'you mean?'

'I would like to offer you a job.'

Giles explained that he needed someone to pick up a consignment in London and deliver it to a location near Manchester. I nearly fell off the roof when he told me what he was prepared to pay. Then the penny dropped, and I felt compelled to ask the question.

'What's in the consignment?'

'I can't tell you that, Nathan. Sorry.'

'In that case I can't accept the job.'

At that moment Ruth appeared, clutching several bulging carrier bags in each hand. The largest, adorned with bright splashes of primary colour, bore the name 'Jackie's Baby Boutique'.

Giles looked Ruth up and down. 'You must be Nathan's girlfriend.'

'That's right. I'm Ruth.'

'Delighted to meet you, Ruth. I'm Giles. Are you expecting a happy event? Only I couldn't help but notice your bag…'

Ruth blushed and smiled at him. 'You're very perceptive, Giles. Yes we are. We only found out recently, and I'm getting ahead of myself by doing baby shopping already, but I don't often get a chance to visit any decent shops, what with living on the boat…'

'So I gathered. Nathan was just telling me about your interesting life afloat. Look, I won't keep you. Nathan, give my offer some thought. I'll come back in the morning and you can let me know what both of you decide.'

17

Giles walked swiftly away, and Ruth watched him go. 'What was all that about?'

After I had helped her bring the shopping onboard, I explained about the offer Giles had made and why we couldn't accept.

'How much did he offer?' asked Ruth.

When I mentioned the sum involved, Ruth took my hand and gently explained how she felt I was being too hasty. She pointed out that the money would enable us to transform the boat into a home fit for a child, which we could never have afforded to do otherwise. It would help us to stay on the canals – the place where I truly belonged. Then she diffused my moral objections by arguing that, if we genuinely didn't know what was in the consignment, we weren't really doing anything wrong. After all, we weren't taking ownership of the goods, just transporting them on someone else's behalf. We were providing a service – end of story. Why shouldn't we take the opportunity to make our lives a little easier, when we worked so hard all the time? We owed it to ourselves, but above all, we owed it to the baby to prepare for his arrival in the best possible way.

We debated throughout the day and on into the evening. Ruth made dinner and opened a bottle of red wine, even though she wasn't drinking, for obvious reasons. She kept topping up my glass, so I finished the bottle with my meal, then rounded the evening off with a few shots of malt whisky. As we sat together on the roof, watching the bright lights of Birmingham dance and waver in the oily waters of the canal basin, Ruth whispered in my ear that our encounter with Giles was meant to be and we should accept the job. The next morning, she stood beside me while I explained how we had reconsidered. It was her hand that Giles shook first.

'You won't regret this,' he said earnestly.

He was right about that. She never did.

3 LOCKED OUT

I didn't see Giles again for a very long time. His business partner Gary got in touch with us later that day and made the arrangements for the job. As requested, we delivered the goods to a remote wharf outside Manchester, and everything went according to plan. Apparently Giles was delighted. Gary and Ruth organised the transfer of funds to our account and the money came through promptly. I breathed a sigh of relief and accepted another job from one of my regular clients in the Midlands. Then Ruth and I headed south.

We were on the Macclesfield Canal when I got the call. I was negotiating a tricky stretch and there was a boat coming in the other direction, so I asked Ruth, who was sitting next to me, to answer my phone.

'Yes, I'm sure that'll be fine. The timings should work out, but you'll need to give us a couple of days' leeway in case we get held up…OK…will do. Bye.'

'Who was that?' I asked her as she smiled up at me. With her round, pink face and shiny blonde bob, she was a poster girl for healthy pregnancy. Untouched by morning sickness, all she had to contend with was an insatiable craving for peanut butter and tuna sandwiches. She reached up to the boat's roof for her plate as she told me Gary had another mission for us. We were to pick up in Birmingham after we had finished our current job, then deliver to various locations in the south west. The fee would be slightly more than we had earned last time. Apparently we qualified for a small bonus, as we had completed the first assignment on schedule.

My stomach lurched as I heard the news. I had assumed the Giles and Gary job was a one-off, was relieved to have got away with it and had been trying to forget it, but clearly Ruth felt differently. In fact, we came close to having an argument, which would have been a first for us. I insisted that Ruth ring Gary and cancel the job, but she refused and, to cut to the chase, she persuaded me to change my mind. Nancy had said she was soft, but in reality I was the weak one. Ruth suggested she deal directly with Gary from then on, to make things simpler, and I let her get on with it. The second job also passed off without incident and, after that, a pattern was established. I negotiated jobs and fees with all my other clients, whilst Ruth became the contact for Giles, Gary and the rest of their team. Gradually, over the next few months, they requested our services more often. Occasionally there were clashes between the jobs for my regular clients and those Ruth had booked. The latter always ended up taking priority, but luckily my other clients could usually be flexible, so we didn't lose out.

By the end of that year, our bank account was looking healthy, and we had our own little miracle who put our newfound wealth into perspective - our son, Arthur. Whenever I held my little boy in my arms, my worries and guilt faded away, and I couldn't get enough of his company. I spent every spare moment jingling a rattle over his head and bouncing him on my knee, desperate to be rewarded with one of his gummy smiles. I read to him every night, hoping that, at some level, he would absorb the magic and musicality of 'Hiawatha', 'The Jungle Book' and countless other classic children's stories and begin a lifelong love affair with books, like I did.

Despite all the happiness Arthur brought into our lives, it wasn't long before the challenges of bringing up a baby on board a narrowboat began to make themselves felt. Arthur soon learned to roll over and shuffle around the floor, so we were forced to move everything off the lower shelves. Soon every storage space was full to bursting and each surface was awash with baby paraphernalia. The interior of a six-foot wide boatman's cabin can never feel spacious, but suddenly it was as though the walls were literally closing in on us. Having shared a similarly confined living space with three other people, I didn't find it hard to adapt, but Ruth really struggled. Often, when we were moored up near a pub, she'd send me off to have a few drinks, just so she could 'breathe', as she put it. Our child was healthy and growing fast, but our living space was diminishing, along with our relationship.

One night, I was sitting alone at the bar of a waterside pub in Warwickshire, admiring the canal art that lined the walls, when this bloke came and sat down next to me. I quickly turned away, as he looked like an undercover cop, and Nancy and I had been trained by Dad to steer clear of the rozzers at all times. He was a big unit; barrel chested and with the faintest hint of dark stubble shading the huge dome of his head. His black padded jacket was pockmarked with raindrops, the bottoms of his jeans were damp, and his trainers were spattered with towpath mud. Effortlessly he caught the barman's eye, ordered a pint, then turned to look at me.

'Refill?'

'I was just heading off, actually...' My voice came out as a strangled falsetto and I silently willed myself to man up.

'And one for my friend here.'

'Well, if you're sure – that's very kind of you.'

When the barman returned with the beer, the man nodded in the direction of a nearby alcove. 'Ruth told me I'd find you in here. I've got something to say, and you need to listen. I won't keep you long. I'm sure you want to get back to your kid.'

At the mention of Arthur, a wave of nausea hit me. I meekly followed the man towards the alcove, my beer slopping over the rim of the pint glass and soaking my trembling right hand.

When we sat down, my companion stared fixedly into my face. His expression was designed to intimidate. I tried hard to meet his gaze, but the intensity was too much. My eyes kept betraying me by flicking away towards the damp and ragged beermats on the table between us.

'I'm a friend of Gary's. He tells me you've done quite a few jobs for him, over the last couple of years.'

'Yes,' I wavered. 'For him – and Giles.'

The man's face darkened when he heard the name Giles. He reached across the table and grabbed my wrist.

'Let me make one thing crystal clear. If ever anything goes wrong, you never mention any of us. You get what I'm saying? You grass on us, you're dead.'

'Is there a problem?' Another high-pitched squeak; so much for manning up.

'There's no problem. We're just making sure all the necessary security arrangements are in place. You just do the job you're on now, plus all the other jobs we ask you to do, and keep your mouth shut. Got that?'

All I could do was nod, but it wasn't enough.

'Sorry, Nathan. I'm not convinced you fully understand. I think I need to give you some examples of what we do to people who tell tales...'

So he did. He described at length, in graphic detail, how a number of people who had indulged in careless talk had met with nasty accidents and been dragged from various canals and locks months, or even years later. He explained how a body could fall into a lock and be pulled down into the murky depths by the flow of water through the open paddles. He boasted that a verdict of accidental death had been recorded every time. Then he drained the rest of his beer in one gulp and placed his glass with exaggerated care on one of the beermats.

'One more thing. Don't think you can outrun us. We've got people everywhere, so we'll always find you and Ruth. Plus that cute little boy of yours.'

After he left, I downed several shots before heading home to face Ruth.

I shakily described my encounter with Gary's nameless friend, expected her to be terrified, and was astonished at how unconcerned she seemed. Apparently the same man who had threatened to kill me was perfectly friendly to her and assured her there was nothing to worry about; he just needed a quick word with me about our next job. While I paced up and down the boat, panicking about how to get ourselves out of the deadly situation into which I had sleepwalked, Ruth told me I was being silly, and we just needed to be careful and keep our heads down. Everything would be alright, she soothed. We just needed to hold our nerve.

This time, though, I refused to be swayed by Ruth's calm reassurances. I knew that, had I been strong enough to stand up to her when we first met Giles, we wouldn't be in this trouble now, so I stood firm. I told her we'd drop off our current consignment as agreed, to avoid arousing suspicion, then that would be it. We'd ditch the boat, dump our phones and laptops, go off grid and lie low for a while, then use the money we had saved to begin a new life away from the canals. Maybe we'd go to Ireland, land of my dad's real, or imagined, forefathers. At any other time, the thought of leaving the canals would have been a real wrench, but now, with all our lives potentially at stake due to my cowardice, I didn't care. I just wanted to save my family.

Ruth argued with me for a bit, then let it go. I think she finally twigged we were in danger and I wasn't going to change my mind. To be honest, I don't reckon she ever wanted to be a boater her whole life and I could tell the thought of getting our own place was starting to win her over. She didn't say much; she just stopped arguing and retreated behind her laptop. Later on, when I looked over her shoulder, I saw she was on Rightmove and knew she was convinced I was right.

Two days later, we arrived on time at the remote Midlands wharf where we were scheduled to drop off our consignment. I was impatient to unload and depart as quickly as possible, so we could begin the journey to the dead end of the Ashby Canal, where we planned to abandon our narrowboat. As it wasn't on the way to anywhere, I figured the location would be off the gang's radar and they wouldn't find the boat in a hurry, if at all.

I tied up at the wharf while Ruth stayed on the boat, giving Arthur his lunch. Then I walked over to a shabby prefab set back from the canal, to find the men who would unload the cargo. As I stepped through the door, I encountered two thickset blokes in jeans and dark hoodies sitting either side of a rickety table, with a flask and two steaming mugs of tea.

'Are you Nathan?' said the one nearest me.

'Yes. You were expecting me?'

'Sure we were,' said his mate.

Then both of them stood up and walked towards me. Their intense, serious expressions told me something bad was about to happen and I instinctively raised my arms in front of my face to ward off the anticipated blows. I realised self-defence was my only option; there was no way I could take both these thugs on. I braced myself for the pain, but it never came. Instead, the first thug pulled my hands away from my face and pinned them behind my back. Cold metal bit into the flesh of my wrists and the shock of what was happening made my head spin. The second guy must have noticed I was struggling to take in what was going on, because he grabbed both my shoulders and put his face close to mine, so I could smell the mix of tea and peppermint on his breath.

'Can you listen carefully to what I have to say. You are under arrest on suspicion of possession with intent to supply a Class A drug. You do not have to say anything, but it may harm your defence if you do not mention, when questioned, something which you later rely on in court. Anything you do say may be given in evidence.'

To this day, I have no idea who tipped them off.

I can't recall how many times I was interviewed, or by how many different officers, during the days that followed. It wasn't like you see in films and on TV, with lots of shouting and fingers wagging in your face, but then again it didn't need to be. The rozzers can be forceful enough, without resorting to those tactics. Even so, I never departed from my story; not once. In a weird way, I'm proud of how I stood up to them. Even when the lawyer they assigned to my case begged me to say who I was working with, I refused to give him a single name or provide the cops with any leads to Giles, or whatever he was really called, and his gang. The only thing I said in my defence was that I was unaware of the contents of the consignment, but I don't think anyone, including my own brief, believed me, despite my genuine shock when I discovered the type and quantity of drugs secreted among the seemingly innocuous cargo. However, when I insisted Ruth knew nothing about the job, the jury readily accepted she wasn't involved. When she was called as a witness, she came across as a sweet, naïve young mother who was not too bright. She was never under suspicion for a moment.

So I went to jail, with a scathing indictment from the judge ringing in my ears. I was almost happy to have the metaphorical book thrown at me; consumed by guilt and self-loathing, I felt it was the least I deserved. I won't dwell much on the years I spent inside, first time round; suffice to say it took me a long time to learn the ropes and I didn't cope well with being incarcerated. Things might have been different if I had a life to go back to, but it disappeared the minute the prison doors shut behind me, or probably even the moment I was arrested. I tried to get in touch with Ruth, as I was desperate for her and Arthur to visit, but I was informed by the prison authorities that she wanted no further contact with me. After hearing the news I began self-harming and virtually stopped eating. I'm not sure I would have come out of there alive, if it hadn't been for Nancy's letters.

I found out years later that my lawyer got in touch and told her I was in jail. I'm sure he only bothered in order to have an excuse to contact her. By that time she was quite a big star, so it would have given him something to brag about to his fellow law students. Yes, that's right – my lawyer was only part-qualified when he was assigned to my defence. That's all you get, when you can't stump up the money to fund your own legal representation. It made no difference to the outcome, though. No lawyer could have kept me out of prison – not unless I had agreed to name names, and I was never going to do that. I didn't care about saving myself – I just wanted to protect Ruth and Arthur.

So Nancy wrote me at least one letter a week, from all around the world, during the whole time I was inside. She never once said 'I told you so' about my relationship with Ruth or mentioned her estrangement from me while Ruth and I were together. Instead, she talked to me about the places she visited on tour, the venues she played and the albums she recorded. Her letters were full of funny anecdotes about her band members, complaints about the stiffs in her record company and stories of fleeting hook-ups with various guys she met on her travels. In her early letters, she mentioned she had told Mum and Dad what had happened but had spun the story slightly so it didn't reflect as badly on me as it might have done. Basically, she played down the drugs angle and portrayed me as an idiot who had been hoodwinked by a sophisticated criminal gang. I guess that isn't too far from the truth - particularly the idiot part. She could truthfully have added that I was weak, deluded and greedy, as I constantly told myself, but she didn't. I guess she figured I had suffered enough.

I'm ashamed to say I didn't answer any of her letters and refused to allow her to visit me when she came back from her tours. The kid who couldn't stop writing poems and stories was long gone. In his place was a man who had sunk so low that he couldn't write a word to the sister who clearly wanted to show she still loved him, no matter what. To Nancy's credit, she kept on writing. Maybe she knew I would read her letters over and over again while I was inside, which I did. I still have them all today and look at them regularly, even though the later ones are darker and don't make easy reading. I should explain that, towards the end of my time inside, Dad got sick, so Nancy's anecdotes were mostly replaced by progress reports on how he was responding to treatment. I struggled to imagine my vibrant and rebellious Dad being weakened and diminished by illness, and when Nancy eventually wrote to say he had died, I just felt numb. The starburst of pain from a razor blade provided fleeting relief from my stupor, but it wasn't enough. The prison authorities offered to let me attend the funeral, but I refused, unable to face anyone else's grief, including my own.

It never occurred to me that my presence could have been a comfort to my mum and sister. Back then, I couldn't accept that anything I might do would have a positive impact on other people.

For the remainder of my sentence I thought constantly about replacing guilt and shame with oblivion. Every water pipe, metal grid, bunk bed and razor blade placed temptation in my path, but there must have been a glimmer of self-preservation in there somewhere, or maybe I was too passive to make that ultimate decision. Instead, I let myself be processed by the system. I shuffled between my cell, the canteen and a succession of mindless prison jobs. My mechanical skills and my literacy could have been my passport to some of the most sought-after jobs in the prison, but I never put myself forward. I felt I deserved nothing, so I received the bare minimum in return.

I was lucky that one person made the effort to jolt me out of my apathy, in the weeks before I was released. I was assigned a resettlement officer called Tony, who is in no way to blame for how things turned out first-time round. I'd definitely have been worse off without him. He tried to track down my narrowboat, only to find out it had been abandoned not far from the wharf where I was arrested. The boat licence expired soon afterwards, and it was eventually removed from the network by the Canal and River Trust. Then he helped me contact my bank and it transpired that Ruth had emptied our account, so I was broke. That was no great surprise. Undaunted, Tony hustled tirelessly on my behalf and managed to secure me a place in a B&B. He advised me how to find a job and claim benefits, and gradually I began to hope it might be possible to rebuild my life. Tony made it clear that looking back was not an option; he gently broke the news that Ruth had married and did not wish me to have access to Arthur. In his opinion, it would be better for both me and my son if I didn't attempt to make contact until my circumstances had improved. Reluctantly I agreed. I didn't have a lot to offer my boy back then.

So Tony did his best to recondition me in preparation for the road ahead. I'm not sure I'd have passed an MOT, but I did come out of prison determined to make a fresh start, which was a big improvement on the leaden, self-destructive state I'd been in just a few weeks previously. The B&B wasn't the sort of place a nice person like you would want to take the family on holiday, but it was preferable to both prison and the streets, and at first I tried hard to make the best of it. I spent my days at the Job Centre, hoping to land a job as a mechanic, but I soon realised an ex-convict with no formal qualifications was never going to be top of an employer's wish-list, particularly during a recession, when unemployment was spiralling upwards, and it was a buyer's market. I managed to land a job as an office cleaner, but I was sacked after a week because I was rubbish. You'd think anyone could clean, but I couldn't. I scrubbed away, but I just seemed to move the dirt from one place to another and I was dead slow. I don't blame them for firing me. Then I got a job in one of those coffee shops where stressed office workers expect their drinks and food to be ready in about twenty seconds. I had to learn a whole other language; I had no idea what a 'skinny americano' was supposed to mean, let alone a 'chai latte'. Coffee and tea, that was all I knew when I started working there, but I was soon immersed in a world of paninis, espressos and mocha frappuccinos. I was gobsmacked at how much people would spend on a hot drink and a filled roll, but it was a job and I tried to do it as best I could. I was slow at first, which drove the boss crazy, but he didn't sack me and gradually I improved. I might have done OK, might even have been promoted to section head or manager, as people were always leaving, so opportunities came your way if you just stayed put. All I had to do was stick at it; but then I met Nina and things unravelled very quickly.

Nina moved into the same B&B as me and was given a room on the floor below. We met in the hallway when I was taking out the rubbish and she was trying to navigate her way back to her room. I remember it was the afternoon - I had been on the early shift at the coffee shop and had just got home – but she was already wasted, and I helped her find her door key, unlock the door and crash out on the bed. I put a bucket and a jug of water by her bedside and left her to it, chalking it up as my good deed for the day, and thought that would be it, but the next day she knocked on my door to say 'thank you', clutching a sorry bunch of flowers which she had obviously picked from a park, or someone's garden. I was touched and pleased to see her in a better state than she had been the previous day. Also, she was cute, in a battered kind of way, so when she asked me to join her for a drink at the pub down the road, I found myself accepting.

Now I've never touched drugs – unless you count booze and a bit of weed. Ironic, really. Nina, though, was into every mind-altering substance she could get her hands on. I begged her to seek help, or at least self-medicate with alcohol instead. I figured drinking was better than taking drugs. The trouble was, Nina was happy to stick to alcohol and weed when she was with me, but the rest of the time she continued using. In the meantime, my drinking spiralled out of control. Like my dad before me, I struggle to find my 'off' switch once I get started on the booze, and suddenly I was drinking with Nina every night after work. It didn't help that I missed my former life on the waterways and alcohol helped me forget what I had lost - for a few hours, at least.

At first we went to the pub every night, but neither of us had much cash, so after a few weeks we figured it made sense to drink in our rooms instead, to save money. So we smuggled in bottles of vodka and spent the evenings swigging, smoking, shouting and arguing. Nina soon got tired of hearing me complain about my life and reminisce about the canals, and I got angry every time I found evidence that she was still using. The next day, I would invariably wake up hungover and full of remorse about what I had said and done the previous night. Every morning I vowed I wouldn't drink that day, but every evening I succumbed and drank even more. I started being late for work and was soon missing entire shifts. I received a written warning and promised my boss it was the wake-up call I needed, and I wouldn't miss work again, but I couldn't stick to it. On the day I was fired, I came home with a litre bottle of vodka, intending to drown my sorrows with Nina, but she had split. I later found out she was living with a fellow addict and small-time dealer. I guess vodka, spliffs and fights just weren't enough for her.

All this time I was still getting letters from Nancy. I reckon the prison service had given her my forwarding address. When things were going better for me, I had been tempted to reply, but somehow I never got round to it and, now I had lost my job, I was too ashamed to contact her. I did manage to find myself some casual work – cutting lawns, that sort of thing – but it wasn't enough to keep me in vodka and I started getting behind with my rent. Soon enough, I received a warning letter telling me I would be evicted if I didn't pay the arrears within thirty days. Predictably, I headed straight down to the off licence and hurried home with my brown paper bag, eager to make the bad feelings disappear. As I approached the front door of the B&B, I saw a tall man in a smart jacket, neatly pressed shirt and chinos standing nearby. When he spotted me, he moved quickly and placed himself between me and the entrance.

'Are you Nathan?'

'Who are you?'

'Someone with a business proposition for you. A chance to make a lot of money. Let's discuss it over a drink.'

When I learned that the man, whose name was Hadley, was an associate of Giles, I stood up and tried to walk out, but he grabbed my arm and pulled me back down into my seat. He explained that Giles, Gary and the rest of the team were 'very impressed' by the way I had refrained from implicating them after I was arrested. They apparently felt bad that I had benefited very little from all the 'hard work' I had undertaken on their behalf. He also reported that Ruth had been siphoning off the proceeds of our illicit jobs into her personal bank account from the start, to finance a new life for her and Arthur away from the canals. Even if I had never been caught, she would apparently still have split once she had squirreled away enough cash. I had no idea how the gang found this out, but it sounded plausible to me and totally consistent with how Ruth had treated me after I went to jail. Hadley sounded almost angry on my behalf, as though he was a mate who thought I deserved better.

Over a couple of pints, he explained that everyone felt I had been unlucky. It was very rare for a person to get caught and they had all agreed that the least they could do was make it up to me. For this reason they were going to give me the opportunity to do a couple of extremely lucrative jobs, to fill my coffers and give me enough money to buy my own boat. After that, if I chose not to work with them again, there would be no comeback. I would be free to resume my previous life as a commercial boatman and purveyor of canal art to tourists. They would never contact me again.

I asked Hadley to give me some time to think about it and we arranged to meet in the same pub a week later. Then I returned to the B&B and thought hard about what to do next. Halfway down the vodka bottle, I decided to bite the bullet and do something I had been meaning to do ever since my release; pay a visit to my mum. In her letters, Nancy had said she was struggling on her own and wasn't in the best of health. She hadn't been able to face life alone on our family boat after Dad died; there were just too many memories. So she had sold up – although our old boat didn't raise much cash – and she was currently boat-sitting for a friend near Rugby over the winter while said friend was visiting family in Australia. So the next day, I walked to the station and bought a ticket to Rugby.

I can't talk much about my reunion with Mum, even after all this time. It's still too painful. Like Nancy, Mum had always been naturally skinny, but even so I was shocked at how emaciated she looked. Her skin was a translucent, sickly yellow, stretched taut across her cheekbones and loosely wrinkled in the hollows of her cheeks. She grasped my arm tightly with one hand and I looked down at her exposed knuckles and the skin splashed with purple bruises. Then I stared into her pale blue eyes, glazed over with tears, and tried to tell her how sorry I was, but she just turned and shuffled away across the cabin. When she came back, she pressed something into my hand.

'What happened to the boy who made this?'

I looked down and saw one of the miniature narrowboats which I had carved as a youngster. It was more intricate than the ones I had sold to tourists, and painted with far more care, so I must have made it specially for my mum. My eyes filled with tears. 'I lost my way for a while, Mum, but I'm getting back on my feet, I promise. I'm going to buy another boat as soon as I can, then you can come and live on it with me. We'll be a proper boating family again, you'll see. I'll make it happen.'

Mum always knew me better than anyone else. I knew her, too – well enough to realise that she was trying hard to believe me but couldn't. I wanted so much for her to look at me with pride, just like she used to. So I told her to wait and see; to have faith. I left shortly after, promising to come back soon with my own boat. The following week I told Hadley I would do two jobs, and no more, and agreed a lucrative fee which would enable me to buy an old boat and do it up. In return I was given temporary use of a battered working boat and details of my first assignment.

I completed this first job without incident and then took some time out to rediscover the canals. It was a huge relief to be back behind the tiller. I immediately found the strength to quit the vodka and stuck mostly to tea, apart from the odd beer in a canal side pub in the evening. I began looking for an old commercial boat to restore and bought a brand-new notebook and a set of paints, ready to resume my poetry and canal art. Things were starting to look up, until one night a text message flashed up on my phone from Nancy.

The text began with the words: 'Urgent – do not delete. Read immediately.' Even if it hadn't, I would have known something was up. Nancy had communicated solely by letter ever since our bust-up over Ruth's pregnancy, so I knew it must be an important message. I clicked on the SMS and received the devastating news that Mum had died. I never got the chance to prove myself to her; on the other hand, she didn't live long enough for me to disappoint her even further.

This time, I told myself to man up and go to the funeral. I had always felt ashamed of my refusal to give Dad a proper send-off and, even though I had one more illicit job to do for the gang, I was already looking beyond that to a new life afloat; impoverished, perhaps, but free. I figured that facing up to my responsibilities by honouring my mother would be a first step towards that new life. So I texted Nancy and told her I'd be there. She responded with a simple thumbs-up emoji. There wasn't really anything else to say.

There weren't many people at the crematorium. It's difficult to gather the boating community together in one place. The small group of mourners followed me and Nancy to a nearby pub for the wake, then gradually said their goodbyes over the course of the afternoon and melted away back onto the canal, while Nancy and I stayed on. The tempo of our drinking quickened with every round and soon what we perceived to be 'the truth' emerged, providing fuel for a bitter fight which had been years in the making.

To those of you who are grieving, I send a big hug and hope you eventually find a way to live with your loss. I'm sure you'll agree there's no 'getting over' these things. Promise me one thing, though. However bad it gets, remember Nathan's Law. You can't drink them back to life, however much booze you pour down your neck. Believe me, Nancy and I tried, that night, but it didn't work and inevitably ended in anger and tears. Nancy started off by asking why I didn't reply to the hundreds of letters she sent me and ended up screaming at me in the street, after the pub had closed, that it was my fault Mum and Dad were dead. I had broken both their hearts, she sobbed. Her strong, sensitive older brother had turned into a coward and she wanted nothing more to do with me.

As she staggered off to her hotel, I followed at a distance, to make sure she got back safely, and no one hassled her. Thankfully Rugby is generally quiet on Tuesday evening and, tottering along in her black funeral coat and huge black hat, she was unrecognisable as The Baroness. I watched her summon the night porter and stagger into the lobby, then turned away, reflecting sadly that I had seen and heard the last of my little sister, and it was all my own fault.

The following week, I got the call from Hadley and headed for a pick-up point near Birmingham that I had been to on a couple of occasions with Ruth. The location didn't exactly bring back happy memories and it didn't feel like a good omen either. As it turned out, my instincts were spot-on. Unknown to me, this was always going to be one of the gang's high-risk jobs, and they had entrusted it to one of the few people who they knew wouldn't grass them up if things went wrong. Which they did. History repeated itself, only with a longer sentence for a repeat offender. This time I was tempted to talk, but I didn't. As before, fear kept me silent.

My first few weeks in jail marked the lowest point in my life. As you've heard, there have already been some dark times; all self-inflicted, I hear you say, and you're absolutely right. I know it. This time, though, I sort of gave up. I started self-harming again, more frequently than before, was barely eating and might well have given in to my suicidal thoughts if I hadn't got one of the luckiest breaks in my life. My cellmate was moved to another jail and his place was taken by Ray.

Tough love doesn't begin to cover it. From the minute he walked through the door of our cell, Ray took no crap from me and showed no mercy for my predicament. He listened to my story and dismissed my self-pity with a few choice words. Then he set about teaching me how to serve a smart term in jail. He respected my wish to go straight, so he never got me involved with anything illegal, but once he learned what skills I had, he set about using them to our mutual advantage. When I told him I could strip down and rebuild a diesel engine, and repair all sorts of other mechanical items, he couldn't believe I had just sewn flags when I was in jail before. He got me to repair his broken items, then used his extensive network of contacts among the prison officers to secure me a job in the workshop, a prestigious and sought-after role. I spent my shifts stripping down televisions to extract the precious metals and reconditioning radios and household appliances. It was far more interesting than my previous prison jobs - and those I had managed to get whilst living in the B&B.

When I got to know Ray a little better, I confided in him about my writing. I thought my revelation would be greeted with derision; on the contrary, Ray saw it as a business opportunity. We established a lucrative side-line in ghost-writing letters and poems to inmates' loved ones, for a modest fee. I'm sure many wives and girlfriends out there wondered how their men had suddenly acquired the ability to write lyric poetry, but they didn't complain. I churned out hyper-emotional, romantic verse by the bucketload, they lapped it up, and Ray and I made a killing. Ray had all sorts of other schemes going on, but I figured he liked working with me because it was completely legit and very easy money.

As well as making good business partners, Ray and I made decent cellmates. It's not that common to be allocated a cellmate with whom you can exist quite peacefully, so we were grateful. As I said earlier, we soon established a well-ordered routine and stuck to it. I was the junior partner, of course. I made tea and coffee, rolled cigarettes and deferred to Ray in most matters. Every evening I read the newspaper to him, as he said he just wanted to lie down after dinner and close his eyes. One evening, after we had been cellmates for a few months, I was settling down as usual with a copy of the Daily Mail, when I made an off-the-cuff remark that changed our friendship for ever.

'Sure you don't want to read the paper yourself, Ray?'

'No. Why would I, when I've got you to do it for me?'

'Not being funny, but I could just be making it all up. If I were to say that England had won the World Cup, or that war had broken out, you wouldn't be any the wiser. Not that I would – make it all up, I mean. But you take my point.'

Ray was silent for a long time, and I started worrying that I'd put my foot in it and would come to regret my loose tongue. Then finally he spoke.

'I can't read, Nathan.'

I couldn't believe Ray had built up a huge criminal network without being able to read, but he explained to me how he skipped school so often and made so much trouble when he did show up, that he got kicked out before he had learned. It didn't hold him back, though. Even as a youngster, he was tough, street-smart and ruthless, which were qualities he needed in his line of work. Only a handful of associates in his inner circle knew his secret and helped him cover up. None of them would ever reveal what they knew; they had no incentive to do so and were well aware of the consequences if they did. Nevertheless, Ray considered it a 'regrettable shortcoming'. His words, not mine.

'I'll teach you, Ray.'

'Could you do that?'

'Sure I can. I'll have you reading in no time. Trust me, it'll change your life.'

After that, I spent an hour with Ray every evening teaching him the alphabet. As I expected, he caught on quickly and soon progressed to simple words and short sentences. Before long he was conversant with the basics of English grammar and started reading The Sun. Eventually he became a regular visitor to the prison library and powered his way through two or three crime novels a week whilst complaining that most of them were 'completely implausible'. When he reported back to me on a piece he had read in the Financial Times, I knew my work was done.

So that was how Ray came to trust me and look out for me. Thanks to his tough love, I stopped self-harming and stashed most of my earnings away in the credit union, in preparation for my release. It seemed like things were looking up.

A few months into my sentence, I got a letter from Nancy. She apologised for her behaviour at the funeral and said she wanted us to have another crack at being brother and sister. We owed it to Mum and Dad, she said. By then I was spending most of my evenings writing letters for other people, to help maintain and repair their relationships, but I couldn't bring myself to reply to my own sister although, just as before, she kept on writing and I read all her letters countless times. She asked when I was being released and said she wanted to meet up when I got out, but I never gave her the date or made the arrangements. Although life had improved so much for me during my second stint in jail, and my self-esteem had dragged itself off the bottom of the ocean floor, the bright water at the surface was still a distant memory, and I couldn't accept that I had anything to offer my hugely successful sister. In fact, no one in the jail, with the exception of Ray, knew we were related. Once in the canteen, I had to sit on my hands when one of my fellow inmates saw her picture in a newspaper and casually described what he'd like to do to her. I was determined not to jeopardise my chances of parole by getting into a fight, so I kept quiet and kept my nose clean.

At last, here I am. Released on parole and washed up in this hostel. I've got a lot more miles on the clock than when I set out on Jeremiah's boat and there are a few grey hairs mixed in with the black. Along the way I lost a child, two lovers, a few teeth, my family, my livelihood and my self-respect, although I'm trying to claw the last two back. Every day, when I wake up, I tell myself, no matter how cheesy it sounds, that today is the first day of the rest of my life, the past is over and done with, and today is a gift – that's why it's called the present. I grasp at any cliché which might help me move forward into a new future. Onwards and upwards, that's where I'm headed. Coming?

4 FESTINA LENTE

On my first morning in the hostel I wake early with a sense of urgency. I can't drop anchor here; I'll only be able to stay for a short while and, in any case, I'm not tempted to hang around any longer than I have to. I must have slept quite deeply during the night, as my roommate is crashed out in the other bed and I didn't hear him come in. Although it looks as though it would take a cyclone to disturb him, I creep quietly from the room, have another shower in my flip flops, return briefly to get dressed and grab my notebook, then drop in on the breakfast room. I smother my gnarly bacon sandwich in copious amounts of tomato ketchup to render it edible, wash it down with black coffee, then I'm out of there. Everyone gets chucked out during the day, but I don't fancy the staff's chances of turfing my roommate out of his pit and onto the street by half eight.

I arrive at the job centre as soon as it opens and approach a guy behind a desk who's tapping away diligently at a keyboard. His name-badge tells me he's called Nick. He stops typing and listens as I explain my circumstances. I mean, really listens; he looks at me the whole time and his eyes don't once flick towards his computer screen. It's a long time since anyone apart from Ray has listened to me this intently and I'm encouraged. However, when Nick starts to search the database for job opportunities, it's the same old story. I have a choice between another job in a coffee shop or stacking shelves in a supermarket. It's not Nick's fault, of course, but he bears the brunt of my frustration, although I do manage to keep my temper, I'm pleased to say. I bend his ear with tales of the engines and appliances I've repaired, both on the canals and in jail, and show him photos on my phone of my paintings and wood carvings. He promises he will keep his eye open for suitable vacancies, but I can tell he doesn't hold out much hope. Then he gently suggests I attend an interview with the manager of the coffee shop, who has a policy of recruiting ex-offenders who are committed to reintegrating into society. I can always do a night class after work, he suggests, to get some formal qualifications. I tell myself this is the best I can expect right now and try not to look too disappointed as I agree to the interview. Nick has done his best.

The coffee shop is indistinguishable from the one I worked in before. Aggressive, entitled customers – tick. Periods of frenetic activity at peak times, followed by hours of boredom spent cleaning tables and worktops – another tick. At least there's less of a learning curve this time; I soon remember how to prepare a skinny latte and a flat white. It's not exactly difficult. Day after day I do my job and am polite to Roksana, Pavel and the rest of my colleagues. Whenever my shifts allow, I return to the job centre, where I always try to speak with Nick if I can. I ask him if anything suitable has turned up and he invariably assures me he's keeping his eyes open and will call as soon as he finds something, so I needn't bother dropping in. I keep on visiting, though. I want to stay in his face and make sure he doesn't forget me. In the meantime, I begin my search for a room in a shared house. I know any place I can afford won't be salubrious, but I have to get away from the hostel, the putrid showers and my comatose, malodorous roommate.

One afternoon, after my shift, I'm just getting my stuff out of my locker when I notice there's a missed call and a voicemail on my mobile, which doesn't happen often. Even though I expect it to be a contact centre asking if I've been involved in an accident that wasn't my fault, I return the call, ignoring the voicemail message. I'm delighted when Nick answers, but if anything, he sounds even more excited than me. I have the feeling he doesn't often get the chance to relay good news. I hear the smile in his voice as he announces he has found me what could possibly be my dream job. He tells me that Bastion Marina, located in the north of the city on the Grand Union Canal, is looking for an odd job man. Better still, they can offer accommodation in the form of a semi-derelict caravan on site, if the successful candidate is prepared to renovate. Nick has explained my history to the manager, who has agreed to see me the following day. All the information is apparently in the voicemail I ignored. I can't say 'yes' fast enough. I negotiate time off from my shift at the coffee shop; the manager is unimpressed, but I don't care. With any luck, I'll be out of there soon. That night in the hostel, I carefully lay out a clean black hoodie and my best pair of black jeans, ready for my interview the following day. I should explain that I haven't turned into some sort of ageing goth since my release. Black clothes aren't allowed in prison, and neither are hoodies, so I scoured every charity shop in the city when I got here, looking for cheap black hoodies, jeans and T-shirts. It was one of the few affordable ways I could find to put some distance between me and my years in jail.

The next day, I show up at Bastion Marina fifteen minutes before the allotted time. The woman behind the desk in the marina office informs me that Geoff, the manager, is doing a tour of the marina with a potential customer, but will be back in time for our interview, and she's right. Ten minutes later, a tall man wearing a Bastion sweatshirt ushers his client into the office, hands her a brochure and shakes her hand. Geoff has a battered complexion, wild grey hair and, incongruously, the upright bearing of someone with a military background. As his customer leaves, he turns to me and holds out his hand.

'You must be Nathan. I'm Geoff. Would you like a coffee, or a tea?'

'Coffee please, Geoff. Black. Thank you.'

'Linda, can you bring us two coffees, please? Come on through to my office, Nathan, and let's have a chat.'

Once we're settled with our coffees, Geoff skips the small talk and asks me to tell him about my life on the waterways and how I came to end up in jail. I know he has heard my story from Nick already, but clearly he wants to see if our accounts match. I figure I might as well be completely honest, so I come clean with the whole sorry tale, but make sure I weave in a few mentions of the engines I've repaired and the boats I've restored over the years. I conclude by saying I'm determined to make a fresh start and would work my socks off for Geoff and his team. I stop short of outright begging, but only just. Then I take a deep breath and ask Geoff if my life story has put him off giving me the job.

'Relax, Nathan. The job centre told me a bit about your background, and it wasn't a deal breaker, or I wouldn't have agreed to the interview. I appreciate you being so honest with me, and now I'll level with you. I haven't always been an angel myself. My navy career didn't end well; I was dishonourably discharged and struggled to get a decent job for years afterwards. This was a failing marina when I first came here; the city location isn't ideal and we had a real issue with break-ins back then, hence the name Bastion, to convey an impression of security to the punters. It has taken me years to turn it around, but now we're doing quite well, although there's still a lot of work to be done, which is why I need someone like you, to tackle all the jobs I haven't got time for and free me up to recruit new customers to fill the empty berths. I'll tell you what. How about I walk you round the site, show you some of the jobs which need doing, and you tell me how you'd tackle them?'

Geoff leads me out of the office into the sunshine and I follow eagerly in his wake. The jobs he points out are relatively straightforward and I'm confident I could handle them all. I talk him through how I would approach each one and point out a number of other things I could do to improve the look of the place, including restoring some of the signs, which are peeling and bleached from the sun. After about half an hour, we reach the far end of the marina and pause outside a battered old caravan. Filthy towels are draped across the windows in place of curtains and one corner is propped up on a precarious pile of bricks, where a wheel used to be.

'OK. If you're willing to take the job, all this could be yours.' Geoff gestures towards the caravan and smiles. I can't quite process what he's saying. For the first time in years, someone is giving me a reason to hope, and it takes me a while before I can babble my incoherent thanks.

'Are you serious? I can't believe…cheers Geoff! Thanks for giving me a break. You won't regret it…I'll do all those jobs we spotted, and more; there must be loads of stuff that needs fixing around the site, and I'll smarten the caravan up as well – you won't recognise it in a few weeks…'

'Woah – pace yourself, Nathan! We don't want our new hire to burn out, before he has even started. Let's go back to the office and I'll introduce you properly to Linda, my office assistant. The lady who brought us coffee. Then we'll call Nick at the job centre with the good news and get started on the admin. I guess you'll have to work a short notice period at the coffee shop, which is fine; I want us to do this properly, so don't leave them in the lurch. If you want to, though, you can move into your des res as soon as you like. You might have to kick out a few rodents, but otherwise it's yours.'

Fast forward a few weeks and I'm the sole occupant of my caravan, having eradicated the mice, and am possibly the happiest odd job man in the east Midlands. I spend my days working through the backlog of repair jobs and my evenings making the caravan habitable. When I'm too exhausted for DIY, I relax with a free book from the marina library or carve and paint my miniature narrowboats. I have access to the shower and toilet block, so for the first time in years I can take a shower in bare feet. I know this is a pleasure you probably take for granted, along with the privilege of using the toilet in private – or maybe not, if you have young children. Whatever; I'm just telling you I appreciate every single one of these showers. I love feeling properly clean and, when I look in the mirror, a more presentable, slightly younger-looking person stares back at me. I'm scarcely recognisable as the floppy-haired canal lothario of my youth, but no matter. Life is improving, that's the main thing. I'm on an upward spiral.

I enjoy working with Geoff and Linda and, over the next few months, I get to know them better. I discover Geoff has been through two acrimonious divorces and we spend many convivial evenings on his boat, sharing a few beers and trading stories about how women have ruined our lives. I know, it doesn't sound like a lot of fun, but it's strangely cathartic. I also meet a few of his friends, most of whom are resident moorers in Bastion, and join them on their regular trips to the local pub. Gradually, I become part of the crew. I haven't felt at home like this since I spent the summer with Jeremiah, Jake and the rest of the old boys in Gas Street

Basin. I don't feel the need for female company; like Geoff, I actively steer clear of women. Not that they're forming an orderly queue for either of us, but I'm not tempted to seek them out. Linda's the only woman in my life right now. We share the daily crossword, a love of chocolate digestives, and that's about it. I listen while she complains about her two teenage sons, then cast my mind back and try to help her understand the primordial soup that is the mind of the adolescent boy. She's divorced as well, and her ex isn't much help.

It's funny, really, how so many people like Geoff, Linda and me, who have been kicked in the teeth by life, find their way onto the canals. On the surface, the waterways appear to be full of happy families and self-satisfied, prosperous couples enjoying holidays afloat. Look a little closer, though, and you'll find the flotsam and jetsam; people who are running away, dropping out, trying to make a fresh start or just struggling to survive. All hoping the canals will provide a refuge where they won't be judged and can live life their way. Here's to us; the underdogs who form the underbelly of the English canal network. The interesting part. I pray we all find what we're looking for.

Through Geoff and Linda, I meet a variety of tradesmen who show up regularly to work on the narrowboats moored in Bastion Marina. Jim the electrician, with his funky facial hair and quirky sense of humour, always has more jobs than he can cope with. Tony spends long days blacking hulls in the dry dock, but it's heavy work and he's not getting any younger. Boats which need repainting get their makeovers offsite but Alan, a talented local signwriter, can change their names in situ, and he's frequently called upon by customers who have just bought a new narrowboat. It's supposed to be unlucky to change the name of a boat, but lots of people are happy to risk it in order to be rid of a name that's inappropriate or just plain embarrassing. Take Gina, for example. Recently divorced and eager to begin a new life cruising the waterways, she searches high and low for her dream boat and eventually finds it. Trouble is, said boat goes by the name 'Old Codger', which is not the image she's looking to portray. In all other respects, though, it fits the bill exactly, so she buys it, moors up at Bastion and commissions Alan to rebrand it. Every time I get a few spare minutes, I pop down and watch as he transforms 'Old Codger' into 'Naiad', or water nymph, which is much more appropriate for a free spirit like Gina.

Once these tradesmen discover what I can do, they start asking me to help them out. I check with Geoff, who's happy for me to develop a few side hustles as long as it doesn't interfere with my main job. Before I know it, I'm swamped with work. None of the tradesmen is based at Bastion, so it helps them to have someone on site who can cover off the smaller, more straightforward jobs, while they focus on the larger, more lucrative assignments and cream off a percentage of the money I earn. Suddenly my days and evenings are fully occupied, and I have to turn down work in order to fit in the occasional pub night with my boating posse. I'm earning enough to make ends meet and living in a place where I feel like I belong. It all sounds perfect, but I'm sorry to say it isn't enough.

The trouble is, every time I see a narrowboat leaving the marina, I want to be on it. It's torture being right next to the waterways I love, but unable to enjoy them. Don't get me wrong; I know I've landed on my feet here and could easily still be in the coffee shop, or worse. I'm grateful for everything I have, and I'm determined not to screw it up, but it doesn't stop me from yearning for a boat of my own. It'll be years before I can afford one, though, even with my enhanced earnings. Ah well. It's my own fault for losing the boat I was given before. There's nothing for it but to knuckle down, save my pennies and stop moaning. I know what Ray would say if he could hear me whingeing, but I won't repeat it here. It's not for your ears.

Occasionally I do get out onto the canals, after a fashion. Our hire boat customers call us up with a whole raft of problems and, if they're close enough and we can't resolve the issue over the phone, we sometimes go out to them. Geoff likes to send me whenever he can, as it can easily mean being off site for half a day. So I hop on Linda's electric bike and pedal to their rescue. You'd be amazed at what constitutes an emergency for some of these people. One family assured me their shower was broken, but when I reached their hire boat I discovered they had just run out of water. Geoff and I always explain how to fill up the water tank, but clearly they weren't paying attention. On several other occasions, customers have been adamant that the propellor has seized up, but when I get there I find out they've just got a load of detritus wrapped around it; waterweed, garden twine, pairs of knickers, you name it. Some of the stuff I've cut off the propellors of hire boats could be entered for the Turner Prize, I kid you not. My favourite, though, was the guy who called up and said all the electrics on his boat had failed. So I grabbed my tools and cycled fifteen miles to the spot on the canal where he was marooned, only to find he had knocked the master switch off with his foot as he was cruising along. From the look of him, I reckon he had been at the gin for several hours, so it's not surprising he didn't notice. The drunken astonishment on his face when I simply flicked the switch and magically restored the power was almost worth the thirty-mile round trip. Almost – but not quite.

While I've been settling in at Bastion Marina, I've still being showing up regularly and punctually, as promised, for my visits to Gemma, my probation officer. Every time, the biscuit tin gets opened for me, as I'm one of her success stories. She was delighted when I secured the job in the coffee shop and ecstatic when I got my lucky break at Bastion, not least because it came with accommodation, thus solving one of the main problems that stops ex-offenders from getting back on their feet. A rodent-infested caravan, propped up on bricks, was more than she had ever dared hope for. Proudly I show her photos of my home improvements and she responds by sharing pictures of her little boy, who's growing fast. By the time our last session rolls around, it feels like we're almost friends. I've told her everything I've shared with you so far and she has listened without judging me. It has been great to have her as a sounding board but, during our last meeting, she goes a bit further and offers me some advice. See what you make of it. To put it in context, I've mentioned to her a few times that I haven't had any letters from Nancy since I was released. It's hardly surprising, really, given that I never told my sister I was getting paroled, so as far as she's concerned I'm still inside. However, in the past she has always tracked me down, and I guess I just expected she would do the same this time, but she hasn't.

'Now that you're sorting your life out, Nathan, I think it's time for you to take the initiative for a change, with regard to Nancy. From what you've told me, she really wants you in her life. Why don't you reach out to her?'

'Because I'm scared. No surprise there. Also, I can't see how I'd add anything to her life. I mean, she's this big star and...'

'Not to you, she isn't. She's your sister. Don't you think it would help her, to be able to talk to the one person alive who has known her since she was a baby, when she's probably surrounded by people telling her what she wants to hear? From what you've told me, she's a forthright kind of person, working in an industry full of pseuds and sycophants. Having her brother to talk to could be just what she needs.'

'Even a brother like me?'

'Especially a brother like you, who's made mistakes, but is moving forward. Nathan, try to think about Nancy for a moment, instead of yourself. Who knows what's going on in her life? I'm sure she has problems of her own, despite what you read in the papers. Just give her a ring. OK, she could say she wants nothing to do with you, but I doubt she will. Also, even if she does, you told me she said that once before and she still got back in contact. I'm going to leave you with two pieces of advice. One, hold onto your job at the marina and two, contact your sister.'

'Thanks, Gemma. You've been a big help.'

'You're welcome, Nathan. You've mostly helped yourself, though. Well done. I'm proud of you.'

Over the next few weeks, I try to summon the courage to call my sister, but I don't. Instead, I distract myself with work, drink beer with the posse, put the world to rights with Geoff and embark on a short-lived fling with Shauna, one of the barmaids in our local. Her boyfriend is in the army and she makes it clear one night that she fancies trying out an older man. It's fun for a while, but then she hooks up with someone her own age, with his own flat and car. There's no contest, really, and I'm cool with her decision, but it doesn't do much for my confidence and I use it as another excuse not to contact Nancy. As you've probably noticed, I'm one of those people who tends to let life kick them around like a football, rather than taking control. The trouble with this approach is that, sooner or later, usually when you least expect it, someone puts the boot in, and you fly off in a whole new direction.

On the evening when the Fates decide to take aim, I'm in the pub with the usual crew. We're all knocking back the beers, and I shoehorn in a few shots as well, because Shauna's there with her new squeeze and I need to take the edge off my petty jealousy. Towards the end of the night, the rest of the guys drift off, but Geoff and I decide to dig in until closing time. Neither of us is feeling any pain when they call time, and we stand up to leave. Geoff needs a slash, so I wait for him by the pub noticeboard, swaying gently. That's when I see the poster for a series of summer concerts at the National Indoor Arena in Birmingham, located just yards from where Nancy was discovered by that record company guy all those years ago. Idly I look down the list of artists who are scheduled to perform and there, near the top, is my sister's name and photo.

At that moment Geoff returns. 'Come on Nathan. Time to travel...what's up, mate? You look dreadful. Maybe that last shot of JD wasn't a good idea...'

He's right; it wasn't, and neither were all the others. If I hadn't drunk them, I'd have been able to control myself better. As it is, Geoff follows my gaze, which leads him to Nancy's photo, and he laughs.

'Forget it, friend. She's way out of your league, although she's more your age than Shauna was...'

'S'not like that...'

'Whatever. Time to go home.'

'No – I mean it, Geoff. She's...my sister.'

'Yeah, right. I think that's the drink talking, mate. Off we go...'

Sober Nathan would have quickly changed the subject, but Drunk Nathan can't let it go. On the way home, I burble a load of nonsense about Nancy. I don't recall most of what I say, but one moment does stick in my mind. I definitely confess to Geoff that I miss her. The next morning, when I'm busy beating myself up for my careless talk, I still remember it was a relief to admit it.

When I pop into the marina office the next morning to check in with Geoff, the paracetamol has not managed to silence the drum solo playing in my head and my stomach's churning ominously. I'm not sure what's worse; my hangover or the fear of what my boss is going to say. Happily,

40

Geoff appears to have forgotten about last night's conversation.

'Morning, Nathan. Epic night out. I have to say I'm feeling it this morning...'

'Me too. What have you got for me?'

'First up, coffee and a bacon sandwich. Then I need you to fix the railing on the swing bridge. Can't have the punters falling into the cut, now can we?'

That's it. I eat my bacon sandwich, start on my list of jobs and make a mental note to ensure that, next time I decide to have a skinful, my companions match me drink for drink.

A few days later I have to borrow Linda's electric bike and head south down the Grand Union to help another hire boater in distress. I make it back just in time for Linda to go home; I've been pedalling hard because I don't want to hold her up and I rush into the marina office, pink-faced, sweaty and oblivious.

'Just made it, Lin! Sorry I took so long, Geoff. It was another case of a prop all snarled up with knickers and tights. I mean, why the hell do people chuck their smalls in the canal?'

'I don't know why you're surprised,' comes a deadpan voice from the corner. 'Have you forgotten how we used to keep a special bread saw for cutting all the crap off our prop?'

Geoff and Linda just stare at me, waiting to see how I react. I turn to Geoff first.

'So you didn't forget what I said that night, on the way home.'

'No chance, mate. You were way more pissed than me. Look, I hope you don't mind me interfering, but I figured you wouldn't do anything about it yourself. I just wanted to help, is all.'

'You have helped, Geoff. I'm sure my brother realises that, even though he seems to have lost the power of speech. Look, is it OK if he takes me on a tour of the marina?'

'No problem. Be our guest. Take as long as you like.'

We walk across the car park in silence then Nancy stops and turns to face me.

'Look, bro, I suggest we forget about all my letters, your time inside, Mum and Dad dying, the lot. Let's just park the past. I'm having a shit time at the moment so I can't deal with it right now, and from the look of you, I'd say you can't either. Why don't you show me around these lovely pleasure boats, and we'll ignore the herd of elephants in the room?'

At last I find my voice. 'Sounds good to me.'

So I take my sister on a tour. I point out bits of signwriting I've done for Alan and tell her about engines I've repaired and cabins I've restored. She seems genuinely interested and I start to relax a bit; enough to show her my caravan and dig out a 'before' picture so she can compare and contrast.

'You've done a good job, Nathan. It's nice to see you carving and painting again, too.'

I should mention that I've painted all the pots, pans and jars in the caravan with roses and castles, and every shelf is adorned with miniature narrowboats. I suddenly realise I've created a living space that bears a strong resemblance to the boatman's cabin in which we grew up.

'You mentioned you were having a shit time, Nan. What's going on?'

Nancy flops down on my little sofa and I sit cross-legged on the floor, just like I used to do when we were kids. I listen while she tells me about the control freaks at her record company and how they're trying to change the direction of her music away from the girl and guitar sound which has always been her hallmark. She clearly has no interest in collaborating with the various artists and DJs they parade in front of her, which has caused some major bust-ups. They continually try to book her for venues and festivals she has no interest in playing and, worst of all, they want her to put her life on show through social media. I can see why this would be Nancy's worst nightmare. When she's offstage, she likes her privacy.

'It wouldn't be so bad if I could just say what I wanted, but they want to "curate" my posts. Censor me, in other words. To them, I'm just an asset they've purchased, and they want to squeeze as much cash out of me as they can by bending me into shape, to fit the image they think the public wants. Then, when I won't co-operate, they throw their toys out the bloody pram. It's happening more often these days, but it's not just me. Plenty of other artists I know are in the same boat, whatever label they're with. I shouldn't complain really. The new album's coming together pretty well. At least I'm still writing songs and making music. And we've managed to meet up, thanks to your boss. He seems like a decent guy.'

'He is. He's helped me a lot.'

'So you're happy here?'

'I guess so, but sometimes it's hard being near the canals and not being able to get back out there. Know what I mean?'

'I do. Sometimes I think that's the reason I bought my house in Islington. So I can walk down Regent's Canal and torture myself by looking at the narrowboats. I reckon it'll always be in our blood – the need to stand on the back counter, grab the tiller and escape.'

'S'pose it will.'

'Look, I've got to get back to London. Are we good, bro?'

'We're good.'

'Then let's make a deal. I won't dredge up the past and you'll answer my calls and texts. Agreed?'

'Agreed. Nan?'

'What?'

'Thanks for coming. I mean, you could have just told Geoff where to stick it, and I wouldn't have blamed you if you had.'

'True – but your boss can be very persuasive. Anyway, I'm glad I came. I'll be back soon. Now I've really got to go; my driver will be going crazy.'

So we walk back to the marina office, where a large black car is parked conspicuously in front of the door. It looks totally out of place. Nancy gives me a quick hug, then slips into the back seat and is gone. As I turn to leave, Geoff opens the office door.

'How was it?'

'Hang on, Geoff. Shouldn't you apologise for interfering in my life?'

'Maybe, but I'm not going to. Someone needed to give you a kick up the backside. Now tell me how it went.'

'It wasn't how I imagined. I thought she'd be really angry, which is what I deserve, but she just wanted to walk round the marina and look at the boats. She's got a lot of crazy stuff happening in her life and I don't think she wanted a heavy scene.'

'There you are, then. Like every human being on this planet, Nancy has her own problems. She's a lovely woman, Nathan. We had a nice chat on the phone. Try not to let her down again.'

'I'm not sure I'll get a chance, what with you breathing down my neck.'

'Glad we've sorted that one out. Now, d'you fancy a beer over at mine?'

'No thanks; I'll pass. I need some time to myself. See you tomorrow.'

After that, life returns to normal, except I get regular phone calls and texts from my sister and I answer every time. There's a big happy hole in my conscience where the guilt used to be. I feel lighter, somehow. I work harder than ever and finally start to feel I deserve my good fortune in winding up here at Bastion.

I'm repairing a customer's starter motor one morning when my phone starts ringing. I struggle to pull it out of my jeans pocket and smile apologetically at the customer, who's hovering around getting in the way. 'Sorry, I need to take this. It's my sister. She hates it when I let her go to voicemail.'

Nancy keeps it brief. She's got a day off later in the week and wants to come back to Bastion and see me. We arrange a time and hang up. I love it that our conversations are becoming routine, with no angst or recriminations. I'm not stupid; I know we'll have to face the difficult stuff at some stage, but by mutual, unspoken agreement, we've agreed a truce, and for now it's holding, which is fine by me.

On the day of my sister's visit, I work through my list of jobs in the usual way, but I can't stop myself from glancing across at the marina office whenever it's in view, to see if the incongruous black car is parked outside the door. Never an early riser, my sister promised she'd show up around lunchtime, but when two o'clock rolls around and she hasn't arrived, I assume she's thought better of it and blame myself, as always. Even when my phone rings and the screen lights up with her name, I figure she's ringing to make an excuse.

'Good afternoon, bro. I'm in the office.'

'What office?'

'The marina office, Einstein.'

'I don't see the car outside…'

'You won't do, 'cos I decided to get the train this time. Geoff picked me up from the station.'

'OK. I'll be right there. Bye.'

What the hell is Geoff doing picking my sister up? What's going on? With improbable scenarios and half-formed suspicions whirling through my mind, I scurry up to the office, preparing myself for some sort of confrontation, but when I get there Nancy's all smiles and Geoff's nowhere to be seen. My sister's wearing one of the wig-and-hat combos she puts on when she doesn't want to be recognised – a sensible precaution on public transport.

'Where's Geoff?'

'Giving a new customer the grand tour.'

'How come he gave you a lift?'

'I fancied taking the train today, so I rang and asked if he could pick me up from the station. I was pretty sure you hadn't passed your test, given that you borrow Linda's bike to do your callouts, so there was no point in asking you.'

'Oh – right.' I decide not to ask Nancy why she didn't just get a taxi. It's not like money's an issue for her. I don't want to risk starting a row, though, so I let it go.

'Come on, let's have a walk around and look at the boats. I've been stuck inside all week, working on a bunch of new songs. I could do with some air.'

So I follow my sister, who's a redhead today, out into the sunshine and we have a leisurely stroll. She tells me about the tracks she's writing – they're doing her head in, but she hopes they'll eventually come right. Then she updates me on her new boyfriend, who is almost young enough to be her son. I'm teasing her for being a cradle-snatcher when I spot something which doesn't look right.

'What's up, bro?'

'That boat, moored up over there next to Dreamcatcher. I haven't seen it before. I know every boat in the marina and I don't recognise that one. It definitely wasn't there yesterday and we're not due any new arrivals today, or Geoff would have told me. It must be moored there illegally.'

'You missed your calling. Should've been a detective.'

'Very funny.'

'Let's go over and take a look.'

'Seriously though, I'd have remembered it, sis. Especially with a daft name like that. What does it even mean?'

'I thought someone like you, with your literary pretensions, would know. Festina Lente means "hurry slowly" in Latin.'

'Since when did you become an expert in classical languages, Nan? Hang on – how…'

Nancy smiles and tosses me a set of keys. 'Go on – take a look. I think you'll find it's no ordinary narrowboat…'

She's right. Festina Lente isn't a pleasure boat, like all the others in Bastion Marina, but neither is it a working boat, like the one we grew up on. It has relatively spacious living quarters, including a double bed which folds down across the entire width of the boat. There's even a small shower room and galley, but the similarity to a floating caravan ends there. Below the side hatch is a counter, complete with a till, and at the front, in place of a saloon, there's a compact workshop, complete with a set of woodworking tools and a workbench.

'It took me and Geoff a few weeks to find the perfect boat for you, but we reckon this is it…'

'I don't understand, sis…'

'Do keep up. You can do your wood carving and painting in the workshop and sell your wares through the side hatch. There are panels on the side of the boat which open out into shelves, so you can create a nice display when you're moored up. You can sell other stuff as well, if you're minded to. Beer, cheese – that kind of thing. There's a big fridge under the counter…'

'Nancy. I can't accept this. It's too much – I mean, it must have cost you a fortune…'

'I can afford it, bro. I'm not short of cash. I would've helped you out before, but I didn't want to put money in Ruth's pocket, which was the right call, as you discovered. After that I never got the chance, what with you ignoring my letters. Look, I'm not suggesting you leave this place behind. Geoff would kill me. We've agreed you can run your business from here in your spare time and use your holidays to cruise the network and sell your stuff. He's given me mate's rates on the first year's mooring fees, which is decent of him. Meanwhile he can rent your caravan to someone else and make a bit of extra cash.'

'You two have really thought this through, haven't you?'

'Yes. It's a win-win. You get back on the canals and Geoff acquires a new revenue stream.'

'But what do you get out of it, Nan?'

'I get to make my brother happy.'

'That's it?'

'Yep – that's all I want.'

'Look, it's sweet of you, but I really can't…'

'You said that already. Just take the bloody keys. End of chat. Now let's go and see Geoff and talk through the details. Maybe he can rustle us up a beer, to celebrate.'

I told you earlier I was a lucky person. I mean, how many people are given not one, but two narrowboats? When I look back on what I've told you about my life so far, I admit I brought all the bad stuff on myself and I'm amazed Nancy wants to give me another chance, after everything I've put her through. Her generosity and faith make me determined to ensure I don't screw up this time. No way will Festina Lente be taken away by the Canal and River Trust like Jeremiah's boat. I'm going to make sure we have some great times together.

As I pack up my stuff, ready to move it onto my boat, I think about where I want to go first, and there's one obvious choice. Bastion Marina is on the part of the Grand Union which forms one of the classic circular routes on the canal network, called the Leicester Ring. Most people take two weeks to complete the one-hundred-mile circuit, but experienced boaters like me can do it in ten days or even fewer, if the Fates are kind. This time, though, I'll take the full fortnight, which will give me plenty of time to moor up in the popular tourist locations and open my onboard emporium for business. Come with me? I can offer you rivers as well as canals and over one hundred locks, plus quaint villages and some excellent pubs. We'll have a blast, and I won't get into any trouble. I promise.

5 RING OF BRIGHT WATER

You're probably wondering why I've chosen this title. By now you know that canal water is anything but bright, although the 'ring' bit should be obvious, if you've been paying attention. All I can stay is – stick with me. All will become clear, so to speak.

Before we get started, I should warn you that my approach to boating is different from your average holidaymaker, who just pootles along looking for the next pub. I was brought up to think of canals as a place for making money, not fooling around, and it's a mindset I'm unlikely to lose. Sure, I enjoy the landscape and the wildlife, but I make progress at the same time, so I won't be describing every lock. I'll point out anything noteworthy, but otherwise I'll crack on. You'll probably find it a relief. I imagine you've had enough of novice boaters in distress, making every possible mistake at each lock they encounter. You can relax. When it comes to locks, I don't make mistakes. I might have screwed up my life, but I know how to work a lock.

So away we go, leaving the first lock behind. Quickly the houses start to thin out as we bid farewell to the city. We pass a marina that's much posher than Bastion, then we glide past a country park on the opposite side. I spot a swan's nest in the reeds, looking like a basket weaving class which hasn't quite gone to plan. The occupants, a pair of regal swans and a clutch of fluffy, scruffy adolescent cygnets, launch themselves into my boat's wake and I throw them the remains of my packed lunch. As I draw away, I stare up at a red kite and a black crow, locked in aerial combat as the crow battles to protect her chicks. Then, just in time, I remember to look down.

Beneath the boat, a miracle is unfolding. The murky canal water is abruptly replaced by water that's gin clear. Under its surface, lime-green waterweed streams in extravagant ribbons, pulled along irresistibly by the momentum of my boat. It reminds me that now, for a while, we're not on the canal anymore. We're on the River Soar and on this balmy, late summer day, with the sunlight dancing merrily on the ripples at the riverbank, it lives right up to its name.

I crank up the engine so we're nudging the four mile per hour speed limit, then settle back and let the remainder of the afternoon unfold. The heat seems to build with every passing hour, and the natural world grows subdued and listless. Sleeping mallards line the riverbank and cows watch with limpid, chocolate eyes as I pass by, swishing their tails uselessly against the relentless flies. In sympathy I sink gradually into my own torpor and am only revived when the evening air cools my skin, and my stomach reminds me I threw most of my lunch to the swans.

I moor up in an isolated spot halfway between Barrow-upon-Soar and Loughborough. I don't feel like spending the night in a town. I'd rather enjoy my own company tonight, so I just carve my miniature narrowboats until it's time for bed. I've built up lots of stock, but I figure you can never have too much. Business could be brisk on this journey, especially if the weather holds. When I finally climb into bed, I feel the warm glow that comes from having something to look forward to. There was a time when I thought I'd never feel this way again.

The next day, Loughborough does a good job of killing my vibe. The town centre might be very nice, but the canal meanders through the drab, litter-strewn outskirts. There's plenty of detritus in the canal and a bunch of it gets wound around my prop, so I spend a miserable morning with my head in the weed hatch. Laboriously I disentangle a cardigan, a length of baling twine and several plastic carrier bags, before I eventually free the propellor and resume my journey. However, I have barely travelled a quarter of a mile before I see an oncoming boater waving frantically, which is rarely a good sign. When I draw alongside, he shouts that a shopping trolley is lurking below the surface near Loughborough Lock. He advises me to hug the left bank to avoid getting marooned on top of it for an hour, like he did. I take his advice and manage to prevent another delay, then decide to make it a relatively short day. There are times when everything's against you, and this is clearly one of those times, so I call it quits in Kegworth, a good place to moor before tomorrow's boating challenge.

The sign warns me about what to expect. 'Emergency Flood Mooring Dolphins', it says. Nothing to do with the slick, smiling creatures everyone loves; these are floating devices to which you can attach your boat if the river's too high to navigate. They rise and fall with the water levels, so you don't end up dangling from your mooring ropes in mid-air. I've been stuck here a few times with my family, unable to proceed until the flood waters subsided. Happily these problems normally occur in winter. There's little chance of a delay at this time of year. I should explain that the River Soar isn't the culprit. The dolphins are here for another reason – the mighty

River Trent, which lies ahead. Before we tackle it, I need a good night's sleep.

I'm on the move early next morning, refreshed and ready to up the ante. We've got a lot to see today. First up is one of my favourite landmarks on this route; the place I used to call the 'Cloud Factory' when I was a little kid, much to my parents' amusement. I really thought that clouds issued from its eight monstrous and majestic cooling towers. Those of a more prosaic nature know it as Ratcliffe-on-Soar power station. Although I love nature, I'm also awestruck by industrial behemoths like this. I gaze up at the smooth, dust-streaked curves looming above me and watch white tendrils of steam escape the confines of each tower, floating to freedom in the clear blue sky. Then I remind myself to face forward; I need to pay attention to what's coming next.

The guidebooks warn boaters to take great care around here, to avoid being dragged towards the infamous Thrumpton Weir, which lurks just beyond the Cloud Factory. It would be disastrous to get tangled up in its thrashing waters, but happily I pass by without incident, then head for a stretch of water best avoided if you suffer from agoraphobia. It's a real shock to the system, if you're used to cruising narrow canals and benign rivers. In an instant, the confines of the Soar are left behind and you emerge into the massive, writhing expanse of water that is the River Trent. Suddenly the safety of the bank is far away, and your narrowboat feels exposed. Most boaters rush for the bank and hug it close, but I know it's easier to cruise down the middle and embrace the fear, so I hold my nerve until I reach the first lock. Afterwards, the river becomes narrower and less threatening, although we don't return to the security of the canal until after lock three, when I can breathe more easily. Even experienced boaters like me get unnerved by the Trent, every time. Now, though, we're on the snug Trent and Mersey Canal, headed for Shardlow, one of my favourite villages on the Leicester Ring.

Shardlow's just as I remember it – compact, with tastefully converted warehouses and traditional canal side pubs. As I anticipated, it's packed with tourists and, as it's the middle of the day and many boats are cruising, there are gaps between the moored craft. I tie up in a central location and start arranging my wares on the shelves that flip down from the sides of the boat. Before I've finished, people are already milling around, so I quickly display my price list and get started. The smaller stuff sells first - miniature narrowboats, wooden spoons, eggcups and pencil cases - but then two newbie boaters buy one of my large planters. They ask me if I take commissions, I agree to customise a water can and we exchange contact details. After that some real ale enthusiasts rock up, enticed by my unusual beers. I sell them a dozen and give them a discount. Then I prepare some small cubes of cheese for the punters to taste, and immediately people swarm from nowhere, eager for free food. The plate empties in seconds. Within half an hour, I've sold nearly half my cheese and made a sizeable dent in my stock of canal art. By the time I shut up shop, I'm starting to worry how I'll restock. I conclude that I'll need to do more carving and painting, but it's a nice problem to have.

I decide to celebrate by spending some of my takings in a pub I visited once with Ruth. Her memory won't haunt me tonight; I'm insulated by today's success. I can't be bothered to change out of the traditional boater's outfit I wear when I'm in sales mode – my trusted floppy white shirt, waistcoat, black trousers and red neckerchief. I'm gasping for a pint, so I head straight over the bridge to my chosen watering hole.

I haven't even reached the bar when a familiar voice calls out.

'Oi – Nathan! What's with the clobber?'

I turn around and there he is. My mate Jake from Gas Street Basin, accompanied by some old boy I don't know.

'You got an audition for Rosie and Jim?' laughs Jake.

'Just dressed up for the tourists. I'll explain over a pint, if you like. My shout.'

'That's my boy. This here's Wilf – my new partner. Wilf – meet my old pal Nathan. Used to be in Gas Street Basin, back in the day.'

'Good to meet you, Wilf. What are you drinking?'

We settle down in the corner and catch up. I tell the old boys about my new start on Festina Lente and today's success. They're apparently scraping a living selling gas bottles to boaters. We reminisce about Jeremiah and the rest of the posse in GSB. Some have died or moved on since I was last there, but most are carrying on as before. It's the only life these old dudes know, and they're too far gone to change.

After a few pints, Jake reveals he has heard about my time inside.

'Word gets around pretty quick on the cut, son.'

'I know, Jake. It's hardly a state secret. I made some poor choices and I'm not proud of it, but I've moved on.'

'Doesn't sound like they was exactly choices. From what I hear, it was that girl of yours got you mixed up in that drugs business...'

'I can't blame her, Jake. It was my fault; I should have stood up to her.'

'I heard you had a kid – is that right?'

'Yes – a little boy. Arthur.'

'Ever see him?'

'No. Ruth married someone else, and she doesn't want me to have any contact.'

'You can do something about that. You don't have to take it lying down.'

'I know, but I don't have much to offer him. He's better off with his new dad.'

'You don't know that.' Wilf has been silent for a while, but now he leans forward and looks at me earnestly. 'I was just the same; I thought my boys wouldn't want anything to do with me after my missus took off. Turns out I was dead wrong. They still needed their dad.'

I decide not to ask Wilf for details. Instead I enquire casually, 'And how are things now?'

'Not perfect, but I'll tell you one thing. I'll never regret the day we found each other again. I'm going to get the beers in, and then we'll talk about something else, but all I'll say is – think about finding your son. Even if you don't, he might track you down someday, and then he'll be sure to ask why you didn't fight for him. Right, enough said. Same again – and how about a chaser?'

It's well after closing time when the three of us roll out of there. We stumble over the bridge together, then hug each other goodbye. Before he lets me go, Jake whispers in my ear.

'You were a mug, son. You know that, don't you?'

'Yes, mate. I know it.'

'And you won't make those same mistakes again, will you?'

'No. I promise.'

'Good. So we'll see you next time you're in Birmingham?'

'You will. Definitely.'

'Right. Now be off with you.'

We head off in opposite directions along the towpath and I turn to watch the two old boys as they totter towards their boat, arms linked, heads bent towards each other. It appears they're having a heartfelt conversation which neither is likely to remember tomorrow. Whatever state they're in, they'll be off first thing in the morning, cruising west towards the Birmingham Canal Network, where most of their customers are based. I wonder if our paths will ever cross again. There's no guarantee, not when you're Jake's age. Or any age, come to that.

I'm sure they're long gone by the time I leave Shardlow. I'm not feeling too fresh after last night, but I try to put on a good show for the tourists who photograph my boat as I depart. A few minutes later, I'm thankful to reach the open countryside. I work my way through a flask of black coffee and a blister pack of paracetamol as the morning wears on. There are very few locks on this stretch of canal, so I make good progress. The noise level increases later, as the canal threads its way between a busy trunk road and a railway line, but by then I've recovered sufficiently to tolerate the decibels. I even manage to appreciate the view as I travel over a picturesque series of aqueducts. By the time I reach Burton upon Trent I'm almost cheerful.

Later on, I tie up in Alrewas and blow away the final cobwebs with a stroll around the village. I admire its historic church, quaint thatched cottages and executive homes, with their manicured gardens. I try to imagine what it would be like to live in these houses and drive the pristine cars parked outside, but I can't. It's way outside my frame of reference. Back on Festina Lente, I carve and paint until my eyes grow sore, then set my alarm for an early start and fall into bed. I try to read, but the words dance before my eyes, so I settle for a few hours of oblivion.

Today's destination is one of the focal points on the Leicester Ring. Fradley Junction is where we leave the Trent and Mersey and join the Coventry Canal, heading south. First, though, we're going to stop here for a day or so, to do some serious business. There's an iconic pub right on the junction, festooned inside and out with traditional canal art. The place really attracts the tourists, so it's an ideal spot to sell our wares. I might even be tempted to have a pint later on. Amazing, isn't it, how fast the memory of a hangover fades, only to be replaced by the temptation to do it all over again? As with so many things in life, we never learn.

As I hoped, Fradley Junction turns out to be an absolute winner; even better than Shardlow. I do a brisk trade in canal art and sell nearly all my remaining beer. I also negotiate several more commissions, which is a welcome bonus. The euphoria of the customers, fuelled by a sunny day out and a boozy pub lunch, takes me back to my teenage years, when the world seemed full of possibilities. A posse of tipsy women on a work outing banter flirtatiously with me. It's just like old times and I'm feeling quite good about myself, until I get a text from my sister:

Nancy: 'Hi bro. How's it going? Having fun?'

Me: 'All good. At Fradley Junction. Punters loving my stuff.'

Nancy: 'Good. Forgot to say – when you get back, get your teeth fixed FFS. You'll sell even more if you lose the prison teeth. Send me the bill.'

Me: 'Cheers for that, sis.'

Nancy: 'No worries. Get your hair cut too. It's a mess.'

I know Nancy means well, but she doesn't exactly bolster my confidence. Still, I get right back to work and have sold so much by the end of the day that I've bounced right back. Even so, I make a mental note to find a hairdresser; the dentist will have to wait.

I decide to celebrate by treating myself to a nice dinner in the pub.

Although I'm a better cook than my sister, which admittedly isn't difficult, I do share her love of a burger, so I order a double cheeseburger and chips, washed down with a pint of real ale.

It's a small world on the canals. If you cruise the waterways for long enough, you'll run into plenty of boats - and people - you recognise. That's why I wasn't astonished to encounter Jake the other night, although it was a pleasant surprise. I wish wholeheartedly that I could say the same for tonight.

I've just finished my dinner when I spot him at the bar. It couldn't be anyone else. He has the same immense barrel chest, and the dome of his head is still shaded with dark stubble. He raises his giant paw and effortlessly attracts the barmaid's attention. As he orders his drink, I gently place my empty glass on the table and ease myself from my seat. I'm about to make my escape when he abruptly turns around.

'Nathan. I thought it was you. Have a drink with me.'

'No. I'm just leaving and anyway, we don't have anything to talk about.' I'm gratified to hear that my voice doesn't sound as squeaky as it did when we met in that other pub, all those years ago. I don't sound super-confident, but progress has definitely been made.

'That's where you're wrong.' The man, whose name I never learned, calls over to the barmaid. 'Can I get another pint, love, for my friend here? Whatever he was having before.'

'You're not my friend,' I hiss as the man picks up our beers and leads me over to a table in the corner.

'That's a shame,' he replies. 'We all see you as a friend, Nathan. Someone who's earned his stripes. A person who, when under extreme pressure, proved he could be trusted; not once, but twice. We'd like to reward you, if you'll let us.'

'You already rewarded me – with two long stretches inside. I promised the screw who showed me the door after the second stint that I wouldn't make it third time unlucky, and I fully intend to honour that promise.'

'I understand, Nathan, and there won't be a third time. We'll give you the pick of the plum jobs. The safe ones. Low risk - and big money.'

I lean back in my chair. 'You never told me your name. I don't normally drink with a man without knowing his name. What's yours?'

'Sebastian.'

I nearly choke on my beer. 'Yeah, right. I don't think I've ever seen anyone who looks less like a Sebastian than you.'

'My parents weren't to know how I'd end up looking.'

'I'm sure they're very proud.'

'Reckon they are, now you come to mention it; what with my nice big house in the country, lovely family – the works. You could have the same thing, Nathan, if you wanted.'

'No. I don't want. In fact, I want nothing more to do with you, Gary, Giles, Hadley, or whatever the hell you're all called. Do not attempt to contact me. If you do, you'll wish you hadn't.'

'Fighting talk, Nathan, but something tells me you'll be back.'

'Really? Don't hold your breath.'

'I'm not often wrong about these things. Look, when you change your mind, just call this place and have a word with Tracey over there, behind the bar. She knows where to find me.'

'I won't be calling.'

'Let's see about that, shall we?'

'Goodbye, Sebastian.'

'Cheers, Nathan. I'm glad we ran into each other!'

Back on Festina Lente, I try to calm down by painting roses on a water can, but I can't focus, and my hands won't stop shaking. Once, I'd have been trembling with fear but now, with Ray's men to call upon if I need them, I'm not scared anymore. Instead, it's rage that stops me from holding my paintbrush steady. I can't get Sebastian's smug expression out of my head. I'm sure he lied about his name, but he was probably telling the truth when he gloated about his big house in the country. I think of them all – Giles, Gary, Hadley and all the others I haven't met – living comfortable, complacent lives, while I wasted large chunks of mine because of them and will live with the consequences forever. What I wouldn't give to get my own back.

Eventually I give up on the painting and pour myself a large JD. I know that, if I let myself be devoured by anger, I'll be the only one who suffers, but my body refuses to get the message. My feet are jittering with nervous energy and the knuckles of my right hand, which is clamped tightly around my whisky glass, gleam sickly white under my skin. Slowly I put my glass down, pour myself a refill, then pick up my phone. Quickly, before I can change my mind, I dial my sister's number and tell her what happened. I don't expect much sympathy from Nancy; she's not really the bleeding-heart type, as you might have noticed. However, she's not always predictable either and tonight she surprises me.

'Look, bro. You've got to let it go. I know it's not easy. I've been done over a bunch of times. I've lost count of the pots I've smashed in place of someone's face. A few guitars too. I made a massive dent in my pink piano after a meeting with some record company suits. Gets you nowhere. Also, I paid a lot for that boat of yours. I don't want you wrecking it.'

'Don't worry. I'm not going to trash the boat. Any other suggestions?'

'No. Park it. I'm a great believer in karma. Those lowlifes will get theirs. Maybe you'll dish it out, maybe you won't. It won't turn out how you expect; that's for sure. Be patient and get on with your life. If you try and force karma, the only person who'll get hurt is you. See what I'm saying?'

'Yeah. File it away until an opportunity presents itself.'

'Spot on. You're not being weak; just smart. And it's time for you to start acting smart, Nathan.'

After we hang up I feel a bit calmer. I don't need any more whisky - just an early night, so I can get up at first light and put as many miles as possible between me and this place. Fradley Junction might be a top location for selling canal art, but I don't plan to return any time soon.

The next day dawns in soft focus, whilst the birdsong begins tentatively with a few isolated early risers, then builds to the full avian orchestra by the time the sun's up. Normally I'd revel in this sensory spectacle, but today it's just background. The Coventry Canal is lock-free all the way down to Tamworth and I blast unseeing through the countryside. It's almost a relief when I reach the outskirts of the town and get a break from the scenic views. The grim suburban landscape matches my mood as I make short work of Glascote Locks and head towards Atherstone. The flight of locks to the north of the town is a pleasant spot, and the quirky display at the top lock usually makes me smile, but not today.

I moor up in Nuneaton for the night and have another go at painting roses and castles. This time, my hand holds steady, and I decorate my water can for hours, until I run out of space and can't see straight. When it goes well, painting absorbs me entirely; I can't think about anything else while I focus on getting those roses just right. It's very soothing, and by the time I fall into bed I find I'm looking forward to tomorrow's destination, which is just a few miles further south, at the point where the Coventry and Oxford Canals meet. Like Shardlow and Fradley Junction, Hawkesbury Junction is another of the focal points on the Leicester Ring. I pray that, for once, I don't run into anyone I know. I'll be more than happy with my own company for the rest of this trip.

The following morning, on my way to Hawkesbury, I pass the entrance to the Ashby Canal, the cul-de-sac where I was planning to dump Jeremiah's boat and escape to Ireland with Ruth and Arthur. As I look left, through the narrow, brick-built bridge and down the shallow canal which causes boaters so many problems, I reflect briefly on what might have been, before telling myself sternly to get real and look to the future. Then I gun the engine, skirt round the side of Bedworth and moor up in pole position on Hawkesbury Junction, right opposite another iconic canal boozer with a bar full of canal memorabilia and a row of picnic tables outside.

Although it's still quite early, the sun is already flexing its muscles. As the day wears on, the heat builds. Coventry is just a few miles away and it seems half the city has decamped out here for a pub lunch and a towpath walk. Soon Festina Lente is surrounded by customers, who make short work of what beer I have left and buy lots of wooden spoons and pencil cases. Everyone is friendly; mellowed out by alcohol and the sun on their backs. I pose for countless selfies and answer lots of daft questions about life on the canals. I don't even get wound up when people peer through the side hatch or sit their children on the roof. It's easy to be tolerant on a lovely day like this, with an appreciative crowd who spend their money, keep me busy and prevent me dwelling on my encounter with Sebastian. As the afternoon draws to a close and the number of customers starts to dwindle, I begin looking forward to a few beers in the pub and pray I'll have no company. Happily, my prayers are answered.

Next morning I leave Hawkesbury Junction at first light. I work the shallow lock in silence and sneak out onto the Oxford Canal before anyone else is around. For a while, this new canal marches in step with the M6, then turns east, passing under the M69 and leaving the Midlands behind. It's time to immerse ourselves in The Shires.

The countryside welcomes me back with open arms. I enjoy the wildlife, as usual, throwing half a loaf to the moorhens, coots, ducks and swans who hustle all morning for food. These birds learn early in life that boats mean bread and they don't give up easily. I know I boasted earlier about being a hardened commercial boater, but when it comes to our feathered friends, I'm a right softie, and these waterborne warriors know a sucker when they see one. I've just finished crumbling up a slice of wholemeal for a particularly persistent posse of greylag geese, when I spot something I reckon most boaters would have missed. A small brown head, fur neatly slicked back with canal water, bobs busily to and fro in the middle of the cut, about fifty metres ahead. The animal has engaged warp speed, desperate to reach the opposite bank before the boat gets much closer. At first I think it's a rat, then I realise my mistake. Rats are a common sight on the canals, whereas this little beast is a rare treasure. It's a water vole; a recluse who's usually too smart to get caught in the open by the likes of me. A brief flurry of thrashing water, a waggle of the reeds beside the bank, and he's gone. At times like these I long for someone to share the moment.

Despite the distractions of the natural world, I make good time and soon approach the outskirts of Rugby, trying hard not to think about the last time I was here. I'd rather not recall Mum's funeral or the bitter, alcohol-fuelled fight with my sister afterwards, so I increase my speed to the four mile per hour maximum as the canal skirts around the eastern side of the town. When I reach the leafy southern suburb of Hillmorton, I make short work of the three locks and move swiftly on.

Soon afterwards, I nip under the M45, then find myself back in open countryside. There are few hedges on this stretch of canal and the fields fall away on either side in an ocean of flowing green. I recall that this area can be bleak in winter but, on a sunny day like this, it's a delight. I soak up the rays and zone out, until the elegant church spire on my left reminds me I'm approaching my final destination. However, before I get there, nature serves up one last surprise. Out of the corner of my eye, I see another sleek, brown, furry head gliding parallel to the bank. This time there's no mistaking the animal; its skull is too broad for a vole or a rat. It's an otter; a previously endangered canal dweller that, happily, is becoming a more common sight on the waterways, thanks to conservation. I'm sure most boaters are delighted to spot him, whilst bemoaning the dwindling tally of ducklings and moorhen chicks. You can't have it both ways, guys. The otter's got to eat.

So here we are in another good trading location. The pleasant village of Braunston is located in a handy spot where the canals on either side form the shape of an 'H'. This means boaters have an unusually wide choice of onward destinations, making it a popular focal point. There should be plenty of customers around.

Once again I luck out and find a mooring just beyond the marina. It's too late to open my shop, so I walk up to the picturesque flight of locks at the far end of the town, which we'll be negotiating tomorrow. Halfway up, I encounter a pretty canal side pub. My family and I were marooned here for a day once, when the gates of the lock outside got jammed shut. I remember the customers in the pub joking that there must be a body stuck under there, but in the end it turned out to be nothing more sinister than a lump of masonry, probably lobbed into the canal by some drunken customers after closing time. Anyway, I digress. I decide to stop for an early evening drink and spend a happy hour outside, next to the lock, sipping beer and helping passing boaters.

After another early night, I open my shop. Before long, the first customers rock up, then I'm busy all morning. The pace isn't as frantic as it was at Shardlow or Fradley, but it's steady enough that, by lunchtime, I'm starting to worry I won't have enough stock for the remainder of my journey. I have one more major canal centre left, and I particularly want to try it out. So, after everyone has gone for lunch, I shut up shop, untie Festina Lente and brace myself for the locks and tunnels which lie ahead.

As I approach the bottom lock, I see the gates are open and there's a boat waiting inside, so I take my place alongside my new lock buddies. A genial-looking bloke is at the tiller and a gorgeous blonde in skinny jeans closes the gates behind us, then trots to the front of the lock to open the paddles. I chat to the guy and discover the golden-haired beauty is his wife, but I can't begrudge him his good fortune as he's so friendly. Indeed, we get on so well that I hardly notice the six locks, the charming lock keepers' cottages and the horses who look on indifferently from their lockside paddock. Turns out I'm headed in the same direction as my new pals. They've just done the Thames Ring, another iconic circular route, and are heading back to base at Crick Marina. They're meeting some fellow boaters at the pub, to celebrate their return, and invite me to join them. I don't make any promises, but I'm tempted.

The next challenge is Braunston Tunnel, whose gaping maw looms up just yards beyond the locks. Even on a sunny day like this, it breathes cool, ominous vapour from the black 'O' of its mouth and the far end is invisible as you approach. There literally is no light at the end of the tunnel. When it was under construction, the unreliable, shifting soil created an unwanted bend, right in the middle. In accordance with Murphy's Law, this awkward elbow is where the hapless boater is destined to meet another craft heading the opposite way. It's difficult enough to pass a boat in a tunnel; there's never more than a few inches of leeway, but Braunston's quirky shape presents an extra, unwanted challenge. Nervous captains have been known to set off at dawn to avoid meeting another boat. Even professionals like me give Braunston Tunnel our full attention.

After half an hour of Stygian gloom, I emerge. The boat and I are splattered with water, but otherwise unscathed. To my right, the land slopes upwards, while to my left, it drops away into a verdant, cattle-strewn valley. Fishermen squat at regular intervals along the towpath, surrounded by mountains of gear and open boxes of squirming live bait. I slow down to tickover every time I pass one of them; the relationship between the fishing and boating communities is tense, so I do my bit for the peace process by playing nice. Soon afterwards, the last junction of the day comes into view. I glide under a little bridge and turn left next to a tiny cottage which would make an ideal home for Bilbo Baggins. The hobbit house marks the start of the Leicester section of the Grand Union Canal. We're on the final leg of our journey. The circle's nearly complete and we'll soon be home.

However, today's graft is far from over. After less than an hour, I reach Watford Locks. I check in with the lock keeper and find that my lock buddies are at the tail end of the uphill batch of boats, while I have failed to make the cut and must wait for the next downhill batch to proceed before I can be on my way. This means a delay of two hours, which provokes a hissy fit from the man on the boat behind me, who vents his frustration on the poor lock keeper. It's not the lock keeper's fault; he has to draw the line somewhere. I imagine he gets this every day, poor sod. As Mr Angry rants and raves, the lock keeper looks at me and raises his eyes to the heavens. I give him a sympathetic smile and retreat to my workshop for some unscheduled painting and carving.

I make it through the locks half an hour before they close. Another pleasant rural interlude awaits me, after which I have to tackle another long tunnel, so I drift along, making the most of the brief respite between challenges. A heron, toothpick legs wedged firmly in the waterside mud, waits patiently to strike, whilst sheep graze peacefully in a field on my left. A few intrepid beasts have scrambled down the bank and are nibbling tufts of grass at the water's edge, which makes me nervous. I've seen plenty of bloated, spherical corpses, floating like woolly space hoppers in the canal, and I've no wish to encounter another today. Happily, all the fearless munchers remain unscathed.

Crick Tunnel is shorter and straighter than its Braunston neighbour, but it's plenty long enough for me at the end of a busy day. It delights in dousing boaters liberally with water, so I'm soaked when I emerge. While I've been underground, the sun has beaten a retreat and it's getting chilly. I need to make a decision on whether to moor here in Crick, and perhaps join my lock buddies in one of the village pubs, or press on and go for a rural, solitary mooring. Often I like my own company, but tonight I'm cold, hungry and fed up. I weigh up my options as I leave the tunnel and pass under the road bridge. Up ahead is a long, straight section of canal and I spot a mooring opposite the marina where my lock buddies and their friends are based. Suddenly I see a familiar figure on a boat roof, bucket in hand. It's the blonde beauty, giving her boat a post-holiday clean. She waves excitedly and lifts an imaginary glass to her lips. That does it; decision made. I give her the thumbs up and prepare to tie up for the night.

It's a good decision. My lock buddies and their friends are excellent company. One guy from Wolverhampton has an accent you could cut with a knife, so obviously we all get talking about the Midlands. I have to duck and weave a bit to avoid revealing too much of my story, but it's still fun, right up to the part where I get a tap on my shoulder and feel the familiar, cold wave of dread.

'Are you Nathan?'

I'm tempted to deny it, but I can't; I've already told my new friends my name. 'Yes. Do I know you?'

'Happen not. You were only a youngster back then, but I'd know your face anywhere. I'm Bill. This is Ambrose. We were friends with your dad, back in the day.'

'We've just been hearing about Nathan's dad,' says Wolverhampton. 'He sounds like quite a character. Come and join us; you can fill us in on the gory details.'

As we listen to the old boy's stories, I quickly relax, as it becomes clear that they last met me when I was a teenager, so can't reveal anything untoward. They're good raconteurs and tell stories about Dad which I've never heard. They recall a man who always had time for his mates and would go out of his way to help a boater in need. Sure, he liked a drink, got into a few scrapes and could be hot-tempered, but he was a good bloke who is sorely missed by his friends. As the night wears on and a mellow beer fug descends, I start to see my dad in a more favourable light. Later, alone on my boat, I think about how I squandered my chance to be a friend to him in his final years, and a wave of anguish washes over me. I'm tempted to reach for the whisky bottle, but I don't. For once, I let myself feel the pain.

The next morning, I feel exhausted, but somehow lighter, for having faced up to my regrets, rather than drowning them. I remember my sister's text, ordering me to get my hair cut, and dimly recall seeing a tiny hairdressing salon on the way back from the pub, so I clear my head with a stroll back into the village. I return with the unfamiliar sensation of the breeze skimming the back of my neck, then check the mirror. As usual, Nancy was right. Without realising it, I had become as unkempt as the old boys in Gas Street Basin, but I'm too young to emulate them. It was an hour well spent.

Now, though, it's time to move on. Today is my last full day of boating, so I settle in at the tiller for the long haul. Ahead of me, as the guidebooks love to proclaim, is a twenty-one mile stretch of lock-free cruising, and it's easy to forget you're in the twenty-first century. The canal meanders in rococo loops to avoid the hills and ancient earthworks. The villages are hidden away, so we see few signs of human life. Horses and cattle graze with focused determination in the early morning, then slump in the shade as the heat grows more intense. Iridescent dragonflies, those gaudy sun worshippers, alight briefly on the boat's roof to catch a few rays and I watch them idly. I manage to keep my brain from dwelling on the past, right up until I reach the junction with the short, scenic arm of the canal leading to Welford. There's a pub at the dead end, where Dad and Nancy would often play to the crowds, while I sold my canal art in the beer garden. We had some happy times there, before life got in the way and I took some wrong turns. As I swing the tiller to the right, leaving the junction behind, I try to remember the good bits and block out the rest.

Husbands Bosworth Tunnel gives a brief respite from the sun's rays and sprinkles me with cooling droplets, which evaporate in seconds as we re-emerge into the glare of the afternoon. I try to enjoy my cheese sandwiches, but the bread has dried out and the sweating cheese and melted margarine slither unappetisingly between the desiccated slices, so I give up. Even the ducks show little interest and the gobs of bread disappear beneath the canal's khaki surface, to be devoured by the pike who lurk, unseen, at the bottom.

Eventually the afternoon's lassitude gives way to evening. The sun's glare loses its grip, and the light mellows to golden. I pass a smart livery stable that reminds me I'm close to my destination. Two glossy, elegant horses look haughtily down their long noses at me as I pass by. I probably don't bear much scrutiny; I'm hot, sweaty and in need of a cool, shady place to tie up. Sadly the best moorings at Foxton Locks are rather exposed, but commerce must take priority over comfort. That's if I'm lucky enough to bag a decent spot, which is unlikely. It's getting late and all the best moorings have probably gone.

Foxton is a full-on tourist destination. The top lock boasts panoramic views across Leicestershire, best enjoyed with an ice-cream from the adjacent café. As you descend the path alongside the locks, you encounter a canal museum and a disused inclined plane, one of the white elephants of waterway history. Beyond the bottom lock is a large pool, where the Market Harborough Arm branches off from the main Grand Union. Two pubs and a shop overlook the water, and half of Leicester swarms out here at the first hint of sunshine. I'm hoping to sell the rest of my stock tomorrow, if the weather's good and I can find space among the traders who throng the towpath at the summit.

Amazingly, the Fates offer me a helping hand. As I pass under the final bridge before the top lock, I see a man untying his boat a few yards ahead. I try to rein in my hopes as I pull alongside and call out:

'You heading off, mate?'

'That's right. I've had a good day, flogged most of my stuff, and now I'm after a bit of peace and quiet.'

'D'you mind if I duck in there?'

'No problem. Just give me a minute, then fill your boots.'

On the towpath next to my new mooring is a statue of a horse; the type that used to tow the working boats before the invention of the diesel engine. I remember begging my dad to let me sit on it as a kid, even though the sign forbids it. This world-weary beast of burden hardly seems to belong to the same species as the disdainful beasts I encountered earlier, but I'm glad to have his company. After I've cleaned up, I get out one of my folding chairs and sit next to him while I enjoy my dinner. Then I decide to grab a quick drink at one of the pubs, before calling it a night.

I have no problem deciding which of the two pubs to visit. One's a destination pub catering for holiday boaters and day trippers. The other's low key, with great beer and no frills. No prizes for guessing which one I choose. I buy a pint of the guest ale and pick up a thriller from the free book exchange in the corner of the tiny bar. I figure it's a great way to make sure no one talks to me. Then I settle down and prepare to zone out.

By the time I'm halfway down my second pint, I'm getting thoroughly hacked off with the main character in my book. It's obvious from chapter one that the dude's going to get the girl in the end; I even know which girl. I've also been told repeatedly how handsome, intelligent and successful this paragon of virtue is, which makes me hate his guts. Time to choose a new book. As I stand up and walk over to the bookshelf, I see a woman sitting by herself, pawing at her phone. She looks up as I approach and I pray she won't talk to me, but she does.

'You gonna change that?'

'I think so. I've read a couple of chapters and I can't get on with it.'

'I would. Change it, I mean. I've read the whole thing and the hero's a right tosser.'

'Funny - I was just thinking the same thing.'

'There you are, then. Want me to pick you something?'

'It's OK. I don't want to disturb you...'

'You're not. My so-called date is over half an hour late and isn't responding to my texts, so realistically he's not gonna show. I might as well talk to you while I finish my drink. No point in wasting perfectly good gin. Right, let's see what they've got. I'm guessing you don't want slushy stuff – am I right?'

'Kind of. I'm not a big fan of Mills and Boon, but I don't mind a bit of emotion.'

'OK. Makes a change from most of the blokes I know. Look – I'm going to go out on a limb and recommend...this one.'

'Interesting choice. I haven't read it, but I did enjoy "Cloud Atlas"...'

'You're kidding! I've never met a man who's read anything by David Mitchell – unless you count that comedian off the TV...'

'Thanks, but I like his books as well...'

Then we're off. An impromptu book club is now in session. In between celebrating and shredding the books we love and hate, I find out Holly lives in Foxton village with her little girl, Stevie. She's a freelance graphic designer and her guilty pleasures are rhubarb gin, cold rice pudding ('gotta be eaten straight from the tin, or it doesn't work') and binge-watching Game of Thrones. I buy us more beer and gin, she returns the compliment, and all of a sudden it's closing time, so we walk outside into the dark.

'Thanks for a nice evening, book buddy. When my date didn't show I thought I'd wasted my babysitter money, but in the end it worked out alright.'

'You're welcome, Holly. I had fun too. Good to meet you.'

'You, too. See you around.' Holly pulls a torch from her bag and I remember my manners.

'Will you be alright getting home? It's very dark on the towpath...'

'I'll be fine. I've done this walk thousands of times.'

'OK then – if you're sure.'

'I am. Goodnight, Nathan.'

'Goodnight.'

I stand for a few minutes and watch the bobbing light of Holly's torch become smaller and fainter, until finally it gets extinguished by the darkness. Then I return to my boat.

I have a brilliant last day's trading. It's another sunny day, but not as hot as yesterday. I put on my canal outfit, sell almost all my remaining stock and pose for countless selfies with customers, beside my old friend the horse. I think he's the main attraction, to be honest. All day long, parents ignore the sign and pop their kids on his back for a photo. The guy in the dodgy waistcoat's an optional extra.

I'm just taking an order for one of my custom-painted water cans, when I catch the eye of a little girl in dungarees, up there on the horse. She smiles at me and waves.

'Hi, Nathan!'

'Shush, Stevie. Can't you see he's busy? You've got to wait your turn.'

I finish serving my customer, then walk over to Holly, who's holding Stevie as she pretends to gallop the horse.

'Hi, Nathan. I made the mistake of telling my daughter I made a new friend who lives on a boat, and she insisted on checking it out. She was interested until she spotted Dobbin here…'

'Don't worry. I'm not offended. Would you like a cup of tea?'

'Are you sure you've got time?'

'Of course. If I get any more customers, tell them I'll be back in five minutes.'

When I return with the teas, I find that Stevie has dismounted the horse and is looking pleased with herself.

'Me and Mummy sold loads of stuff!'

I raise an eyebrow at Holly, who smiles.

'Slight exaggeration. We flogged a set of coasters and a watering can. One guy wanted a planter, but I couldn't see any, so I said you had none left.'

'Correct. I've sold out of nearly everything. Well done, Stevie. I should pay you commission!'

'What's commission?' asks Stevie.

Holly spots the packet of digestives I've brought out with the tea. 'It's when you sell something for Nathan, and he gives you a biscuit.'

I look around frantically at the few remaining items on the shelves. 'A biscuit and maybe – a special pencil case, to take to school?'

'What d'you say to Nathan, Stevie?'

'Thank you,' mumbles Stevie, suddenly all shy.

'Stevie – I think Mummy deserves a present too, for helping you sell stuff to my customers. Do you agree?'

'What kind of present?'

'How about this little boat? Would she like that?'

'Yes, she would,' Holly says. 'But she's worried Nathan won't make enough money if he gives away all his stock.'

'Don't worry. It's the least I can do, for my two top saleswomen.'

Holly and I drink our tea, while Stevie eats several biscuits, washed down with a Fruit Shoot, which her mother produces from the massive bag all parents seem to lug around with them.

'I hope you didn't mind us coming.'

'Not at all. It was nice to see you – and meet Stevie, of course.'

'Great. Right, I must be off. My dad's coming over for tea and he's a creature of habit – likes to be fed bang on time.'

'No worries. Look – do you and Stevie ever make the trip to Leicester?'

'Of course. It might seem far away if you're on one of these things, but not if you've got a car – even a crappy old thing like mine.'

'I take your point. Anyway, what I was going to say is – if Stevie wants a boat trip some time – I'm in Bastion Marina.'

'That's a nice offer. I'm sure she'd like that. Give me your number and I'll get her to ring you next time she fancies a day out.'

So I write down my number and Holly pockets it, then she leads Stevie away down the towpath, back towards the village. As I watch them go, I have the uncomfortable feeling I've failed. As the saying goes, I've snatched defeat from the jaws of victory, but it's too late to do anything about it now and, in any case, it's probably for the best.

Suddenly the towpath is empty; people eat early in this part of the world, and I guess they've all gone home or retired to the pub, so I pack up my few remaining trinkets and climb back onto the boat. It's time to prepare to head home tomorrow. My inaugural trip on Festina Lente is nearly at an end.

The following morning, I'm first in the queue for the staircase. When I book in with the lock keeper, I make a point of mentioning that I'm boating solo, and my plan works. When I arrive at the top lock, both lock keepers are in position, ready to help me through. They want to make sure I don't hold up the boats behind me; a delay at the head of the queue means playing catch-up all day. So I get through Foxton Locks quickly, and it looks as though I'll make it back to Bastion by lunchtime. As I pass the pub where I met Holly, I feel a brief pang of regret, then chalk it up to my ineptitude with the opposite sex.

My last morning serves up another feast of rural boating, as the canal weaves its way around woods, hills and villages. I almost forget our last tunnel, until I see the gaping black hole of the tunnel mouth and hurriedly switch on my tunnel light.

Compared with Braunston and Crick, Saddington Tunnel is short. You can see a golden circle of light at the far end as you enter, and you soon emerge on the other side. There are some widely spaced locks on this stretch, which occupy me intermittently, but I still get a final chance to enjoy the wildlife. A heron stands like a sentry on the bank at Fleckney, as if to bid me goodbye, until next time. Then, just as I'm gearing up for the many locks which punctuate the route back into the city, there's a vivid blue flash in my peripheral vision. I instinctively turn my head, just in time to see a kingfisher hit the water like a neon dart and emerge triumphant, with a silver fish wriggling in its beak. I feel blessed; many boaters never spot the elusive kingfisher, and few see one make a successful catch - but now I've got work to do. I pick up my windlass and prepare to toil my way downhill, through the locks into Leicester and back to Bastion.

So here we are. We've come full circle. Geoff has given me a massive to-do list, so I'm going to be busy for the next few weeks. I hope you've enjoyed the journey and we know each other better than before. That'll come in handy later on. I'm sorry I'm not a perfect action hero, like the bloke in the book I rejected on the night I met Holly. I know I've got lots of flaws, but I promise you one thing. For the rest of our time together, I'll do my best.

6 PAYBACK TIME

Thank you for indulging me in the last chapter by travelling at narrowboat pace. I hope you found it relaxing, but now it's time to speed up a bit.

After I return to Bastion, I'm either busy with the long list of repair jobs Geoff lined up for me or working for one of the tradesmen I told you about before. Jim, in particular, is constantly on the phone. Everyone's electrics seem to be playing up and he's glad to have his little helper back to cover off the minor jobs. Meanwhile I try not to dwell on how I messed up with Holly. I'm positive I've heard the last of her, but it turns out I'm wrong.

One Friday afternoon, I've just finished covering one of the jetties with a new layer of chicken wire to make it non-slip ready for winter, when my phone buzzes with an incoming SMS.

Holly: 'I'm sending this text against my better judgement, but Stevie won't stop pestering me. She wants a trip on your boat. Any chance you can oblige?'

I'm not going to make the same mistake twice.

Me: 'It would be great to see you – and Stevie. How about this weekend? The weather's going to be nice.'

Holly: 'I could do Sunday.'

Me: 'Great. Would eleven work for you? I'll make a picnic.'

Holly: 'Alright. See you then.'

It's not the most effusive exchange, but it's better than I ever expected. I hope I managed to make up for my previous faux pas and convinced Holly that it's her I want to see, not just Stevie.

So Sunday arrives, and so do Holly and Stevie. I'm awkward and tongue-tied with Holly in a way I never was around Ruth, and I get the feeling she picks up on my nerves and decides she can't cope. Stevie's oblivious to the tension between me and her mum; she's just excited to be on the boat. As we leave the first lock and head north, Holly quietly asks if she can go and sit at the front, leaving me and Stevie at the tiller, and I have no choice but to agree. I'm flattered she's happy to leave me in charge of her daughter, but disappointed to be deprived of her company. Meanwhile Stevie bombards me with a relentless barrage of questions. In response, I explain how the boat works and name every bird we see along the way. When a fish breaks free of the water, twists in mid-air, then drops back in with a splash, the little girl squeals with delight. Later, when we moor up to eat our picnic, she drags me off on a quest for feathers and flowers to take to school on Monday for show and tell, leaving her mum behind to gaze silently at the water. When we return to Bastion, I realise Holly and I have exchanged no more than a few sentences. As I watch her drive away, I expect never to see her again, so I'm astonished when I get a text the following week, asking for another trip. Apparently Stevie had an amazing time and is desperate to return.

Fast forward a month, and Holly and Stevie have visited several more times. However, each trip has followed a similar pattern to the first, and I don't feel I know Holly any better. I can't regain the sense of easy camaraderie I felt when we happily discussed books for several hours on the first night we met. Perhaps we're destined just to be friends, or maybe not even that. To be honest, Stevie feels like a much better friend than Holly right now. On our last trip, she revealed she was going to stay with her dad for half-term. When I asked her if she was looking forward to it, she replied in her usual candid style.

'No. I like being here better. Mummy likes it too.'

I was tempted to press for more details, but Stevie had already moved on, demanding I explain why leaves turn yellow in autumn and fall from the trees, so I let it go. That night, not for the first time, I lay awake for hours trying to figure it out. When I woke the next morning, I was overwhelmed by the urge to get away again, put some distance between me and Holly and try and gain some perspective on the whole thing. So, before I had time to change my mind, I went to see Geoff and negotiated a few weeks of unpaid leave. The backlog of repair jobs was under control, so he was happy to comply and keep his costs down. Also, when I said I was going to visit my sister, he was pleased, as I knew he'd be. Having engineered our reunion, he wants to see us become a devoted brother and sister. I wish I could explain to him that, with Nancy and me, it's never going to be that simple.

Before I leave, I call Holly. I explain I'm going to London to see my sister, but that I'll be back. She doesn't say much, apart from to thank me for letting her know, which I guess is something. Then I head south on the Grand Union, through Milton Keynes, Hemel Hempstead and a host of other forgettable places, and drop into the city from the west.

I moor up in Islington, just east of Danbury Road Bridge. From here, I can easily walk to Nancy's house and back again later. I don't plan to stay the night; my sister and I aren't on a secure enough footing yet and besides, she's living with someone, and I don't want to get in the way. Some guy called Johnno, a drummer in a supposedly up and coming band. As usual, the guy's decades younger than her, but I've promised myself not to have a go at her, even though I worry he's just using her to get on in the music business. Clearly I've got no moral high ground from which to lecture her on her choice of boyfriends, and I'm determined not to provoke one of our rows.

Don't get me wrong; I'm pleased to have Nancy back in my life, but I still struggle sometimes with how it happened. I love my new boat, but at the same time I can't forget it was Nancy's money which made it all possible. I know it's pride talking, but I do feel indebted to her, and I can't see how I'll ever pay her back, which makes me feel guilty and resentful. I shouldn't, but I do. Having once been my sister's protector, her dependable older brother, I now hate the notion that the tables have turned. I'm proud of her success, but it does throw my own failures into sharp relief. I know she doesn't see things the same way, but that's hardly surprising. It's easy to sugar coat reality, when you're the one on top. As I approach Richmond Crescent, I tell myself to man up, enjoy some time with my sister and go easy on the JD. I know if I drink too much, all this stuff I just told you will come pouring out, and I'd rather keep it between ourselves.

Most of the houses in the crescent have clearly been converted into apartments. Beside each front door is a row of doorbells, with a name plaque next to each one. However, when I find Nancy's house, I see there's just a single doorbell, with no name displayed next to it. I hesitate, then press the bell and listen to it echo in the hallway beyond. I look around for security cameras but see none. After a couple of minutes, I hear the sound of approaching footsteps, then the door opens just a little and my sister peers through the gap.

'Hi, bro. Sorry about the chain thing. I just needed to check it was you.'

'They have these things called security cameras now,' I say as I follow her up the stairs. 'So you can see who's at the door, even when you're out. You can access them via an app on your phone…'

'Look, bro – if you're planning on being this boring all night, you can just jog on back to your boat…'

'Don't listen to her, Nathan. I've been telling her to get a security system installed, but she takes no notice. Good to know I'm not the only one she ignores. I'm Johnno, by the way. Pleased to meet you.'

I soon feel ashamed that I thought the guy was just using Nancy to further his career. It's obvious he's devoted to my sister; I can tell by the way he looks at her. He brings us a cold beer, asks me a few polite questions about my boat, then makes his excuses. He says he's got band practice, but I reckon he's just giving me and Nancy some space, which is decent of him. After he leaves, Nancy flops down on the sofa and stares as me defiantly.

'S'pose you're going to accuse me of cradle snatching, as usual.'

'Actually, no. He seems like a nice guy. You've lucked out there.'

Nancy smiles. 'Who are you and what have you done with my brother?'

'Very funny. Anyway, are you going to give me a tour of the house, or what?'

'OK - but let me order a takeaway first. I've got no food in the place.'

'Why does that not surprise me?'

'Pizza work for you?'

'Sure – as long as it hasn't got pineapple on it.'

'God no – gross. Right, where's my phone…'

Once the American Hot is on its way, Nancy shows me around her house, and I'm overwhelmed. Obviously, I've known for years how successful she is, but this is the first time I've seen tangible evidence, and I have to admit it's intimidating. It's suddenly very clear to me, now I've seen her home, that my boat was nothing but small change to my sister. No one could describe her as houseproud, so the place isn't super-tidy, but it has been expertly done over by an interior designer in a minimalist, faux-industrial style which reflects Nancy's no-nonsense approach to life, and it's filled with the kind of stuff most people could never afford. Huge, walk-in wardrobes, a massive wet room, an immense waterbed and a range cooker more suited to a professional kitchen than to my sister, who can barely boil an egg. It's the music room which really knocks me sideways, though. Nancy has told me about her pink grand piano, and it's nice to see it in the flesh, as it were, but she has never mentioned the display that covers the wall opposite.

'What's all this, Nan?'

'I call it my altar. It's the reason I don't show many people my music room; it's kind of personal. All my favourite female artists are up there – the women who inspire me. It helps me to look at them, when I'm at the piano writing my songs.'

'It's nice of you to show me, sis. Can I take a closer look?'

'If you like.'

Nancy's altar is plastered with photos, concert tickets and posters, but tucked in between are all these little notes. As I start to read, I realise they're from some of the women in the photos. These artists, who are household names to you and me, clearly know and like my sister well enough to reminisce about happy times and offer support and encouragement. I'm not allowed to reveal who they are, but here are a couple of examples. They've both used their real names, not their stage names, so we should be OK.

'To Nan, aka The Baroness – we'll always have Camden, girl. Keep the faith and keep on rockin'! Marianne xoxo'

'I'm glad we got to meet – just in time. Remember – never compromise. Mary.'

As I stare at Nancy's altar, and the gold discs which line the wall opposite, my eyes fill with tears. Suddenly I can't control myself. I start sobbing, and Nancy jumps up from the piano stool, where she has been sitting.

'Hey, bro. What's brought this on?'

'I-I'm sorry, sis. It's just that, I don't think I ever really got how successful you are. How well you've done. I'm so…proud of you.'

'I just got lucky, Nathan. I was in the right place at the right time. End of chat. There are plenty who are way more talented than me but will never make it. That's life.'

'Maybe so, but you made the most of your chances, and what did I do? I screwed up, every time. I made mistakes, didn't learn from them, then made them all over again…'

'Quit beating yourself up, bro. Man up instead – and put it behind you!'

'I'm trying, but the truth is I don't trust myself. I'm so scared of messing up again. That gang I got involved with – they don't fool about – but at least I've got back-up now. And then there's this woman I met…'

'Hold on; you're not making sense. Look, there's the doorbell. That'll be the pizza. Why don't we grab a bottle, have something to eat, then you can tell me the whole story. It's time we got things straight.'

It's very late when I leave Nancy's house. She wanted me to sleep over, but I refused; I told you earlier I wouldn't stay the night, and I've stuck to it. I also said I wouldn't drink too much JD, but that particular resolution went right out of the window, once we got talking. You see, I told my sister everything, but I couldn't do it sober and I'm conscious I might regret it when I wake up in the morning. Still, it's done, and I can't unsay any of it. Nancy knows the lot, now. She knows the full truth about Ruth, and she knows all about Giles, Hadley and the rest of them. I told her about prison too; in a lot more detail than I had time for, with you. She listened in silence as I explained all about my cellmate Ray, whom I taught to read, plus the resettlement officers and everyone else who helped me. In fact, I've never known her so quiet – until we got onto the subject of Holly. By this time I was well stuck into the JD, so my loose tongue didn't hesitate to reveal that I liked her a lot but had probably blown it.

'Don't be so sure, bro. Sounds like she's the kind of chick who needs time before she can trust you. Probably Stevie's father, or some other dude, stomped all over her life and she doesn't want to go through that again. Just be patient. Get on with your life, keep her in it and see what happens.'

'Good advice, sis. Don't tell me you're getting all sensible in your old age...'

'Not a chance.'

The next morning, I turn my boat around and begin the long journey home. As I cruise west on Regent's Canal, en route to the Grand Union, I think hard about my evening with Nancy. It dredged up a lot of emotions: pride, jealousy, shame and fear, to name but a few. Afterwards, all I wanted was to be alone on my boat to think it through. In a way, I feel more vulnerable, now I've revealed all my secrets to Nancy. I felt safer when it was just you and me, but even so, I'm sort of glad we've got her on side. My sister can be quite formidable; you wouldn't want to cross her. Sorry if that sounds conflicted.

Once I get home, life carries on as normal. Autumn grows progressively colder and darker, then segues into winter. As the weather worsens, boats trips lose their appeal for Stevie, who doesn't like the cold. For a while it feels as though my friendship with my new buddy and her mum has run its course, but just as I'm about to lose hope, Holly texts me to say that Stevie misses her friend Nathan. I don't know whether her mum feels the same way, but I decide not to push it and end up visiting their house in Foxton every couple of weeks, for tea or an early dinner. Holly picks me up in her car and delivers me back to Bastion afterwards. On each occasion, I spend a happy hour or so playing with Stevie and her collection of Barbie dolls; a garish line-up which would put the cast of RuPaul's Drag Race to shame. While we eat, Holly and I compare notes on the books we're reading, and I gradually rediscover some of the ease I felt with her on the first night we met. Whenever I'm tempted to steer the conversation in a more intimate direction, I recall Nancy's advice and back off.

Just before Christmas, I stop by the marina office at closing time to report back to Geoff on the jobs I've completed that day. Usually, it's a five-minute conversation but today, Geoff has a special request for me.

'Nathan – have you got any plans for the run-up to Christmas?'

'Yes, of course; a different party every night and a string of hot dates...'

'Thought as much. In that case, do you fancy a trip down to Stratford-upon-Avon? The owners of Meander 2 have sold to a couple who live there, on condition they move the boat down to Bancroft Basin by the end of the year. They looked into road transportation, but it was too expensive, so they asked me if I could help, and I thought of you. I reckoned the extra money might come in useful, for Christmas.'

For a moment I hesitate; I'm not sure if this is a good time to go away, when Holly and I seem to be getting on OK at last, but then I figure a week won't make much difference. What with Christmas shopping and all the other festive nonsense, she'll barely notice I've gone. Also, the Stratford Canal is one of my favourites. Then there's the cash, of course. Before I can change my mind, I tell Geoff I'll take the job.

The weather during my trip is excellent for the time of year. Obviously it's cold, but each day dawns bright with sparkling frost and the sun remains unclothed by cloud until it dips below the horizon for an early night. To make the most of the daylight, I set off with the sun and cruise continually until nightfall. I power down the Grand Union Canal, through Braunston, then turn right at Napton Junction towards Warwick. At Stockton Locks I'm tempted by the two lovely pubs located, like bookends, on either side of the flight, but I resist the urge to stop and push on towards one of the most iconic and strenuous locations on the network. Hatton Flight is an imposing edifice of twenty-one locks that stretches mercilessly up the hillside north of the town. Hours later, I shut the gates of the top lock, admire the view south across the majestic spires of Warwick and text a photo to Holly and Stevie. Then I wiggle through the hairpin twists and turns of scenic Kingswood Junction, and there it is – the Stratford Canal.

Novice boaters who have struggled through the deep-throated double locks of Stockton and Hatton tend to breathe a sigh of relief when they see the quaint single locks on the Stratford, but the feeling is invariably short-lived. The gear on those locks is so antiquated that they're incredibly difficult to operate. Even I had forgotten what a trial they are, but it soon comes back to me. I curse the clunky mechanics and distract myself by taking photos of the quirky lock keepers' cottages, with their white walls and barrel roofs. That night, I go straight to bed with the Complete Works of Shakespeare. It feels appropriate, seeing as we're getting near the home of the bard.

The following lunchtime I reach my final destination – Bancroft Basin, next to the Royal Shakespeare Theatre. I've made good time; the owners aren't scheduled to pick the boat up until tomorrow, so I have a free night before I hand the keys over and take the train back to Leicester. I manage to moor right next to the statue of Hamlet, and it feels like a sign, so I walk over to the RSC to see if I can get a cheap last-minute ticket for tonight's performance of Macbeth. Sadly they're sold out; not surprising, I guess, as it's so close to Christmas. When I get back to the boat, I text Holly a Hamlet picture and mention I've missed out on my chance to see the Scottish Play. I'm heating up some soup for lunch when my phone pings with her reply:

Holly: 'Just checked the website. I can get us two tickets for tomorrow's matinée.'

Me: 'I've got to hand over the boat tomorrow morning – then I'm going to get the train back.'

Holly: 'No worries – I'll drive you home afterwards. Save you the fare.'

Me: 'What about Stevie?'

Holly: 'My Dad will have her for the day.'

Me: 'OK then – sounds great.'

The next day, Holly arrives just as I'm completing the handover to the new owners of Meander 2. She's amazed boaters can tie up in the shadow of the RSC. We have lunch in a nearby pub and admire the pictures of Shakespearian luvvies that paper the walls, then enjoy a spectacularly blood-soaked performance of Macbeth. For most of the dark drive home, we dissect the play; we're both back on comfortable territory, in a world of literary make-believe where we can talk freely, without sharing too much of ourselves.

I don't know what makes Holly break out of this safe space and tell me about Stevie's dad. Maybe the darkness of the car makes her feel secure, almost as if I'm not there, or perhaps it's just the right time. Anyway, she suddenly starts talking, and I remain silent as she describes her years of torment at the hands of a controlling, serially unfaithful bully with serious alcohol and drug problems. After she finally found the courage to leave, he managed to get clean and begged her to return, but the damage was done. She has no contact with him now; her dad organises the access visits with Stevie and she worries herself sick until her daughter is returned safely to her. She says she's telling me this so I understand why, ever since, she has limited herself to the odd Tinder hook-up, and why she doesn't think she can ever trust a man again.

I have a choice here. Either I can play safe and just sympathise with her predicament, or I can jump right in, reciprocate with my own history and give her plenty of reasons not to confide in me ever again. She might even throw me out of her car, here in the middle of nowhere, and I wouldn't blame her. Even so, I decide to risk it. After all, I'm getting used to telling people my sorry story. Ray heard it first, then you. After that there was Gemma, my probation officer, then Nick at the Job Centre, followed by

Geoff, and finally Nancy. The last time was the scariest so far, but I know telling Holly will be even more frightening. It feels like the right thing to do, though. 'Screw your courage to the sticking place,' as Lady Macbeth said earlier. Good advice, scary bird. So I take a deep breath – then I talk.

I'm still speaking when I see the first signs to Leicester. There's a lay-by up ahead and Holly indicates left, ready to pull in. I figure it's decent of her to wait until I'm within striking distance of the marina before she chucks me out. As the car comes to a halt, I undo my seat belt.

'So you got done over as well. By Ruth – and that gang of lowlifes.'

'Sure, but I brought it on myself. I can't claim to be a victim.'

'Like me? Is that what you mean?'

'Not at all. Your story's completely different.'

'Maybe, but I'm not entirely blameless, either.'

'That's kind of you to say. Anyway, I thought I should tell you my story, seeing as you were brave enough to tell me yours. I wish I had a better one for you. Thanks for dropping me off...'

'Hang on; that's not why I stopped.'

'I don't understand.'

'Look, I can either carry on to Leicester from here, and drop you back at your boat, or I can cut across country to Foxton, if you fancy – staying over.'

'Oh – I see. Er...cross country sounds fine.'

So that's how Holly and I finally get together. By unspoken agreement, we make a cautious start; I guess we're both terrified of making a mistake. We mostly see each other at weekends, when Stevie's around, and we keep things low key in front of her. In fact, we're so successful that, at first, I don't think she realises anything has changed between us. Then, as winter releases its grip, we start taking longer boat trips. Stevie sleeps in a folding bed in the workshop while Holly and I share the cabin. She doesn't waste any time; on our first trip, she collars me while I'm steering and Holly's in the galley making coffee.

'So Mummy says you're her boyfriend now.'

'That's right.'

'Does that mean you're coming to live in our house?'

'No, Stevie. I live here, on the boat. It's my home.'

'Don't you like our house?'

'Your house is lovely. But your mum and I need to get to know each other really well before we think about living in the same place.'

'Why?'

'So we're sure it's the right thing for all three of us. So we don't make a mistake.'

'Like Mummy did with Daddy?'

'I don't know your dad, so I can't really say...'

'He made Mummy cry. She cried a lot of the time, when I was little. She thinks I don't remember, but I do.'

'Come here.' Stevie climbs down off the roof and stands next to me at the tiller. I put my arm around her. 'I promise you I'll be kind to your mummy. I'll try to make sure she's happy and has fun. I'm not a super-hero, so I might mess up sometimes, but I promise you I'll do my best.'

Stevie seems content with my response, and even happier when her mum brings her a chocolate croissant to enjoy with her morning milk. On that trip, we travel south to Crick. She enjoys helping the lock keepers at Foxton, then I don't think she's silent for more than two minutes. Holly retreats to the prow with her book, leaving me to field endless questions about the wildlife alongside the canal. Six hours later, we moor up near Crick Wharf. Stevie devours a large bowl of homemade ice cream, Holly has a pot of tea and I down my first pint in about two seconds, then order another. I reckon I deserve it. I'm exhausted, but in a good way. Funny how kids make you see the world differently, isn't it? It's a though they have their own crazy, perspective-altering Instagram filter.

During that trip, Stevie mentions she likes drawing, so I buy her a sketchbook and a set of coloured pencils to keep on the boat. I've seen some of Holly's awesome graphic designs and I figure her daughter might have inherited her mum's artistic talent. I'm not trying to keep her quiet, I promise you. Anyway, the little girl is absurdly delighted with her present and I wonder whether her dad ever bothers to get her anything.

Over the next few months, we make a series of short trips to Braunston, Welford and Market Harborough. Holly brings her laptop and works on her latest commission; she always seems to have a deadline looming. Stevie asks loads more questions – the sketchbook wouldn't have stopped her talking, even if I wanted it to – and produces a host of drawings I think are brilliant for her age. Her mother's less impressed; I guess she's used to Stevie's precocious talent. Every evening she reviews what Stevie has done and suggests how she could do better next time. This leaves me to play the role of uncritical, besotted fan, which suits me fine.

At the start of the summer holidays, Stevie's supposed to be spending a few days with her dad, but when her grandad tries to drop her off, there's no one at home and Dad's not answering his mobile. None of us, including Stevie, is particularly bothered; in fact, Stevie seems quite relieved. She tells me she's looking forward to staying with her grandad in his static caravan in Great Yarmouth, and in the meantime she seems quite happy hanging out with her friends in Foxton.

While Stevie's in Yarmouth, Holly and I make our first solo trip. I've often waxed lyrical to her about the beautiful Shropshire Union Canal and the stunning Pontcysyllte Aqueduct in Llangollen, so she suggests we see it for ourselves. I'm nervous about how it'll work out, but I agree anyway. We might as well find out if we can be happy together, just the two of us.

The Fates provide us with a long period of warm, sunny weather, which always helps when you want your companion to fall in love with the canals. Holly lies on top of the boat, reading her book and soaking up the heat from the steel roof like a lizard basking on a rock. She works the locks efficiently, cursing occasionally when she comes across some antiquated gear that she struggles to budge, but she makes few mistakes, and Festina Lente belies its name by making rapid progress. During the early part of the trip, we cruise from dawn to dusk as we head north, skirting around the western edge of Birmingham. At lunchtime, Holly makes sandwiches, which we eat on the run. We blast through endless lock flights and skim across the pages of the guidebook.

Once we reach the 'Shroppie', everything changes. Maybe it's the glorious views across open countryside, interspersed by secluded, deeply wooded cuttings. Perhaps it's because there are relatively few locks; who knows? Anyway, for whatever reason, we finally start to relax. Holly suggests stopping for lunch, which goes against my commercial boater's instincts, but I agree. From then on we spend a couple of hours, most days, on the towpath in our deckchairs with a book each. Holly asks me to teach her to paint roses and castles and picks it up annoyingly quickly, decorating a set of six mugs over several lunchtimes. She breaks with convention whenever she chooses, and the end result is better for it. I joke that we'll set up shop in Llangollen and split the profits.

At Wheaton Aston, we spot a canal side pub and moor up for an early evening drink. The beer's excellent, Holly gets stuck into the white wine and when we totter back to the boat, the cabin seems a more appealing prospect than the tiller. Before we know it, a new regime is in place. More downtime, more booze, lots more sex. I decide I could get used to this new, hedonistic approach to boating. As we approach Llangollen, we're languid and lazy. Holly hasn't opened her laptop in days, and I stand at the tiller with a dazed, dopey expression on my face. We wake up temporarily as we look down from the Pontcysyllte Aqueduct at the valley floor, over a hundred feet below, then we arrive in Trevor Basin and prepare to zone out for a day or so. It's then the Fates decide they've been kind for long enough.

We've just finished tying up when my phone buzzes in my pocket. I stare blankly at the screen, then the adrenaline kicks in as I read my sister's text:

Nancy: 'Hi bro. I'm jacking it all in and joining you on the canals. Fancy meeting up when I reach Leicester?'

Me: 'What's going on, sis?'

Nancy: 'I'll explain when I see you.'

Me: 'Nan, I'm in Llangollen with Holly.'

Nancy: 'No drama. We can do it another time.'

Me: 'Can I call you?'

Nancy: 'No. I'm not in the mood. I'll be in touch.'

I try calling anyway, but Nancy's one step ahead of me, as usual, and has switched her phone off, so I ask Holly's advice. I'm rattled by Nancy's bombshell, but Holly's pragmatism steadies me. She reminds me Nancy isn't ill, and she doesn't appear to need anything from me other than to be left alone until we get a chance to talk face to face, so there really isn't anything to worry about. She says that from what I've told her, it never sounded as though Nancy was content, despite her wealth and success, so perhaps this latest move shouldn't come as a surprise to me. She's right, of course, so I accept the beer she offers me and gradually calm down. Later on I leave a voicemail for my sister, saying I'm here for her whenever she needs me, then I let it go. Nancy has always needed her own space to figure things out, so I leave her to it, just like she wanted.

In the end, I manage to recover my chilled vibe and Holly and I stay in Llangollen a couple of days longer than planned. There are loads of tourists swanning around Trevor Basin, so we decide to open up my shop, and we get mobbed. Holly sells most of my stock and takes orders for commissions, while I beaver away in my workshop, trying to replenish the lines which have sold out. After two days we concede we can't keep up with demand, so we pack up and count our pennies. Our takings have more than paid for our holiday, so we high five each other and head for home. It has been a good trip, so far. We've had fun and worked well as a team. Neither of us is the type to dissect our relationship, but it feels to me as though something has solidified between us. After a few weeks spent floating on murky canal water, we're somehow on firmer ground.

We're still on the 'Shroppie' when I get another text from Nancy:

Nancy: 'Hi bro. You home yet?'

Me: 'No - we're up near Market Drayton. What's wrong?'

Nancy: 'I'm south of Foxton, rescuing a novice boater. I could use an extra pair of hands, but you're not around. No worries - I'll sort it.'

Me: 'I can speed up and get back more quickly...'

Nancy: 'No. It'll all be over by then. I've got this. Chill.'

So I do. Growing up, Nancy and I helped countless novice boaters with every conceivable problem, so I've no doubt she'll be fine. Whatever trouble this person's having, Nancy will have encountered it before, no question. I don't want to be accused of being in her face, so I leave it a few days, then drop her another text:

Me: 'All OK, sis? Did that novice boater get sorted out?'

Nancy: 'Yep – all good here. See you soon x'

That's odd. Nancy's not normally one for adding kisses at the end of her messages. I decide not to knock myself out by over-analysing it.

I don't message Nancy again until I'm back in Bastion. Holly has gone home and I'm spending the first night in weeks on my own.

Me: 'Hi sis – I'm back now. Where are you?'

Nancy: 'Closer than you think.'

Me: 'Where?'

Nancy: 'Allenby Marina. South of Leicester.'

Me: 'You should have told me! I went past there yesterday – I could have stopped by.'

Nancy: 'I'm not ready for company. I'll message you when I am.'

Me: 'What are you doing settling into a marina? Has someone body-snatched my sister?'

Nancy: 'No chance ☺. Now sod off.'

So I wait a couple of weeks. As I said earlier, I learned in prison how to wait, and I haven't lost the knack. I don't message Nancy once, until I receive her promised invitation. I reply immediately and check out the bus timetables.

Nancy's message says her boat is called Warrior and is moored at the far end of the marina. It doesn't take me long to spot it. Most of the narrowboats at Allenby are fancy craft that have been lovingly maintained – all shiny paintwork and gleaming chrome. This is clearly a more upmarket marina than Bastion – a place where the fat of wallet park their floating caravans. However, even in this exalted company, Warrior stands out. It's one of these faux-industrial craft; meant to look like a well-preserved relic from the nineteenth century, when in reality it's bristling with twenty-first century technology. I tease Nancy about this, but in reality I'm impressed, and I also understand. After a childhood in a basic boatman's cabin, I can see why a washing machine, remote control central heating and touch screen controls would appeal to her.

My sister grabs us a couple of beers and a family sized bag of Monster Munch. As she does, she witters on about this novice boater she helped, whose husband had apparently done a runner and who was then accused of stalking or something. I'm only half listening, as I'm still checking out the very impressive interior of her boat. Also, I can't raise much interest in a person I'm never going to meet.

'So that's how I wound up here,' she concludes, as she hands me my beer.

'OK, but why have you stayed?'

Nancy pauses for a moment and takes a swig of beer. 'I've been hanging out with an old friend. His name's Dan. He's a session musician – played on some of my albums and came on tour a few times.'

'So you kicked Johnno into touch?'

'Yeah – along with the rest of my old life – the house, the recording contract, the lot. I'll tell you all about it over dinner.'

'What dinner? I thought these Monster Munch were it.'

'No – you're in luck. Dan's cooking on his boat, but don't read anything into it. He's just a friend.'

'Let me guess. With benefits.'

'Whatever.'

'That's nice, but I'm sad about Johnno. He was a solid guy.'

'Still is, and he'll get over it. Probably already has.'

The three of us have a pleasant dinner. Dan, a charming Irishman, turns out to be a great cook, although his galley is nowhere near as flash as the one on Warrior. In a break with tradition, Nancy has chosen someone about the same age as herself, and the difference is immediately apparent. Whilst Dan doesn't hang on her every word, like Johnno, he and Nancy laugh at the same jokes and occasionally finish each other's sentences. Although she maintains it's just a casual thing, Dan clearly didn't get the memo, and I think she's kidding herself as well. It's obvious to me that the two of them just click, but I decide to keep my thoughts to myself.

Throughout the evening, Nancy insists she's done with the music business, but Dan gently tells her not to be too hasty. He maintains that talented artists don't need a record company these days; apparently, digital and social media skills are all you need to forge a successful career as an independent. Nancy's not convinced and says she and Warrior will shortly be heading north, but I don't buy it. I think she's staying put, and I'm glad. It'll be nice to have her around.

It turns out I'm right. Nancy remains in Allenby with Dan and only takes occasional holidays on the network. She's busy with her new recording studio, housed in a converted widebeam boat, and with the new fans who have discovered her music via social media. It's Holly and I who do most of the travelling. During the school holidays, Stevie comes with us, but in term time she stays with her grandad and we enjoy some adults-only trips.

After we return from one, my sister invites us over for dinner. Dan cooks and I lend a hand, trying not to eavesdrop while Nancy and Holly chat quietly over a drink. My glass constantly gets topped up with real ale while I'm stirring the risotto and chopping the salad. It's a lethal brew, so by the time we sit down to eat I feel no pain. The alcohol does its usual job of compressing time and, before I know it, Holly's driving me back to Foxton. I fall asleep in the car and have only a vague recollection of going to bed.

The next afternoon, I'm back at Bastion in the dry dock, replacing the sacrificial anodes on a boat's hull, when my phone rings. It's Nancy.

'Hi bro. How's your head?'

'It'll be fine once the drum solo finishes.'

'You never learn, do you?'

'Pot? Kettle?'

'Yeah, I know. Thanks for coming over.'

'Thanks for inviting us. I had a good time – I think.'

'I enjoyed my chat with Holly. She's cool.'

'I'm glad you think so.'

'You've done well, Nathan. You did the right thing by taking it slow. Holly was telling me about her ex. I get why it took her a long while to trust you – but she does now. Do me a favour – don't balls it up.'

'I'll try.'

Nancy puts on a croaky voice. 'Do or do not. There is no try.'

'Thanks, Yoda. I never had you down as a Star Wars fan, sis.'

'I had to do something on all those long-haul flights. Anyway, that little dude gives good advice. Holly's one of the good ones. Look after her.'

So I do. I pass my bike test and renovate a beaten-up Vespa, which I use to shuttle between Bastion and Foxton, so I can stay with Holly and Stevie several nights a week and get back to Bastion in time for work. I have a toothbrush in Holly's bathroom and clothes in the wardrobe. I help Stevie with her homework, and she starts getting better marks in her essays and spelling bees. Holly and I cruise the Warwickshire Ring and explore the Oxford Canal, with its easy single locks and cosy canal side pubs. We've just had dinner in one of them, at Aynho, when she decides to level with me.

'Nathan. You know I love our boat trips...'

'You do seem to, most of the time. Especially this morning...' I give her a playful nudge.

'Be serious for a moment. What I'm saying is – I enjoy taking holidays on the boat – but I couldn't live on the canals full time. Just so you know.'

With someone as reserved as Holly, you learn to read between the lines. I think over our conversation and conclude she's ready to consider moving in together, but only if I stop living on my boat – and I'm not sure I can. I love Holly, but the canals gave me my life back and I don't know if I can turn my back on them and live in a regular house. Also, our semi-detached relationship works well, and I'm frightened of changing it. So I decide to ignore the issue for the moment. Christmas, that great friend to procrastinators, is coming up, so I use it as an excuse to forget what Holly said until the New Year and just enjoy the festive season. Holly seems OK with my lack of response; at least, she doesn't raise the subject again over the holidays.

Despite the co-habiting elephant in the room, I have the best Christmas ever. I stay over at Holly's on Christmas Eve, so I get woken up at six by Stevie, desperate to open her presents. We leave her mum to sleep in, and I make us a jug of hot chocolate while Stevie roots delightedly through her stocking. She's at the age where she's just as happy with her chocolate orange and scented highlighters as she is with her bigger presents, and I pray for her not to discover the world of Fortnight and designer trainers too soon. Once she falls victim to the power of branded merchandise, my meagre bank balance will be shot.

After the presents have been opened, Holly asks me to watch Frozen with Stevie for about the millionth time, while she cooks up a storm. Nancy and Dan join us for a long, relaxed Christmas lunch, and by early evening the table is a wasteland of empty bottles, shredded crackers and dirty plates. My sister and I offer to clear up and install Dan and Holly on the sofa with a bottle of JD, while Stevie dresses up her new dolls with their terrifying, dinner-plate eyes and neon-pink, nylon tresses.

'Happy, bro?' Nancy asks me as I hand her a tea towel.

'Yeah, actually. You?'

'Weirdly enough, I am. Who'd have thought it?'

'You realise something's bound to go wrong...'

'That's what I've always liked about you, Nathan. Your positive attitude to life.'

'Just being realistic, that's all.'

'Christmas is no time for realism. Now scrub those bloody pans, or those two will have necked all the JD by the time we get finished.'

I'm right, though. In the New Year, the Fates decide to twist the knife; or maybe they just want me to make an actual decision, for once in my life. I've just finished a finger-numbing day blacking a boat's hull in the dry dock at Bastion, when I get a text from Geoff, asking me to come up to the office immediately, which is odd. I normally join him for a cup of tea at close of play, and God knows I'm desperate for a brew on a frigid day like this, but I'm not due to finish for another half an hour. However, Geoff never uses words like immediately unless it's something urgent, so I quickly pack up my toolbox and head on over.

As soon as I walk in the door, I see from Geoff's face that it's bad news. His ruddy cheeks have paled and his shoulders slump in defeat. His voice is unusually quiet as he tells me his news – Bastion Marina is sold. He has tried his best to keep the place going, but the bank refused to loan him any more money and without the capital to invest in upgrading the facilities, he just can't compete with the big boys.

'The small independent marina has had its day, Nathan. I'm sorry; I did my best to keep going, but there comes a time when you just have to call it quits.'

'Why didn't you tell me you had a problem?'

'What could you have done, mate? Anyway, I didn't want to worry you – and I was hoping I might be able to save your job…'

'Was?'

'I'm afraid so. With your skills, I thought the new management would take you on, but they want to bring their own people in…'

'So I'm out of a job.'

'Yeah, that's about the size of it. I'm sorry, Nathan.'

'It's OK, Geoff. Don't sweat it. You did your best and anyway, it's time I made some changes.'

'How d'you mean?'

'Holly's been hinting she wants us to move in together, but she doesn't want to live on the boat, so now seems as good a time as any to sell up.'

'Oh mate – are you sure? I reckon you belong on the canals…'

'But it's like you said, Geoff – there's no place for us small guys anymore. The canals have gone all corporate – like everything else.'

'I'd like to disagree, but…'

'You can't. Anyway, what are your plans?'

'Pay off my debts and use whatever's left to buy a retirement bungalow.'

'There you go. I rest my case.'

So I tell Holly I'm going to sell Festina Lente and move in with her, if she'll have me. I say I'll get another job, go to college on day release and obtain some qualifications. I promise to split everything 50/50; childcare, housework, costs – the lot. Then I sit back, expecting her to be pleased, but as usual she surprises me by suggesting a cooling-off period.

'I can't afford to make a mistake, Nathan. Not again. It wouldn't be fair on Stevie. That's why I want you to take a long trip on your boat and think it through. At the moment you're in shock, after getting that news. Take some time out and get your head together. Stevie and I will be waiting for you, when you get back.'

I know there's no use arguing – and I think she has a point. Holly knows I've let life kick me around in the past, rather than making my own choices, and she's clearly worried this is just another of my knee-jerk decisions. I'm determined to prove her wrong so, in defiance of the freezing weather, I head north, in a bid to remind myself how tough boating can be. I'm sure a few weeks on the Leeds and Liverpool Canal in the depths of winter will help me bid farewell to the canals for good.

I'm moored up in Skipton when I get the call. The weather has confounded my plans by turning clear and sunny, and I'm feeding my stash of stale bread to the numerous swans and ducks which converge on the canal in this quaint market town. My phone vibrates in my pocket and I'm tempted to ignore it, figuring it's probably someone offering to sell me car insurance or interest me in equity release. It isn't, though; this time it's Nancy.

My sister sounds flustered, which is unusual for her. She begins by asking me if I remember the novice boater she helped out, when Holly and I were on the Shroppie. When I confess I wasn't paying much attention, she asks me to take a seat and listen to the whole story, some of which she's only just discovered herself. So I obediently settle down on the back counter and idly continue distributing my sourdough nuggets to the birds while I try and take in what she tells me.

Apparently Stella, this novice narrowboater, had been abandoned on a hire boat by husband Alex, who had deserted her for another woman. Nancy reluctantly came to her aid by steering the hire boat back to Allenby Marina and was about to make her escape, when Stella was arrested for stalking. Nancy hadn't a clue what was going on until after Stella's release, when she explained how her husband and his new girlfriend had attempted to frame her. My sister could never understand their motive, but she put the incident to the back of her mind and embarked on her new life with Dan. However, she kept in touch with Stella. The two of them are clearly chalk and cheese, but their shared experience has obviously created a bond of sorts. Evidently Stella trusts Nancy, as she has just confessed to my sister that Alex didn't abandon her – she tried to kill him.

I have to say I admire the woman's ingenuity; she chose a creative, if not particularly effective, method. What she did was spike her husband's drinks, wrap the mooring rope around his ankle, while he was off his face, then kick the rope off the back counter of the boat, right by the prop. Of course the inevitable happened – the rope got tangled round the prop and dragged the unsuspecting bloke into the murky waters of the canal, where he got well and truly mangled. He wasn't killed, but he was gravely injured. He lost half his leg and would have bled to death if he hadn't managed to drag himself onto the towpath and been rescued by a cyclist.

So it turns out Alex is an alpha male who is not going to let a deed like this go unpunished. From his hospital bed, he manages to come up with a plan to get his wife arrested on a trumped-up stalking charge. He knows it'll never stick, but with a bit of help from his adoring girlfriend, he manages to procure Stella a brief stay in a police custody suite, which is extremely traumatic for a sheltered, middle-class housewife who's never had so much as a parking ticket.

'You with me so far, bro?'

'Yes, but all this was what – two years ago? And anyway, what's it got to do with you and me?'

'Patience, dude. All will be revealed. So Alex starts a new life in leafy Cheshire with his girlfriend, who gets on well with his kids…'

'How old are the kids?'

'Student age, I reckon. Anyway, Alex and Stella get divorced, and Stella starts up her own business. She's trying to move on, when she gets a call from Jennifer.'

'Who's Jennifer?'

'Alex's new squeeze.'

'The girlfriend?'

'Yes, Nathan. Do keep up. So the two of them meet up in Manchester, because Jennifer wants to talk…'

'I hope Jennifer paid the train fare. I'm not sure I'd have gone. I mean, the woman nicked Stella's husband and tried to frame her for stalking. You're not exactly going to share a bottle of Pinot, are you?'

'This is Stella we're taking about, dude. She's way too nice…'

'If you say so. So, what did Jennifer want?'

'Help. Once they started living together, lover boy morphed into a monster. He was always a control freak, but now he gets violent and starts playing nasty in bed. Jennifer wanted to know if he was the same with Stella.'

'And was he?'

'Yeah, but not so bad. They both figured he was way worse this time round.'

'Talk about karma. I bet Stella had a good laugh!'

'Not really. Turns out Alex had it in for both of them…'

'How come?'

'He was trashing Stella's new business – warning clients off, that sort of thing.'

'I see.'

'Also, the creep was trying to turn her kids against her…'

'So he wasn't content with divorcing her…'

'No. He wanted to ruin her life. She started seeing this guy Chris, but Alex put the frighteners on him, so Chris dumped her.'

'Chris sounds like a bit of a wuss.'

'Alex is a piece of work, more like. Also, I forgot to say – Jennifer got pregnant.'

'That's going to complicate things.'

'Too right. Once the pregnancy was confirmed, Alex tried to turn her into a nun, while all the time he was playing away with a bunch of different women…'

'What a snake.'

'Indeed. So Stella and Jennifer had a talk and admitted they wished Stella had bumped him off on the narrowboat.'

'Let me guess. The wife and mistress joined forces to get their revenge…'

'That was the idea. Stella, who was tanked up by now and had popped a few pills, came up with another plan to finish Alex off…'

'You're kidding.'

'No; but remember, this is a nice, middle-class lady we're talking about – not a ruthless killer. She sometimes thinks she's a badass, but she so isn't.'

'So the plan was crap.'

'It was. Luckily Jennifer, who's more streetwise, clocked this and told her it wouldn't work.'

'So what did they decide to do?'

'Nothing much. Just try and keep Alex in check.'

'I guess they weren't successful?'

'No. What happened was - Alex carried on treating Jen like crap and playing away. So Jen called him on it, tried to leave, they had a fight, and she lost the baby. Stella said she was in a bad way afterwards…'

'I suppose she would have been…'

'But it got even worse…'

'How could it get worse?'

'Alex found out Jen was in contact with Stella…'

'He must have flipped out…'

'No, he didn't. He didn't tell Jen he knew. Instead he drove to Stella's house in Surrey, broke in during the middle of the night and pulled a knife on her. Stella thought she was dead. Next time, she reckons she will be.

That's what he told her.'

'Have they been to the police?'

'No. Stella might have, in a previous life, but after her mini-break in custody she doesn't trust them.'

'What about Jennifer? Hasn't she reported it?'

'No. She's too scared. Alex warned what he'll do to her if she contacts Stella again, or talks to anyone about losing the baby. The nurses asked questions when she was in hospital, but she said she had a fall, and they let it go.'

'OK, sis. It's a sad story – but I don't see where you and I come in.'

'I'm coming to that.'

'Sorry.'

'Look, I know it sounds weird, but I care about Stella. We've got nothing in common, but we're friends, and I can't let this scum hurt her – or worse.'

'I get that…'

'Do you, though? She's shit scared, Nathan. Desperate enough to do something stupid and wind up in jail.'

'So, let me guess. you're going to ride in on your white charger and save her.'

'Yes…with a little help from my brother and his pals in Birmingham…'

'I don't like the sound of this, Nancy.'

'Don't worry; I've thought it through.'

'That's what I'm afraid of…'

'Remember when you were teasing me for being a Star Wars fan?'

'Yeah…'

'Well, I was thinking about a line from The Phantom Menace. "There's always a bigger fish". You know it?'

'This is relevant - how?'

'Alex is a big shot in the commercial world, but I reckon he'd soon back off if he ran into that gang who put you in jail.'

'What are you suggesting?'

'Nathan, those guys owe you. Twice you went inside and didn't talk. It's time they did you a favour by getting Alex to leave Stella and Jennifer alone – for ever. You told me they don't take prisoners…'

'You're not suggesting I get them to put Alex at the bottom of a lock? That's their speciality…'

'Christ no; nothing like that. Just…'

'Intimidate him?'

'Yes.'

'And if they refuse?'

'Then you remind them you know enough to put them away for a long time.'

'Nancy, that won't work. I've told you how they operate, so you can imagine how they respond to threats like that...'

'Ah, but it's like I just said. "There's always a bigger fish". And from what you told me about your second stint inside, you've got the biggest bloody fish in your corner. That cellmate of yours. The one who's been eternally grateful ever since you taught him to read.'

'You mean Ray?'

'That's him. From what you told me, he's not just a big fish; he's the whale shark of the underworld, and he made it clear he's got your back. Him and his people.'

'That's true.'

'So if you mention Ray's name, I'm sure they'll do one small favour for their old mate, whose silence has helped them line their pockets.'

'So you want them to frighten the shit out of Alex and rescue your two damsels in distress?'

'That's about the size of it.'

'I'm going to need to think this through, sis. Leave it with me.'

'Sure, Nathan. Don't take too long, though.'

That night I settle into a corner of an old pub in the canal basin. As I start working my way through their wide selection of real ales, I try to decide what to do next. Clearly I want nothing more to do with Giles and his pals, but I can't stop thinking how much I owe Nancy, and that this is my chance to do something for her in return. After all, she never gave up on me, through all my years in jail. She kept on writing the whole time, even though her letters went unanswered, and once Geoff brought us together, she turned my life around by buying me Festina Lente. Even now, after I've earned money from that boat and am planning to sell it, probably for a decent profit, she won't take a penny off me. Invest it in a home for you and Holly, she said. She even paid for me to get my teeth fixed, like she promised. I can never pay her back financially, so perhaps I should show how much I appreciate her kindness by helping her friend.

I'm on my third pint when I start thinking how much I loathe men like Alex, who use women as punchbags. Ray feels the same way. If ever he heard of anyone beating up on a woman, he'd make them regret it. I'm sure he'd support my efforts to nail Alex, even if it meant one of his people had to apply a little pressure to a bunch of middle-ranking drug dealers. I hope I never have to involve them, but it's reassuring to know I can call on them if need be.

By the time I finish pint number five, I'm beginning to see how this little favour could actually benefit me. I figure that, once Giles and Co. realise I have a powerful guy like Ray behind me, they won't bother me again, once this is all over. They'll leave me alone, and I'll finally be free. I'll never have to worry about being accosted in some canal side pub. I'll be able to wipe the slate clean and begin a new life with Holly and Stevie.

Suddenly it all makes sense. Smiling to myself, I look around the bar. The buttery, muted light makes everyone seem attractive and cheerful. The punters are having the time of their lives. Life is good. I pull my mobile from my jeans pocket and find I've got a decent signal, which is unusual in a place like this. So I Google the number of the pub at Fradley Junction, ring it and ask for Tracey, the barmaid, who doesn't sound surprised to hear from me. She says she'll make an appointment for me in Birmingham with Sebastian, that inappropriately named member of Giles's gang. I tell her I'm in Skipton and it'll take me a while to travel back to the Midlands, and she says she'll factor that in and get back to me. Then I hang up and call my sister.

'Hi, sis. How's it going?'

'Fine. Dan and I are working on a new track. You sound pissed...'

'Slightly. I'm just calling to say I'll help your mates out.'

'Thanks, but I hope this isn't a beer decision you'll regret in the morning.'

'Too late, if so. I already arranged the meeting in Birmingham. Obviously it'll take a while to get there, given I'm in Skipton in my four mile an hour Ferrari.'

'No problem. It'll give me time to speak to Stella and get you some background information about Alex.'

'OK. Speak soon...'

'Nathan?'

'Yeah?'

'Thanks, bro. This means a lot, even if you had to get shitfaced to do it.'

Nancy was right, of course. My decision was beer-enabled. All I want to do now is get it over with as quickly as possible. Next morning, while I'm coming round with the help of a pot of black coffee, I call Holly and say I'll be home within the month. I tell her how much I miss her and how I'm longing to see her and Stevie. My voice turns hoarse as I insist I'm finally ready to leave my floating life behind. As usual, Holly's response is muted.

'That's nice - but see how you feel when you get back. Stevie sends her love.'

The trip from Skipton to Birmingham is far from straightforward. The town lies at the northernmost point of the Leeds and Liverpool Canal, so I have to head south via numerous canals, tunnels, aqueducts and locks. Lots and lots of locks. To add to the challenge, the days are short at this time of year, so I don't have much time to spare and there's little margin for error. It's probably just as well I'm under pressure; it stops me from dwelling on what awaits me at my destination.

The venue is a gin bar near Gas Street Basin, and I moor up nearby, just before the appointed time. One of the fearsome locks in the Wolverhampton flight was playing up, so I got stuck there for half a day, and for a while I thought I wasn't going to make it. As I walk past GSB, I think of my old mate Jeremiah, who sat on this towpath with me for many happy hours and gave me my first boat. I know exactly what he'd say if he could see me now.

The gin emporium is dimly lit, with fashionably distressed wooden floors. It appears empty and is dead quiet, so my footsteps reverberate like gunshots as I walk towards the bar. I search in vain for a beer pump, but all I can see are hundreds of gin bottles, glittering gothically under the artfully placed downlights. I feel like I'm in a Potions class at Hogwarts. To add to the magical vibe, a barman dressed all in black appears out of nowhere and makes me jump. Thin and pale, he has the habitual stoop of someone who is acutely conscious of his extraordinary height. His hands shake slightly as he proffers an inch-thick gin menu, which appears to be made of Egyptian papyrus.

'What kind of gin would you like, sir?'

'Have you got any beer?'

A raised eyebrow tells me all I need to know.

'In that case – is there like – a house gin?'

'Yes, sir. It's an interesting mix of botanicals. Juniper-led, of course, but accented with notes of...'

'Whatever. Make it a double, please.'

'Of course, sir. And what kind of tonic would you care to try? We have elderflower, Mediterranean...'

'Just - normal tonic. Please.'

'I'll get that, mate.'

I recognise the voice behind me and turn to face Sebastian, who looks me up and down with an irritatingly smug smile.

'Welcome, Nathan. I knew you'd be back.'

'Don't hold your breath, Sebastian – it's not what you think.'

'Course it's not. We've found a nice little snug where we can talk in private.'

'We?'

'Yeah – we. I've brought along an old friend of yours. I'm sure you'll be excited to see him again.'

As I follow Sebastian through a maze of darkened rooms, it's apparent why Tracey chose this venue for our meeting. The hundreds of hipster gins are incidental; this is a hiding place, where dark deeds go unnoticed. I'd never have spotted the man at the corner table, if Sebastian hadn't pointed him out.

'Over there.'

As I approach the table, my stomach lurches as I recognise him.

'Good evening, Nathan. Nice to see you again.'

'Hello, Giles. I didn't think you'd bother with a low-level meeting like this.'

'Then you underestimate how delighted I am to welcome you back into the fold.'

'That's not why I'm here, Giles.'

'Is that so, Nathan? In that case, why don't you take a seat and tell me what's on your mind?'

The three of us cluster around the small table. Sebastian sits opposite me, and I'm uncomfortably conscious of his knees almost touching mine. I place a slim cardboard folder on the table and pray my voice won't betray my fear.

'I want you to do something for me.'

Sebastian laughs. 'That's not how it works, pal…'

Giles holds up his hand, with the palm facing his colleague. 'Hang on, Sebastian. Let's hear what Nathan has to say.' He glances at the folder, then focuses his full attention on my face. 'Tell us what you need, Nathan.'

So I do. I tell him about Alex and what he has done to Stella and Jennifer. I'm careful to present the propellor incident as an accident, just as Stella initially did with Nancy, but otherwise I stick to the facts. When I get to the part about Jennifer losing the baby, Giles drains the last of his gin and holds out his empty glass to Sebastian.

'I can't abide violence against women. Get us another round, Sebastian.'

As Sebastian leaves the table, Giles lowers his voice and nods at the folder. 'Tell us more about Alex. Is that him, in there?'

'Yes.' I take Giles through the contents of the folder and he stairs intently at each page. I also tell him about my cellmate Ray who, like Giles, abhors men who hurt women. I explain that Ray and his people would be pleased if he helped me. My implied threat is clumsy – I'm no good at this stuff – but Giles immediately picks up on it. He checks to make sure he has understood who I mean, then abruptly falls silent when Sebastian returns with the drinks. He takes his drink from the tray, raises his glass and clinks it against mine.

'Cheers, Nathan. That's all very interesting. Now, if I understand correctly, you'd like us to – shall we say – apply some pressure to this gentleman? Make him leave these ladies alone, once and for all?'

I clutch my hands together under the table to prevent them from shaking. 'That's right.'

Sebastian laughs again. 'And why should we do anything to help you?'

'To pay me back, for keeping silent. Twice.'

'You've got to be kidding. We don't have to do a thing for you. If you've got nothing for us, then you can do one, and be thankful we let you leave in one piece. Isn't that right, Giles?'

'No, Sebastian, it isn't. Nathan's quite correct. We have a moral obligation to him, and he's not asking much from us. The gentleman in question regularly spends time in Birmingham, so the job requires minimal effort. We'll be happy to help, Nathan. It's the least we can do.'

Instantly my hands stop shaking and a warm tide of relief washes over me. Sebastian glares at me over the rim of his glass and it's my turn to look smug.

'Nathan, you should know I'd have done this for you anyway, even if you hadn't mentioned your friend.'

'What are you talking about, Giles? What *friend?*'

'Never mind, Sebastian.'

Suddenly it all seems too easy. I pick up the folder and clutch it defensively to my chest. 'Thanks for agreeing to help, Giles. I don't mean to sound suspicious, but how will I know you've kept your word?'

'Don't worry, Nathan. I'm not expecting you to take this on trust. We'll give you a visual on the whole thing.'

'What d'you mean?'

'We'll need to work on the details, but when we're ready to act, we'll inform you and let you observe the discussion, as it were. Then, after it's done, we'll go our separate ways and have no further contact. All obligations will have been discharged – on both sides – and you will make no attempt to hinder our activities going forward. Is that clear?'

'Yes.'

'Good.' Giles holds out his hand and I pass him the folder. Swiftly he grabs a briefcase from beneath the table, flicks it open, places the document inside and clicks the briefcase shut. 'Now I'm sure you've got things to do, and Sebastian and I have a lot to discuss.'

Leaving my second gin untouched, I stumble back through the maze of darkened rooms towards the exit, barrelling into tables and chairs on my way. As I reach the door, a group of women in business suits burst in, nearly flattening me in their quest for gin. Their laughter fills the bar, instantly dispelling its sinister gothic vibe, but I still can't leave quickly enough. I rush out into the fading light and hurry along the towpath towards the city centre. I don't stop when I reach my boat; I can't bear to be alone right now. I need people, lights – anything to distract me from what just happened.

I pause at the apex of a metal bridge which spans the canal. The guardrail is festooned with padlocks, each a symbol of eternal love. That's the idea, anyway. I imagine the keys, sinking into the mud on the canal bed, and long to be back with Holly, so I decide to leave for home at first light. Decision made, I continue over the bridge towards wine bars, restaurants and the beguiling glitz of an upmarket shopping centre. It's a more affluent version of the place in Leicester which overwhelmed me on the day of my release. These days I'm accustomed to the sensory overload. The escalator carries me down, past towering shots of fashion models with chiselled cheekbones, towards the shops where people spend fortunes emulating them. One of the models is holding a guitar but has clearly never struck a chord in her life. The sight reminds me to call Nancy.

My sister picks up on the first ring.

'Hi, bro. How's it going?'

'I had the meeting, if that's what you mean.'

'How was it?'

'Giles was there, as well as Sebastian.'

'So not just the foot soldier, then. I wonder why the big boss was interested?'

'Who knows? Sebastian didn't want to play ball, but Giles agreed to everything.'

'Let me guess – *after* you told him about Ray.'

'Yes, but he said he would have agreed to help anyway.'

'He would say that, wouldn't he?'

'He seemed sincere…'

'Course he did. The dude has made a fortune out of sincerity.'

'Whatever. The main thing is, they agreed to do it.'

'Good work. So, what happens now?'

'I head back to Leicester and they call me when they're ready. They're giving me a front row seat, so I'll know they've kept their promise. Afterwards we go our separate ways forever. Their words, not mine.'

'Sounds good to me.'

'It sounds *too* good, Nan. I can't believe they agreed so easily.'

'That'll be the Ray factor. The bigger fish, like I said before.'

'I hope you're right.'

'I am. Don't worry. Go home to Holly and wait it out.'

'Will do – but, in the meantime, I have a lot of beer to drink.'

At the other end of the shopping centre I find a trendy bar, pulsating with dance music curated by a liberally pierced, heavily bearded DJ. It's almost impossible to convey my order to the barman, but after much yelling I succeed and retreat into a corner with my beer and JD chaser. I down the whisky in one, the beer in two. It takes a few rounds, but gradually my fear subsides, and the world seems a better place. In a few weeks, I'll have repaid my debt to my sister and stopped a bad guy in his tracks. I'll have severed my ties with the gang, and I'll be free to start a new life with Holly and Stevie. I tell myself it's natural to feel nervous, but the hard part's over now.

Things are looking up.

7 OVER DELIVERY

When I get home, I go straight to Holly's house in Foxton. I've barely made it through the door before I clumsily blurt out that I'm ready to move in. I can tell she knows I mean it. She doesn't say anything, just pulls me in for a long hug. Stevie's delighted, as we both knew she would be. We take her out to McDonalds to celebrate, then I stay over, and after that I never leave.

Holly and I spend many evenings discussing what to do with Festina Lente. We'd like to use the money from the sale to get a new place, but neither of us can bring ourselves to leave the canals behind completely and give up our boat trips. Also, I need the workshop so I can keep some money coming in while I look for another job and try to get a place in college.

Then the Fates intervene via a casual chat in the village pub. One of the locals knows a farmer a few miles south of Foxton, whose fields adjoin the canal and who has a side hustle renting out moorings to boaters. It's way cheaper than marinas like Bastion and Allenby, and it doesn't matter that there are no on-site facilities, as we live nearby. So we go and see him, do a deal and arrange to move the boat from Bastion to its new abode. I'm not looking forward to saying goodbye to Geoff, but when I visit him in the marina office he proudly announces he's put in an offer on a retirement bungalow in nearby Gumley, so we'll practically be neighbours. Then the local shop at Foxton Bottom Lock agrees to stock my canal art in return for a modest commission. If it wasn't for the spectre of the brief encounter coming up in Birmingham, I'd say everything was working out nicely.

It hasn't escaped my notice that the field where I'm moored isn't far from where my sister's friend Stella took her revenge on her husband. Whenever I'm down there, painting and carving in my workshop, the location keeps the whole saga at the forefront of my mind. Mostly I think about whether to tell Holly about this latest instalment; after all, it was only after I came clean about my two spells in prison that she began to trust me, and our relationship got started. Nevertheless, something stops me from sharing Nancy's request and the trip to Birmingham which I'll have to make sooner or later. Having just moved in, I'm desperate not to mess things up. Also, it's just a one-off, so it hardly seems worth the risk. Holly believes I've broken free of my past, and very soon that will actually be true. In the meantime, I figure all I need to do is stay quiet, although my silence keeps me awake through those relentless early hours of the morning, which force guilty people like me to examine their sins.

A few weeks later, Sebastian calls, but this time it's like talking to a different person. The aggression is gone; Sebastian v2.0 is business-like and civil as he describes how he has reviewed the dossier on Alex and tracked his movements regularly since our meeting. Happily, the information Nancy gave me was correct. Alex is on assignment in Birmingham three days a week and has rented a stylish penthouse apartment in the Jewellery Quarter. I guess that, after decades of business travel, posh hotels have lost their appeal.

According to Sebastian, Alex is a creature of habit. Every morning at the same time, he walks briskly from his apartment to his client's office in Brindley Place. His journey takes him along the canal towpath, uphill past the Farmer's Bridge flight and over the bridge by the National Indoor Arena. Then, every evening, whatever the weather, he retraces his steps. He invariably leaves the office late, long after the rush hour has finished. When he gets home, he discards his business suit in favour of skinny jeans and a leather jacket, then hits the town, returning several hours later. Sometimes, he comes back alone, but often he doesn't. When he does have company, the person always leaves before dawn.

Sebastian and his accomplices have agreed a plan. He tells me the date and exact time at which they will intercept Alex alongside one of the locks on the Farmer's Bridge flight. I've worked those locks countless times and I can visualise the exact location. It's a good choice. The lock is hidden away under the exposed foundations of a modern apartment block and, after dark and in the middle of winter, the area is bound to be deserted. I'd never walk that route at night, but Alex probably thinks he's invincible. Soon he'll find out otherwise.

Giles has kept his word about arranging a vantage point for me. Across the road is a modest block of flats which overlooks the lock. One of the top floor flats, number twenty-six, will be unlocked and empty on the night in question, ready for me to observe proceedings. Sebastian tells me to bring night vision binoculars, otherwise I'll see nothing, just like the residents of the other flats. Even so, he has picked a moonless night, just to be absolutely sure.

We check over the details one more time, then I hang up and call Nancy to tell her we're good to go. I don't share the date, though. I'm probably being over-cautious, but I reckon it's better if she doesn't know.

'So I guess it was convenient, sis, that our friend took this assignment in Birmingham?'

'Of course; that was what gave me the idea of asking you for help in the first place. I was talking to Stella, and she mentioned in passing that Jen was looking forward to some respite, as Alex was going to be working away in Brum three nights a week.'

'So you thought of me and my old pals in the Midlands?'

'Yes – and I figured it would be good if Alex ran into trouble well away from home.'

'So Stella and Jennifer were unlikely to be implicated?'

'Precisely.'

'I kind of wish the guy had gone to Glasgow instead.'

'I know, Nathan, but it's just one night, then it'll all be over.'

'You're right – and Giles and his cohorts have kept their word so far. They've done everything I asked.'

'Stella's very grateful. She wanted to meet you…'

'I don't think that would be wise.'

'That's what I told her.'

'Good. I'll be in touch again once it's all over.'

That evening, I casually mention to Holly that I'm going to be meeting up with some old boating pals near Gas Street Basin in a couple of weeks. I say I'm not planning to stay over, so I'll buy a return ticket for the cross-country train from Leicester to Birmingham New Street. Holly, bless her, offers to pick me up from the station afterwards to save on the taxi fare, even though I say I'll be late. Her kindness makes me feel sick with guilt. I thank her and tell myself I've lied to her for the very last time. Only a week to go, then I'll be able to afford the luxury of telling the truth.

The appointed day is bright, cloudless and sharp with cold, but the light is fading fast as I board the train at Leicester. Predictably, the heating is out of action and I shiver my way through the journey, then wind my woollen scarf tightly around my neck as I take the escalator up from the platform at Birmingham New Street. On the airy concourse, a sign proudly proclaims 'Grand Central', but any similarity with Manhattan disappears as I leave the building and walk up the darkened street towards a looming concrete flyover. On the far side is the shopping centre with its trendy bar, where I drowned my fears on my last visit to the city. Beyond that lies the canal.

All along my route are sights which force me to recall my last encounter with Giles and Sebastian. Once again I gaze at the huge picture of the model with the sculpted cheekbones, whose guitar playing skills haven't improved since my previous visit. At the back of the shopping centre I watch shoppers and office workers crowd into the canal side restaurants and bars, noisily clamouring for food and drink, and I envy them their carefree evening. Once again I walk onto the metal bridge and stop in the middle. I put my hand in my coat pocket and locate a small metallic object that's cold to the touch. My hands are shaky, so I fumble with the mechanism, but I finally manage to secure the padlock around the handrail, alongside all the others. Then I look down, drop the key into the dark water below and pray for eternal love; for me, Holly and all the other lovers whose symbols of hope adorn this bridge. Then I walk on down the canal.

I try not to look as I hurry past the gin bar where I met Giles and Sebastian, but I suddenly have a vivid flashback and desperately need a drink to take the edge off my fear. Further ahead, three canals merge in front of the National Indoor Arena where, during the daytime, narrowboats have the unusual task of negotiating an aquatic roundabout. On the far side of the junction, near the top of Farmer's Bridge Locks, is a pub, whose curtained windows reflect a welcoming glow onto the surface of the water. I cross the same bridge which Alex will soon use on his way home from work and take refuge there. I'm conscious that time is short, but I can't be completely sober when I watch what's about to happen.

Three shots later, I leave the pub and locate the quiet street which runs downhill, parallel to the flight of locks. My heart races and my footsteps resound as I walk. At every moment, I expect an assailant to leap out of the darkness, but nothing happens; all is quiet. The top locks are completely hidden from sight, but further on I spot the overhanging apartment block which conceals the target location. Slowly I approach the tall metal railings which separate the road from the towpath. Beyond them, just as I remembered, are the balance beams, tucked away behind the concrete pillars that support the building. I can just about make out the oily surface that tells me the lock is full.

I check my watch; fifteen minutes to go. Perfect timing. I walk over to the block of flats on the other side of the road and key in the entry code Sebastian gave me. Instantly the light on the keypad flashes green. I push the door and it opens inwards. There's a lift on the right-hand side of the entrance hall, but I choose to take the stairs. I don't want to risk getting trapped. By the time I reach the top floor I'm breathing heavily, but I've encountered no one and the corridor that stretches ahead of me is empty and quiet. I count the numbers on each door until I reach number twenty-six. I grasp the door handle, twist it firmly and push. The door opens quietly. So far, so good.

Silently I creep from room to room. I check behind every door, peer into the cupboards and look under the beds. Once I'm satisfied the flat is empty, I return to the front door and lock it from the inside. Then I place a chair next to the living room window, overlooking the street. I open my bag, take out my night vision binoculars and train them on the concrete pillars next to the lock. I have a perfect vantage point; Giles and Sebastian have chosen well. Everything is going according to plan.

Five minutes to go. I scan the towpath above the lock, but no one approaches. The minutes tick by and the appointed time passes. Despite the chill of the unheated flat, my palms are slick with sweat and I struggle to hold the binoculars steady. My brain serves up a stream of nightmare scenarios which threaten to eclipse the view from the window, so at first I don't realise what's happening. Then relief floods through me as I spot a tall, upright figure in a dark overcoat, his silhouette distorted by the laptop bag slung across one shoulder. The green and black picture rendered by the night vision binoculars isn't crystal, but it's clear enough. This is the man photographed in the dossier I showed Giles. He walks briskly downhill, oblivious. Obligingly he glances to his left and for an instant I get a good look at his face.

'Hello, Alex,' I whisper.

Sebastian comes out of nowhere. Running flat out, he gives Alex no time to react as he grabs him by the neck and hurls him to the ground. The victim's mouth opens in a scream of pain as his right elbow takes the full impact of the fall. His bag thuds onto the concrete. Agony makes Alex clumsy; it takes him a moment to struggle onto his back. When he succeeds, Sebastian stands over him, using his dominant position to add weight to his threats. I watch his mouth open and close as he speaks.

For a moment Alex just lies there. Then he struggles to his feet. Clearly his prosthetic leg places him at a disadvantage, but it doesn't stop him from trying to take Sebastian on. He rushes at his opponent, fists flailing wildly, but Sebastian effortlessly blocks his every move, laughing and taunting. Then he apparently decides it's time to get serious.

Sebastian places himself squarely in Alex's path. He continues to deflect Alex's blows, moving gradually closer until he's right in Alex's face. His lips curl into a snarl and he jabs the index finger of his left hand towards his victim's chest. Alex immediately stops lashing out and tries to regain his composure. He picks up his laptop bag and attempts to face off to Sebastian, chin tilted defiantly upwards. His posture gives him away, though; he clutches his bag defensively to his chest and his shoulders slump. He shakes his head and Sebastian laughs in response.

Alex tries to sidestep his adversary, but Sebastian's too quick for him. There's another heated exchange and Alex shakes his head again. My stomach churns as I realise he's not co-operating. He still thinks he's a master of the universe, and Sebastian is starting to get impatient. He grabs the lapels of Alex's overcoat and stares right into Alex's face. Whatever he says clearly hits home, as for the first time Alex looks really frightened. I pray he feels threatened enough to do the sensible thing and back down, but he doesn't. Instead he swings his laptop bag, which connects heavily with the side of Sebastian's head. It's an amateur, almost comedic blow, but it's enough to knock his opponent to the ground.

Alex looks jubilant at having overcome his enemy. As Sebastian struggles to his feet, he presses home his advantage with a solid left hook. Sebastian staggers backwards towards the lock but remains upright this time. I wait for him to fight back, but instead he raises his hand, and a second figure slips out from behind the pillar. Oblivious, Alex tries to floor Sebastian with a second punch, but his new assailant locks him in a stranglehold from behind and rams a gag into his mouth. Sebastian grabs Alex's flailing legs, but still fails to subdue him. The fight moves closer to the lock and one of the pillars gets in my way. I jump to my feet, desperate for a better view, but most of the action is obscured. The exception is a raised fist which suddenly appears from behind the pillar, clutching a glinting knife. The fist arcs swiftly downwards, vanishes, then reappears a second later. The knife is streaked with blood. Through my night vision binoculars I see it gleaming black. Another blow is struck, then another. The tempo increases to a frenzy and the knife is saturated. Then, abruptly, the struggle ends, and all is still.

I press the binoculars against the windowpane and lean heavily on them, unable to process what I have just seen. I can't bear to watch any more, but I'm unable to tear my eyes away as the scene slowly comes to life. Sebastian is the first to emerge. His opponent's legs flail no longer, but he and his accomplice still struggle to carry Alex over to the lock. I see the strain on their faces as they squat down and carefully release the body into the water, where it disappears below the oily surface, weighed down by its heavy woollen overcoat. Sebastian walks away as the body sinks, returning seconds later with an object that's less cumbersome, but still heavy. Alex's laptop bag joins its owner at the bottom of the lock. The dark waters ripple briefly, then recover their calm, as if nothing ever happened.

The two men head in opposite directions. Their clothes must have blood on them, but both are dressed in black, so I can't see the stains from here. Sebastian heads uphill, in the direction I came from less than half an hour ago, in a previous life. His partner goes downhill, towards the ring road. In seconds, the darkness consumes them both.

I shove my binoculars in my bag and bolt towards the door of the flat. As I run down the corridor I punch Sebastian's number into my mobile. His phone is switched off; of course it is. I take the stairs two at a time, sprint across the road and grab the railings with both hands, gasping for breath and looking fruitlessly up and down the towpath. Then I try to intercept Sebastian by running back up the road and catching him at the canal junction, but it's no use. Bent double in front of the National Indoor

Arena, my ragged breath knifing at my lungs, I'm forced to admit defeat.

I sit down on the steps, trembling and sobbing. My first impulse is to tell Nancy what has happened. My hand hovers over my phone, then I order myself to get a grip and think it through. Once I reflect on what just happened, the excuses come thick and fast. I haven't killed anyone, nor did I ask for it to happen. However, I have witnessed Sebastian and his accomplice committing murder and, should I be called upon to do so, I can reveal the location of the body. What's more, having arranged my vantage point, Giles and his cohorts know that I know. The more I think about it, the more it makes sense simply to keep quiet. I'm positive they won't say anything to anyone. After all, they've done this before and got away with it. From where I'm sitting, I can just about see the sign warning boaters that the Farmer's Bridge Flight is closed for repairs, so the body won't be discovered until the spring. There's plenty of time for the dust to settle.

Then I recall what I know about Alex. Clearly he was a villain who was wrecking women's lives. If left unchecked, he might well have committed murder himself; indeed, an unborn baby is already dead because of him. Even so, I would love to undo what I've just witnessed, but I can't, and telling other people won't bring him back. If Stella and Jennifer don't find out what really happened, they can live the rest of their lives in peace and if I keep the secret from my sister, she'll be able to think she's done them a favour, ably assisted by her dear brother. Most importantly, I'll be able to go home to Holly and Stevie and start my new life.

Of course, I won't come out of this unscathed. I know I'll be compelled to live with the guilt. The slate I was hoping to wipe clean tonight will forever remain tarnished. Ever since Giles first walked into my life, just yards away in Gas Street Basin, guilt has sat on my shoulder like a malign familiar. I desperately want rid of it, but that's not going to happen. Not now. I think of calling Ray's people but decide against it. What would be the point? The deed is done. No one can undo it.

So there you have it. We first met on Day Zero, but I know there won't be another one this time round. I've been sentenced to a life of guilt; I just have to accept it. The alternative is unthinkable, so I need to find a way to live with what I've done.

I have no choice.

JENNIFER

8 FATEFUL ATTRACTION

Hello, strangers. I assume you know who I am, so I do not expect you to like me very much, but that does not bother me. I will not attempt to influence you. As you know, I am a communications specialist; an expert in delivering messages and changing minds. A spin doctor, in other words; but rest assured I am not going to practise on you. I merely intend to tell my side of the story and let you form your own view.

You should know that I am not comfortable writing about my personal life. Normally I can detach myself from my subject matter, which is just how I like it. A corporate change programme, a new IT system, a product launch – I can leave them all behind, but I am stuck with myself. I was not inclined to rake over my past, but they persuaded me that I owed it to myself to have my say. Frankly, I would prefer to put the past behind me, but it is too late to back out now.

My profession means I am conditioned to focus on the recipient of the message; in this case you. I cannot help wondering who you are and what your own life is like. I imagine you are married or have a long-term partner. Maybe you were both single when you met, and you fell in love in a nice straightforward way. Your families and friends were all pleased for you and many of them became friends with each other. If this is true, then good for you. I hope you deserve your life and do not lose it through complacency, or bad luck.

Or perhaps you are looking for love. Swiping left and right, checking out strangers in bars and supermarkets. Avoiding people who are attached. It is difficult sometimes, but you call time immediately if you find out someone has deceived you. Only the unprincipled and amoral cheat, you tell yourself. You would rather be alone than stoop to that level. I salute you, up there on your high horse, and hope your virtue is rewarded.

Or maybe you are like me and picked someone who was already taken. You tell yourself your affair is not like those sordid entanglements you read about in the popular press. It is serious – and temporary. As soon as certain conditions are met, your lover will be yours alone. Perhaps the right moment needs to be found to tell the truth to the current incumbent. Children need to start or leave school, so their educations are not disrupted. Finances need to be sorted and fallout minimised. The list is endless, but you are confident things will work out and you will get what you want. If this is you, we have a lot in common. I have been in your shoes, so I feel compelled to warn you. Be careful what you wish for. I know it is a well-worn phrase, but there is a reason for that.

My background should have ensured I never went near someone like Alex. The truth is it did not, but I am not going to use it as an excuse. These days people like me, with a privileged upbringing, have lost the right to complain. Our pain does not count. I beg to differ. I bleed, just like anyone else, or at least I used to, but I do not expect you to be sympathetic.

My father was a civil engineer who ran major construction projects all across south-east Asia. Bridge building was his speciality. As a child, I spent several years each in Hong Kong, Kuala Lumpur, Manila and finally Singapore. Ours was a classic ex-pat lifestyle – luxury apartments, weekend retreats, live-in help. In Hong Kong, we lived up on The Peak, with one of the most iconic views in the world. In KL, I watched the construction of the Petronas Towers from my bedroom window. Only a few memories from those early years stand out. My father teaching me to swim in the rooftop pool of our apartment block. A birthday trip to Ocean Park with my mother and a group of schoolfriends. Nancy, our Hong Kong amah, tucking me up in bed.

Manila was my favourite posting. We had a huge penthouse apartment in Makati, and I was old enough by then to meet up with my friends at the Greenbelt shopping mall for a milkshake after school, with just one amah in tow to keep an eye on us. Poverty was only yards away, in the form of cardboard communities clinging to the banks of the poisonous river Pasig, but we seldom caught a glimpse of those less fortunate than ourselves. Instead we played in the sun on our roof terraces and in Ayala Triangle Gardens. Some weekends, my parents and I flew down to our beachfront house in Borocay and I went snorkelling. On the surface, life was idyllic, and I took it for granted, just like my friends.

None of us saw much of our parents during the week. My father worked long hours and my mother was always busy being the perfect hostess. In the afternoons and evenings our penthouse buzzed with party guests, drinking tea or cocktails and emptying their wallets for charity. I was happy to remain behind the scenes with Agnes, my Filipina amah, who was the centre of my world. On the occasions when I was required to step outside my comfort zone and be shown off, I disappeared as soon as my mother's back was turned. Her brittle glamour made me uneasy.

Although, or maybe because I saw little of him, my father was my hero. Charming and kind, he swept into my life at weekends on a wave of fun. Together we did things my mother would never have allowed. I was always sworn to secrecy and I never broke my promise. The rollercoasters, the junk food, the Jeepney trips amidst Manila's anarchic traffic; all went unreported. I loved the covert activities we shared.

The most difficult part of my childhood was the inevitable disruption every time my father finished one project and started another. Changing countries, cities and schools every few years was hard. Friends quickly fell by the wayside and were replaced. It was easier to slough off one skin every few years and grow another. Gradually I became adept at reinventing myself, a skill I have never lost, and which has served me well.

When I was fourteen and we were preparing to move to Singapore, my parents decided my education had been disrupted enough and arranged for me to go to boarding school in England. At the time, I was so distraught at leaving Manila that my next destination made little difference to me. I arrived in England with conflicted feelings; sorrow at leaving the Philippines and being separated from my father, mixed with anger at having been sent away and a glimmer of excitement at being set free to reinvent myself, *sans* amah and parents, in a completely new world.

My new school was in a quaint market town buried in the English countryside. After a lifetime of city living, I found most of the pupils naïve and sheltered. Inevitably I gravitated towards a small group of fellow ex-pats for whom parents were largely cheques in the post. How smug we were when those living in England were summoned home at weekends. Most of us had English guardians who showed minimal interest in our welfare, which suited us fine.

Uncle George, my mother's older brother, was my guardian. A successful journalist and notorious bon viveur, he was happy for me to stay with him in his Pimlico flat whenever I had a free weekend and seemed unaware, or at least unconcerned, about my age. During the day I was allowed to roam London by myself and do as I pleased, as long as I returned to share a late dinner and a couple of bottles of wine. Afterwards, as he worked his way down a bottle of brandy, I would listen through my wine fug to his stories, which were often repeated, but always entertaining. My favourites were the ones about my mother's youthful exploits. I could never reconcile the rebellious sister Uncle George described with the glamorous but conventional hostess I knew. When I returned to Singapore during the holidays, I looked for signs of the fun-loving person she had been, but I never found them. In fact, each time I returned, she seemed more unhappy, but I told myself it was my imagination.

The school ensured we were fully occupied, either with studies or sport. I was useless at the latter, but my classroom teachers were surprisingly inspiring, so I worked harder than ever before. In science, my diligence earned me only average marks, but I did well in all my other subjects, particularly English. It was obvious I was never going to follow my father into engineering, but Uncle George was delighted with my English results and regularly arranged for me to spend a Saturday running errands in his newsroom. I was immediately hooked on the frenetic atmosphere and convinced myself that my future lay in journalism. There were a few fearless, battle-hardened women on the editorial team, and I watched in awe, determined to emulate them. When I aced my English GCSE at sixteen and my teachers said I was destined to read English at Oxford, life seemed firmly on track. With hindsight, I think that was the happiest I have ever been. I studied for my A Levels, worked my way through the first fifteen rugby team and enjoyed carefree weekends in London. Life was good.

The following year, everything changed. I was in my French class when the headmaster's secretary walked in and asked me to come with her. From her face, I knew something bad had happened, but she refused to tell me anything. A few minutes later, in his office, the headmaster broke the news that my mother had died from a heart attack. Dazed, I entered the parallel universe inhabited by the bereaved and allowed myself to be processed. That evening, I boarded a flight to Singapore and was met at Changi by my father's PA. At home, the kind man who used to be my father had been replaced by a grim-faced stranger who recited the funeral arrangements in a monotone and hardly seemed to know who I was. The only sign that he cared came on the night I flew back. This time, he accompanied me to the airport, and we sat together silently in the rear of his chauffeur-driven car. As we pulled into the drop-off zone, he turned to me and grasped my hand briefly.

'Don't let this derail your life, Jennifer.'

I couldn't think of a reply, so I simply stepped out of the car. The chauffeur helped me load my bags onto a trolley, then I walked alone into Departures. As the automatic doors swished shut behind me, I turned to look for my father's car, but it had already gone.

Back at school, I was summoned to the headmaster's office, where I received the news that my father had changed my arrangements without consulting me. Uncle George was no longer my guardian, and I was forbidden to visit him. His place had been taken by two of my father's old friends, whom I hardly knew, who lived in a small village an hour's drive away. I tried to protest, but the change was non-negotiable.

After that, I found it impossible to focus on my studies and my grades nosedived. My friends were uncomfortable with my grief and I drove them away. I had never felt close to my mother, but my devastation at her sudden loss showed it was irrelevant that we did not see each other very often, or even get on particularly well. She was my *mother*.

A few weeks later, I was in the bathroom early one evening, lying in a tub of water which had long since cooled, when a third former burst in and announced that there was an urgent phone call for me, from a man whose name I didn't recognise. I was tempted to ignore it, but instead I dragged myself from the tub, wrapped a towel around me and dripped my way to the phone.

Uncle George was not exactly sober, but I understood him well enough. He had used a false name as he was not supposed to contact me. He was staying the night at the Bull Hotel, just up the road from my boarding house. Could I come and have dinner with him? He had something important he wanted to show me. I immediately agreed, hung up and went to find someone to cover for me if anyone came looking, which was unlikely. Sixth formers were not monitored closely in the evenings. As long as I returned before ten thirty, when the house was locked up, my absence would go unnoticed.

Uncle George ordered me a large glass of white wine, then pulled me into his arms and hugged me. It felt good to be with someone else who was grieving, but the relief was short lived. My uncle sat me down in a quiet corner of the bar and showed me an email my mother had sent him. In it, she described how she felt unable to go on after decades of putting on a brave face and playing the perfect hostess. She said she could no longer pretend to ignore my father's affairs and make polite conversation at parties with people who knew the truth, but feigned ignorance. She apologised to her brother and told him how much she loved him, and how he was her only true friend in the world. Finally she confessed that she hated to leave me and asked him to look after me once she had gone. Then she said sorry again. She had tried her best for so many years but could no longer cope. It was time to go.

As soon as Uncle George received the email he called our house in Singapore, but my mother was one step ahead of him. She had timed the email to send several hours after she checked out, to prevent my uncle from trying to stop her. Our distraught amah broke the news. Uncle George declined to speak to my father and did not fly out for the funeral. He said he could not trust himself to be in my father's presence and did not want to ruin the dignity of the occasion, as his sister had struggled for so long to remain dignified whilst alive.

Finding out that my mother had committed suicide, and my father had lied to me about it, was the defining moment in my young life. My father, who had been my hero throughout my childhood, was instantly dead to me. I made a conscious choice, then and there. He simply ceased to exist. I discovered, the hard way, that I had the ability to extinguish a source of pain through an act of will, and I have put this talent to good use on a number of occasions since then. Of course, there was a price to pay. My childhood ended that night, and I found I was able to trust no one. Not even my kindly uncle, of whom I was very fond.

I went back to my boarding house and quietly fell to pieces. I stopped eating and abandoned any pretence at studying, but no one noticed. Pupils and teachers alike were preoccupied with our impending A Levels and my excellent marks were a distant memory. No one mentioned Oxbridge to me anymore and all the attention was focused on those most likely to succeed. I spent my eighteenth birthday alone in my study, covertly drinking vodka from my coffee mug and trying to feel happy that I was now technically an adult who could make her own decisions. My father's birthday card lay in pieces in the bin, but I responded to a long letter from my uncle, in which he invited me to stay with him for the summer.

A few weeks later, I left school behind and caught the train to London, convinced I had failed all my exams. One hot August day, I was proved right. Uncle George was at work when the post arrived and I spent the day wandering aimlessly through the Tate Gallery, hating my life. That evening I walked back along the Embankment and sat with my uncle on his balcony, getting drunk on red wine and pouring scorn on the world. Uncle George listened patiently until bedtime, then steered me towards my room. As he hugged me goodnight, he whispered in my ear.

'Enough now, Jen.'

The next morning, I stumbled into the kitchen to find the table littered with application forms for London crammers where I could retake my A Levels. There was a Post-It note on top of one of them.

'Time to turn things around.'

I wish I could say that I wholeheartedly followed my uncle's advice, but things were not that simple. I did get a place at a crammer, financed by my uncle, but the inspiration I felt at school never returned; neither did my Oxbridge ambitions. I studied moderately hard, partied much harder and got respectable A Level results. The following autumn, I hugged my uncle goodbye and boarded the train for Manchester to begin my English degree.

I got a good feeling about the city as soon as I stepped off the train at Piccadilly. Over the coming weeks, I began to feel at home for the first time since leaving Manila. I was grateful to my uncle and had enjoyed staying in his flat, but it was a relief to have my own room in a hall of residence and be able to shut the door on the world whenever I chose. Sometimes, though, I did not choose. I loved the gritty, down-to-earth vibe of the city and walked the streets at all hours. I deliberately kept my friendships superficial and created for myself an exotic persona, based on a selective account of my Asian childhood. Thus armoured, I studied, partied, racked up lots of one-night stands, kept my secrets and completed my degree unscathed, without revealing myself to anyone. It was a perfect three years, and when I graduated I knew I was not going anywhere. My so-called friends headed south and were swiftly forgotten, but I stayed behind in the place where I felt in control of my life.

My uncle was disappointed that I declined to take on London. An old-school hack, he felt the capital was the only place to be if you wanted to make it in journalism. Nevertheless, he was determined to help me break into the profession, so he got me a job as a trainee reporter in the Manchester office of his newspaper. I revelled in the relentless pace and intense competition, but with hindsight, the knives were out for me, right from the start. My posh accent didn't go down well, and as I was uninterested in making friends with my fellow trainees, I was labelled snotty and cold. I did not think it mattered, but it did. Once they found out who my uncle was, they had the perfect stick with which to beat me. I was dogged by accusations of nepotism and eventually my position became untenable. I resigned before I was pushed and resolved to set a new course for my career, without help from anyone else.

I decided to give public relations a try, as it seemed to provide an alternative outlet for my writing skills. Eventually, after weeks spent surfing job websites and going for uninspiring interviews, I spotted an opportunity with the PR department of a management consultancy whose Manchester office was located just off Deansgate. After a string of challenging interviews, I was delighted to land the job.

Working in consultancy suited me perfectly. The corporate culture was governed by the project-based nature of the work, which meant that no one stayed in the same place for very long. The consultants were a transient bunch and even in support functions like PR, people moved around a lot. There was no need for me to form lasting relationships or try particularly hard to fit in. Professional competence was the yardstick by which success was measured, which suited me perfectly. I discovered I was good at PR. The learning curve was steep, but I had useful mentors. The writing part of the job came naturally, whilst the social interactions were conducted at a superficial level with which I was entirely comfortable. I was able to keep my barriers firmly in place. I concluded that I had chosen my ideal career.

Fast forward a couple of years and I had one promotion under my belt and was on track for my next. I had rented an apartment in one of the new tower blocks which were transforming the low-rise city centre and my social life was frothy and insubstantial. I saw no reason to change any of this until I met Stefan.

It happened in my favourite city centre bar, down by the canal. We will visit it again later. I was having a drink with some colleagues after hosting a successful corporate event. Stefan came in with a group of friends; one of his party knew one of mine and we all got talking. He was gorgeous, with bright blonde hair and a clear, blue-eyed gaze. As the night wore on, people gradually started leaving, but Stefan remained behind. I suspected I was the reason for this and decided to stick around as well. I ordered more drinks and teased Stefan for sounding like The Swedish Chef. It turned out he was actually from Sweden. I flirted away and pretended to be interested while he talked about Stockholm. I was only half listening; my main concern was how soon I could suggest getting a taxi to my apartment without blowing it by seeming too predatory. Stefan seemed quite happy where he was, so I resigned myself to more conversation, making a mental note to timebox it to half an hour.

We discovered we had both studied at Manchester University. At one point we even lived in the same hall of residence in Fallowfield. Stefan was a year above me, studying psychology. Like me, he loved the city and wanted to stay put after graduation. He took the academic route, studying for a PhD and landing a job as a junior lecturer in his old department. Apparently he was renovating a rundown terraced house in Didsbury. When he started talking about patios and decking, I quickly called time.

I invited Stefan back to my flat and he immediately accepted but, to my surprise, he ignored my unsubtle hints and installed himself at the breakfast bar in my kitchen. I opened a bottle, hoping more alcohol would do the trick, but instead he just began asking questions about my life. I tried my best to divert his attention onto other subjects, but by the time we had finished the second bottle I was quite drunk, and he deployed his psychology skills to good effect. To cut to the chase, I told him about my mother, and he did not seem surprised. Then he said he had to be getting back and politely declined my offer to stay over. He just took my number and left.

Confused and frustrated, I finished the bottle and went to bed. The next morning, I made a hungover start to the weekend and chastised myself for letting my guard down and spilling my secrets to someone I hardly knew, whom I was unlikely to see again. I was wrong, though. Stefan called two days later but held out on me for several months before I finally got him into bed. This was a smart move on his part. I was unaccustomed to delayed gratification where men were concerned and by making me wait, Stefan transformed himself from a good-looking man I fancied taking home for one night into a prize I was determined to win. When I eventually succeeded, my sense of achievement was so great that I broke the habit of a lifetime and embarked on a relationship.

Stefan was devoted and steadfast, but he was no pushover, and he had a few tricks up his sleeve which kept me interested in the early days, so I gave up the lease on my apartment and moved into his house in Didsbury. At first, being coupled up was a novelty. Stefan cooked healthy meals and we went running together. We socialised with other professional couples in wine bars and restaurants. We recycled and gave to charity. Our careers flourished. My life lacked some of its former excitement, but most of the time I was too busy at work to give it much thought. With hindsight, I was suffocating – or maybe marking time.

Meanwhile, my firm was at the critical stage of a high profile, five-year assignment called Leviathan. Based in Leeds but with a national reach, it was the biggest IT implementation programme in the UK public sector. Like all endeavours of its kind, it was politically sensitive and required careful engagement with the different stakeholders, many of whom were opposed to any form of change. Despite his best efforts, the communications manager had lost the confidence of the client and the partners were struggling to find another consultant to step in. When my manager put my name forward, it raised a few eyebrows, as I was part of the corporate PR team and had never worked as a consultant. Nevertheless, I was asked to attend an interview with the programme director. I had never met him but knew him by reputation as one of the rising stars in the firm, hotly tipped to land his senior partnership off the back of Leviathan. The night before I travelled to Leeds to meet Alex for the first time, Stefan advised me to 'bring my A game'.

The junior analyst who led the way to Alex's office confided that the boss was in a bad mood. This fact was clearly important to her, but I did not care. I enjoyed my current role and was not keen to spend weeks on the other side of the Pennines. If Alex did not want me on his team, that was his loss.

He was glaring at his screen when I walked in. Without looking up, he pointed to a chair and growled:

'Take a seat.'

I sat in silence and watched him while he ignored me. The sleeves of his expensive white shirt were rolled up to the elbow and he jabbed aggressively at his keyboard with neatly manicured fingers. Every so often his honey blonde hair fell across his face and he pushed it away impatiently. From eyebrow to cheekbone, two circles of pale skin around his eyes contrasted sharply with his bronzed face - clearly a goggle tan from a winter sports holiday. I was idly speculating whether he preferred skiing or snowboarding, when he spun his laptop around so that the screen faced me.

'OK, communications expert. Look at this email from one of our client sponsors, who is mightily pissed off, and advise me how you would respond.'

I read the email and asked a few questions about the client and his team. Then I did what I had been trained to do and put myself in the client's shoes. I grabbed Alex's laptop, ignoring the look of surprise on his face, and started typing. I avoided anodyne corporate speak and addressed each of the client's concerns in turn, acknowledging the challenges he and Alex were working to surmount, whilst emphasising the personal benefits he stood to gain from Leviathan. I thought it was an excellent effort, given my superficial knowledge of the programme. I handed the laptop back and Alex stared at the screen, his expression unreadable.

'This phrase isn't appropriate. Not for this client...'

He backspaced through five words and replaced them with five different ones. The difference was barely noticeable. Clearly pride dictated that he had to alter something. He was so full of himself.

'That change is OK, Alex.'

'I'm glad it meets with your approval, Jennifer.'

I registered the sarcasm and was about to retaliate, when he smiled at me and pressed 'Send'.

'Did you really send that to the client?'

'Of course.'

'I thought it was just an exercise – for the interview...'

'I haven't got time for that. Besides, it was fit for purpose.'

Then he stood up and shoved his laptop into his bag along with his phone and a few papers.

'I have another meeting. I suggest you contact the programme administrators and get them to book you a hotel for next week. See you on Monday.'

When it came to stakeholder engagement, Leviathan was on the back foot and I had to fight hard to turn the situation around. This meant working closely with Alex, so I was constantly under the microscope and each of my early communications was subjected to scrutiny and criticism. Work of which I was justly proud earned me no more than a cursory nod and a reluctant 'OK', but I was fine with that. I do not require validation from others. I am quite capable of being my own cheerleader.

One afternoon, I walked into the programme office to chase up an overdue report and found the admin team in a huddle, giggling away. Not everyone has the same work ethic as me.

'What's so funny?' I asked.

'Hi, Jennifer. Laura was telling us about her photo shoot with Alex – for his new ID card.'

'What do you mean, Margaret – photo shoot? Laura points a camera at us, and it's done.'

'That may be true for us, Jen, but not for our esteemed leader. Twelve goes to get one shot which met with his approval – and poor Laura had to adjust the lighting between each take.'

'Tell me you're joking, Margaret.'

'Wish I was. Dude thinks he's David Beckham.'

'Got to admit, though, the end result's quite easy on the eye…' Laura winked suggestively at Margaret.

'Guess so, Laura. The boss is looking good…'

I had heard enough. 'He's OK, I suppose - if you like older men.'

'Ah c'mon, Jen. He's not that old and you've got to admit – he's hot. Blonde hair and ice blue eyes – works for me every time.'

'Alex might float your boat, Mags, but you don't have to work with him all day like Jen does. Also, I gather you're happily bloked up, Jen?'

'If you wish to put it like that.' Clearly the admin team had checked the firm's personnel records. I suppose it is one of the perks of the job.

'So Jen might be immune to his charms, but the rest of us aren't…'

'The guy's married, Mags.'

'I know, but I can still look.'

The team was right. I had no interest in Alex back then. He was not on my radar. I privately agreed with the admin team that he was very good looking, but I was not prepared to admit it to them. Girly gossip is not my style. More importantly, I did not want to give them ammunition which they could later use against me.

At first I was relieved to escape from Leeds every Friday. I am not quite sure when things started to change; it happened so gradually. After a while, the communications problems were resolved, thanks to my efforts, which meant Alex started to relax. With the senior stakeholders on side, his sense of humour began to emerge, and I discovered he could be just as bitchy as me. We shared secret jokes about our most difficult clients; it was fun being nice to their faces, to keep them sweet, whilst performing character assassinations behind their backs.

Alex was well known for retreating to his hotel room every night, but now he started to join the team for dinner twice a week, and I enjoyed seeing how everyone deferred to him – and, by extension, to me, as I was clearly in favour. He exuded power and volatility, with a temper that could flare instantly, then dissolve into laughter moments later. The contrast with steady, reliable Stefan could not have been more marked.

Most people were a little scared of Alex; unlike me. Even so, I never suspected him of having a softer side, until I heard him speak to his daughter.

I walked into his office one Friday afternoon and was astonished to hear him talking on the phone in a completely different tone of voice. I had no idea he could sound so gentle. The conversation seemed rather intimate, so

I made a show of retreating towards the door, but Alex waved his hand to indicate I should stay.

'No, darling, I won't forget. As soon as I hang up, I'll call and make a booking. I'll order some flowers as well, I promise. And when I get home later, we'll celebrate your good news with a glass of champagne…oh, I see. I might have known you wouldn't be in on a Friday night. Tomorrow, then – OK? It's a date. Right, I have to go. I've got some work to finish before I catch my train. Love you too, angel. Bye.'

Alex leaned back in his chair and smiled at me.

'She thinks she's my PA…'

'Your wife?'

'No. That was Minnie, my daughter. Short for Imogen. She was ordering me to book a table for dinner with my wife next weekend. Apparently Stella's fed up that we only seem to go out with friends these days and she's obviously been complaining to Minnie. The two of them are close.'

'I see.' This was the first hint that all was not well with Alex's marriage. I filed that scrap of knowledge away for later and leaned forward, eager to learn more.

'Also, Minnie got great marks for her latest assignment, so I promised to break out the champagne, as you heard. Even though she's a bit too young to be drinking…'

'How old is she?'

'Seventeen.'

'Should have seen how much I drank at that age.' The words were out before I realised I had said them. I had not planned to confide in my boss, but now I had no choice. I knew he would not let it go.

'How come?' Alex stared at me grimly.

'My uncle liked a drink – or ten. He was my guardian when I was at boarding school, as my parents were overseas. We'd drink wine together in the holidays…'

'But you didn't drink at school?'

'Not at first – but I did later. Like a fish, but I never got caught. It's easy to hide vodka in your coffee mug…'

'Why, Jen?'

I stood up. 'You don't want to know, Alex. You have dinner to book, flowers to order and a train to catch.'

'Just tell me, Jennifer.'

I took a deep breath. 'Sure you want to hear? It's not pretty…'

'I'm sure.'

'Alright then - my mother killed herself when I was seventeen and my father …well, let's just say he wasn't as kind to me as you are to Imogen.' I had said too much. I pulled the drawbridge up and marched towards the door.

111

Alex did not try to stop me, but as I left he simply said, 'Thanks Jen – for confiding in me.'

When I returned to the office on Monday there was a huge bouquet of flowers on my desk. The message on the card read, 'You are very special. A.'

After that, Alex remained a tough boss, but he was more appreciative of my efforts. He would often call me his 'work wife', even in front of others, and say that he did not know how he had ever managed without me. Colleagues credited me with making the boss more relaxed, thereby improving the atmosphere in Leviathan HQ. It was the closest I've ever come to being popular. I no longer missed being in Manchester and was happy to remain in Leeds.

After a few months, Stefan started to get fed up with me being away every week and asked me to try and get transferred off the programme. I refused and the atmosphere at home became tense. On Mondays I would confess to Alex that Leviathan was driving a wedge between me and Stefan. I pretended it bothered me, but in reality I did not care. Stefan was too nice for me. Frankly, I was bored.

Gradually Alex began to reciprocate, telling me how years spent working away from home had taken its toll on his marriage. Apparently his wife focused all her energy on the kids and the house, and he often felt like an unwelcome stranger when he arrived home on a Friday night. I told him I could relate.

An idea was starting to form. I know you probably do not approve, but really it was Stella's fault. She took her eye off the ball and presented me with an opportunity. All I did was take advantage of it. Who knows? Maybe you would have done the same in my position.

Look at it from my perspective. Reliable Stefan, in his terraced house, was no longer right for me. To be honest, he never was. However, I did not want to go back to my previous diet of one-night stands and casual hook-ups. There is only so much fast food you can eat. I wanted a real man – with looks, power, charisma and money. So I set my sights on Alex.

As we approached one of the major programme milestones, our team had to work even longer hours, which provided plenty of scope for subtle flirtation and in-jokes. Without being too overt, I stepped my work outfits up a gear. Higher heels, shorter skirts, brighter colours, fitted jackets. I claim no marks for originality, but it worked. I could tell Alex noticed, and liked what he saw. I imagine the view was much better than at weekends. Men are such simple creatures.

Pressure of work meant that team dinners became less frequent; instead we ordered in pizza and carried on working. After one of these late-night sessions, Alex and I shared a taxi home. The rest of the team had gone ahead but we had stayed behind as we had a presentation to finish. As we pulled up at the door of our hotel, Alex suggested a nightcap.

There was only one table left in the bar and someone had left a trash mag on it. Over drinks, we amused ourselves with the latest celebrity tales of weight loss, relationship breakdowns and fashion disasters. A glamour model had apparently announced her engagement to a footballer she had met only weeks previously. I remarked that it was undoubtedly a publicity stunt and would be over in months. I fully expected Alex to agree, but his response astonished me.

'So cynical, Jen, for one so young. It could be true love…'

'But she only met him the other week!'

'Doesn't matter. In my experience, when you know, you know. Elapsed time is irrelevant when it comes to matters of the heart. Take you, for instance…'

'What about me? Stefan and I aren't getting engaged…'

'I'm not talking about Stefan. I'm talking about you – and me.'

'What do you mean, Alex?'

'Oh, Jen. I'm in love with you. Have been from the start – since you came for your interview. I know I shouldn't be, but I can't help it. It's out of my control.'

It was the moment I had been waiting for, but it had happened much more quickly than I had expected, and the shock made me clumsy. I pushed my chair back and tried to stand up, but my knees knocked the underside of the table and our glasses crashed to the floor. People turned to stare at us. A few of them clapped. Alex grabbed my hand.

'Jen – stay. Please. I didn't mean to upset you. Let me get some more drinks and…explain. Don't go anywhere. I'll be right back.'

A nice girl would have fled to her room, but I did not. Now that I was over the initial shock, I was thrilled. After Stefan's measured approach to love, the idea that Alex had fallen for me at first sight and could not control his feelings for me was intoxicating. I am sure you can understand. After all, everyone likes to be desired. I was busy planning my next move, when Alex came back with the drinks and poured cold water on my plans.

'I mean obviously, Jen – I'm married, and you're with Stefan, so I know nothing's going to happen between us. It's just that – we've become so close, and I can't lie to you any more about how I feel. We can't be together, but it's wonderful just seeing you every day. That's it – enough said.'

After that, he abruptly switched to work matters. We finished our drinks and retreated to our separate rooms. After a sleepless night, I went into work determined to ask Alex to replace me so I could return to Manchester, but he was in meetings all day, so I never got the opportunity. Then, as the week progressed and the flirting not only resumed, but intensified, I realised that all was not lost. That weekend, I listened to Stefan complain about how

I had changed, since I joined the programme, and he was right. I could not wait to get back to Leeds.

Back in Leviathan HQ, the tension was mounting as the next major milestone loomed ever closer. The future success of the programme depended on it being a slam dunk. The whole team knew we could not afford to fail, and emotions were running high. In parallel, a whole other type of tension was gaining momentum. All my thoughts of leaving the programme had long since disappeared. I was doing some of my best ever work and I knew that the admiration Alex felt for my professional skills fuelled his other, more personal feelings. Then, suddenly, there was no more time to think. The deadline was upon us. It was time to go flat out.

On the day of the rollout, Alex and I were at our desks by 6am along with the rest of the team. All day long I fielded questions, dispatched communications and diffused potential issues before they occurred. Inevitably there were a few minor problems, but overall things went according to plan. The hours flew by and suddenly the working day was at an end. I was oblivious; busy wrangling my inbox and making sure every query received a considered response. Suddenly a new email popped up onscreen and demanded my immediate attention. It was from the Chief Technology Officer and was entitled, 'Please Read'.

I opened the email, anticipating a major issue. The CTO never emailed me unless something had gone badly wrong, so I was surprised and gratified to read an effusive 'thank you'. Apparently he was very impressed with the way I had communicated with the different stakeholders and supported them through the rollout. I looked across the room at Alex, who was grinning broadly. I thought it was because he had just read the email – the CTO had copied him in – but I discovered he had received a similar message, telling him this was 'the sweetest IT rollout in the history of the organisation' and praising his 'outstanding leadership skills'. The CTO asked us both to thank the whole team on his behalf for doing a sterling job, so we gathered everyone together to share the good news. Alex concluded by inviting everyone to a celebration dinner the following night and promised to foot the bill himself, including our drinks. Company policy forbade us to expense alcohol, so the prospect of free booze prompted a huge cheer.

The dinner was a riot. I do not recall any of us eating much, but we drank a lot of wine. Afterwards, we went on to a club and started doing shots. I downed a few flaming sambucas, surprising the younger members of the team with my fire breathing party trick. Then they dragged me onto the dancefloor, where I remained far longer than I might otherwise have done, as I noticed that Alex was watching me intently. Eventually I made my excuses to my colleagues and left the dancefloor. It was time to take a chance. I pushed my way through the crowds to where he was standing.

'I'm going to head back to the hotel,' I yelled, trying to make myself heard above the noise. 'Thanks for a brilliant evening.'

Alex leaned in close and shouted in my ear. 'You looked beautiful, out there on the dancefloor. Will you be OK getting home?'

'I'll be fine. I'm going to get an Uber. See you tomorrow.' Then I left without a backward glance.

The cold air hit me when I stepped outside, and the wine and sambuca made their presence felt. I pawed at my phone, clumsily summoning an Uber, and swayed slightly as I waited for it to appear. Then someone tapped me on the shoulder. I smiled briefly to myself, then turned around.

'Only me,' Alex whispered in my ear, putting his arm around me. 'I thought I'd leave the youngsters to it. I've left the rest of my cash with them – should keep them going for a bit. Can I share your Uber? Christ, it's freezing out here.'

It was scarcely any warmer inside the car, so we huddled together on the back seat. At first we gossiped about the antics of our younger colleagues and speculated who might end up in bed with whom. Then Alex turned serious.

'You know, this rollout would never have been a success without you.'

'Nonsense.' I waved my arm dismissively. 'You'd have been fine.'

'No, we wouldn't. None of us would – especially not me. You're brilliant, Jen…'

'I'm so not.' False modesty is not normally my thing, but in this case I made an exception. It gave me an excuse to look up at Alex in a way designed to engineer my intended outcome, and I am happy to say it worked.

Alex stared fiercely into my eyes. 'Yes, you are.' Then he kissed me.

Back at the hotel, I took control and made sure Alex had a night to remember. I enjoyed showing him what he had been missing in his lacklustre marriage and his surprise and delight were a powerful aphrodisiac. After he finally fell asleep, I lay awake, replaying the night's events and planning my next move.

The next morning, I reminded myself to be cool. After all, there was a chance that Alex would wake up full of remorse and insist that last night was a terrible mistake. Whatever his reaction, it was essential to be smart. I crept back to my room, showered and dressed, packed my suitcase and caught a cab to the office. I was grateful it was Friday, so I could escape to Manchester at the end of the day if things did not work out.

Alex arrived half an hour later.

'Where did you sneak off to?'

I played my next card. 'I knew you'd regret what happened last night, and I didn't want to be around to see it.'

'You couldn't be more wrong, Jen. I don't regret a second of what happened last night. Quite the opposite. I know things have got to change in both our lives for us to be together properly, but I'm willing to make it happen. The question is – are you?'

Talk about a result. I was delighted that Alex was prepared to tear apart his whole life to be with me, but I did not let him see how I felt. I have always had a good poker face. Instead I told him to go home to Surrey and think it over, to give him the chance to change his mind. I thought it was sensible to suggest a cooling off period, to ensure he was serious. The following Monday, it appeared he was. He insisted we were the real deal. Although he was discreet at work, he made his feelings clear whenever we were alone. He urged me to join him in planning how we could leave our respective partners and be together. He said it drove him crazy to think of me being with another man at weekends, so I left Stefan and rented a flat in the city centre. Stefan was devastated, but I did not care. Whenever he could, Alex pleaded pressure of work to Stella and said he needed to remain in Leeds over the weekend. Then, instead of heading south, he would cross the Pennines with me. On those memorable weekends, we rarely left my flat.

I suppose you are wondering whether I ever felt guilty about Stella. The short answer is no. Alex told me all about her and I concluded that she had brought this on herself. Once a high-flyer, she had clearly let herself go a long time ago, both professionally and physically. Now she was merely a dowdy housewife. There was nothing left for Alex to respect, let alone fancy. Frankly, I was astonished that he had not strayed before. I concluded that Stella had squandered her chance. Now it was my turn.

Naturally I expected Alex to make changes in his life, as I had done by ditching Stefan. He insisted he was married to Stella in name only and the marriage had run its course. However, whenever I asked him to make the break, he said that it was not the right time. Apparently, his main concern was Imogen. After struggling at school for years, she was finally doing well in the sixth form and he did not want to run the risk of her failing her A levels. He was desperate for her to follow her brother Hugo to a top-flight university. Having messed up my education so spectacularly at the same age, I sort of understood, although I hated being forced into the role of 'other woman'. I repeatedly told Alex I was worth more and each time he agreed. He urged me to be patient, but I struggled. I sensed that I was losing control of the situation and I did not like it.

Meanwhile, the subsequent Leviathan rollouts went as well as my first and before long, the end of the programme was imminent. I was not looking forward to it. It would be difficult for me to see Alex regularly once we no longer worked together; the firm had made it clear I was required back in Manchester and Alex would return to the London office until his next assignment, which could be anywhere. It was clear that my window of opportunity was in danger of closing. Also, I knew Alex was under pressure to take Stella on a luxury holiday once the programme wrapped. I could not risk them reconciling under a tropical sun, so I made Alex promise not to take her anywhere exotic. When he took me at my word and booked a narrowboat holiday in Leicestershire, despite Stella's protestations, whilst promising me a trip to The Maldives, I was encouraged. I realised I should have walked away, rather than settling for such meagre crumbs of comfort, but I could not. I find it difficult to admit but, somewhere along the line, I had fallen for him. It was never part of the plan, but I could not help it. All I could do was attempt to retain a semblance of control while I fought for what I deserved.

At that point fate provided me with a helping hand, and my luck changed.

My mobile rang in the middle of the night. At first I could not work out what Alex was saying. I thought he was drunk, until he managed to tell me he was in hospital, gravely injured and fighting the effects of his sedatives. I started to ask about the nature of his injury, but he silenced me. He did not have much battery left, so he only had a few minutes to explain. He told me Stella was responsible for his accident. He did not say exactly what she had done to him, but he was clear about her motivation. Somehow, he was not sure how, she had found out about our affair and tried to exact revenge. Now he wanted to return the favour, with my help. His idea was that I should present myself as his partner and frame Stella as an obsessive ex-girlfriend who had been stalking him. I said I doubted I could fool the police for long, but Alex said I did not need to. Just getting arrested would be enough to destabilise Stella and, most importantly, demonstrate that he knew what she had done. Then he said he had to go as his phone was about to die. The last thing he said before he rang off was that he would never return to Surrey and his future lay with me. Whatever happened, he would protect me.

Whatever you think of me, I hope I have convinced you I am not stupid. I knew the sketchy plan which Alex had concocted was full of holes, but at the same time I was elated to think that any feelings Alex might have had for Stella had abruptly been extinguished. He was mine now, and I was determined to prove my worth. Never have I used my professional skills to more devastating effect. I fabricated hundreds of emails and text messages; a body of digital evidence which would temporarily convince the police that Alex was being stalked and would lead them to arrest Stella. In the event, luck was on our side. A series of chance events – a lawyer's delayed train, the appearance of a surprise witness – meant the police could not immediately run their background checks, so Stella was held in custody for some time following her arrest. Once the truth emerged, the police immediately released her and clearly suspected Alex of foul play but, given the nature of his injuries and the drugs he was on, he was able to plead that he was confused and had lied to me about being married. Reluctantly, the officer in charge of the investigation decided to take no further action, so Alex was in the clear. Of course, so was Stella. I hated the fact that she had got away with attempted murder, but Alex urged me to let it go. He told me I had more important things to worry about, like helping him recover from his injury.

When I first learned that Alex's leg had been amputated below the knee, I was devastated, of course. I was also concerned that things would not be the same between us, and I was right. At first, they were better. Alex made a rapid recovery and was soon fully mobile once again. Now that he was free of Stella, he delivered on all his promises. He bought us a beautiful house in Wilmslow, an affluent suburb of Manchester. At my instigation, he left our firm and went freelance, so he could work locally and come home every night. I was determined not to throw away everything I had worked for by risking a long-distance relationship. In return, I stayed out of sight until I could be presented to his children, after a decent interval, as his new partner. In the meantime, I too made a fresh start in my career, by getting myself a job in one of Manchester's top PR agencies. The success of Leviathan was well documented by then and I was able to take full advantage.

After a few months, Alex and I officially became a couple. Our diaries were soon full of social engagements with other upwardly mobile couples. It finally seemed as though my plan had come to fruition. I had the powerful man I desired and the luxury lifestyle with which I grew up.

Alex was devotion personified. He constantly told me that he adored me and was much happier with me than he ever had been with Stella. At weekends, he loved to take me clothes shopping and help me pick out new outfits. He called me his 'clothes horse', as he thought everything looked great on me, whereas the same could not be said for Stella. Even so, he urged me to abandon my sexier clothing in favour of a classier, more grown-up look. Money was no object, so my weekend wardrobe of bodycon dresses was consigned to the charity shops and replaced by tasteful designer clothing. He took me on surprise dates to all the best restaurants in the area and booked a series of exotic holidays, including that romantic getaway to The Maldives he had promised me. In fact, it was during that trip, while we were enjoying cocktails on the terrace of our luxury villa, that he told me he wanted us to have a baby. He said it would 'cement our relationship'.

I did not think our relationship needed cementing and told Alex as much. I said I would like to have children one day, once we had spent more time together, although in truth, children had never figured in my life plan. However, he would not let the subject drop. He kept telling me how much he loved me and insisting that, if I loved him back, I would give him the child he craved. He suggested that my refusal to comply meant I was not committed to our relationship and I felt him begin to withdraw from me. I could not face losing Alex, so eventually I gave in, pushing aside the notion that I was being manipulated, when it used to be me who controlled the agenda. I threw out my pills, crossed my fingers and hoped I would not get pregnant for a while, but my prayers went unanswered. In the end it all happened so quickly, before I could catch my breath.

So there you have it. I got the man I wanted - and he adored me. I played for high stakes and thought I had won. Of course, hindsight is twenty-twenty. What I know now, but was unable to see at the time, is that I picked a man who was exactly like my father.

9 BOILING FROG

Imagine a small frog, swimming alone in a pond. One of those jewel-bright frogs you find, deep in the rainforest. Around he swims in the warm water, disturbing the reflections of the trees towering above. Every so often, his sticky tongue snaps out and ensnares an unsuspecting fly. Food is plentiful and life is good.

But unknown to him, change is afoot. Deep in the earth below, the gods have lit a fire. Gradually the water temperature in the pond increases, but the change happens so slowly that our frog doesn't realise. He just keeps on swimming, thinking how cosy warm it is, until suddenly it is not. The water is boiling, the earth is burning up and the rocks have turned to molten lava. The frog wants to escape, but he is unable to free himself. It is too late. He is doomed.

Or imagine you are the frog. Perhaps you have had a stressful day and are treating yourself to a warm bubble bath. You lie there for a while, with a magazine and a glass of wine, until you notice the temperature has cooled. So you add some more hot water. You make the bath so hot that your skin glows pink and you feel light-headed. Normally you would stop right there, but this time, you do not. You keep adding more water, until the skin peels from your arms and legs in little scrolls. Until you pass out. Until you boil.

Of course, you would not do that. I know you are far too sensible. You would stop when it started to hurt. You would recognise the tipping point. You would realise that what you were doing was no longer good for you and would call a halt. I know you think that, because I thought precisely the same thing.

The water was pleasantly warm for some time. Unlike me, Alex was delighted when I got pregnant so quickly; he could not do enough for me. He bought me flowers several times a week, lit scented candles all around

120

the house every evening and surprised me regularly with spa days and beauty treatments. Admittedly it was nice to be pampered. I felt I deserved it after everything I had done for him.

He also bought every baby book going. I was surprised by this; I thought that, having already had two children, he would be somewhat blasé, but he was extremely vigilant from the start. He read in one of these books that expectant mothers should not wear high heels, and that was that – my beloved Louboutins and Jimmy Choos were consigned to the attic. The old me would have protested, but the new me had more important things to think about.

At his instigation, I took an early blood test and discovered that we were having a son. I know the romantic souls among you want the sex of your baby to be a surprise, but for Alex it was a no brainer. He had to know, so he could *plan*. Paint the nursery the right colour, buy the appropriate clothes, put his name down on the waiting list for the best schools. I am sure it has not escaped your notice that I am big on planning too, so I could relate to his need to know. Anyway, he was delighted with the test results. For Alex, a boy was the preferred outcome. I would have been happy either way.

You are probably surprised that I used the word 'happy', given that you know I did not want this baby, so I need to explain. Hormones have a lot to answer for. Sometime early in my pregnancy, I fell in love, despite myself. To my astonishment, my feelings for my unborn child eclipsed even my love for Alex. I felt like I had begun a private journey with someone whom I had known for ever, but could not wait to meet, and I knew without a doubt that I would do anything to protect my son from harm. I called him my Little Flea. I have no idea why. It was my own secret name for him. No one else knew; not even Alex. I had never used a slushy pet name in my life, but my pregnancy changed me. It brought out in me a fierce tenderness I never knew I possessed.

Even so, I did not lose focus on my career. I was still enjoying my job with the PR agency and working hard to get promoted. Long hours go with the territory in my line of work, but that never bothered me, and I did not see any reason to scale back just because I was pregnant. I was not ill; in fact, I felt great. Alex, though, had other ideas. One night I was talking on the phone to my manager about an upcoming event. It was a lengthy discussion – there was a lot to get through – and finally Alex saw red. He marched into my study, grabbed the phone from my hand and told my boss I had to stop working in the evening 'for the sake of my health'. Afterwards, I tore him off a strip, telling him in no uncertain terms that he had overstepped the mark. He apologised and admitted he had overreacted, but said it was only because he loved me so much. Anyway, after that the evening phone calls stopped. I only found out later that my manager had asked other colleagues to take on my after-hours work, when one of them let slip he was grateful for the opportunity which my 'scary boyfriend' had gifted him. Apparently, my boss had decided it was not worth incurring the wrath of Alex. I confronted her about it, but she did not reverse her decision. The damage had been done.

As you already know, Alex likes clothes shopping. Sometimes we bought clothes for him, but after I got pregnant, the focus was firmly on maternity wear. I protested that I did not require new clothes, as I was not even showing, but Alex insisted he wanted me to look 'more discreet', so he bought me lots of perfectly tailored maternity dresses in expensive black and navy fabrics. And beige. Lots and lots of beige. My colleagues, who mostly lived in city centre apartments, like I used to, started teasing me about being a 'suburban housewife', but I told myself they were just jealous. After all, Wilmslow is a highly desirable location. The Beckhams used to live down the road in Alderley Edge. I figured my co-workers would all love to live in a stunning, seven-figure house like mine.

I adored our modern home, with its huge rooms and clean lines. I have always had an eye for interior design and Alex gave me free rein to decorate and style as I saw fit. Money was no object. He loved the result and said how proud he was to invite friends around for supper. However, when it came to feeding those friends, it was a different matter. By the way, I use the term 'friends' loosely. These were strictly dinner-party chums; affluent, stylish, status-conscious and judgmental, but that did not bother me. Having led a transient life and discarded people along the way, superficial acquaintances work fine for me, whilst Alex revelled in the not-so-subtle one-upmanship which passed for friendly banter among the men. The only thing that bothered him was that, unlike them, he could not boast about my culinary skills.

At first he laughed it off, saying my PR career left me with no time to be a domestic goddess. When we entertained, he hired the best caterers and joked about it, until one of the wives, a corporate lawyer, produced a meal worthy of MasterChef. After that, I was under pressure to practise at home. It did not matter that Alex could barely make toast; the onus was on me to compete, and I lost count of the dinners Alex scraped contemptuously into the bin. I protested that cooking skills were never part of the deal, but to no avail. Alex appeared conveniently to have forgotten how he used to joke affectionately about my culinary incompetence, when we first got together. He even used to say he liked the fact that I was different from Stella, who was an accomplished cook. He would smile and observe that I had other talents, then invite me to remind him what they were. I was always happy to oblige, but now things had changed.

Imogen used to visit us quite frequently in those days, as she was studying in Manchester and liked to escape the city from time to time. She picked up on the tense atmosphere one evening, when yet another meal had been consigned to the trash, and I confessed that I felt under pressure to compete on the dinner-party circuit. Sweetly, she promised to share some recipes with me, but also advised me to decline the culinary challenge.

'Mum's a brilliant cook, but Dad found plenty of other ways to show her she wasn't good enough. Don't let him pull the same trick on you. He's already changing you – I can see it. You probably don't realise it, but he's clever like that. You have to fight back.'

At the time, I was surprised at her apparent disloyalty to her father, but I put it down to the bottle of Sauvignon Blanc she had drunk instead of eating my disgusting dinner.

The following week, the former members of the Leviathan admin team, who had all been deployed on different assignments, were in town for a training course and asked me to join them for a reunion drink afterwards. Normally I would have turned them down, as reunions are not my style, but Alex had told me he was working late, so I decided to drop in briefly on my way home. They all said I was looking well, although they did remark on my 'different' clothes. After forty minutes spent watching them down gin and tonics while I stuck to sparkling water, I made my excuses. I was on my way to the tram stop when Margaret caught up with me.

'Jen,' she puffed. 'Hang on a moment. I need a word.'

'What's wrong, Margaret? Did I forget something?'

'No, but you have lost something.'

'What d'you mean?'

'Your sparkle. It's gone AWOL.'

'It's called being pregnant - it takes it out of you.'

'That's not the reason. I can tell. I've seen this happen before – to my mum. My stepdad was a bully, like Alex – and she became just like you. She was feisty and strong, but he beat her down. Don't let it happen to you, Jen.'

'Are you sure you're not just jealous? You've always fancied Alex.'

'I admit, he's fit, but would I want him in my life? No chance! You're welcome to him.'

'You've got it wrong, Margaret. Alex and I are very happy…'

'Sure you are. Look, I've got to get back, or they'll wonder where I am. You've got my number – call me when you need help.'

Much later, I remembered that Margaret had said 'when', not 'if'. At the time, I did not notice. I was too busy being annoyed at her for interfering in my life, but if I had been honest with myself I would have acknowledged that she had a point. I had started trying to please Alex, in the kitchen and elsewhere, which was unlike me, as I have never been a people pleaser. It is funny how even women like me, who regard themselves as tough, can get suckered into that role, although it did not sit well with me and I was no good at it. The harder I tried, the more extreme his response. He would be silent and cold for days on end if I made even the slightest mistake and he progressed from scraping food into the bin to throwing full plates and glasses across the kitchen. I was constantly touching up the paintwork and using sex to gloss over the invisible stains which were more difficult to eradicate. As it turned out, this was the worst thing I could have done.

I do not like sharing this sort of thing, so I do not intend to give you too much information. All I will say is that, when the lover I thought I knew morphed into a whole different person between the sheets, I told myself to be more broad-minded. I rationalised Alex's behaviour by telling myself he was not going far beyond what you read about in a certain type of novel which has become popular these days. As I rubbed arnica into my legs and applied concealer to my neck before leaving for work in the mornings, I longed for the sensuality of our early days, but consoled myself with the thought that he would only ever go so far. I knew he would never risk hurting the baby.

Even so, I did acquire some bruises outside the bedroom as well. The incidents were never very serious, but they happened frequently enough to make a mockery of what must have looked like a dream life to outsiders. Let me give you an example by explaining what happened during a typical evening out on our dinner party circuit. I was in the en suite, putting on my make-up, when Alex stormed in and said he wanted to shave. I told him to wait a minute, as I was just finishing up, or alternatively to use one of the other bathrooms. His response was to scream at me.

'Don't you dare tell me what to do in my own house!'

Then he grabbed a handful of my hair and yanked me out of the way. He threw my make-up bag onto the floor and the contents spilled across the tiles. I knelt down and gathered them up, then retreated to the family bathroom. As I applied my lipstick with shaking hands, my only thought was that this would not be the end of it. There would be more to come, later.

I was right. At the dinner table, I contributed to the banter, but I should have kept my head down. By then, no attempt from me to take an active role during a social gathering went unpunished, but I forgot myself and started recounting a funny story from work. As the others listened intently, obviously interested and amused, it was too much for Alex, so he grabbed my hand under the table. A casual observer would have thought it an affectionate gesture, but it was the opposite. As I continued talking, he squeezed my hand progressively harder, until I thought my bones would crack. At the same time, he put his foot on top of mine and pressed down on the bare skin exposed by my sandal. I tried to carry on despite the pain, but it was no use, so I admit I gave up and allowed someone else to grab the limelight.

There were many evenings like this, but there were good times too. Alex could still be the charismatic man I fought so hard to get. When things were going well, the bad memories melted away and I told myself I had overreacted. When he booked another exotic holiday for us and my dinner party friends told me how lucky I was, I believed them. When he bought me a top of the range SUV 'to keep our son safe' they remarked on what a great father he was going to be. When he flirted openly with them, and they whispered to me afterwards how hot he was, it did not bother me that much. I reasoned that a sexy man like Alex was always going to flirt and at least he was doing it out in the open. I defended the life I had built for myself and ignored the fact that the water was coming to the boil.

When Alex and I moved in together and he went freelance, he promised me he would only accept assignments in the north west, so he could come home every evening. We agreed we would never replicate his life with Stella, only seeing each other at weekends and leading a semi-detached existence. For a while, he kept his promise. His reputation as the man who delivered Leviathan, the most successful IT implementation in the public sector, meant he could pick and choose his jobs and command a spectacular day rate. After a while, though, things changed, and he started to work further away from home. When I challenged him, he replied that he could not pass up the opportunities and insisted we needed the money, as I only earned 'pin money' from my PR job. Clearly this was nonsense; although I brought home only a fraction of what Alex did, my salary was generous, and money was absolutely not an issue. Then he started accepting invitations to speak at overseas conferences and was often away for several days. None of this would have mattered if he had been the same person when he came home, but there were changes in his behaviour that I could not ignore.

For instance, he began wearing trendier clothes. He had always been a fan of quality, classic leisurewear; I use to tease him about it, calling him 'Man at Gant'. Now, though, he started seeking out edgier labels and got a new haircut. His floppy blonde fringe was replaced by a sharper style, with the sides shaved close. I had to admit it suited him and thought maybe he had been influenced by the European consultants he met, whose dress sense was typically less conservative than their UK counterparts. What I could not explain away was how he behaved with his phone.

In the early days, Alex used to leave his phone on the charging pad every evening. He would check it a few times in case there was an urgent message from work, but otherwise he would ignore it. He always said our evenings were precious and he did not want to let them slip away by being constantly on his phone. If a call came in and he was busy, he would tell me to answer it and take a message. Now, though, his phone had taken up permanent residence inside his back pocket. Imogen noticed immediately, when she visited us one weekend.

'I see Dad's phone has migrated to his back pocket – again.'

I asked her what she meant, and she revealed that he always carried his phone in his back pocket when he was at home in Surrey, with her and Stella. She made some remark about old habits dying hard. Even so, I could have blamed it on pressure of work, had it not been for the calls which were hastily terminated and Alex's defensive response when I asked him who had phoned. One night, I waited until he was asleep, then crept round to his side of the bed and picked up his phone. I promised myself I would not check his messages; I was determined not to become a suspicious, pathetic person. However, I suspected this would not be my choice to make, and I was right. Alex had changed his password without telling me. When we first got together, I always knew the password for his phone and laptop. He informed me every time he changed them; he said it was his way of proving we had no secrets between us. Now I could not ignore the fact that those days were gone.

Later that week, I ran into Margaret when I was shopping during my lunch break. I had not contacted her since our last encounter, and we made awkward small talk for a few minutes. Then, as I turned to leave, she grabbed my hand.

'I hardly recognised you when I saw you, Jen.'

'I know – I've blown up like a beached whale since we last met.'

'You so haven't. You're the skinniest pregnant woman I ever saw. No; what I meant was – you look different. Your clothes, your hair – even the way you walk. I wondered who you reminded me of, and it came to me while we were talking. You look like his wife.'

'Stella? How d'you know?'

'We met her at the Leviathan wrap-up party – remember? She seemed like she had to apologise for existing, if you know what I mean. He did that to her – and now he's doing the same to you.'

Later, at home, I cast my mind back to when I met Stella briefly at the party. I took a long look in the mirror, then I searched online for Stella's digital advisory service to refresh my memory.

I have to admit I was astonished at how professional her website was. Either she had employed a superb web designer, or her own skills were very impressive. Her photograph was a surprise as well. Clearly she had dropped some weight since the party and her pleasant, unthreatening face was expertly made up. Her shiny, dark hair was cut in a classic bob not unlike mine. In short, she was way more attractive than I remembered. In no way did she look browbeaten or apologetic. On the contrary, she looked like an approachable purveyor of professional advice. I felt sure her clients would have no problem admitting to her their inability to operate the smartphones and tablets their children had bought them. She looked like the sort of person to whom fears could be confided and secrets confessed.

Talking of secrets, I should have deleted my browsing history, or changed the password for my laptop, just like Alex had done, but I did not. I made a schoolgirl error and I got caught out. I should have known Alex would check up on me. He mentioned it casually a few days later, as he was pouring himself a glass of wine.

'I see you've been researching an old rival.'

'What d'you mean?'

'Stella. You looked at her website.'

'Have you been on my laptop?'

'Of course. We always said…no secrets.'

At that point I should have challenged him about changing his passwords without informing me, but I let it go, which would not have happened in the early days.

'It's a nice-looking site, isn't it?'

'Yes, it is.'

'Well, don't be fooled. Appearances can be deceptive…'

'I don't understand.'

'The website might look impressive, but Stella's business is always going to struggle. I've got a good network in Surrey. My friends are highly influential. They're making sure she doesn't build up a decent client base, but she'll never suspect I'm behind it. She'll just blame herself and say she needs to improve her marketing. Well, she can market all she likes, but she's doomed to failure. I've seen to that.'

I thought back to Alex's accident and how I hated Stella for what she did to him. Then I looked at his face and saw he was not annoyed I had checked up on his ex-wife. On the contrary, he was pleased to discover my interest in her and had enjoyed boasting about how he was wrecking Stella's business from afar. He was controlling us both – and loving it. I instantly vowed that I would not permit this situation to continue.

Not long afterwards, Imogen came over for Sunday lunch. She was on a high after a successful climbing trip to the Peak District the previous day and Alex popped open a bottle of champagne to celebrate. They finished it between them before lunch and washed down my overcooked roast beef with copious quantities of red wine. As I was serving the trifle, which had failed to set, Imogen babbled away in the background; her stream of consciousness was rapid and loose-tongued. She was talking about her recent visit to Surrey and fleetingly mentioned the name Chris. I hoped for her sake that Alex would not pick up on it, but he did. It takes more than a bottle of wine to make him miss a trick.

'Who's Chris?'

'What?' Poor, tipsy Imogen was immediately on the back foot.

'You mentioned a man called Chris – with a narrowboat?'

'He's – just a friend of Mummy's...'

'Just a friend? Is that all?'

'It's nothing serious....no big deal.'

'What's the boat called, Imogen?'

'Why d'you want to know?'

'What's it *called*?'

'I can't remember...'

'Come *on*, Imogen. Of course you can...'

'Honestly, I can't. It's a French name. Mummy said it meant 'whale' – that's all I know.'

'Sorry, Minnie.' Alex was immediately contrite. 'I didn't mean to get on your case. Let's change the subject.'

Later that evening, I drove Imogen to the station to get the train back to Manchester, then Alex and I watched TV until bedtime. Afterwards, I was in the en suite, taking my make-up off, when he burst in.

'Good old Google Translate. *Baleine*. That's the name of the boat. Kind of appropriate, for my wife...'

'Your ex-wife...'

'Whatever. Anyway, lucky it's an unusual name, although I confess I have no idea why Stella would hook up with a canal boater. You'd think she'd want nothing more to do with narrowboats...'

'Alex, just let it go. Forget about Stella – that's all in the past!'

'No, it's not. If you think I'm just going to let her 'move on' after what she did to me, you're mistaken. I'm going to make sure this Chris breaks it off with her...'

'And if he doesn't?'

'Not an issue. Trust me - he will.'

That is what finally made me decide to contact Stella. I had been thinking about it for a while. Ever since I checked out her website, then discovered what Alex was doing to her, I had stopped thinking of her as a rival and started seeing her as a fellow victim. I wanted to find out if Alex had treated her the same way as me and warn her about the damage he was still inflicting on her. Above all, I needed her take on how we could get ourselves out of this mess. Female solidarity is not usually my thing, but I was willing to try anything to protect my baby. For the first time, I was starting to entertain the notion of bringing up my son alone, and I needed to work out what to do next.

It took me a while to reach her. The first few times I called her, she hung up on me, but I persevered. Eventually we spoke, and I asked her to meet me on home turf, at my favourite canal side bar in Manchester. Remember I said earlier that we would go there again? Anyway, she finally agreed, although it took some persuasion.

At first it was not an easy conversation, as you can imagine, but gradually the atmosphere thawed. As well as warning Stella about what Alex was doing to her, I found myself telling her all about how he had treated me. I told her things I have never revealed to anyone else, apart from you. She is the sort of person you confide in, despite your best intentions and even though it is not appropriate, given your history. It is a gift she has. She never once told me I got what I deserved. The nearest she came was when she used that old line about creating a vacancy, by moving in with Alex. We both had a laugh at that, just for a moment. We needed a brief distraction from our shared predicament. Having compared notes, we concluded that Alex's behaviour was escalating, and we needed to co-operate in order to regain control of our lives.

Stella had persuaded me to have two small glasses of wine; the first alcohol I had drunk since finding out I was pregnant. As I stood up and walked to the Ladies, I felt its effects. I clung to the washbasin as I made the decision to ask the key question. As soon as I returned to the table, I blurted it out, before I could change my mind.

'D'you ever wish that it had worked?'

Stella asked what I meant, but I could tell she knew, and was playing for time. I clarified, asking if she wished she had finished the job, that day on the narrowboat, and she admitted that it would have 'made things simpler'. Then she asked if I felt the same way. I admitted that I would have been devastated at the time but that now, with the benefit of hindsight, I realised it might have been for the best. Then we sat there for a moment in silence, contemplating our new status as co-conspirators.

It was Stella who made the first move.

'So, here we are. Two intelligent, educated women with lots of skills, including our ability to lie convincingly. Surely we can find a way to get ourselves out of this?'

I struggled to reply. By then I felt guilty about how I had treated Stella, even though I do not usually do guilt. I had stolen her husband and conspired with him to frame her, and now I regretted doing both these things. I knew she was far from blameless, but I understood how Alex had driven her to do what she did, that day on the narrowboat.

I tried to apologise, but Stella silenced me. She had moved into solution mode. I asked her what she thought Alex would say if he knew the two of us had met, and she answered that he would never envisage us getting together. In Alex's mind, she said, we both exist only in relation to him, but his arrogance could be his undoing. Then she asked me to give her a moment.

I watched her as she wandered across the terrace and stood by the lock. A narrowboat was passing through and she watched its owner expertly open and close the gates. I guessed she was reliving her own experiences on that fateful holiday in Leicestershire and momentarily shared Alex's surprise that she would ever willingly step on board a narrowboat again.

When Stella walked back to our table, she seemed to have had a lightbulb moment. She had drunk nearly two bottles of wine, but its effects appeared miraculously to have vanished, and she radiated clarity of purpose as she announced that she had found the perfect solution. Apparently she knew exactly what we were going to do next. She sat down opposite me, rested her elbows on the table and I leaned forward, eager to know the answer.

By the way, scientists have established that Boiling Frog Syndrome is a myth. Thermoregulation, as they call it, is an essential survival strategy for frogs. When the water becomes unbearably hot - they jump out.

10 GONE, BUT NOT FORGOTTEN

I am sorry to report that the lightbulb moment was a mirage. The supposed plan which Stella had concocted would have landed us both in jail. I have no intention of revealing it here; I do not want to embarrass her. She can tell you herself if she chooses.

After Stella proudly revealed her solution to our problems, it was my turn to play for time by ordering a pot of coffee, to sober her up. Then I explained all the reasons why her plan would not work and would play right into Alex's hands. When I had finished, she admitted:

'You're right. It would just end up another botched job, but I wouldn't get away with it this time. Lucky you're more streetwise than me. So, have you got a better idea?'

I had to admit, my mind was a blank. We sat and talked for a long time, but neither of us could come up with any other ideas. By the time office workers started flooding in for happy hour, a bond of sorts had been formed, but we had to leave. We both had trains to catch.

I accompanied Stella back to Piccadilly and put her on the London train. We said goodbye and agreed to remain in touch. As I scanned the departures board for a suburban train to Wilmslow, I wondered whether she would keep her word.

At home, I tried to focus on the baby and avoid incurring the wrath of Alex, but it was becoming increasingly difficult. We used to enjoy lively debates about a range of subjects, but now any attempt to challenge him was met by shouts of rage, followed by slamming doors and aggressive silences that could last for days. For someone like me, who communicates for a living, the silent treatment was the worst part. Alex was aware of this, of course. Having worked with me on Leviathan, he knew exactly how to push my buttons.

Then, for no apparent reason, everything would change. Charming Alex would be back in the room. The bad times would recede into the background and I would tell myself I had overreacted. Life would return to relative normality – until the next time. It was exhausting.

As I mentioned before, I thought about leaving. On some days, I could think about little else, but I was not naïve enough to imagine I could escape simply by moving out. Alex would find me, wherever I was, and I did not like to think about what he might do when he caught up with me. Then there was the baby. Ideally I wanted him to have two parents, so I told myself I owed it to him to try and make it work with his father.

During the week following our meeting, I heard nothing from Stella. Then, one lunchtime, I was queuing in Pret when I got an incoming call from a number I did not recognise. I assumed it was a nuisance call, so I did not pick up, but later I saw that the caller had left a voicemail, which nuisance callers tend not to do. I hit 'Play' and put the phone to my ear.

'Hi, Jen – it's Stella. I got myself a different mobile to call you on. Pay as you go. I'm sure Alex trawls your phone, and I don't want him to recognise my number. I suggest you save this number under a different name. Call me back when you get a minute. Hope you're OK – talk to you soon. Bye.'

I smiled at Stella's clumsy attempts at subterfuge. I saved her new number under the name 'Jane' – after DCI Tennison from Prime Suspect. I thought it was the least I could do.

After that, we spoke regularly. During the week, we talked in my lunch hour, but at weekends I could sometimes escape for a walk on Alderley Edge, if Alex was trying to curry favour with the local movers and shakers by playing golf. I would stand on those extraordinary landlocked cliffs, looking right across Manchester to the moors beyond, and talk to the woman I had misjudged. She confided that she had warned Chris about Alex, who had apparently not made contact. Her business was doing OK, and she had acquired some new clients. All was quiet in Surrey.

Meanwhile in Cheshire, things were changing. One evening over dinner, Alex reported that he had been offered an assignment in Birmingham which would require him to be away from home three nights a week. He did not normally consult me before accepting new jobs outside the north west, despite having originally promised to come home every night, but this was an 18-month project, so I suppose he felt obliged to ask my opinion. Once I would have vetoed a long-term assignment in another city, but these days I had different priorities.

I quickly weighed up the pros and cons. Clearly I would have to cope alone with a new-born for half the week. Also, I figured that Alex would probably stray if he were away regularly for so long. Maybe I would end up in the same position as Stella. However, these objections were dwarfed by the relief I felt at the prospect of having some respite from Alex on a regular basis. I also hoped that spending time apart might remind him what he was missing and enable me to reboot our relationship. So I told Alex I was happy for him to accept the job.

At first, the Birmingham job did seem to mend things between us. Alex enjoyed the work and seemed relaxed and happy when we spoke on the phone. He did not want to stay in a hotel long-term, so he rented a penthouse in the Jewellery Quarter. He waxed lyrical about the city, saying the restaurants and bars were as vibrant as in Manchester, but I was sceptical. In my opinion, no other place in England could compare with my adopted city, so Alex suggested we spend a weekend there. Birmingham would not have been my ideal choice for a romantic mini break, but I quickly changed my mind when I got there.

The weather was fine and dry, so we walked everywhere. Alex showed me his 'commute', a pleasant uphill stroll alongside a flight of locks and across the canal to the client's office in Brindley Place. We shopped for designer baby clothes in a glitzy arcade, then Alex bought me mocktails in the bar at Harvey Nichols. Later, we had dinner in a stylish restaurant, run by a celebrity chef, on the top floor of a modern office block. As we looked down on the city lights, winking cheerily in the velvet darkness, I hoped that things might be improving.

When I got home, I rang Stella and suggested that things could be looking up, but she did not agree. She was not in a good place. Chris had dumped her that same weekend. He swore it had nothing to do with Alex, but she was not convinced. Even so, I did not allow her news to puncture my new-found optimism. I thought she was using Alex as an excuse, to avoid confronting whatever had gone wrong in her fledgling relationship. With hindsight, I had better stick to PR. I would make a lousy psychologist.

On the day that changed everything, Alex was working from home, as it was not one of his Birmingham days and he had to finish a report for another client. He got up early to get ahead of the game, and when I came downstairs I found a flask of coffee and a lunchbox full of peanut butter toast waiting for me.

'I know you never have time to make breakfast, darling, so I prepared this for you. Save you having Pret porridge – again.'

'Thanks, Alex. That's thoughtful of you. I have to go - see you tonight.'

Towards lunchtime, I started to feel unwell. At first I ignored it, thinking I shouldn't have eaten the entire contents of the lunchbox in one go, but the nausea began to build, rolling over me in waves, until I was forced to run for the toilets, convinced I was going to throw up. It did not happen, but as I stared at my grey face in the mirror, I became aware of a sensation I had not experienced for months. I rushed for the nearest cubicle, praying I was wrong, but no one up there was listening. As I stared at the spots of bright blood, I reminded myself about what the baby books said. I repeated my new mantra over and over, as I packed up my things and rushed for the office door. 'This is perfectly normal. It happens to lots of pregnant women. It doesn't mean anything.' On and on, over and over, as I jumped in a taxi and made the driver's day by asking him to drive me all the way to Wilmslow.

As the taxi headed south, out of the city centre and into the suburbs, the nausea subsided. I prayed that the scare was over, and it was just one of those things. The taxi dropped me off at the end of our driveway and I bargained with God as I walked towards the house.

'Please let my baby be OK. Please don't hurt my Little Flea. I promise to rest up and take it easy until he's born. Just let him be OK. My Flea. Please. I'll stop work, I'll put up with anything Alex does – just as long as you let my baby be alright. Please…'

I knew Alex would be in his office at the back of the house. Probably with his headphones on, playing white noise or binaural beats to help him concentrate. I crept into the downstairs toilet, discovered the bleeding had stopped, put my head in my hands and sobbed with relief. Then I wiped the trails of molten mascara from my face and went to make a cup of tea.

As I walked into the kitchen, I saw two mugs on the counter. One was Alex's favourite; the other was a guest mug. Then I noticed a trademark, heady scent. My sense of smell had become particularly acute since getting pregnant, and I could not mistake the distinctive odour of Opium perfume. At school, one of the girls in my dormitory used it in copious quantities and the rest of us grew to hate it.

I felt quite calm as I opened the office door.

'Christ!' Alex shot out of his chair and ripped the headphones from his head. 'You nearly gave me a heart attack, Jennifer! What the hell are you doing here?'

'I didn't feel well, so I came home. Alex, who was here earlier?'

'What d'you mean?'

'There are two mugs on the counter. Yours – and a guest mug. Who stopped by?'

'Oh – that was Steven. You know – my financial advisor? He came by with some documents for me to sign.'

I have met Steven a few times. He is a pleasant, grey-suited, fifty-something accountant, not given to wearing Opium.

'I don't believe you…'

Alex dropped his voice to a low growl, like he always does when he is angry.

'What are you accusing me of, Jennifer?'

'Do I really need to spell it out?'

He fixed me with a menacing gaze, and I stared right back. I refused to be intimidated by him, when he was the guilty one. Then it struck me. I was in exactly the same position as Stella, on that narrowboat holiday. Trading accusations and denials with a man I no longer trusted. I had grown to like Stella, but I was determined not to emulate her. It was time to leave. Without a word, I turned my back on Alex and headed to the bathroom to begin packing. When he heard me open the bathroom cabinet and start taking things out, he followed me.

'What are you doing?' he screamed.

'What does it look like?'

'Don't you dare walk out on me.'

'Just watch me…'

'Don't bother, Jennifer. It's a waste of time. Wherever you run to, I'll track you down. You're the mother of my child; you don't get to leave me!'

'Yes, I do.' Alex had given voice to my fears, but I refused to respond to his threats. I put my head down and continued filling my washbag. As I zipped it up, Alex grabbed me by the shoulders and shook me roughly.

'Stop this nonsense – now!'

He took hold of my bag with one hand and tried to prise it out of my grasp. I clung to it with both hands, determined not to let go, so he braced his other hand against my shoulder to gain more purchase and force me to yield. As I resisted, my stockinged feet slipped on the marble tiles and flew out from under me. Instinctively I released my grip on the bag to try and break my fall. After that, my world slid into slow motion. I calmly observed my feet in the air above me and felt detached from them, as though they belonged to someone else. I remember thinking that feet had no business being up there. The sharp crack of my lower back on the rim of the bathtub distracted me briefly from these idle thoughts. Then someone flicked the 'off' switch.

When I came to, I felt relieved that our bathroom was tiled right to the ceiling. It would make it so much easier, I thought, to clean off the splashes of scarlet which had unaccountably appeared. They seemed to be everywhere; I could not imagine where they had come from. In the background, a male voice was sobbing and shouting. He did not appear to be talking to me, so I ignored him. I did not feel up to speaking, or to making a start on the cleaning. It would have to wait. What I really needed to do was go back to sleep. Lucky I was already in the bathtub, where it was nice and cosy.

I do not recall the paramedics lifting me out of the tub and carrying me to the ambulance, and the journey to hospital is a blank. The next thing I remember is seeing a kindly nurse looking down at me. Her face and voice were familiar, and I asked her if she was from The Philippines. She nodded and said she came from Baguio. Where the rice terraces are, I murmured. That's right, she replied. Then she took my hand, told me I had lost my baby and held me while I cried. Just like my amah used to do, back in Makati, when a childhood trauma made my world seem like it was ending.

Afterwards, I would wake every morning with a smile on my face. For a few blessed moments, I thought my Little Flea was still there with me and we remained on our private journey together. Then I remembered what had happened and the emptiness flooded in. Alex took compassionate leave so he could stay at home and bring me food which stuck in my throat. When he clasped a remembrance bracelet around my wrist I longed to tell him how much I hated him for what he had done, but I held my tongue. Nothing I could say would bring my baby back. Instead I called on the skill I discovered when I found out that my dad had lied to me about my mum's suicide. I simply switched Alex off and extinguished the source of my pain. From that moment on, he meant nothing to me.

I began working from home as it allowed me to shut myself away in my study. Meanwhile, to my immense relief, Alex made arrangements to return to Birmingham the following week. I saw I had a voicemail from Stella, but I decided to ignore it until I had the house to myself.

On the day before he left, Alex went shopping. When he returned, he asked me to join him in the garden. He led me to a sheltered, south-facing spot where he had dug a hole in the flower bed. A spindly sapling rested against the garden fence; its roots cocooned in a plastic bag.

'I thought it would be nice to plant a tree – in his memory.'

There was nothing I wanted less, but I figured it was easier to go through the motions than protest. Carefully we teased out the roots, then placed the tree in place and filled the hole with soil, tamping the surface down firmly. When we had finished, we stood back and stared at the tree in silence. I remember hearing birdsong and thinking that, although it sounded harmonious, in reality it was anything but. Those birds were singing to defend their territory from their enemies; their beautiful songs were really battle cries. Then Alex spoke.

'This was your fault,' he said quietly. 'You and your false accusations. I will forgive you, in time, but I can never forget that you killed our son.' Then he walked back to the house, leaving me alone in front of the flimsy tree. He stayed in his office all day and departed for Birmingham that night.

In a way, Alex helped me out. By blaming me for my miscarriage, he enabled me to associate it with the demise of our relationship and draw a line underneath it. With his assistance, I said goodbye forever to my Little Flea and resolved never to have children. It was almost a relief.

As soon as his car left the driveway, I called Stella. She listened while I told her about what had happened and how Alex had blamed me.

'Look, Jen. We've wasted far too much of our lives on this man. We've both suffered enough. I'm going to get us out of this, but I can't do it on my own. Fortunately, as I mentioned in my voicemail, I know someone who might be able to help.'

Obviously Stella had mentioned Nancy before – her friend who came to her aid on the canals. I had always thought it an unlikely friendship; the two of them are clearly so different. I was also intrigued by the notion that Stella was friends with a celebrity, although from what she has told me about her, I am sure Nancy would hate to be described that way. I could not imagine how Nancy could possibly help us, but Stella seemed convinced that she could, and I did not have any better ideas, so I just went with it.

For a while I heard nothing, but it did not bother me. I could not imagine that anything good would ever happen again, so I just tried to numb the pain. I returned to the office and put in long hours, ignoring my colleagues' advice to take things easy. At home, I drank vodka out of a coffee mug, just like I used to do at school. If Alex was away, I stared unseeing at the TV, then collapsed into bed. If he was at home, I stayed out of his way.

When Stella finally called back, she was jubilant. Nancy had apparently come up trumps.

'You don't need to worry. Alex isn't going to be hurt – more's the pity, although it's probably just as well, for both our sakes. However, he will be out of our lives, permanently. It's best you don't know the details. Just carry on as normal and I'll let you know when it's all over.'

So I did as Stella said and carried on with my new normal. Work, drink, repeat. I started drinking as soon as I got home and collapsed early into bed, so I could still function the next day. My colleagues all told me how well I was coping, although the more observant remarked on how much weight I had lost and brought me cakes and sandwiches, which I discarded discreetly. Alex still accepted dinner party invitations on our behalf, and at weekends I sat quietly through some excruciating evenings. At least, this time, my hands and feet remained intact. I had no funny stories to tell anymore.

The next time Stella called; I did not hear the phone. It was not that late, but I was already in my vodka-induced oblivion. I picked up her voicemail on the train the next morning.

'Hi – it's me. Just to let you know it all went perfectly. Our mutual friend was not harmed – but he won't be contacting you again. Call me when you get this message.'

I spent the rest of the train journey in a daze and had walked as far as Piccadilly Gardens before I realised I was nearly at work and should call back. When I did, Stella was all business.

'Right, Jen. Am I right in thinking that Alex isn't due back from Birmingham until tomorrow night?'

'That's right.'

'OK. Don't report him missing until later on tomorrow night; a few hours after he was due home.'

'Won't the police think it odd that I didn't realise he was missing before then? Won't they expect us to have spoken on the phone daily, while he was away?'

'I was just coming to that. You need to tell them you were having problems, so you often went days without speaking. Tell them about the baby and how you've both struggled since then.'

'Won't that make them suspect me?'

'Jen – you've been telling me how you've been working long hours, to try and block things out, and I've told you my opinion on that, which you've ignored. What time did you leave the office last night?'

'About half seven.'

'And given that PR is notorious for its long hours, I assume you weren't the last to leave?'

'No. There's a big pitch happening this morning, so the team was still there last night, rehearsing and doing the usual last-minute stuff with the slides.'

'Did they see you leave?'

'Yes. Before I went home I offered to help, but they said they were all good, so I left.'

'Just as I thought. You have a cast-iron alibi, so don't worry. Just report him missing, sound upset, which shouldn't be difficult in your current state, then leave the police to look into it. Nancy said it won't be a priority for them, and she's right. Look at it from their point of view, Jen. A healthy, wealthy man, who previously deserted his wife in odd circumstances, and possibly even tried to frame her, absconds without telling his lover. The couple have been having problems following a tragic miscarriage, but there is no evidence he intended to take his own life. I think I know what the police will conclude.'

Stella was absolutely right. The police took a statement from me and from Alex's client in Birmingham, who had tried unsuccessfully to contact him when he failed to show up for work. They even got Surrey Police to interview Stella. They were thorough, but I imagine they knew what the outcome would be.

It was not difficult to resume my old life. I am sure you are not surprised to hear that the house was in Alex's name and he had always insisted we keep separate bank accounts. I contacted his financial advisor, Steven; as I suspected, he did not smell of Opium. I informed him that Alex had relocated, and I was moving out. I said he would be in touch at some point to make arrangements to sell. Then I packed up my stuff and moved back to the city, where I rented a high-rise apartment not unlike the one I used to have. I took Stella's advice and booked myself in for counselling. I replaced vodka with meditation and started doing weekly Park Runs, like I did when I was with Stefan.

I wish I could say that I am back where I started, or even wiser and warier, but neither is true. It is not like when you throw a pebble into a pond, and the water closes over the pebble, ripples briefly, then is still. In reality, I feel more like the little stuffed monkey which our Hong Kong amah – also called Nancy, oddly enough – made for me when I was little. I was born in the Year of the Monkey, and she always said I was true to type. Monkeys are lively and quick-witted, but they can also be selfish and jealous. Anyway, I loved that monkey so much, and would not be parted from him. He remained with me, day and night, and got cuddled half to death. Nancy was frequently called upon to repair him, until he was reduced to a ball of lumpen stuffing, held together by mismatched patches. I still have him; in fact, he is sitting here on my desk as I finish writing to you. He is battered and worn, but if you look very closely, you can just about tell that he was once a monkey.

STELLA

11 NIGHT FEVER

Well done you. I can't believe how much you got out of Jen. As you probably gathered, she doesn't find it easy to open up. The trouble is, she doesn't know the whole story, so they've asked me to retrace my steps and fill in the gaps. I hope you don't mind us getting together again. I'll try not to repeat myself but do forgive me if I have the odd senior moment.

Talking of which, I hope you've had a coffee, because I'm going to ask you to cast your mind back to when I was released from custody in Leicester, halfway through the night. I was in a right state, as you may remember. The staff practically had to carry me out to reception, where that hot shot lawyer from London whom Nancy had hired for me – Alastair, I think he was called – was waiting.

'I trust you will drive my client back to Allenby Marina, to collect her vehicle,' he said in an imperious tone, looking down his nose at the custody sergeant.

'Yes, we can do that. She'll have to wait a while, though.'

Then Alastair handed me his card and took his leave. He couldn't get back to London fast enough.

I waited in reception for hours, shivering and drinking bitter machine coffee. Looking back, I could have ordered a taxi, but I wasn't thinking straight. I was still in shock, so I sat there passively until they found time to give me a lift in a patrol car. By the time I got back, it was already light.

Still on auto pilot, I packed up my stuff and loaded the car. I even cleaned the boat. I don't know about you, but I can never leave a place dirty. My hands were shaking so much that I broke a glass while I was putting it away, so I stuck a couple of pound coins in an envelope, along with the boat key, and pushed it through the letterbox at the marina office, just before they were due to open up. I didn't want to risk running into

Ron, Eddie or any of the other staff and being faced with a barrage of questions. Then I went in search of Nancy. I was pretty sure where I'd find her.

I tapped on the window of Slowing Downe and waited for its owner to appear. A couple of minutes later, Dan stumbled into the saloon, pulling on his T-shirt. Even in my traumatised state, I could appreciate why Nancy might want to stick around. As soon as he saw me, he unzipped the cratch cover. I still hate that word, by the way.

'Stella. Good to see you...back.'

'I'm looking for Nancy. Is she here?'

'Yes; just give us a second. Nan – Stella's here! Come on in, Stella. She'll be out in a moment.'

'Sorry to drop by so early.'

'Not a problem – look, here she is. Our little morning ray of sunshine – not. Look, Nan. Stella's back.'

Nancy's hair was like an exploded bird's nest and her face was streaked with last night's mascara. She was wearing nothing but a tatty old band T-shirt and what looked like a pair of Dan's boxer shorts, but she still managed to look gorgeous. When I saw her, I burst into tears of relief and she awkwardly stepped forward and took me in her arms. She's not a natural hugger, but on that occasion I was glad she made the effort.

'So they let you out.'

'Yes. Thank you so much, Nancy, for hiring that lawyer – I'm sure I'd still be locked up if it weren't for him.'

'They'd have released you anyway, as soon as they realised your story checked out, but I thought you needed someone to fight your corner. I don't imagine you're used to being banged up.'

'I've never even been inside a police station. I hadn't spoken to a police officer until yesterday...'

'Well, you can forget all about it now. Normal service can be resumed, back in leafy Surrey. What's the deal with your husband, by the way?'

'I'm really sorry, Nancy, but I don't feel up to talking about it yet. I just wanted to say thank you. That's about all I can manage right now. Give me your number and I'll call you once I'm settled in at home. I need to go.'

Dan's face was full of concern.

'Stella – I don't think you're in any fit state to drive. At least let me make you coffee and breakfast.'

'That's kind of you, Dan, but I'm just going to head off.'

Nancy joined in the protests and I couldn't help noticing how natural and comfortable they were together.

'You're the one who's always nagging me about not eating properly.'

'I know; but being incarcerated didn't exactly give me an appetite.'

'Incarcerated. How you talk. Look, at least have a coffee.'

'No; you're OK. I'm just going to go.'

'As you wish. Look, here's my number. Call me when you get home.'

'I will. I'll keep in touch. Thanks for everything, Nancy. I don't know what I'd have done without you.'

'Neither do I. Try not to prang your car and I'll talk to you later.'

Dan was quite right; I was in no fit state to drive. Twice I changed lanes on the motorway without checking my mirrors, causing other drivers to swerve and hoot, but I kept going and somehow made it home in one piece. As I walked through the front door, it felt as though I was stepping into someone else's life, which in a sense I was. It was a different woman who cancelled the papers and set the burglar alarm, what seemed like months ago.

I headed straight for the litre bottles of 'weekday wine' in the garage, then I grabbed my largest wine glass, sat down at the island, right where you first met me, and tried to process the idea that Alex was never coming home. Clearly his future lay with Jennifer; I had made sure of that. I might even have felt relieved, had I not known he would never stop trying to get his revenge. I was convinced he would contact me as soon as he was released from hospital, but in the event I didn't even have to wait that long. He called our home number from his hospital bed that night. We hardly ever receive calls on our landline, and when the phone rang I just knew it was him. Weirdly, it never occurred to me not to pick up.

'Hello?'

'Well done, Stella. You got away with attempted murder. Not bad for a first go...'

'Alex, I...'

'Be quiet! You do *not* get to speak. Here's what you are going to do. You will talk to our children and present your crime as an unfortunate accident. Of course, they will want to visit me. When they do, rest assured that I will never tell them, or anyone else, the truth about what you did. I don't want to destroy them by showing them what their mother is really like.'

'Can I just say...'

'No. You can't. What I *will* tell them is that I plan to make a fresh start away from Surrey. Later on, I will say I intend to file for divorce. I will also inform Imogen that you told me about her abortion...'

'Alex, no!'

'I thought that might upset you. It will be interesting to see what my revelation does to the 'special relationship' you think you have with our daughter...'

'Please...'

'Save your breath, Stella. In addition, I will tell Hugo that you told me he's gay. Ooh...tumbleweed. Don't you want to protest, Stella? Or are you not as bothered about our son? Or – let me think – did he ask you to tell me? Of course, that's got to be the answer. He always was a wimp.'

'Don't say that.'

'Shut up! I will not tell them about Jennifer. Not yet. After a few months, when the time is right, I will present her to them as a new partner and you, Stella, will go along with my story. You will do this because, if you don't, I will tell them what you did. I don't want to, because of how much it would hurt them, but if you force me to choose between making them hate you, and making them hate me, I'll choose you. Every time. Now give me a one-word answer to a closed question. Do I make myself clear?'

'Yes.'

Immediately the line went dead.

It took a long time for me to heal my relationship with Imogen. The counsellor I hired, a wonderful woman called Rachel, did a lot of work with us both, to help us 'move on', as she would put it. I know Imogen has told you about this, so I won't dwell on it. Suffice to say we both bear the scars, but our relationship is stronger now than it was before. Alex doesn't think so; he believes that, because he's closer to Imogen, the opposite must be true of me, but he's wrong. He sees the world as a zero-sum game; for him to win, someone else has to lose, but I don't care. I'm happy for him to think himself victorious.

I shouldn't give Rachel all the credit; Hugo was a big help too. Coming out gave him a strength I never knew he possessed. Alex was so wrong when he called our son a wimp. Hugo helped Immo cope with the fallout from Alex's 'accident' and encouraged her not to judge me too harshly for breaking her confidence. He also spent hours on the phone to me from Scotland, urging me not to blame myself and reassuring me everything was going to be OK. I'm so proud of the man he has become, and I'm delighted he and Rob have found each other.

Even though I knew it was going to happen, I was still shocked when Alex filed for divorce, but I kept it together. It helped that he only communicated with me via his solicitor but even so, I would never have coped without Madeleine. As I expected, most of our so-called 'friends' here in Surrey melted away when Alex and I split up. After all, he was the one with the power and influence, whilst I was only ever the 'plus one'. Madeleine was the one exception. Do you remember her? If you had met her in real life, you definitely would. She's colourful, glamorous and very vocal. She was the one who asked if I was OK, at that lunch party we held, before we went on our canal holiday. At the time I remember wondering whether her concern was genuine, and I can tell you now – it absolutely was. With her help, I negotiated all the practical stuff: the divorce settlement, the sale of our family home and the purchase of my cottage. I owe her a lot.

Nancy was also a big help. We're too different to be really close, but she's a great person to talk to when I need some light relief. She's always got an irreverent take on things and I love hearing about her new life. It's like having access to my own private mini-series. I adore the fact that she's crazy about Dan, but totally won't admit it and tries to play it cool, whereas he's the opposite. I admire the way she has reinvented herself as an independent artist and resisted all attempts by her old record company to woo her back. I also think it's amazing how she has embraced all things digital. When I first met her, she barely knew one end of a smartphone from the other and hated social media, but now she has a huge community of followers and a legion of new fans.

I don't want to overstate my role in Nancy's success, but I think I did play a small part. Quite a few of the decisions she made were clearly informed by the business plan I prepared for her, when we were on Two's Company together. Also, if it hadn't been for me, she would never have moored in Allenby Marina, so she wouldn't have been reunited with Dan and relaunched her career. All this helped me justify asking her for help later on – but I'm getting ahead of myself. Sorry.

So the divorce came through, I moved into my cottage and started my digital advisory service, which was tough. While the children were growing up, I always kept in touch with all things digital, so I was sure I had a lot to offer my clients. I just had to find those clients in the first place, and I was surprised how difficult this was for me. I was used to marketing on behalf of others, but this was the first time I had tried to put myself 'out there' and I struggled. I thought my divorce from Alex had nothing to do with it, but my counselling sessions with Rachel showed me it was all interlinked. My confidence, which had gradually been eroded over the course of my marriage, was shot. Rachel levelled with me; getting my self-esteem back was going to be a slow process, and she was right. I'm still not there yet, and I don't know when I will be. One piece of advice Rachel gave me was to avoid trying to drink my way to confidence. I have to be honest with you and admit I mostly ignored her.

Alex got the vintage wines as part of the divorce settlement, but that was fine by me. Quantity, rather than quality, was my focus back then. There was always a litre bottle of white in the fridge, waiting for me at the end of my working day. I knew just the right amount to drink, to take the edge off, whilst still enabling me to function the next day. The trouble was that this amount increased as the weeks went on and my tolerance grew. Also, at the weekends, the brakes were off. If I wasn't going out at night, which was most of the time, as my social life was practically zero, I would drink all evening. Sometimes, I'd throw in a couple of the strong painkillers I'd been prescribed for my dodgy knees. Often, I couldn't remember going to bed. I stopped burning scented candles, which I love, as I was worried I would forget to blow them out and burn my cottage down. I wasn't out of control, but I knew I had a problem. I just didn't want to do anything about it. I felt I had been through enough. Life without wine, or even with less wine, was unthinkable.

When I was drinking, I would normally slump in front of the TV, but sometimes I'd surf the net or send ill-advised emails, usually to Imogen. My sensible daughter always knew when 'drunk Mum' was at the keyboard, and mostly ignored my rants, although they didn't help us reconcile. Often I had to duck and weave the next day, to patch things up.

One Saturday night, I was finishing off a litre of Chardonnay and browsing various clothing websites, thinking I might buy myself a treat. I've lost count of the number of unsuitable garments I've had to return after sessions like these. Anyway, for some reason the word 'whale' sprang to mind. Maybe the thought of me in a pair of skinny jeans triggered it – who knows? So 'whale' led to 'baleine', which made me think of that guy Chris I met when I was working the locks on my holiday with Alex. The man who alerted me to the dangers of getting tangled up in a mooring rope and mangled by the prop. Before I knew it, I was Googling 'narrowboat Baleine', as he advised. There are a few boats with this name, but even so, it wasn't difficult to find Chris, navigate to his website and blog and track down a contact email address.

The next morning, once I remembered what I had done, I stumbled downstairs to my desk, praying I had forgotten to press 'send' – but I hadn't, of course. Thankfully, I had kept it brief and didn't sound too crazy, so I relaxed and decided just to forget about it. I was astonished when I logged on the following day and found a reply in my inbox.

Apparently Chris did remember helping me through the locks that day. He wrote that he and Baleine were doing the Thames Ring and were currently near Watford, heading south. In my not too crazy email, I had told him I had split from Alex and was living in Surrey, although thankfully I stopped short of giving him my actual address. In his reply, he asked me whether I would like to meet him for a coffee in Kew, when he reached west London. Before I could overthink it, I told him I would. I remembered him as really sweet, and I was lonely. Besides, I figured it would take him quite a while to travel from Watford to Kew, so I had plenty of time to think up an excuse if I changed my mind.

In the end, I didn't make an excuse, and morning coffee in Kew was followed by a leisurely walk around Kew Gardens and lunch afterwards. I was driving, so luckily I couldn't drink. I felt so comfortable with Chris, right from the start. If you remember, he was with me when I found out

Hugo was gay, so I told him how my son was so much happier since coming out and how he had supported me through my divorce. I avoided talking too much about Alex and, crucially, did not reveal to Chris the role he had unwittingly played in our split.

Chris told me funny stories about his kids and made me laugh with tales of his failed attempts at dating. Obviously, it isn't easy to form relationships when you're constantly on the move, but he seemed to have had a particular run of bad luck. I admired the way he was making light of his problems and appreciated him keeping things relaxed. When lunch was over, he asked me if I would join him when he reached Hampton Court, for a tour of the palace and grounds, which he had never visited before. Then, if it was OK with me, he'd like to cook me lunch aboard Baleine. I wasn't sure how I'd feel about being on a narrowboat again, but I agreed anyway. Again I figured that I had time to back out.

In the end, we had a brilliant day. I don't live that far from Hampton Court and I've been there many times, when the kids were young and we were trying to take them somewhere 'educational' instead of Thorpe Park or Chessington, which they obviously preferred. It was fun to discover the palace through the eyes of someone who had never seen it before and the weather was hot and sunny, which helped. We got lost in the maze and sat on the lawn for ages, not talking much. Already, Chris was someone with whom I could be silent. Later, as we walked along the riverbank towards his narrowboat, I felt nervous, but I needn't have worried. The interior of Baleine was completely different from that of Two's Company, so it didn't trigger any bad memories. Whereas Two's Company was all about practicality and function, Baleine was the opposite. It was a real 'Rosie and Jim' narrowboat, painted and decorated with love. The varnished wooden door panels were covered with traditional roses and castles, which Chris had painted himself, along with the stencils which adorned every wall. The upholstery and curtains were chintzy and charmingly mismatched. Next to the front door were rows of metal badges, each commemorating a place, flight of locks, tunnel or junction visited by Baleine on its travels. Every kitsch ornament and picture had a story to tell.

The galley was cramped and cluttered, but Chris produced from it a wonderful lunch and a chilled Sancerre, with a vintage which would not have been out of place in Alex's wine fridge. Again I was driving, so I just accepted one small glass. We ate and talked, then sat in the sun on the roof of the boat, drinking coffee and watching other boats drift past. Finally I realised how peaceful the waterways could be, if you were with the right person. When the sun began to set and Chris gently asked if I might like to stay over, I said I would. So he fetched another bottle, which we shared as we watched the sunset. That evening, half a bottle was plenty for me.

The next day, Chris headed west towards Windsor. He promised to keep in touch, and I hoped he would, but I kept my expectations low. I resolved to cherish the memories and not seek anything more. I told myself I wasn't ready for a relationship, especially not a long-distance romance with a moving target, but Chris changed my mind. He phoned me from Reading and asked me to meet him there, so I did, then later on I joined him at Oxford. I had to drive home the next day because of work commitments, but I agreed to clear a few days in my diary and cruise with him on the Oxford Canal, north of Banbury. He had a friend at Braunston who would drive me back to my car afterwards. A journey which takes days on a narrowboat can easily be retraced by car in an hour or so.

The Oxford Canal was a revelation. I found the single locks easy to operate and Chris even let me have a go at steering, staying remarkably calm as I veered from one side of the canal to the other. He reassured me that everyone does this when they're learning, until they get used to the boat's delayed reactions and remember to push the tiller in the opposite direction from where they want to go. Gradually, I got the hang of it all. My stomach no longer lurched when the balance beams of a lock came into view. On the lock-free stretches, I basked in the sun on the roof of the boat. In the evenings, we shared barbecues on the towpath or had dinner in a lovely canal side pub. It was brilliant.

After I got home, Imogen came to stay. She instantly picked up on my improved mood and quizzed me over dinner. Finally I caved in and confessed I had been seeing someone but emphasised that it was early days and very casual, as he lived on a narrowboat and was constantly on the move. Immo's response was predictable.

'Weird that he's got a narrowboat. I thought you'd want to steer well clear, after everything that happened with Daddy...'

'So did I, but he changed my mind. Anyway, don't make a big deal out of it, darling...'

'I won't, but it's good to know you're having some fun. You deserve it, Mummy.'

When I first split from Alex, my daughter would never have wanted me to have fun. As I topped up our glasses, I reflected that we had made progress.

One evening soon afterwards, I had just poured my first glass of the evening when my mobile rang. I didn't recognise the number so I picked up, hoping it would be a potential client, but as soon as she said my name, I knew who it was, even though we had only met once. I hung up immediately and downed that first glass in two large gulps. The following day, the same thing happened again, and the day after. Then, the next night, I got a text.

'Please meet me, Stella. I need to ask you a question - and to warn you about something. I can't discuss it over the phone. We're both in trouble. Call me – please.'

If I had received the text in the morning, I might have ignored it, but yet again the wine made my decision for me. I was curious as to what Jennifer might want to warn me about and gratified that she sounded unhappy, so I picked up the phone and did my best to sound sober. Eventually she persuaded me to meet, and we made the arrangements. For a moment I considered tying in the trip to Manchester with a surprise visit to Imogen, but the next day I thought it through and concluded it was best to keep the two trips separate. With hindsight, I'm glad I did.

So I met up with Jennifer, fully expecting to gloat over the problems she was having with Alex but, as you know, the meeting turned out differently. I'm aware that Jen has told you what she went through with Alex, so I won't go over it again here. Suffice to say that by the end of our meeting, we weren't friends – not even close – but we both understood we were in it together. She was no longer the enemy; Alex was. He was trying to destroy my business and any relationship I might have with Chris, and I realised my only option was to fight back.

By this time, I had drunk the best part of two bottles of wine, swallowed several painkillers and was filled with false bravado. I came up with what I thought was a cunning plan to eliminate Alex from our lives, but thankfully Jen had only drunk a tiny amount of wine, because of the baby, so she put me straight. I'm not even going to tell you what my plan was; I'm far too embarrassed. Suffice to say it was a crock, but we couldn't think of anything better, so we both went home in defeat, promising to keep in touch while we tried to work out what to do.

Back in Surrey, I confided in Madeleine that Alex had been warning people not to do business with me and asked if she could discreetly find out more. It turned out Alex didn't have to do much to start the rumour mill going. He just hinted that I had left our old firm under a cloud, which is why I chose not to resume my career after having children. According to Alex, I was only starting up my new business 'out of desperation' because no one would employ me and my digital skills were obsolete, as I had been absent from the workplace for so long. That was it. A few lies were all it took. He didn't have to try very hard to cause people to doubt me and make my business suffer.

Initially I was sceptical about whether Alex would go to the trouble of contacting Chris, but once Madeleine told me about the rumours he had been spreading, I decided to take no chances, so I called Chris and told him Alex might attempt to warn him off with a pack of lies. By then, Chris had heard enough about Alex to know what he was capable of, and he reassured me that nothing Alex could say would make the slightest difference to how he felt about me. I believed every word, and we spent the rest of the conversation making arrangements to meet up on the Stratford Canal a few weeks later.

After that, when I didn't hear anything more from Chris for a week, I wasn't too concerned, even though he normally called every few days. Mobile reception on the canals is patchy, and Chris often spent long days at the tiller, so I told myself he hadn't been able, or had time, to make contact. Finally, though, I decided to call him. It took me a few attempts to reach him and when I did, he sounded like a different person as he told me we couldn't meet up in Stratford, or anywhere else, ever again. He swore Alex had nothing to do with it and hadn't even been in contact. The truth was that he didn't want to have a long-distance relationship; he wanted someone who would share his life aboard Baleine, and clearly that wasn't going to be me. So I put down the phone, blamed myself for not being interesting enough and got my litre bottle out of the fridge. As I drank, I replayed our time together and tried to identify all the times when I had got it wrong. I found plenty of reasons why Chris might have had second thoughts about me.

I always tell Imogen self-pity is a most unattractive quality, but I must admit I did wallow for a bit, until I got the phone call from Jen which changed everything. I had been trying to reach her for days, to keep in touch as agreed, but her phone had gone to voicemail every time, so I figured she didn't want anything more to do with me either. At that point my self-esteem was so low, it never occurred to me there might be another reason.

When Jen told me she had lost the baby, and how it happened, I was gutted for her. It confirmed what I discovered when we met in Manchester; she was Alex's victim, just like me. Then I thought about Nancy and reflected that she wouldn't take this from a man. Someone like Alex would never be able to mess with her. She'd kick him into touch and forget him; or write a song about him, humiliate him and make millions. Nancy would know what to do. I told Jen I would call her and ask for advice, but after I put the phone down I hesitated. Nancy had done so much for me already and I was reluctant to ask for her help again, so I decided to sleep on it.

I was awoken by a loud knock at the door. At first I thought I had dreamt it, but then I heard it again; it was louder and more prolonged, this time, so I pulled on my dressing gown and hurried downstairs. I was concerned that my elderly next-door neighbour might be in trouble, but even so, I kept the chain on when I opened the front door. You can't be too careful.

Alex snapped the chain with one swift kick. He burst through the door, grabbed me by the throat, flung me against the wall and pressed a knife to my neck while he told me he knew about Jennifer and me.

'I checked her call records as usual and saw she phoned you a few times

– then nothing. I was going to dismiss it as a sad mistake on her part – an obsessive desire to contact the ex-wife, which she had fortunately overcome – when I noticed all these calls to a new number; one I didn't recognise, so I dialled it – and guess who answered? Stupid Stella, who thought she'd outsmart me by getting a second phone.'

I remembered the phone call. When the caller didn't speak, I assumed it was a nuisance call. You'd have done the same, right? I hung up and never gave it a second thought, and now Alex was here, in my home. Marching me into my sitting room, flinging me onto the sofa and threatening me with a knife. Screaming at me, but with tears in his eyes.

'If you and Jennifer had not tried to conspire against me, my son would still be alive…'

For one sick moment, I thought he meant Hugo, but then I realised he was talking about Jennifer's baby.

'It's you I blame, not her. You were the one who encouraged her to leave…'

'I didn't…'

'Shut up! You *do not* get to speak. If you could have seen the face on that poor sod you were dating, when I told him what you did to me. You won't be hearing from him again, that's for sure…'

He laughed in my face, but the tears were still there.

'You might have failed to kill me, Stella, but you succeeded in murdering an innocent, unborn child. I hope you're satisfied, because if you ever try to contact Jennifer again, I will find out, and I will kill you. I won't hesitate.'

For a few seconds Alex stood over me, looking down on me with contempt as I huddled on my sofa, sobbing. Then he was gone.

12 FRIEND WITH BENEFITS

For a while I just lay there, stunned, but eventually I noticed the cold breeze coming from the hallway and struggled to my feet. It took me ages to get the front door closed; the door frame had splintered when Alex kicked the chain off. By the time I had wrestled it shut, I felt exhausted, but I was too scared to go upstairs and sleep. My first thought was to take refuge in a bottle, but I didn't, oddly enough. Alex had shown me I was in real danger. The shock of him breaking into my house and threatening me woke me right up. I realised it was time to stop self-medicating and start being smart. So I went into my office, arranged for a carpenter to come and fix the door and booked a visit from an emergency locksmith. Then I ordered a home security system which would link to an app on my phone. Afterwards, I sat back with a cup of coffee and replayed what Alex had said about Chris.

Obviously my ex-husband's little chat with Chris was more effective than he could possibly have imagined. I thought how delighted Alex would have been, had he known it was Chris who had unwittingly given me the idea which caused his injury. He would love the idea that a nice guy like Chris would be plagued with guilt, even though the accident was not his fault. I'm sure Alex had threatened Chris, just like he did me, but he didn't need to. By revealing what I had done, Alex had guaranteed that Chris would never contact me again.

Clearly there was nothing I could do to fix me and Chris, so I concentrated on what I could control, and made the decision to call Nancy in the morning, despite my reservations about asking her for help again. I needed to talk to someone who was detached from the situation and I was counting on her to advise us on how to get out of this mess. I reminded myself about what I had done to help her and told myself she owed it to me to listen, at the very least.

Nancy turned out to be a surprisingly good listener. I spent ages on the phone to her, telling her about what had happened to Jen and how Alex burst into my home and threatened me. She said very little in response, and when I had finished, she didn't dole out any platitudes. I guess you know her well enough by now to realise that's not her style.

'So I take it you both want this snake out of your lives?'

'Yes, but I'm not sure how to make it happen, Nancy. I've had loads of fantasies about what I'd like to do to him, but when I think about it rationally, I realise I don't want him harmed, for our sake as much as anything…'

'Yeah, I get that. You don't want your lives ruined by guilt, take it from me. I've seen what that can do to a person…'

'What d'you mean?'

'That's a story for another time, Stella – but you've just given me an idea. Tell me everything you know about Alex's new life. Home, friends, work, the lot.'

So I recounted everything I knew about the house in Wilmslow, the awful dinner party friends, who sounded just like our old pals here in Surrey, and the lucrative freelance consultancy work. When I mentioned his eighteen-month contract in Birmingham, Nancy asked for more details, but there wasn't a lot I could tell her. When Jen had reported back on her supposedly romantic mini break, she had mentioned a posh flat in the Jewellery Quarter and a walk alongside the canal, into the city centre, but that was about it.

'Leave it with me, Stella – I'll see what I can come up with. I'll get back to you once I've worked something out.'

I didn't hear anything for a while, and I reluctantly concluded that Nancy didn't know what to do, any more than Jen and I did. All this time, I was desperate to contact Jen, but I was too frightened of what Alex would do if he found out. So instead I just carried on with my life. I advertised my digital advisory service in all the local papers and answered a few enquiries from potential clients. I spent my evenings working and trying to avoid the lure of the wine bottle, with limited success. Then, at last, Nancy called back.

'Hi Stella. Sorry it's been a while. I had a few things to work out, but now I've got a plan to make this loser leave you two alone and find someone else to bully.'

'Nancy, that's brilliant. What do we need to do?'

'Nothing. No offence, Stell, but this isn't your forte. You're better off out of it, so I'm not going to give you any details. You can't implicate yourself if you don't know anything. All you need to do is wait – I'll let you know when it's done.'

'Look, Nancy – I never meant you to actually *do* anything – I was only looking for some advice.'

'I know. So I've overdelivered.'

'I don't understand why you would do that, Nan.'

'Let's call it a win-win situation. I saw an opportunity to help you, and someone else, at the same time. Kill two birds with one stone.'

'I don't want you to put yourself at risk...'

'That's not going to happen. No one's at risk, but when this is all over, three people will have their lives back. Two of those people are you and Jennifer. That's all I'm saying.'

'Thank you so much, Nancy.'

'You can thank me when it's over. In the meantime, tell Jen what I told you – everything's in hand. She just needs to stay in Manchester and sit tight.'

'I can't. Remember what Alex threatened he'd do if I called her? I've already thrown away the pay as you go phone I used to speak to her.'

Nancy sighed, then spoke clearly and slowly, in the sort of tone I would use with my children, when they were small. 'Here's what you do, Stell. Find a pay phone. Call Jen when she's at work and Alex is in Birmingham. Tell her you've got everything in hand but won't contact her again until it's a done deal. Also, warn her not to call you. That's it.'

My little Surrey village is home to many old age pensioners, some of whom don't have, or want, a mobile phone. There was an outcry when moves were announced to close the phone box and residents petitioned the local authority to raise an objection, so it was given a stay of execution, which was lucky for me. After I shut the door of the phone box and dialled Jen's number, I looked around nervously, as though Alex could see what I was doing.

I kept the call as brief as possible. I didn't even tell Jen about Alex breaking into my home. I just said I had found 'a way forward' and instructed her to carry on as normal and wait for my next call.

As it turned out, we both had quite a long wait. I immersed myself in work and gained temporary respite when I was with my clients. Their problems helped me forget my own, but as soon as each meeting was over, my stomach retied itself in knots. Finally, early one evening, I was bingeing on a bottle and a box set when my phone rang.

'Hi, Stell. Just ringing to tell you it's all sorted. Alex won't bother you again.'

'Seriously?'

'Yep.'

'You're kidding! Nancy, I can't believe you actually did it – I never thought...'

'OK, Stella – calm down. Quit flapping and do me a favour.'

'What's that?'

'Pop round next door and borrow a cup of sugar from your neighbour. Have a little chat. You get me?'

'Er…yes. I see.'

'Also, tell your mate Jen to do something similar, and warn her to wait until well after Alex is due home before reporting him missing – understood?'

This time I caught on more quickly. 'Absolutely. We could all do with some breathing space…'

'That's right. Gotta go. Take care of yourself, Stella.'

'Will do. Nancy?'

'Yeah?'

'Thank you.'

I didn't realise how tense I had been until the relief flooded through me. I burst into tears and sobbed for what seemed like hours. Afterwards, my hands shook uncontrollably as I tried to clean up my face so as not to shock Maisie, my elderly neighbour. Once I stopped looking too scary I knocked on her door and asked to borrow some eggs for a cake I needed to make that night. For the next twenty minutes Maisie, a Bake Off afficionado, doled out recipes, baking tips and cake decorations, along with the eggs, before I finally made my escape. Alibi firmly in place, I dialled Jen's mobile number. It felt good to be able to call her from my regular phone. When she didn't answer, I left a voicemail:

'Hi – it's me. Just to let you know it all went perfectly. Our mutual friend was not harmed in any way – but he won't be contacting you again. Call me when you get this message.'

I drank more wine and watched a few more episodes, but my phone remained silent, so I finally gave up and went to bed, where I slept peacefully for the first time in ages.

The next morning, my appetite seemed to have kicked in, so I scrambled the eggs which Maisie had given me, dug some bread out of the freezer for toast and made a big pot of coffee. I was at my desk in my PJs, answering an email from a client, when Jen called back in response to my voicemail. I told her not to report Alex missing until the following night, several hours after he was due home. She was concerned that the police would expect her to have noticed his absence earlier, but I reassured her that they would back off once she told them she and Alex were estranged due to the loss of their baby. Then I asked her how she spent the previous evening, knowing what the answer would be. As usual when Alex was away, she worked late, then took the train home. A group of colleagues spoke to her just before she left the office. Should the police decide to check the CCTV at Piccadilly, they would see her boarding the suburban service to Wilmslow.

I closed off the call by insisting that Alex's disappearance would be a low priority for the police. Their IT systems were more joined up these days, so they would obtain case details from Leicestershire Police and conclude that, if Alex had abandoned his wife in dubious circumstances, he would have no qualms about deserting his new partner. While he might be traumatised at the loss of the baby, there was no evidence he was suicidal; nor did he have any money, health or career issues. I said I was sure the police would conclude he had simply absconded. All Jen needed to do was report him missing and sound upset, which shouldn't be too much of a stretch. Then I wrapped up my speech and let her get to work.

A few days later, I received the expected knock on the door. I invited the police officer in and made her a cup of tea. I told her I was not surprised Alex had left Jennifer, given how he had treated me. I speculated that he had found someone else. If he'll do it with you, he'll do it to you, I said. I confirmed that I was at home on the night he went missing, apart from one brief visit to my elderly next-door neighbour. She's always in, I said, if you want to check with her. I recounted Alex's clumsy attempts to frame me and voiced the opinion that his new relationship was always doomed to failure. I hinted at his violent and controlling tendencies. In short, I played the part of the embittered ex-wife with the cast iron alibi. The officer didn't stay long.

The following week, Jen called me. She said she was planning to move out of the Wilmslow house. She was heading back to the city, where she belonged. In the meantime, she was consuming the contents of Alex's wine fridge, starting with his vintage champagne. She popped a cork over the phone and we both laughed. Then I left her to it. I needed to work out what to tell my children.

In the end, I told them the truth; or part of it, at least. I said that Jen and Alex had split up, as they couldn't make things work after the loss of the baby. I reported that their father had gone away on an extended holiday to 'get his head together', as Imogen might put it. He would be in touch as soon as he felt able to talk. As I expected, my children were very understanding. They both knew how much Alex loved them, despite everything, so it wasn't hard for them to imagine how devastated he would be by the loss of his child and agree to give him some space.

For months afterwards, I couldn't believe I was really free. I kept expecting another knock at the door, although no one would ever be able to pull that trick on me again, not with my new security system. But neither I nor Jen heard anything, so gradually we both picked up the pieces of our lives. I have no idea what Nancy did, and I know she wouldn't tell me if I asked. I just hope it was a win-win, like she said, and that the mystery third person got something out of it as well.

I'm very busy these days; my digital advisory service has finally taken off. There is no shortage of people who want to catch up with the twenty first century. I work most evenings, so I've given up wine. On weekends I'll treat myself to a glass or share a bottle with Madeleine if she drops round, but that's about it.

I try not to dwell on the last few years; I think guilt and regret are a waste of time. Having said that, I can't help feeling sad about Chris. I really liked him.

NANCY

13 ROLE MODEL

I hear you've met my brother, so I guess you get why I didn't want to talk about him last time. The dude does my head in and I'm not looking forward to telling you about him, but it's got to be done, so we might as well crack on.

So what d'you make of our Nathan? Let me guess. The word 'sucker' might spring to mind. I mean, who gets stitched up by a gang of drug dealing scum, twice over? I wouldn't blame you for thinking my bro's not too smart. You probably reckon he's weak, too. The kind of guy who sits back and lets others drive his life. Not big on taking responsibility.

And what about the way he writes? OK, I'm not great at it, but I don't pretend to be. Unlike Nathan, who thinks he's bloody Shakespeare. Never uses one word when ten will do, and half of them I don't understand. I hope he dialled it back for you, but I'll never know. I haven't read what he wrote. Like I said last time, books aren't my thing. If I'd known they'd ask me to do this again I'd have fired up Warrior's engine and hidden on some remote canal, where no one could find me. But I didn't, so here we are. Nothing personal, by the way.

Right. Time to defend my brother and change your view of him. OK, so he's got his faults, but at least he admits it. I bet he said his problems were self-inflicted – right? He knows he's been weak and done wrong, but he always tries to put it right. It just seems like every time he gets back on his feet, fate kicks him in the teeth again, and back down he goes. I've tried to help him, but I'll let you be the judge of how well I've done, once we get to the end.

Also, if this were a film, I guarantee you'd like him a whole lot better. It sounds wrong to say this about your brother, but the guy is hot. When he was younger, he was fighting girls off with a stick. Even now, after two stints inside, he still gets a second look from most women, and quite a few blokes. He was in a right state when he came out last time, but I made him have his hair cut and paid for him to get his teeth fixed, so now he's back to his old handsome self. A bit battered, but still fit. He's modest about it, though. The dude hasn't let it go to his head, and he has always treated women with respect. More respect than some deserved, but we'll come on to that. First let's start at the very beginning, as someone once said, and tell the truth about his childhood.

I bet he told you how happy he was, growing up on the canals. He always puts a brave face on it, but the truth is our dad gave him a rough time. Nathan was a poet and a dreamer, which wound Dad right up, as he thought writing was a big fat waste of time. Poor Nathan would show him his poems and stories, but at best he'd just get told to find something useful to do. If Dad was in his cups, all Nathan's hard work would end up in the stove. Paper makes a great firelighter.

It didn't help that Nathan was rubbish at music. He couldn't sing a note or play an instrument, so Dad paid more attention to me. You remember how I told you we used to perform together, on the towpath and in canal side pubs? Most brothers would've hated their sister getting all the attention and would've taken it out on her, but Nathan never did. Sure we fought plenty, but he always had my back and would defend me against anyone. He didn't need to, as I can look after myself, but it was good to have him in my corner.

Nathan never gave up trying to please Dad, so he made sure he learned how to repair diesel engines. He got very good at it, which helped make Dad a bit happier, although he still made my poor bro feel he wasn't good enough. Dude kept trying, even so. He learned wood carving off Dad, and then this guy Terence taught him to paint roses and castles. He was brilliant at both and made all this amazing stuff, which he sold from our boat. The punters lapped it up, but Dad just had a go at him for not making enough money. Mum would sometimes try and defend Nathan, but it only wound Dad up even more, so mostly she just kept quiet.

Once Nathan set up shop he started to get a lot of attention from girls. I reckon he got from them the approval he wanted from his father. As we moved around so much, he met a lot of girls, and he never had to try too hard. Sadly, being a babe magnet didn't make up for the bad vibes he got from Dad.

Like Nathan, I had my fair share of admirers, and many of them were creeps. Nathan chased the creeps away, along with some of the good guys, which caused a few fights, but I always forgave him in the end. I knew he only wanted the best for me. Back then he was my role model and I looked up to him.

As my brother got older, I could tell he was desperate to strike out on his own. I guess he finally figured he was never going to win with Dad, and got sick of trying, but he stayed put a lot longer than he wanted, all because of me. You see, the two of us were dead close. It was like we were two halves of the same person. I was good with numbers; he was good with words. He loved nature, whereas I couldn't tell a duck from a swan. He was my sensible older brother, and I was his wild little sister. He preferred to keep his head down, while I was a big show-off.

Nathan wasn't the only one who got a hard time from Dad. Even though I was Dad's music buddy, he'd often have a right go at me for a whole bunch of reasons – mainly my clothes, plus what he saw as my 'bad attitude'. Mum would try and stick up for me sometimes, like she did with Nathan, but my brother always waded in, even though he knew Dad would just take it out on him instead. He was like a kind of forcefield, deflecting Dad's rage onto himself, and I know he was scared of what might happen to me if he jumped ship and wasn't there to protect me anymore.

In the end, I got out just before him. Remember I told you how that record company guy spotted me, when I was gigging in a pub in Birmingham? So I upped and left, which meant Nathan was free to take on that old guy Jeremiah's boat, after he had a stroke. I was sorry for the old geezer but pleased for my brother. I thought he was set up for life, with his commercial narrowboat and his painting side hustle. So did he.

As you know, I quickly hit the big time and scored a fair bit of cash, unlike my brother. He got by, but as you can imagine, you're never going to get rich on a narrowboat. Even so, he was never jealous. He was pleased for me and very proud, in both senses of the word. I'd try and help him out, but he'd never take any money off me, so I did my best to spoil him whenever he visited, which was fairly often back then, as he had quite a few London customers. Each time he showed up, I'd buy him a nice dinner and a few beers. If I was recording, I'd take him along to the studio, plus I got him tickets for all my London gigs, although he'd go all shy if he met anyone famous. I reckon my lifestyle would have been his idea of hell, but his life suited him fine and he was doing OK. Until he met Ruth, that is.

What a piece of work. I bet Nathan went easy on her, didn't he? Even now, he sees that bitch through rose-coloured glasses, but I don't. As soon as I met her, I clocked what she was like. She saw him coming, right from the start. I tried to warn my brother, but he wouldn't listen. People never do when they're in love. You have to let them find out the hard way.

So when Ruth met Nathan in that pub, she was on her uppers. She had lost her job and was about to be evicted from her flat. She also had a list of creditors as long as your arm, chasing her down. I found that part out later. Some of them were dodgy characters who wouldn't think twice about punishing people who didn't pay up. Then along came her escape route and meal ticket combined, and she didn't hang about. She moved out of her flat and onto Nathan's boat, then cruised away from her creditors, with no forwarding address. The canals are a great place to disappear.

When my brother introduced us, he looked so proud. I have to say, she was attractive, if you like that sort of thing. Blonde, curvy and smiley. Looked like butter wouldn't melt. The opposite of me, in other words. She acted all friendly, but once we got talking, I twigged what she was really like. I see plenty of her kind in the music business. Girls – and blokes – who are all over you like a rash when you're on your way up but drop you like a hot brick the minute your luck changes. That was Ruth. She was very into public displays of affection, but I could tell she didn't love my brother and had no loyalty, no steel. With hindsight, I should've kept my mouth shut, but that's never been my strong point. I told Nathan what I've just told you, he told me to butt out, and we weren't so close after that. I wasn't too worried; we've always had our ups and downs so I reckoned things would come right in the end.

I was wrong, of course. What happened next was Ruth got pregnant. Nathan expected me to be pleased; maybe he thought the baby would fix the problems between us. Doh. Why do people even think that? I've got nothing against babies, but they don't solve problems. How could they? They just create them. I was gutted he had hitched himself to this snake for life by having a child with her, but I didn't say those exact words. I was quite tactful, for me. I just said he had got himself in too deep, but even so, he took it badly, and we didn't part on good terms. After that, he stopped returning my calls and answering my texts, but I refused to give up. I kept on calling and messaging, because I'm not like Ruth. Sure, I can be rude and aggressive, but I can also be loyal. So can Nathan. Often to the wrong people.

The first thing I knew about that bunch of lowlife drug dealers was when I got a call from his lawyer. If you could call him that. The dude was only part qualified. I was annoyed when I found out, because I could have hired Nathan a much better lawyer if he'd told me what was going on, but it was too late. My brother had already been convicted and sentenced. He would have been given a shorter jail term if he had named the gang members, but he refused, which I could understand. We both know the penalties for grassing.

I asked what happened to Ruth and the lawyer told me Nathan had sworn she wasn't involved. He'd stuck to his story, even under intense questioning from the rozzers, but I knew different. He'd taken the rap for her, to protect her and their son. It was the lawyer who told me they had a little boy. Of course, Ruth repaid Nathan's loyalty by breaking off all contact and refusing him access to his child. No surprise there.

So I was right about her all along, but I figured there was no point rubbing my brother's nose in it. Instead, I wrote to him every week, all the time he was inside, but he never wrote back. Not once. I didn't judge him, though; I figured he was ashamed, and maybe embarrassed at being taken in by Ruth and those dealers.

All this time, Mum and Dad were still grafting away on the canals. They were used to going long periods without hearing from us, but even so, I knew they'd be bound to notice if Nathan was silent for months on end, so I bit the bullet and told them he was inside. I played down the reason and just said he fell in with the wrong crowd. I never mentioned drugs, as I knew that would destroy them. Sure, my dad drank like a fish and chain-smoked rollups, but for him alcohol and tobacco didn't count. Illegal drugs were a whole other ballgame.

Not long after that, Dad got sick. I'm sure it would've happened anyway, but the Nathan thing didn't help. I sent my brother a letter, but I still got no reply, and what happened next is Dad died. Sorry to be blunt, but I don't do all this 'passing away' business. You should expect that by now. Again I wrote and told Nathan. I also contacted the prison and got permission for him to attend the funeral, but he refused to come. Mum was gutted, and I had the job of helping her hold it together. It was tough doing it on my own.

In the weeks after the funeral I nearly gave up on my brother. I was livid with him, but somehow I managed to go on writing, and I'm glad I did. Much later, he told me how close he'd come to topping himself at that point. He was constantly working out ways to do it, but my letters helped him hang on.

After he was released, I kept on writing. The prison gave me his forwarding address and I was tempted just to rock up, but I didn't, and I regret it now. Maybe if I had, I could've stopped the things that happened afterwards. Or maybe not, but at least I'd have tried. The thing was, he still hadn't answered any of my letters, so you can't blame me for thinking he didn't want to see me.

In my letters I told him how Mum had got really sick, but by then I didn't expect him to do anything about it, so I was gobsmacked when Mum said he'd been to visit. Maybe something I wrote got through to him. She said he'd lost his boat while he was inside and kept going on about how he was going to get another one and take her on a trip. Seems like he was trying to make her proud of him, but he never got the chance. She died soon afterwards, but at least he came to the funeral this time. When I saw him shuffle in, wearing a long black coat which had seen better days, I told myself this was my chance to make things right. Don't blow this, Nancy, I said to myself, but I did. Well done me.

At the wake, we both got off our faces. The other mourners made their excuses and left, once they could see the way things were going. The booze loosened my tongue, and my rage at the years of unanswered letters all

161

came pouring out. I had seen the pain my brother had caused Mum and Dad, but that's no excuse for the low blows I struck. I blamed him for both their deaths and carried on ranting for ages, even though I could see how much I was hurting him. Grief and booze are a lethal combination. After the pub closed, we spilled out onto the street, where I made a right spectacle of myself. I remember screaming that he was a coward and I wanted him out of my life. Even so, he still followed me at a distance, as I staggered back to the hotel. Obviously he wanted to make sure I got back OK. He tried to hide from me, but I spotted him easily, even though I was shitfaced. He'd be no good on a surveillance team.

Maybe if I'd behaved better that night, my brother wouldn't have ended up back inside. Who knows? I've often beaten myself up about that, but it's a mug's game, so I'll stick to the facts. In the months after the funeral, I stayed angry at my brother. It was easier than dealing with the loss of my mum. So, for the first time since we both left the family narrowboat, I stopped writing to him, and guess what happened? Another lawyer, not much better than the first, contacted me to say he was back inside. Afterwards I held out for a bit longer, then finally caved and picked up my pen again. I told myself we only had each other, and we owed it to ourselves, and to Mum and Dad, to have another go at being brother and sister. So I wrote to him and said sorry for how I carried on at the funeral. Guess what, though? No reply – but still, I kept on writing, just like before. I pestered him for a release date and said I wanted to meet up when he got out. Maybe I put too much pressure on him – who knows? Anyway, after a while, my letters started getting returned, so I contacted his lawyer, who confirmed he had been released. Thanks for telling me, dude. I asked where he was and the brief informed me that he had been in a hostel but had checked out, without leaving a forwarding address. He had no idea where Nathan was and no way of contacting him. The mobile number he had on file was unobtainable, so Nathan must have changed it. Maybe he didn't even have a phone. So that was it. I had officially lost contact with my brother. I've never felt so alone.

Looking back, that was the worst time of my life. I had no family anymore, but I told myself I was lucky to have no ties and focused on my career. I was still on the record company treadmill – album, tour, rinse and repeat – and I had convinced myself it was what I wanted. Whenever the suits tried to make me do something I didn't want to do, like duet with some sad sack pop idol or plaster myself over social media, I fought my corner and battled on. I was doing OK, or so I thought – right up until I got the call from Suzi.

You remember Suzi? Well done, if you do. She's the receptionist at the record company and an expert in filtering out nutters. When she says I need to take a call, I believe her, even if it's from someone I don't know. That's how I came to be talking to a bloke called Geoff, who said he was my brother's new boss.

So it turns out this Geoff runs a marina in Leicester and employs Nathan as a handyman. The two of them get on well and often go out drinking. On one of these nights out, Nathan apparently got wasted, saw one of my tour posters in the pub and let slip I was his estranged sister. Geoff was in a marginally better state, so next morning he remembered what Nathan had told him but had enough sense not to let on. Instead he tracked me down via my record company, so he could try and persuade me to pay my brother a visit. He was convinced Nathan would love to see me, even though he'd never admit it.

I like to think I'm a decent judge of character and the guy seemed genuine enough. He told me Nathan was brilliant at painting roses and castles and knew his way around a diesel engine better than anyone he'd ever met. I replied that he hadn't met me yet, then made arrangements to pay a secret visit to Bastion Marina. Suzi arranged a car and driver for me, so I could make a sharp exit if need be.

You should have seen Nathan's face when I stepped out of the shadows in the marina office. He looked terrified, but so was I. We went for a walk around the marina, and I suggested we park all the difficult stuff. I was scared I'd blow it otherwise, what with my temper. So we chatted about his job and he showed me the little caravan where he lived. It was crammed with his canal art, just like our narrowboat used to be, and I felt as though I'd stepped back in time. I admired his handiwork while he made me a cup of tea, then he asked me about myself. I was about to fob him off, but then I remembered what a good listener he was when we were young. So I told him about how my record company wanted to turn me into someone I'm not and put my whole life out there on social media for the world to see. It felt great to share my problems and Nathan hardly got a word in edgeways, which is probably just how he wanted it, I reckon. It was only when I was about to leave that he let slip how hard it was to be near the canals, but not on them, if you know what I mean. It was the only time he shared a bit of himself, but it was a start. It also gave me an idea.

After that, I found I was getting on well with my brother for the first time since before he met Ruth. He replied every time I texted and answered all my calls. We began to share a few laughs and life started to feel less lonely. I was grateful to Geoff for meddling, so I rang and told him so. Then I asked him a favour. I wanted him to help me find a narrowboat for Nathan. Sure, I could easily have bought a bog-standard boat myself, but I had some unusual requirements and knew there weren't many boats that would meet them. Being in the business, Geoff was best placed to help me find what I was looking for. Instead of a saloon, I wanted a workshop for

Nathan's carving and painting, plus a side hatch and some outside shelving, where he could display his stuff. I also wanted the mod cons we didn't have as children, like a shower room, a decent galley and a big comfy bed. I knew it would be hard to find a suitable boat, but luckily Geoff agreed to take on the challenge. Like I expected, it took a while, but in the end he came up trumps. The boat in question had been owned by a canal artist who had to leave the waterways behind when he got sick. Geoff was worried about the price, but to be honest it was small change to me. Sorry to sound like a prat. So I arranged a bank draft and Geoff gave me mate's rates on a year's mooring fees. He planned to rent out the caravan which Nathan had done up, so he also got something out of it.

The boat was called Festina Lente. It means 'hurry slowly' in Latin, or so I'm told. Geoff arranged to have it transferred to Bastion and when it arrived, I hopped on the train to Leicester, where he met me at the station and drove to the marina to surprise Nathan. I saw no need for a car and driver this time. Geoff was sound and I didn't think I'd need to make a quick getaway from Nathan second time around.

As I expected, Nathan refused to take the keys off me when I first showed him the boat. He said he couldn't accept my 'charity' and it took a long time to persuade him. I told him he had always looked out for me, when I was little, so I was just returning the favour. I also said he deserved a fresh start and I wanted to help him make one. I reminded him it was just the two of us and we needed to help each other. Finally he gave in, and I could see how chuffed he was to have a new boat, but I was worried he thought he owed me, when he really didn't. At the end of the day, he's my big brother. I just want him to be happy. I also told him Geoff had found Festina Lente and didn't want to be rewarded by losing his handyman, so he couldn't just do a runner and would need to confine his trips to the holidays. Nathan agreed, so the three of us had a deal.

The first chance he got, my brother took one of the best-known round trips on the canal network, called the Leicester Ring. At the time I was stressed out, trying to nail the songs for my new album, so it was nice to think of him drifting along at four miles an hour on his new boat, selling canal art to the tourists. I left him alone to enjoy it at first, then started up a bit of banter. I nagged him to get his hair cut and his teeth fixed, and he told me to get off his case. That kind of thing. Then, one night, he called instead of texting, and it was obvious something was up. Turns out he was in one of our favourite canal side pubs, up on the Trent and Mersey, when he ran into one of the gang members who had stitched him up. Not content with putting him inside twice, the bloke tried to get his claws into him again, but Nathan told him to stuff it. I felt pleased he was able to tell me about it, and I hoped he wouldn't be tempted to go back down that route, but I sensed that wasn't the end of it for him. It seemed like meeting this guy had stirred up all the anger he had buried down deep, and he wanted to lash out and get his own back. I know I'd have reacted the same way, but I persuaded him to let it lie. It was a case of 'do as I say, not as I do'. I gave him a load of crap about karma and how those lowlifes would get theirs, but the truth is, I was desperate to stop him getting into any more trouble. Not when he was finally turning his life around. Thankfully he listened, and the rest of his trip passed off without any more drama.

Nathan still enjoyed working for Geoff at Bastion, but before long he started planning his next trip. The canals are addictive that way. This time he decided to head south to London and visit me. I realised he'd never been to my house in Islington, even though I'd lived there for years by then.

When Nathan showed up, Johnno (remember him?) said hi, then left us to it, which was decent of him. I phoned for a pizza, cracked open a bottle of JD, then showed my brother around the house – and he was gobsmacked. I don't think he'd twigged how successful I was; not until he saw where I lived. I have to say, the place is huge, and it looks the business, thanks to my talented interior designer. The only thing I contributed was the mess, most of which Johnno tidied away.

It was my altar that did for Nathan, though. Remember my altar, on the wall of my music room – my tribute to all the women in the music business who inspired me? When my brother saw the handwritten notes up there, and I told him who they were from, he burst into tears. Once he started crying, he couldn't stop. He just kept on bawling his eyes out, saying that I was brilliant, and he was crap. He carried on like that until the pizza delivery guy rang the doorbell.

We left most of the pizza but drank almost all the JD. As we worked our way through the bottle, my brother started talking. Ever since, I've been grateful I had the sense just to listen as he told me all about what those guys did to him. I reckon he told me more than he did you. I mean, did he let on how shit scared he was, as well as angry, when he ran into that lowlife Sebastian, while he was on his trip? When he realised the gang now knew he was out of jail and had got himself another boat, so was useful to them again? He confessed to me that he lived in fear of them coming after him. I hated the thought of my brother going through life like that. Always looking over his shoulder.

Then he told me about his time in prison, and it sounds like the second time was much better than the first, although neither was exactly a picnic, as you know. I made sure I didn't miss a word as Nathan described his cellmate Ray and his massive criminal network. He sounds like a proper scary dude, does Ray. Dead smart and proper ruthless. I'm grateful he took a shine to my brother. From what I hear, it could easily have gone the other way, like it did with most of his other cellmates, but it didn't. Nathan helped

Ray out and taught him to read, so Ray looked out for Nathan in return. We've got that in common, me and Ray. We're naturally suspicious and normally think the worst of people, but once we do let a person in, we're loyal to them. Unless they betray us, then all bets are off.

Both times, after he came out of jail, Nathan struggled to get back on his feet. As he told me about the string of dead-end jobs he did when he got released the first time, I felt like smacking him for not picking up the phone and calling me, but at the same time I got it. Dude was ashamed of how things had turned out. He probably thought I'd rub his nose in it, but at least he knows better now. I wasn't too impressed either when he told me about that chick Nina he hooked up with, after he was released the first time. An addict – just what he needed. Not. Anyway, at least she split before she could do too much damage. I wish Ruth had done similar.

Finally, we reached the end of the story and Nathan mentioned Holly for the first time. He described how they met, then hung his head as he confessed he'd blown it. I decided it was time for some sisterly advice, so I told him to hang in there, be patient and take things slowly. From what I'd heard, the woman was no pushover and I respected that. Clearly she wanted to be sure about Nathan, especially as she had a kid to think of. He just needed to take his time and put in the spadework.

I tried to get Nathan to stay the night, but he was determined to totter off to his boat, so I let him go. It was a fair walk from my house to his mooring, so I told him to text me when he got there and hoped he was up to it. He'd drunk a lot more whisky than me; I'd been too busy listening and didn't want to miss out by being off my face.

Half an hour later, I got a message saying he was back on board, then the next morning he texted to say he was heading home to Bastion. After he got back, he kept calling and messaging as normal. He sounded happier than before, and I was glad he'd confided in me. I was also pleased I'd advised him about Holly, as he revealed they'd finally got it together, but were taking things slowly, like I said they should. Her daughter was OK with it, which was good news, and the three of them had taken a few short trips on Festina Lente. The little girl loved the canals, so he said. I was pleased for them, but that summer I put my brother's life on the back burner as my own imploded, big time.

Remember what happened? How my record company did the dirty on me, so I told them where to stick it, bought Warrior and left them all behind? Well, when I started heading in the same direction as my brother, west and then north, up the Grand Union, I texted him and told him what happened. I wanted to talk it over with him, and I was planning to reach Bastion as quickly as possible, so we could meet, but he wasn't there. He was in Llangollen with Holly; about as far away as it was possible to be on the canal network. Just my luck. He was out of reach, and I didn't want to discuss it over the phone, so I told him we'd speak when he got back. Then I switched my phone off, as I knew he wouldn't take no for an answer and would keep trying to call me, which he did, although he gave up after a while and just left me a voicemail saying he was there for me, whenever I needed him. I figured we'd have plenty of time to catch up once he got back, and in the meantime I'd take time out to get my head together. However, as you know, the forces which spin this crazy world had other ideas. I was just south of Foxton when I ran into Stella, our damsel in distress, and this whole story kicked off.

I'm not going to go over old ground again, but I do have to tell you one thing I left out first time round. Cast your mind back to when I came across Stella's boat, the not so aptly named Two's Company, floating in the middle of the canal. As you might remember, I tied the boat up, woke Stella, who was passed out on the bed, tried to work out what was going on, then ran off down the towpath like a headless chicken to look for Alex, her missing husband. So here's what I failed to share last time, as I didn't want to talk about my brother back then.

The first thing I did, once I was out of sight of the boat, was text Nathan for help. I figured he might be nearly home, but I was wrong. Clearly he and Holly had decided not to rush, as they had only made it as far as Market Drayton on the Shropshire Union Canal. My brother offered to up the pace and get back as soon as he could, but I predicted the Stella issue would be done and dusted by then, however quick he was, so I told him to forget it, and he backed off. He knows I can handle myself on the canals, so he wouldn't have been too worried about me. Even so, he texted me a few days later, just after Stella had been released from custody, to check I was OK. I must have been feeling relieved; it wasn't until after I had hit 'Send' that I realised I'd stuck a kiss on the end of my reply. That's not my style, and I'm sure my brother thought it was weird.

After that, Nathan and I carried on rebuilding our relationship, or whatever the shrinks like to call it. Things started to settle down. I thought the whole Stella business was over and done with and I never dreamed I'd need to get my brother involved. Turns out I was wrong.

14 QUICKSAND

So Dan persuaded me to stick around in Allenby Marina. At first I didn't invite my brother to visit, even though Bastion was only a few miles up the canal. I wanted Dan to myself for a bit – I reckoned I deserved some fun for a change. Also, I needed to make sure Dan was worth it before I introduced them. After a couple of weeks, I decided he was, so I asked Nathan round for dinner. Based on my crap cooking skills, I figured he'd be expecting a takeout, or even just a bag of Monster Munch, so I had a laugh at how gobsmacked he was when Dan served up a proper meal. Dude's an excellent cook. We had a fun evening, and Nathan clicked with Dan right away, which was both a good and a bad thing. Good, because I wanted them to get on and bad, because Nathan sided with Dan when he said I should start over as an independent recording artist. However much I protested that I was done with the music business, neither of them would let it go.

All the time we were talking, I couldn't help noticing how much my brother was drinking. I know – pot, kettle and all that. Granted we both like a drink, but even by our standards Nathan was caning it, and it seemed to me like he was drinking to forget. Occasionally I'd catch his eye and see the pain lurking under the surface. I didn't think it was anything to do with Holly; things seemed to be going well there. I reckoned it was the memory of that gang that was bothering him. He couldn't get them out of his mind, and it was doing his head in. He said as much, when I poured him into a taxi later on. When I asked if he was OK and gave him one of my looks, to show I knew something was up, he replied:

'As OK as I'll ever be, given everything that's happened.'

That told me all I needed to know. In vino veritas and all that crap. I was just thankful he'd got Holly in his life. Without her, I didn't think he'd be able to hold it together. I decided I needed to meet her, so I told him to bring her along next time.

I got a good feeling as soon as I met her. The woman's battle-scarred, wary and tough. My kind of girl. She wasn't fazed by me being famous; but she didn't deliberately ignore it either, to make a point, like some people do. She was just cool, and it was obvious she didn't take any crap from my brother.

After our first meeting, the two of them often rocked up at Allenby and when Christmas rolled around, Holly invited us to her house. We had a chilled time, and I enjoyed meeting her little girl, Stevie, who's as cute as a button and just as bright. Nathan and I offered to clear up after dinner, as we hadn't lifted a finger all day. We plonked Dan and Holly on the sofa with Star Wars and a bottle of JD, then got stuck into the washing up, trying not to drop anything, as a lot of booze had been drunk. I looked at my brother with a tea towel in his hand and ribbed him about getting all domesticated. He said it was worth it, to be with Holly. Then he confessed he was shit scared about the future.

'You realise something's bound to go wrong, Nan...'

Cue a load of piss-taking from me about his positive attitude to life. Looking back, I should have taken him more seriously, because it turns out he was right. In the New Year, things went downhill fast.

First up, Geoff announced he was selling Bastion Marina. The poor sod had been trying to make the numbers stack up for years, but in the end it got too much for him and he decided to retire. He had hoped the new owners would want to keep Nathan on, but they preferred to bring their own people in, so my brother was out of a job. His immediate reaction was to tell Holly he'd sell Festina Lente and move in with her, which wasn't quite as knee-jerk as I've made it sound. They had already been talking about living together and Holly had confessed that, while she had built up enough trust for her and Stevie to share their space with him, she could never live on the canals full-time, which I respect. It's not for everyone, particularly in winter, when conditions get harsh. So it seemed like fate had helped her get what she wanted, but unlike Nathan, Holly doesn't allow life to push her around. Also, I imagine she was frightened of making a mistake, given what she had been through with her ex, and she wanted my brother to be dead sure, before he made the commitment. So she told him to take a canal trip by himself and think it over. A kind of cooling off period, as the contract lawyers call it. She's a smart girl, is Holly. Nathan wasn't wild about the idea, but he knew he'd have to play ball if he wanted to keep her and Stevie in his life, so he agreed, and off he went. He headed up north; I reckon he wanted to remind himself just how tough conditions can be up there, in the depths of winter, to make it easier for him to leave his precious waterways behind. Like that was ever going to work.

Meanwhile, fate also decided to point its bony finger at me. I was working away on one of my new songs, when Stella rang. I should've let it go to voicemail, but I gave in and picked up, as I fancied a break. Some break it turned out to be. At first, all I got were floods of tears. It took me ages to calm her down enough to talk. When she did, she told me how Alex had broken into her home the previous night, assaulted her and threatened her with a knife, because he found out that she and Jennifer, his girlfriend, had got together in Manchester. They had compared notes and realised they were both victims of this creep. Jen told Stella how Alex had been trying to destroy her business, plus her relationship with her kids and some guy she was seeing. She described how Jen lost her baby due to that scum and – get this – he blamed Stella. Easier than blaming himself, I suppose. Finally he threatened to kill her if she ever contacted his girlfriend again.

I guess that must be your nightmare scenario, if you're a controlling, violent cheat. The wife and girlfriend getting together and deciding they both want you out of their lives. Of course, it wasn't that simple. Alex wasn't about to let either of them walk away. Then Stella revealed she was responsible for the accident that almost killed him, which was why he tried to stitch her up on the stalking charge.

It's always the quiet ones, I tell you. Who'd have thought she had it in her? Knocking her husband out with booze and pills, then tangling him up in the mooring rope, so he got dragged into the canal and mangled by the prop? I've heard of it happening by accident, but it's very rare, and Christ alone knows how a novice boater like Stella thought that one up. She wouldn't say, and I was more worried about stopping her having another go at nailing the creep than about finding out where she got the idea. She told me she did come up with a Plan B, but Jen talked her out of it, which is just as well. After that, they both agreed to back off, in the hope that things might sort themselves out, but of course they didn't. After Alex broke into her house, she was forced to accept they never would, unless she did something about it, which is where I come in. You see, Stella wanted my help in getting rid of Alex.

The poor moo tends to overestimate my abilities. I'm no criminal mastermind, but then again, neither is she. It was obvious that, if I didn't stop her from trying to get shot of Alex, she'd likely wind up in jail. I didn't want that to happen, but I couldn't work out what to do about it, so I played for time. I asked her to tell me everything she knew about Alex's new life – where he lived and worked, what he did in his spare time, that sort of thing. When she mentioned that he was working three days a week in Birmingham and had rented a swanky penthouse in the Jewellery Quarter, I had a lightbulb moment. My mind took a trip down Memory Lane, around Gas Street Basin and the nearby canals. Right into the heartland of the gang who screwed up my brother's life. I wasn't sure if my idea would work, so I told Stella I'd think it over and call her back.

Look, I know Nathan's told you it was me who asked him to get that nasty bunch of lowlifes to warn Alex off. You might be wondering why I bothered, and I don't blame you, so I'm going to try and give you an answer. I think it's important you understand my motives, given what happened afterwards, but let's get one thing straight. I'm not about to apologise for what I did. I don't regret it. Sure some bad stuff went down afterwards, but none of that was my fault.

Maybe you think I did it because I reckon I owe Stella. If so, let's knock that one on the head right away. OK, so I wouldn't have got together with Dan, if Stella hadn't brought me to Allenby Marina. Also, her business plan came in handy when Dan and I set up our recording studio. She's got a great business brain and I realise I'd have paid big bucks for that advice, if I'd hired a fancy consultant. I've offered her a share of our royalties, but she won't take a penny. What I'm saying is, I'm grateful for her help, but not enough to stick my neck out for her.

I've already told you she's a mate. Even though we're chalk and cheese, we went through something together, and that created a bond of sorts. I didn't like Stella at first, but somewhere along the line that changed. It's weird, really. Anyway, however strange it might look to you, we're pals. Stella's one of the few women I'll always look out for. Val, my lawyer, is another, although with her it's normally the other way round. I'd help Holly, too, providing she stays loyal to my brother. Maybe Suzi as well, but that's about it. So my friendship with Stella meant I wanted to help her, if I could, but was it enough to get my brother to put his head in the lion's mouth? No chance. Truth is, I didn't do it for her. I did it for Nathan.

See, this was my brother's chance to free himself from that gang, once and for all. I figured the timing was perfect, and it needed to be done. My brother was about to make a new life for himself, with Holly and Stevie. He had his best ever shot at a decent existence; who knew if he'd ever get another chance? But while the gang continued to lurk in the background, there was always a risk he'd blow it, either by drinking himself to death, or falling back into their clutches. You know what he's like, so I'm sure you agree he's capable of that. Sure he said he was going to sell his boat, but he won't, I tell you. He'll find a way to hang onto it, and a guy like him, with a commercial narrowboat, is always going to be a magnet for those scumbags. I figured they were bound to come calling again before long, so Nathan's only way out was to take control. Fortunately, he now had the back-up he needed to make it happen.

When I asked Nathan to confront the gang and get them to warn Alex off, I didn't tell him any of this. I just painted a picture of two innocent women, whose lives were being ruined by a violent man and who needed his help. Nathan's one of life's rescuers, who hates violence. Our Dad often threw a few punches when he was drunk, and Nathan was always there to defend me and Mum. We saw much worse men than Dad, though, growing up on the canals, and my brother always swore he wouldn't go down that route. So I made it clear he should tell the gang not to use violence and I was positive it wouldn't be necessary. I knew a guy like Alex, who operates in the safety of the business world, would soon back off when confronted by a bunch of dangerous criminals with a whole different set of values.

My brother has never been the confident type, so he doubted he could get the gang to agree to a favour. I reminded him they owed him, after he had gone to jail twice without grassing them up, but even so, I knew he was right. These scumbags were experts in exploiting weakness, and there was no chance Nathan could stand up to them by himself. They'd just hit back harder. Instead he'd need to play his trump card by telling them about his close relationship with Ray, his old cellmate. The guy was so powerful; I knew they'd have heard of him by reputation and encountered his associates. They'd be sure to agree that a small, low risk favour was a tiny price to pay for keeping on the right side of Ray. Afterwards, they'd drop Nathan like a hot brick, leaving him to get on with his life.

I knew Nathan would need some time to think about it, so I was surprised when he called back that evening to say he had already contacted them and set the wheels in motion. He sounded a bit pissed when he gave me the news, but I figured he just needed some Dutch courage to make the call. I hoped he wasn't doing it because he felt he owed me for his boat, or for all those years of unanswered letters, but being realistic, I figured that might be part of it. Whatever. The main thing is, I knew he was desperate to be free, and he was never going to make it happen by himself. He needed a push from yours truly. Now all I could do was wait. I had kicked things off; it was time to be patient. I knew it would take Nathan ages to get from Yorkshire to Birmingham on his narrowboat.

When Nathan did call, it was like I had got my brother back. His voice sounded like it used to when we were growing up. Sort of younger and lighter, if that makes any sense. He told me the gang had agreed to warn Alex off. They had sworn to him that Ray had nothing to do with their decision, but I knew different. Bullies only respond to bigger bullies. The important thing was, they were playing ball and planning to confront Alex alongside one of the Farmer's Bridge Locks, on his way home from work – date to be confirmed. The boss had even arranged a vantage point for Nathan, in an empty flat overlooking the lock, so he could see for himself that they had kept their word. After that, whatever happened, there was to be no further contact. It would be as though they and my brother had never met. My brother would be free.

So I called Stella and told her I'd found a way out for her and Jennifer. I said Alex wouldn't be harmed, but he'd be out of their lives for ever. I refused to tell her anything else, to protect her and Jennifer. I just said I'd be in touch again on the day, so she could make sure they both had watertight alibis, but it was best if we didn't talk in the meantime.

As I waited for my brother to name the day, I asked myself whether a few choice threats from that gang would be enough to make Alex leave Jennifer and Stella alone. To be honest, I didn't care about Jennifer, but I did hope it would be a win-win and Stella would be able to escape, just like Nathan. In the end I decided it would. You know why? Because although Alex had put the frighteners on his ex-wife, he had one thing in common with her. That snake had led a sheltered life. I'm sure he strutted around his office like he was a master of the universe, and he probably was, in that corporate world of rules and logic. What he didn't know was, there was a whole other universe out there. One that didn't operate according to his rules. Where the laws of the jungle were different, and the fish were a whole lot bigger than him.

The more I thought about it, the more I felt confident Alex would back right off, once he realised these guys had him on their radar and were way tougher than him. He'd never find out who was behind it, but he'd know for sure that Stella and Jen had ruthless friends in low places, so he'd figure it was best to move on. As you've seen, Alex always does what's best for Alex and he has no trouble jumping ship. I knew he wouldn't hesitate to save his own skin, once he realised he was in danger.

Then, one afternoon, Nathan called. The signal was poor as he was on a cross-country train, heading west towards Birmingham, but he managed to tell me the encounter was on for that night. So I told Stella, who predictably got in a right flap and needed precise instructions. I had to advise her to pay her next-door neighbour a visit and ask to borrow something. A cup of sugar – that old chestnut. Anything to prove she was in Surrey that night and couldn't have made it to Birmingham without the Tardis. I also warned her to call Jen and tell her to do similar. I said Jen should report Alex missing only after he failed to return home for the weekend, to allow some time for the dust to settle. Then I poured myself a strong one and waited for my brother to call and tell me it was all over. Luckily Dan was in the studio, tinkering about with one of our tracks. He's a perfectionist so he often spends hours in there, getting everything just so. I hadn't told him about any of this. I didn't see the point, as it was all going to be over very soon, and I figured the fewer people who knew, the better. So I holed up on Warrior and waited for Nathan to call and tell me it was done and dusted.

When the call didn't come, I wasn't too bothered. I rang my brother's mobile, and it went straight to voicemail, but I figured he was either celebrating in a noisy pub or heading home on the cross-country train, with its crap reception. Right after I hung up, Dan came back from the studio in a good mood, as things had gone well over there, so I suggested an early night. Good call, as it turned out.

The next day, I rang Nathan again, and this time he picked up. He told me everything had gone according to plan, but he didn't sound relieved, like I expected. In fact, he seemed pretty wound up, but when I asked if he was OK, he said he was fine. Just waiting for the adrenaline to wear off, he said. It sounded like a crock to me, but then he said he had to ring off as it was time to collect Stevie from school, so I let it go. My brother has always been a moody kind of guy, so I figured I'd just leave him be. I expected him to be fine next time we spoke.

After that, I called a few times and left voicemails, but he didn't call back, which was weird. Sure, Nathan spent years not answering my letters, but since we got together in Bastion he'd always returned my calls. I thought maybe all his time was taken up with adjusting to his new life with Holly and Stevie, and now he had done me a favour, he wanted his sister to take a back seat for a while. So I did what always works best for me. I picked up my guitar and grafted away on one of my new songs. I had been tinkering with it for months, but the chorus still wouldn't hang together, so I decided it was time to put Nathan out of my mind and give the song my full attention.

One night a few weeks later, Dan had gone down the pub with his mates and I was alone onboard Warrior, just me and my guitars. It was late in the evening when I got a call from a number I didn't recognise. I figured Dan's phone might have died and he could be using someone else's, so I picked up, but it wasn't Dan. It was my brother, who sounded like he was wasted, but I guess he needed to be, given what he had to tell me.

I listened as Nathan told me how everything had gone wrong, that night. How Alex had tried to stand up to the gang and paid with his life. How his body lay at the bottom of a lock in the Farmer's Bridge flight.

When my brother finished talking, I told him I'd call him back. Then I put down my phone and threw up in the sink. Suddenly I was freezing, but my hands were shaking so much I struggled to put on Dan's baggy jumper which he'd left on the sofa. When I finally managed it, I didn't want to press redial, but I knew I had to stop my brother from doing something stupid.

It took me a long time to talk him down and I'm not sure I succeeded, but I did my best. He kept saying it was all his fault, so I reminded him that he hadn't harmed anyone. In fact, he'd done the opposite. He'd specifically said no violence; it wasn't his fault the gang had ignored him. I reassured him there was no evidence to link him to the crime and told him the world was a better place without a creep like Alex in it. I threw in every argument

I could think of and I don't suppose I made much sense half the time. The main thing I tried to get across was that he wasn't to blame for Alex's death. I said it was me who had asked him to help Stella. Then I told him to get on with his life. Easier said than done, I suppose.

I reckon Nathan still feels guilty. He was always big on guilt, and I can't kid myself I made it go away by talking. I'm not that bloody eloquent; no one is. As for me – if I catch myself feeling bad about what happened, I just tell myself to get a grip. I don't do guilt; it's a waste of time. At the end of the day, a guy got murdered, but I didn't kill him, and anyway, some good has come out of it. Two women are free from a nasty dude who would probably have wound up killing them both. Granted it's not easy, living with my secret, and I wish things had worked out as intended, but that's life. Sometimes things go to shit, and you just have to suck it up.

Stella doesn't call so often these days. She's maxed out at work now Alex isn't around to ruin her reputation, so she doesn't have much time to chat. When we do speak, she always thanks me for helping her and Jennifer 'turn their lives around', but when she does, I quickly change the subject.

Right, I'm off. I'm spending today recording a bunch of new material in our widebeam studio. Dan and I are planning a small tour to see how our fans like our new songs. We're going to rope in some local musicians and play a bunch of small, intimate venues – just how I like them. No more stadium gigs for me.

So you see, I've got a lot on, and I refuse to dwell on the past. Only losers do that. Soon enough, it'll seem like it never really happened. Or like it happened to someone else.

DAWN

15 HAPPY EVER AFTER?

I'm uncomfortable discussing my personal life. I don't mind sharing details of my police work; I'm proud of what I do. Where it's relevant to the story, I'll even talk about Craig, my teenage son, and my poor widowed Dad. To be more specific, I don't like discussing my relationship with Alan. We kept it secret for so long that covert operations have become a habit, if you see what I mean.

It's my fault, really. Last time you met me, I finished my statement with the news that Alan had asked me to dinner at a fancy French restaurant and signed off his text message with two kisses, which was totally out of character for him. So they demanded I tell you what happened next. I would have preferred to fast forward to the police investigation, but they weren't having any of it. They said you'd want what they called the 'backstory', so here we go.

So, if you recall, I was dating Superintendent Alan Hamilton. We had both been divorced for years, and each had a few scars on our back. We also had three teenage sons between us, so things weren't straightforward. I'd had a few failed relationships since my divorce, and I was wary of getting too involved, particularly with a colleague, but I couldn't help it. Alan and I had great chemistry, we respected each other and, most importantly, we made each other laugh. The job always makes it difficult to have a personal life, but I had thought things were going well, until an awkward phone conversation made me think I was about to be dumped. Remember? Anyway, I put it to the back of my mind until I had concluded the canal investigation, then I called Alan back, which was when I got the dinner invitation and the text with two kisses.

At this point, I didn't know what to think, so I went home to get dressed up for this posh dinner. I was glad Craig was staying at his grandad's that night; I didn't want him teasing me about having a 'hot date'. Actually, who am I kidding? He probably wouldn't notice if I walked into the kitchen wearing a dinosaur costume, as long as there was bread for toast and a big jar of peanut butter.

I only wear make-up on special occasions, which means I'm not great at applying it. I had several goes, progressing through 'deranged panda' and 'drag queen' until I toned it down and finally managed to look half decent. Back then, I used to wear my hair scraped back in a ponytail for work, so I untied it and fluffed it up with the aid of a few styling products. Then I put on a floaty dress, but I drew the line at heels. I only own one pair of stilettos, and I can't walk in them. Car to bar? Forget it. I'd be sprawled flat out in the car park and wouldn't get anywhere near the bar. So I put on a pair of biker boots, with lots of zips and buckles. I thought I had read somewhere that the contrast between a feminine, floaty dress and rough, tough footwear was supposed to be trendy. Whether or not I was right, it would have to do.

Alan picked me up on the dot at half seven. He's always on time. That's one thing about dating a fellow cop; they're generally punctual. We hadn't seen each other for a while, because of the investigation into that odd canal crime you know all about, and the conversation in the car was a bit awkward at first. So we broke the ice by talking about that investigation, and the reasons for my decision to NFA it – sorry, take No Further Action. I explained my colleague Dave Langley's theory that the wife, Stella, had spiked her husband Alex's drinks, surreptitiously wrapped the mooring rope around his leg and dropped it into the canal, so it got wound around the propellor and dragged him into the water, causing him grievous injuries. I also described what we believed to be a clumsy attempt by Alex and his girlfriend Jennifer to frame Stella for stalking in a bid for revenge. I voiced the opinion that two intelligent people like Alex and Jennifer knew their botched job would never stand up to scrutiny. They just wanted to punish Stella. I concluded that it was an odd crime of passion and revenge, perpetrated by a bunch of amateurs, but I had to NFA it as I could never have made it stand up in court.

Alan agreed with my decision.

'But it must've been a frustrating call to make, Dawn.'

'Tell me about it. I mean, if Dave's theory is correct, the wife got away with attempted murder.'

'Indeed. The question is – who put her up to it? I mean, the woman's never set foot on a canal boat before. She's hardly going to think that one up herself. God knows there are more straightforward ways of seeing off your cheating husband. In all my years in the job, I've never heard of anyone doing that to a person. That thing with the mooring rope. Where the hell did she get the idea?'

'Don't suppose we'll ever know.'

'The husband sounds like a piece of work, as well. If that's what he's capable of when he's drugged up in the ICU, I hate to think what he could come up with when he's fit and well.'

'Let's hope we never find out. Everyone involved lives outside our patch, so chances are we'll never come across them again. Hopefully they'll go back to their middle-class lives and leave us to deal with real villains.'

'They're villains too, Dawn. Attempted murder and conspiracy to pervert the course of justice – and that's just for starters. You were right to NFA, but I'm not sure they'll just toddle back to their offices and behave themselves from now on. After all, they've all got away with something. In my experience, that tends to encourage people to have another go.'

'Well I hope someone else gets to clear up the mess, if so. I'll never make DI off the back of cases like that.'

'Of course, you will. You aced the exams and you're brilliant in the field. You'll make an excellent DI.'

'If I ever get the chance.'

'You will. Just hang in there. Right, here we are. Shall we agree not to talk shop during dinner?'

'Sounds like a plan.'

We both ordered gin and tonics, which surprised me. Alan doesn't normally drink at all when he's driving, but I decided not to mention it and focused my attention on the menu. I chose fish, he followed suit and asked for an expensive white burgundy to go with it. Then, as the waiter left us, he leaned forward and said:

'Dawn, I have some news.'

Uh-oh, I thought. Here we go. Unusually for Alan, he looked nervous, which didn't feel like a good sign.

'The thing is, Dawn – I've got a new job.'

That was the last thing I expected to hear.

'I'm transferring to Warwickshire Police – as Detective Chief Superintendent.'

'That's amazing, Alan. Well done!'

I meant it. Once you reach the rank of Superintendent, it's hard to get promoted any further up the food chain. The pyramid narrows and competition for the most senior posts is fierce.

'So I guess you're planning to move?'

'Maybe, but there's no rush. I'll be based at HQ in Warwick, which isn't so far to drive. I might stay over on the odd night.'

'But the traffic's bad, and you'll be pulling some long hours. You need to be careful you don't burn out.'

'That's typical of you, Dawn. Always thinking of others, instead of yourself. Anyway, there was a reason why I applied for that job.'

'To get away from me?'

I was only half joking.

'Kind of. The truth is, I decided to transfer to another force so I could offer you this.'

Alan pushed a self-sealing evidence bag across the table towards me. Inside it was a large diamond ring.

'I'd get down on one knee, but I don't want everyone staring at us. Not unless you're going to say yes, but I don't want to put pressure on you to give me an answer right away. I just want you to know I love you; I want to stay with you forever, and I'm sick of sneaking around. Like I said before, you're a very talented detective, but if we go public and remain in the same force, I worry your brilliant career will be tarnished by accusations of nepotism. You know what some of our colleagues are like. So I decided to move. This way, everyone will know you got there on your own merit.'

'So you're moving forces because of me?'

'Yes. I'd have happily made a sideways move and taken another Superintendent's post. The promotion to Chief Super was a bonus.'

'I see. And you'd willingly shackle yourself for life to my stroppy teenage son?'

'That's a daft question. Of course, I would! You'd be taking on my two as well, and anyway, they won't be teenagers for ever. They'll improve with age, whereas I doubt I will. You'll have to take me as I am. If you want to, that is.'

'In that case, Alan – it's time.'

'Time for what?'

'Time for you to make a spectacle of yourself.'

So he did. He got down on one knee, took the ring out of the evidence bag and held it up to me.

'Dawn Burrows, will you make me the happiest man in this restaurant by agreeing to become my wife?'

'I believe I will – on one condition.'

'What's that?'

'No flouncy white dress.'

'You can get married in your riot gear, Sarge, if that's what you want. Now can I put the ring on? Everyone's staring and my knee's starting to hurt.'

On went the ring, and our fellow diners clapped and cheered. We'd given them more entertainment than they'd bargained for on a weekday evening. The waiter brought us two large glasses of champagne and the rest of the meal was a bit of a blur, although I do recall the white burgundy was excellent. Afterwards we retreated to one of the squashy sofas in the lounge for coffee, brandy and a spot of planning. After a long discussion, we agreed to start looking for a house about halfway between Leicester and Warwick. The Rugby area was our preferred option.

'I think there's a canal near Rugby, Dawn. Maybe we can get ourselves a narrowboat?'

'You've got to be joking.'

Eventually we asked for the bill and Alan picked up his phone.

'I'll just call a taxi. I'll come back and get my car tomorrow.'

I should have realised something was up when he called the person on the other end of the phone 'Dev', asked him to 'swing by that new French place', then hung up without giving his name, but I was too happy and wasted to notice. Even so, I couldn't fail to spot that the vehicle which picked us up wasn't a taxi. It was a plain clothes police car.

'Thanks for doing us a favour, Dev,' Alan said.

'No problem, boss. I just booked off. You two had a nice night?'

'Certainly have. In fact, the lovely Dawn has just agreed to be my wife!'

Luckily the drive home was short, so I didn't have to endure too much noisy enthusiasm from Detective Sergeant Dev Sastry. A few minutes later he dropped us outside my house and peace was restored.

'Alan – I hope you realise DS Sastry is the biggest gossip in Force Headquarters?'

'Absolutely. The news'll be all over HQ by tomorrow morning. Told you I was sick of sneaking around!'

'OK, I get it. I just hope you don't regret this tomorrow, once you've sobered up.'

He didn't, I have to say. The gossip about our engagement surged, then rapidly subsided. Marriages between police officers are commonplace, and our story soon became old news.

Personally, I wasn't too worried about the chitchat. My main concern was how my son Craig would respond to my news. For so long it had just been him and me, and I was worried he wouldn't take kindly to another man in his life, so I decided to tell my dad first and ask his opinion on how to break it to Craig. My son's close to his grandad; he often gets on better with him than he does with me. Surprisingly, Dad predicted Craig would be fine with it, and he was right. I introduced him to Alan and the two of them hit it off straight away. It turned out that Craig had missed having a man around but had never mentioned it to me. I guess he thought there wasn't much I could do about it and didn't want to hurt me. My ex, Fraser, hangs out with him when he can be bothered, or when there's a crisis in Craig's life, but he's got a new family to worry about, so he's not the most reliable, whereas Alan is solid and dependable, which was just what Craig needed back then. Far from being traumatised by my engagement, my son flourished. My dad was delighted, by the way. Since my mum died, he has been alone, and he misses sharing his life with the right person, so he was pleased his daughter was getting a second chance.

But back to Craig; his main worry was moving away from his mates in

Leicester. He had recently started driving lessons and I promised to practise with him, to help him get through his test as quickly as possible so he could visit them at weekends. I also reminded him he'd be going to college in a year, and his friendship group would be scattered around the country, but that didn't cheer him up. A year is a long time in the life of a teenager.

Talking of time, Alan and I decided we didn't want a long engagement or a formal wedding. Now the decision was made, we saw no point in hanging about, so we chose to get married abroad. In an all-inclusive resort in Mexico, to be precise. We thought it made sense to combine the honeymoon with the wedding and take our three sons with us – Craig, plus Alan's two boys, Brendan and Finn. People thought we were crazy, but we asked my dad along as back-up, which we figured would lighten the load. Alan's parents didn't want to join us; they hate flying and have a menagerie of needy pets. We arranged to celebrate with them when we got back, then we flew away from the English winter for our sunshine wedding.

Mostly it worked out well. Craig is slightly older than the other two, so he became the self-appointed leader of the band of three. Every morning they'd cheerily demolish the huge American-style breakfast buffet before heading off to the main pool or the beach, sometimes with Dad in tow. Either we'd join them or grab some time to ourselves in a more secluded part of the resort. At the end of the first week, once we'd built up a decent tan for the wedding photos, we had a simple, beautiful ceremony on the beach at sunset. I wore a sundress and kept my feet bare; I decided it was too hot for riot gear. Everyone else wore white shirts and chinos. Brendan and Finn were best men and Dad and Craig both gave me away, so everyone had a role to play. Afterwards we had a celebration barbecue on the beach, then checked out the cheesy cabaret and pulled some shapes in the disco. It was perfect.

During the second week we all crammed in as many activities as we could, conscious that our days in tropical paradise were numbered. Dad and I took some cultural trips together and we all enjoyed a day's snorkelling in an idyllic lagoon. Alan and I led the boys on a high-octane day out where we zip-lined, jumped off cliffs into river gorges and raced each other in kayaks. My new husband and I were first down the zip-wires and off the cliffs, every time, much to the surprise of our sons. Clearly it was a sad attempt by two middle-aged cops to show the youngsters we had still got it, but it seemed to work.

In the evenings, it was remarkably easy to squeeze in a few quiet dinners. Dad had struck up a good rapport with Brendan and Finn, so he was happy to graze the buffet in the early evening, then take them off to play air hockey or watch movies on the big outdoor screen. Meanwhile, Craig had embarked on a holiday romance with a sweet Scottish girl called Elspeth, so he was fully occupied. It was difficult for him to leave her and fly home, but

I gather they have stayed in touch via social media. Parting is still 'sweet sorrow', as someone once said, but it's not so final, these days.

For Alan and me, returning to an English winter wasn't so bad. We found a house on the outskirts of Rugby which we both liked. It actually backs onto the canal, but I decided I could cope. Alan started his job in Warwick and immediately loved it. Life was good, until DI Andrew Gillespie threw the proverbial spanner into the works.

Here's another memory test. Do you remember Andrew? He was the DI on the Alex and Stella case. He's one of the good guys and has always been supportive of my career. Anyway, I was on my way to the HQ canteen one morning, a few weeks after our return from honeymoon, when he waylaid me.

'Dawn! Just the woman I wanted to see! Where are you off to?'

'Canteen. I need coffee and cereal bars before I tackle my inbox.'

'OK. Get me a bag of wine gums, while you're there, then swing by my office on the way back.'

'Still can't quit the wine gums, then?'

'Never. Quitting smoking wasn't too bad, but now those pesky wine gums have enslaved me forever.'

'I'd better make it two bags, then.'

A few minutes later, I settled down in Andrew's office. The two of us often met for an informal chat about the various cases we were investigating, so I thought it was just routine. I was wrong.

'You've been after a DI post for a while now, Dawn, but nothing's come up.'

'I'm aware of that, Andrew. You don't want to see a grown woman cry, do you?'

'Absolutely not, which is why I called you in. I was just on the phone to an old mate of mine in West Midlands Police, who told me they're desperate for DIs to work in central Birmingham, so of course I mentioned you.'

'What did you say?'

'I told him you're a highly experienced DS, who aced her Inspector's Exams a while back and is frustrated because a suitable DI post hasn't come up. To cut to the chase, they're interested in taking you on secondment as a temporary DI, but you need to move fast.'

'Thank you, Andrew. That was so worth two bags of wine gums.'

'It will be, if you nail the secondment, which I'm sure you will. Do your time in Brum, then you'll be in a great position to jump into a substantive DI post when you come back. There's his name and number. Give him a ring.'

So that's how I came to be living near Rugby and working in

Birmingham, which is where my story really starts, this time round. Time to put my personal life to one side and get to work. It'll be a relief.

16 DUMMY RUN

I enjoyed my secondment from Day One. Right after my induction, I was assigned to a GBH case, the result of an unfortunate encounter between a stag party from out of town and a bunch of locals on the lash. The best man came off worst; a few ill-chosen words landed him in hospital.

All the officers gave me a warm welcome. They were seriously overworked and desperate for reinforcements to lighten the load. I expected some to imply that Leicester was an easy patch compared with Birmingham, and I had a lot to learn, but actually I found the opposite. My new colleagues were happy to ask for my advice, when they needed it.

One of the first to do so was DI Natasha Frantz, known as 'Tash', an experienced detective whom I had met briefly during my induction. I was surprised, but flattered, that she wanted my take on a missing person case she was leading. I was pushed for time and could have done without the interruption, but I was eager to please, so I resisted the urge to hurry her up as she explained the background.

Apparently the man in question was reported missing by his client the previous Thursday. He had been due to attend a business dinner the night before but didn't show up and wasn't answering his mobile. When he was also absent from work the next day and still couldn't be contacted, the client became concerned and sent one of his team to call at the man's apartment, where he got no answer. At this point the client called the police. I suggested it was a bit early to involve us, and Tash agreed, but apparently the caller was adamant that foul play was the only possible explanation for the no-show. Apparently the missing man was a paragon of virtue – completely reliable, professional and punctual to a fault. He would never have switched off his phone and failed to honour his business commitments. Tash wasn't so sure and was maxed out, so the case was a low priority for her, until the man's partner called the control room, late on Friday night, to report him missing. She was expecting him home several hours earlier, but he hadn't shown up.

'Odd that she didn't call it in on the Wednesday, Tash, when he first went missing.'

'I thought so too, at first, but they live in Cheshire, so he stays down here during the week, in a rented place, and only goes home at weekends.'

'Even so, you'd expect them to talk on the phone every day, or at least text each other. They wouldn't have had zero contact for over forty-eight hours. She should have realised earlier that something was up.'

'That's sweet, Dawn. Spot the newlywed! Seriously though, turns out they were having problems. They'd recently suffered a miscarriage and were estranged as a result. They weren't talking much.'

'Ah, I see. My friends Sophie and Tom had a miscarriage and it nearly split them up. So, have you taken statements?'

'Yes. My team interviewed the guy's client and drove up the M6 to see his partner in Cheshire – the posh end. Seven-figure house; clearly he's not short of cash.'

'And did the partner have an alibi for Wednesday night?'

'Yes, she did. She was at work in her office in central Manchester until 7.30pm. Before she left, she checked in with a group of colleagues to see if they needed help. We have contact details for all of them. Also, we checked CCTV and have footage of her boarding a train from Manchester Piccadilly just before 8pm and arriving at Wilmslow station half an hour later. By this time her partner had already failed to show for his business dinner in Birmingham.'

'OK. If you want my opinion, Tash, the most likely scenario is that this man has simply absconded. He's decided to call time on his relationship and he's not the dedicated professional his client thinks he is.'

'That was my take on it, too.'

'So why are you asking my opinion? Don't get me wrong; I'm always happy to help, but...'

'Because of this.'

Tash pushed a piece of paper across the desk.

'We looked our guy up on PNC and found details of this woman who spent a night in custody, accused of stalking him. Weirdly, she turned out to be his wife. The record says you were the investigating DS. Remember?'

'Do I ever? The missing man's name is Alex Pitulski. I was hoping I'd never hear that name again. It was one of the most frustrating cases I've ever worked on. I couldn't prove a thing, so I had to NFA it, but they were both up to something. Him and his wife.'

'So, does this change your opinion about what might have happened?'

'You know, I'm not sure it does. It could still be the right call – Pitulski might simply have jumped ship. He left his wife for his lover, and it looks as though things haven't worked out. This man has a low tolerance for anything in his life that's less than perfect, and probably sees a miscarriage as a massive failure, so he could just have had a meltdown and decided to start over.'

'Makes sense, I guess.'

'Having said that, I recommend you take a statement from his wife, Stella. Find out where she was last Wednesday night. She looks like butter wouldn't melt, but she's very smart. We suspected she was responsible for her husband's injuries...'

'What injuries?'

So I explained to Tash, who listened to me open-mouthed. I then promised to get some additional paperwork sent across from Leicestershire Police.

'Right. The last thing I need is extra work, but I'll definitely make sure we take a statement from the wife. Thanks, Dawn. You've given me more than I bargained for, but I'm grateful, I think.'

'You've seen she lives in Surrey.'

'Yes; lots of time wasted on the M40 and the M25. Deep joy.'

'You could get someone in Surrey Police to take the statement for you. Do you know anyone down there?'

'No, and I'm not going to delegate this one. Given what you've told me, I want my team to meet this Stella in person.'

That night at home, I poured two large glasses of Malbec and gave Alan a debrief on the case which seemed to be following me around. Alan, calm and rational as ever, agreed with me that it was probably just a domestic, and to be grateful someone else was in charge this time. The combination of wise words and red wine soothed me, and the next day I redirected my attention to my own case.

A couple of days later, Tash gave me an update. Her team had taken a statement from Stella, who was unsurprised that they knew all about the Leicestershire case. Apparently, she even congratulated the officers for being 'joined up'. Her opinion on Alex's disappearance was predictable; she was convinced he wouldn't hesitate to leave Jennifer, his new partner, when he had callously abandoned *her*, after so many years of marriage.

'Did she have an alibi, Tash?'

'Yes, she did. Guess what she was doing on the night Alex went missing?'

'I can't begin to imagine.'

'She was baking.'

'Of course, she was. Bake Off has a lot to answer for – but since when does a Victoria Sponge provide you with an alibi?'

'She ran out of eggs, so she went round to her neighbour to borrow some. My officers called round to see said neighbour, a very prim elderly lady who was terrified by the sight of them. She couldn't have lied to save her life.'

'OK. So Stella hates her ex-husband's guts, but she was over a hundred miles away when he went missing, so she couldn't be responsible. You have no evidence Alex was suicidal, although he was probably traumatised by his partner's miscarriage. He has no career, health or money issues...'

'Particularly not money, Dawn. He's a very wealthy guy.'

'I know. Which makes it much easier for him to leave his life behind than for us mere mortals, and it looks to me like that's what he's done.'

'I'm inclined to agree. Thanks for your advice, Dawn. We'll keep a watching brief on it, but we've got higher priorities to focus on, as you know.'

'Absolutely. Everyone is maxed out. I understand why you're so keen to take people like me on secondment.'

'It can be a mixed blessing, in my experience. Some secondments don't work out, but that's not the case with you. I'm glad to have you on board.'

'Thanks, Tash. Good to know.'

After that, I heard nothing more about Alex, which was fine by me, especially as I was soon just as busy as everyone else. I concluded my work on the stag night GBH case and was immediately assigned to a huge new investigation into a double murder, along with many of my fellow officers. The team was so big, we even had our own dedicated canteen. I'd never worked on such a massive case before, and the learning curve was very steep, but it was an amazing experience.

As winter gradually loosened its grip, life was working out well. Craig managed to pass his driving test, even though I hadn't spent as much time practising with him as I would have liked, due to the long hours spent at work. Alan and I had to plan our schedules carefully to ensure we got enough time together, which maybe doesn't sound very romantic to you, but it works for me. I like the fact that Alan diarises our downtime. It's one of the reasons why my second marriage is much more successful than my first. Alan makes an effort, whereas Fraser just expected everything to turn out perfectly, without him having to lift a finger. Fraser resented my professional ambitions, but Alan's my cheerleader, and his can-do attitude has rubbed off on my son, as well. Under his influence, Craig has started working hard at school, for the first time in living memory, and my dad has benefited too. Soon after we returned from honeymoon, Alan took him out for a beer, just the two of them. Shortly afterwards Dad joined a rambling club and started volunteering at his local hospital. He has been much happier ever since.

One evening, I was about to head home for some scheduled 'quality time' with my husband, when a call came through from Tash.

'Dawn. I need to show you something.'

My heart sank.

'OK. Will it take long?'

'A few minutes, that's all.'

I messaged Alan to say I would be late, then took the lift to the fifth floor, where I found Tash at her desk, munching on a Yorkie as she stared at her screen.

'They're not for girls, you know,' I quipped.

'No advertising campaign's going to dictate what chocolate I choose to eat – and what I need right now is full-on chocolate. No air bubbles or biscuits to get in the way.'

'That bad, huh?'

'Are you familiar with a flight of locks called Farmer's Bridge?'

'I'm getting a bad feeling about this...'

'The locks start at the National Indoor Arena and go downhill from there – know where I mean?'

'Yes, I do.'

'Great. Anyway, they've been closed for repairs over the winter, and the Canal and River Trust just drained one of them, to patch up some of the brickwork. It was one of their last jobs before reopening. I want to show you what they found, at the bottom. Come with me.'

Tash stood up and walked away. I followed glumly in her wake.

'You wouldn't believe what people throw in locks,' Tash continued through a mouthful of chocolate. 'Normally the Canal and River Trust would've just chucked this stuff away, I'm sure, but we got lucky. One of their team used to be in the job, before he retired to do good works on the waterways. He made the team hold onto both items and called his findings in to his old colleagues in the Evidence Review Team. Right, here we are.'

The glass windows of the room opened out onto the corridor. Someone had pulled the blinds to prevent passers-by from seeing what was inside. As Tash ushered me in, I immediately saw why. The room contained a large table, and on the table lay a body. My brain struggled to process what I was seeing; corpses belong in the mortuary, not a fifth-floor meeting room.

Tash laughed.

'Your face is a picture! Don't be shocked - take a closer look.'

As I approached the corpse, I realised why Tash was amused. What I had initially taken for a dead body was in fact a male mannequin; the type you see in the windows of Moss Bros. It was dressed in a long, thick overcoat, a sports jacket, a white shirt and a pair of dark trousers, all of which were liberally streaked with mud. The top two buttons of the shirt were open, revealing a glimpse of moulded collarbone and the top of what appeared to be some impressive pecs. Then I noticed something else.

'What d'you see?' asked Tash.

'Puncture holes – to the neck and chest.'

'All over the body, Dawn. We've checked.'

'So this wasn't a case of high jinks; a bunch of students on their way home from the pub, finding a shop dummy and chucking it in the canal for a laugh.'

'No. You're right. Someone wanted this sucker to drown and remain submerged.'

'Any idea why?'

'Not sure – but we do have an idea of *who*. Take a look at this.'

Tash handed me a black rucksack, of the type commonly used for toting one's laptop and lunch box between home and office. I have something similar myself.

'We found it in the same lock,' Tash explained. 'It was full of bricks.'

'Was there anything else in it?'

'We thought not, at first. As you can see, it's got loads of pockets, but they were all empty – except for one, tucked away right at the bottom. Even we nearly missed it. Here's what we found inside.'

Tash handed me a small square of plastic, the same size as a credit card. It was warped and stained from its long immersion in murky canal water, but nevertheless it was clearly identifiable as a loyalty card from a well-known airline. Its owner had Silver status, which undoubtedly bothered him greatly. I'm sure he was gunning for Gold and resented those who had already acquired it.

The name on the card was Alex Pitulski.

Poor Alan. He had other plans for that night, but instead he ended up discussing the latest twist in the canal case and listening to me complain that it would never let me go. He's a patient man, but finally even he had heard enough.

'You know what, Dawn? You need to make what Brendan describes as an "attitude adjustment". Stop moaning about this weird case and wishing it would go away. It sounds to me as though it's just getting going, so stick with it. You never know, it could end up being very challenging. It might even be the investigation which makes your career.'

'I'm not so sure about that, but I'm involved, whether I like it or not. I've got to help Tash, so I might as well try and enjoy it.'

'That's my girl. Now, what's your take on it?'

'It looks to me as though Alex tried to fake his own death, but conceal his identity at the same time, except he slipped up with the loyalty card. Why would he do that? It doesn't make sense.'

'You're right, it doesn't add up – yet. But you'll find the answer, Dawn.'

'I'm glad you're so confident of the outcome.'

'Always.'

'Do you reckon Alex had help with this mannequin business?'

'Quite possibly. He's unlikely to have received assistance from his ex-wife or his lover, although you can't rule them out.'

189

'Agreed. Anything's possible with this lot.'

'Equally, if he did have help, it could have come from an entirely different source. People you know nothing about. Who knows? You'll just have to cast your net wider. Right, enough of all that. I'm officially calling time on shop talk tonight. "And now for something completely different," as someone once said.'

'You got it.'

For the remainder of the evening, Alan took my mind off the canal case. It wasn't until the following day that my husband's words gave me an idea. I immediately rang Tash and told her I knew what to do next.

17 MUSIC THERAPY

I explained to Tash that there was another person involved in the canal case, whose name didn't appear in any of the paperwork I had shared with her, as it didn't seem relevant to include her in the investigation when we thought we were simply dealing with a missing person case. Also, unlike Stella and Jennifer, she was never suspected of any wrongdoing.

'So how was she involved, Dawn?'

'She was the one who found Stella, after the canal incident I told you about. She was on her own narrowboat when she came across Stella's boat drifting across the canal, with no one at the tiller. So she made like a good citizen, moored up and tied the other boat up as well. Then she took a look on board and found Stella passed out in the cabin.'

'What did she do next?'

'Revived Stella, searched for the missing Alex...'

'There's a theme developing here...'

'Certainly is. Anyway, she couldn't find him, for reasons you already know, so she agreed to accompany Stella back to Allenby Marina, just outside Leicester, from where she and Alex had hired the boat.'

'That was good of her. Was she heading in the same direction?'

'Sorry. I didn't explain properly. We're not talking about a convoy. Nancy – that's the woman's name – left her own boat behind and took Stella's back to base, as Stella had no idea how to steer a narrowboat. Her husband had been in the driving seat, and she had been working the locks.'

'Figures. This Nancy sounds like a very kind person. There aren't many people who'd go to such trouble for a total stranger.'

'She's not a kind person, as you'll discover. She's a tough cookie, but I don't think Stella gave her much choice. She was very distressed and there was no one else around to help. Anyway, Nancy made the return trip with Stella, which took about a day and a half, I understand.'

'So they had time to get to know each other.'

'Exactly. They're chalk and cheese, but they apparently bonded on some level. Must have done, because after I arrested her, Nancy immediately arranged legal representation for Stella from a fancy London lawyer.'

'You're kidding. How could she afford the legal fees? It must have cost a fortune.'

'Maybe, if you're a police officer, but it was small change to Nancy. You see, she's a musician. Quite a successful one.'

'What's her surname?'

'Parkinson.'

'Doesn't ring any bells.'

'Sorry. She doesn't use her real name. She's very protective of her privacy, although she has loosened up recently. Her stage name is The Baroness.'

'You're joking! My nephew's a huge fan. He follows her on Instagram and streams all her songs as soon as they're released. What on earth was a big star like her doing on the Grand Union Canal?'

'Escaping from her record company. She's an independent recording artist now and the funny thing is, she has stayed on the canals ever since. Or maybe it's not so surprising, given that she grew up on a narrowboat.'

'Ah. So we might have difficulty tracking her down.'

'No, we won't. I know precisely where she'll be. She has a permanent mooring in Allenby Marina.'

'The same place she returned to with Stella?'

'That's right. She hooked up with some guy she met there, who used to play in her band, and they set up a recording studio on site.'

'So you think we should go and interview her, in case she's still in touch with Stella and knows something that could help lead us to Alex?'

'It's a long shot, but it's worth a try. I don't think your team should interview her, though.'

'Why not?'

'Nancy can be difficult, and she's very clever. If she doesn't take to your officers, which is highly likely, there's a risk you'll get nothing out of her, and the whole thing will have been a waste of time. She doesn't trust the police, you see. Her dad had a few run-ins with us when she was little and taught her to see the rozzers as the enemy.'

'Sounds like we're on a hiding to nothing.'

'No, we're not. I have a solution. My colleague, DC Dave Langley, who worked with me on the original case, gets on quite well with her. He's a big fan of her music and they stayed in touch after the investigation concluded. I wouldn't say they're close, but I know he messages her sometimes and she always responds. I think she sees him as less of a police officer and more of a superfan, these days. If she'll talk to anyone, she'll take to Dave.'

'OK. Get DC Langley to take the statement, Dawn, and let's hope it leads to something. God knows I've drawn a blank everywhere else.'

'Don't get your hopes up, Tash. Nancy still might not talk, and even if she does, it's likely she doesn't know anything. She might not even be in touch with Stella anymore.'

As I expected, Dave was hugely excited at the prospect of interviewing Nancy again. Apparently he had just secured tickets for one of the intimate gigs which The Baroness prefers to perform these days. He was planning to take a bunch of his mates along, and Nancy had promised to have a beer with them backstage, after the performance.

As luck would have it, I was scheduled to go back to Leicester that week for a commendation ceremony for DI Gillespie, so I arranged to brief Dave in person at HQ before the ceremony. I asked him to try and set up the interview with Nancy for the same day, so I could hang around and do a debrief with him afterwards. It would be good to see him again and it would also give me the opportunity to catch up with my colleagues. I didn't want my home force to forget about me while I was on secondment, as it would make it more difficult to reintegrate on my return and secure that DI's promotion. I needed to maintain my relationships with my most influential colleagues, and this was a chance to get in their faces and remind them of my existence.

Later that day, Dave called me back and said Nancy had agreed to be interviewed on board her boat on the day of the ceremony. He reported that she sounded wary, which didn't surprise me, but at least we hadn't fallen at the first hurdle. So I emailed the people I wanted to meet and collated the briefing notes and photographs I needed to share with Dave.

When he walked into the canteen at HQ, I did a double take. As I told you last time, Dave's a big strapping lad, with a massive chest and huge guns, but he has always been a bit chubby round the middle, due to the typical detective's diet of doughnuts, burgers and the like. Now, though, the love handles were gone, and he was looking pretty buff. A couple of uniformed officers at the next table gave him a second look as he sat down, and I couldn't resist teasing him.

'Hi Dave. Good to see you. Tell me, since when did you become a babe magnet?'

'What d'you mean?'

'The women at the next table were checking you out as you walked over here.'

'I've always been a babe magnet, Dawn, but I guess you're referring to my impressive physique...'

'Indeed. Looks like you've been working out.'

'I have. The wife and I decided to shape up together, so I quit with the Krispy Kremes and joined a veteran rugby team. I go with her to yoga as well, when it fits in with my shifts.'

'You never struck me as the yoga type.'

'She had to drag me there the first time, but now I'm hooked. It's good for flexibility, which really helps with...'

'Woah! Too much information!'

'...with rugby, I was going to say. All the top players do yoga. Anyway, you're looking well, Dawn. I like your new haircut.'

'Thanks. Alan persuaded me to ditch my trademark ponytail.'

'I'll have to inform Nancy when I see her. Did I tell you she nicknamed you "Croydon Facelift?" She let it slip one time when she replied to one of my messages. She'll be disappointed she can't call you that anymore.'

'I'm sure she'll think up something equally flattering. Anyway, talking of Nancy, shall we get to it? We've got DI Gillespie's commendation ceremony in half an hour and I need to take you through a bunch of stuff.'

First I updated Dave on what Alex had been up to since we concluded the canal case to our mutual dissatisfaction. I explained that he had been living with Jennifer in Wilmslow, but the relationship had been under pressure due to a miscarriage. They had remained together, but Alex had been on assignment in Birmingham so was away three nights a week. Then I explained to Dave about Alex's disappearance, which was initially reported by his client, and the whereabouts of Jennifer and Stella on the night he went missing.

'I guess Jennifer could have jumped in the car after she got home, driven to Birmingham and bumped Alex off.'

'Unlikely, Dave, as he had already failed to show up for his business dinner by then.'

'I know. Just wishful thinking on my part.'

'Yeah, I can relate. I'd love to get shot of him too, believe me. Anyway, at this point I thought he had just done a runner, and the DI in charge of the case agreed. She was maxed out and the case dropped down the priority list – until we got given this lot by an ex-cop, who now works for the Canal and River Trust. Take a look and tell me what you think.'

I pushed a photograph across the table.

'This dude was found at the bottom of a lock in central Birmingham, when the Canal and River Trust drained it for repairs.'

'His clothes have seen better days, but he was probably quite smartly dressed before he drowned. Is that a puncture wound, just near his collarbone?'

'One of many. Here he is naked...'

'It's a bit early for a full frontal – oh, I see. More holes than a Swiss cheese.'

'Exactly. Whoever did this wanted to make sure he drowned – and remained permanently submerged. We also found this, in the same lock. It was full of bricks.'

I showed Dave the photo of the rucksack.

'Looks a bit like yours, Dawn. Was there anything in it?'

'Just this. We nearly missed it, as the bag has so many pockets. You're right, it is similar to mine, and I'm always losing things, then finding them months later in some obscure pocket or other.'

'A frequent flyer reward card. Silver status. I bet its owner wasn't happy about that. Sees himself as a Gold status guy.'

'Funny – that's what I thought, when I saw the name on it.'

'So it looks as though the bag belongs to our friend Alex. It would appear he meant to empty the bag but overlooked the loyalty card.'

'That's my take on it too, Dave.'

'And in the same lock, we find a mannequin full of holes, which would indicate an attempt to stage a death. The question is, are the two items related?'

'I'm assuming so, for the moment.'

'They might not be. People ditch all kinds of stuff in the canals, particularly in urban areas. But if they are, the next question is – who was the intended audience for this little charade? Someone was meant to see it, I'm sure.'

'Probably, but DI Frantz and her team are looking into all that. Just focus on the interview with Nancy and leave the rest to them. You've got enough to do here, and I've already taken up half a day you don't have to spare.'

'Sorry, Dawn. I can't help myself. I have to think these things through.'

'I know. I'm the same.'

'I reckon the answer will be found in the area around that lock – not from an interview with someone who's probably got nothing to do with all this.'

'I know; it's a long shot – but in my experience they do occasionally pay off.'

'It's worth a try, I agree, and there are plenty worse tasks on my to-do list than interviewing Nancy Parkinson. Can I take these photos to show her?'

'Be my guest. You can tell her everything I just told you. Find out if she has been in contact with Stella recently and, if so, what they talked about.'

'I know what questions to ask, Dawn.'

'Sorry. I'm micro-managing as usual, and it's time for the commendation ceremony. Good luck, Dave – and thanks for helping me out. Give me a ring later when you're ready for our de-brief.'

After the ceremony, I stood in line to congratulate Andrew Gillespie and thank him for recommending me for the secondment.

'Nothing to thank me for. I've received positive reports about the way you've fitted in and the quality of your work. DI Frantz, in particular, was very complimentary. She's a good person to know, Dawn. Extremely well connected.'

'So if Tash has been in touch, you probably know that the weird canal case has raised its ugly head again.'

'Yes; that's an odd one. It'll probably come to nothing, in my view, but at least it has put you on Tash's radar.'

I spent the next few hours drinking endless coffees and catching up with my colleagues, including Fraser, my ex. It was quite satisfying to be able to tell him how well Craig was doing at school although, predictably, he gave the school full credit for his son's improvement, rather than admit the positive influence of my new husband. Once I would have pressed the point, but now I was happy to let it go and allow him to delude himself.

I was just running out of people to distract from their work, when the call came in from Dave. He was on his way back and was gasping for a cup of tea, so I agreed to get the drinks in and meet him in the canteen.

'So I guess Nancy didn't make you a brew?'

'No. She's not what you'd call a perfect hostess. Her other half might have done, but he was in the recording studio.'

'How did it go?'

'She wasn't that friendly at first. In fact, she was quite off with me, which I found surprising, given I'm such a big fan and we'd messaged each other and the like. Anyway, I told her about Alex going missing in Birmingham, and it turns out she already knew. Stella had told her about it and described her interview with the police. They don't speak that often, but they do tell each other about big stuff, like this. Then she asked me why I was involved, and I explained about your secondment. I said I was helping you out by doing the interview, as I was closer to Allenby Marina than you.'

'Let's cut to the chase. Did she tell you anything new?'

'Not a thing. She doesn't know any more than we do.'

'Sorry, Dave. Looks like I've wasted half a day of your time.'

'Hang on a minute; I haven't finished. It wasn't so much what she said. It was how she reacted, once I showed her the photographs. She catches on quick, as you know, so when she saw the image of the mannequin full of holes, and I said it was found submerged in a lock, she immediately responded, "So someone faked their own death. What's that got to do with me?" Then, when I shared the pictures of the bag, and the card with Alex's name on it, her voice went all shaky and she whispered, "Are you saying it was Alex who faked his own death? Made it look as though he'd drowned in a lock?" So I said that was our theory, and immediately she burst into tears.'

'Now there's a surprise. I wouldn't have thought Nancy did tears.'

'Nor me. It was the last thing I expected. I asked her why she was so upset, and she didn't answer for a bit. When she finally calmed down, she apologised. Said she was just upset for Stella, as she has already been through so much.'

'So she was crying for her not very close friend, with whom she's not in frequent contact?'

'I know. It does sound odd, Dawn, when you put it like that. Her point was that Alex had cheated on Stella, tried to ruin her business and driven a wedge between her and her kids. Stella had lost her home and most of her friends, and Nancy interpreted this latest move as a sign that Alex still wasn't done with her.'

'She could be right, but I still don't see why she was crying. It's a bit of an overreaction.'

'I agree. Anyway, she reckons Alex is up to no good. She said something along the lines of, "One thing's for sure. Alex has faked his own death for a reason. He wants Jennifer and Stella to think he's out of the picture, so he can return when they least expect it, and do something much worse. You rozzers need to be on your guard." Then she said we were no match for people like Alex. That we couldn't stop him from doing what he wanted and could only pick up the pieces afterwards. Same old, same old.'

'Still doesn't explain why she was so upset.'

'I know – but here's the thing. After she had stopped crying, she was much friendlier. She tried to laugh the whole thing off and blame it on her age. According to her, being a woman in your mid-forties sucks. Your hormones are all over the place and you cry and shout for the most trivial reasons.'

'She's got a point, Dave. It still doesn't add up, but I'll give it some thought. Anything else?'

'Don't think so, except I now know a lot more about the peri-menopause than I ever wanted. Too much information, as you said earlier.'

'Don't knock it, Dave. Forewarned is forearmed. I hope I haven't blown your chances of the backstage meet and greet with your friends, after her gig?'

'Not at all. She was positively matey, by the time I left.'

'Talking of which, I have to go. Email me the recording, will you?'

'Sure thing.'

'Thanks for doing the interview, Dave.'

'No problem. I don't feel like I've helped much.'

'Who knows? But thanks, anyway. I owe you one.'

After that, the investigation stalled. Tash's team did a thorough search of the surrounding area, but it yielded no results. Her officers returned to Wilmslow for another chat with Jennifer, who was making arrangements to relocate nearer her office in central Manchester. They probed further into Jennifer's movements after she returned home on the night of Alex's disappearance, whereupon Jennifer produced her trump card. She didn't think of it when they interviewed her before, as she was in pieces back then, but she thought she had the recordings from the home security cameras. The officers were lucky they caught her before she moved out, as she was planning to delete them as soon as she left. She scrolled through an app on her phone and quickly located the recordings from the evening Alex went missing. A review of the images taken throughout the night clearly showed her car hadn't moved since she drove back from the station just after 8.30pm and there was no record of anyone entering or leaving the house after she returned home. So the officers returned to Birmingham empty-handed, and Tash ran out of options.

Meanwhile I passed on the recording of Dave's interview with Nancy and focused on the double murder investigation. My team was tasked with following up the thousands of calls and messages from members of the public, each claiming to have a lead which would give us the breakthrough we needed. It's a painstaking task, as I'm sure you can imagine. As usual in high-profile cases like this, a large number of calls were from so-called futurists who claimed they could lead us to the perpetrators and the weapons they used. I've always wondered why these prophets don't come forward earlier and warn us about the crime before it is committed. It would make our lives so much easier.

Anyway, I was on my way back from lunch when it happened. The weather was wet and cold, and my team had found nothing of interest that morning, so I had bought myself a wodge of cake which I planned to eat al desko after my sandwich. I'm normally quite disciplined, as you know, but this was a day for comfort food, not cereal bars.

As I walked into HQ reception, the receptionist called me over.

'DI Burrows! I was just about to phone you. There's someone here to see you.'

'I'm not expecting anyone. Let me check my diary.'

'He hasn't got an appointment, but he says it's urgent.'

The receptionist pointed towards the far corner of reception, furthest away from the window, where a tall, dark haired man was seated, his face hidden behind a copy of Police magazine. He was dressed in jeans, a black leather jacket and a white T-shirt. The pages of the magazine trembled as he turned them.

'If you haven't got time to talk to him, I'd be happy to conduct an in-depth interview,' joked the receptionist.

'Sorry, I'm going to have to disappoint you.'

'Story of my life.'

As I approached my unscheduled visitor, he lowered the magazine and I saw what she meant. He was very good looking, in a craggy, faded rock star kind of way. If there were a mid-point between Harry Styles and Keith

Richards, that's where he'd sit. I might have been a newly married police officer, but I could still look. I stopped beside his chair held out my hand.

'Good afternoon. I'm DI Burrows.'

The man leapt to his feet, fizzing with nervous energy.

'DI Burrows. Thank you for agreeing to see me.'

'I haven't agreed to anything. I don't normally see people without an appointment.'

'I understand, but I'd be grateful if you could make an exception in my case.'

Despite trying his best to sound assertive, the man couldn't hide his agitation, nor was he able to look me in the eye. Instead he kept glancing over my shoulder at the main entrance.

'Are you expecting someone?' I asked.

His voice dropped to a whisper. 'Is there somewhere private we can talk? An interview room or something? Please, Inspector.'

Clearly this man was not a time waster. I know a vulnerable adult when I see one.

'Come with me.'

THE OTHER SIDE

18 FREEDOM PASS

I know you don't want to hear this, but those women have lied to you, so now I'm giving you the chance to open your mind and discover the truth. I have to say I don't relish the task. I could be doing something much more interesting and lucrative, but I feel I owe it to you. In return, all I ask is that you hear me out.

After I divorced Stella and moved in with Jennifer, we were very happy. I'm sure Jen told you we weren't, but that woman suffers from what I believe psychologists call 'hindsight bias'. Her memory of our life together has been distorted by the outcome, but mine has not, and I plan to be honest with you.

I remember very clearly the wonderful life I created for us. Jennifer wanted for nothing. I bought us a stunning house in Wilmslow, just south of Manchester. It's one of the most prestigious towns in the country, part of the famous 'Cheshire Golden Triangle'. Jennifer could never have lived in a place like that, had she not been with me. We took luxury holidays in stunning locations like The Maldives and she had a wardrobe full of designer clothes. She would never have attained that lifestyle, had she stayed with boring old Stefan in his terraced house in Didsbury.

However, I don't want you to think our happiness was purely based on material possessions. The most important thing you should know is – we were devoted to each other. After what Stella did to me on our canal holiday, I was no longer torn between her and Jennifer. I'm sure that comes as no surprise. What's more, Jen stood by me, helped me gain an element of revenge and rebuild my life, so I loved her more every day, and I know that devotion was obvious to the new circle of friends we acquired in Wilmslow. At every dinner party we attended, at least one of the men would tease me for being 'loved up', and I could tell the women were all jealous of Jen. Some of them hinted they would happily take her place, but they had no chance. I was absolutely committed to my new partner.

Only one thing was missing. I desperately wanted a child with Jen. After all, it's the ultimate pledge, isn't it? Way stronger than walking up the aisle and making a vow before God, whoever he might be. Anyway, I needed Jen to prove to me that she was ready to make that commitment. When she tried to put me off I was disappointed, but not discouraged, as I knew it was what she really wanted. After all, what woman doesn't want to have children with the man she loves? So I persisted and soon persuaded her to get on board with the idea. She probably made out I put pressure on her, but I didn't. She just needed time to get her head around being a mother. Once she did fall pregnant, she was delighted, and I rewarded her by being a solicitous father-to-be. After all, I had been through it all before – twice. I knew what to do and which pitfalls to avoid, so I made sure she received the benefit of my experience. Mostly she was grateful, but occasionally she didn't realise what was good for her, so I had to put her right.

The high heels had to go, for a start. If Jen had tripped and fallen, she could have hurt the baby, so I bought her a selection of smart, flat shoes. That was a minor issue, though, compared with finding out the sex of our baby. Jen suggested we might want it to be a 'surprise'. How utterly ridiculous. As a PR professional and consummate planner, she should have recognised the value of knowing in advance. How else were we supposed to decorate the nursery, purchase appropriate baby clothes and put the child down for the right schools? When I pointed this out, she immediately saw sense, and when we went for our next scan, we were told we were having a boy.

I know Jen would have been happy either way, but for me a boy was the right result. I longed for another son. I promised I would be honest with you, so I admit it probably had something to do with my son Hugo coming out. I've got nothing against gay men, but I wanted Jen to give birth to a son who was straight and would one day have children of his own.

Another area where Jen needed a steer in the right direction was work. Thankfully she was fit and healthy in the early stages of her pregnancy, but she continued pulling the same long hours, despite me telling her repeatedly that she needed to cut back. It all came to a head one evening at home. She was on the phone to her boss for hours, when she should have been resting. I was watching TV, trying not to get wound up, but eventually it got too much, so I marched into her study, grabbed the phone and gave her boss a right telling off. Jen wasn't very pleased, but she should have been grateful. I was only doing it for her own good.

After that, I checked her diary and picked a day when she was out of the office hosting a PR event. Then I paid a call on her boss and told her to assign the evening work to someone else. I didn't put it quite like that at the time; I was more forceful. Anyway, whatever I said, it worked. Jen never found out I had an impromptu meeting with her immediate superior, but she did notice her diary was cleared of all evening engagements. It probably didn't do her career much good, but who cares? PR isn't the most prestigious line of work, we didn't need the money and she was going to quit anyway, after the baby was born. That was my plan. My experience with Stella had taught me careers and motherhood don't mix. Stella tried to carry on working, but it was a disaster. All she did was delay the inevitable. This 'having it all' business is a myth perpetrated by the media. Mothers must be at home with their children. It's as simple as that.

Looking back, I don't think Jen had got the memo about the full implications of being a mother. For one thing, she was still trying to look hot, which was inappropriate. Unlike Stella, she had kept her figure, so she could still fit into her bodycon dresses and leather leggings, but it was time for her to switch to a classier, more mature look. After all, she had got her man, and she no longer went clubbing in Manchester. Even though she wasn't showing, the disco gear had to go. It wasn't suitable for the dinner parties we attended. A few shopping trips and discussions later, it was all sorted. The charity shops had a field day.

Next I turned my attention to Jen's skills as a hostess, which were appalling. She could be entertaining company, but too often she tried to be the centre of attention, which was just embarrassing. Also, unlike the other women, she couldn't cook. At first I hired caterers and tried to laugh it off, but it didn't work; not in the circles we frequented. Some of the wives had much more demanding careers than Jennifer's but were excellent cooks. Why couldn't she be like them? How hard can it be? Even Stella was fairly competent in the kitchen. So I bought a pile of cookery books and told Jen to start practising. Some of the dishes she concocted were edible, although hardly dinner party standard, and many of her attempts ended in abject failure. I did sometimes lose my temper at her ineptitude and toss some plates around, but that was only to be expected. She just wasn't trying.

Anyway, a few stains on our kitchen walls were no big deal. I had given Jennifer free rein to decorate and style the house as she wished, plus a budget to match, so she could easily repair the damage. She was better at interior design than cordon bleu, which is just as well, given the money she spent. I should have bought shares in Farrow and Ball.

So we had a few domestic issues. Who doesn't? I know lots of men who let these squabbles spill over into the bedroom; but not me. I always made sure things stayed exciting in there, no matter what was going on outside. I know women love that 'Fifty Shades of Grey' stuff and I was more than happy to oblige, although I had to tone things down a bit, as she was pregnant. I bet she told you it was too much, didn't she? That's the hindsight bias again. I didn't hear her complain at the time, and she knew what she was getting into, when we got together. She was perfectly well aware that I was passionate and dynamic. In fact she loved me for it. She dumped that wimp Stefan as soon as we hooked up, because she preferred what I had to offer, and if I occasionally overstepped the mark, those incidents were outweighed by my considerate, romantic gestures. The trouble was that Jen got used to all the wonderful things I did for her. She began to take them – and me – for granted. I started to feel as if I couldn't do anything right.

Take the car, for instance. I bought her a top of the range SUV, to keep her and the baby safe, and all I got in return was a barbed comment about it being 'dull'. At dinner parties I was always sociable, but if I so much as exchanged a few sentences with another woman, I was accused of 'flirting'. Even though I was happy about the baby, I began to feel undervalued. Trapped, even. I was working hard and earning good money, but nothing I did or said met with her approval.

When we moved in together, I agreed only to take on assignments which allowed me to return home every night, which basically confined me to the north west. At first this worked well, as I had spent five years living in hotels whilst directing the Leviathan programme and I enjoyed sleeping in my own bed. After a while, though, I longed for the pressure release valve; a night on my own in a hotel room, with time to myself. I was also missing out on some very lucrative offers; not just consultancy projects, but invitations to speak at international conferences. I reflected on this and concluded I hadn't spent decades building my profile as one of the most respected programme directors in Europe to let my career stagnate for domestic reasons. By restricting myself to the north west, I was slowly strangling my professional life to death, so it was no longer appropriate to keep my promise to Jennifer.

Besides, that woman was costing me a fortune. I've already told you about the clothes, the holidays, the cars and the rampant interior design. Someone had to pay for all this, and her salary wouldn't have covered the cost of our curtains. So you see, I had no choice but to accept the opportunities I was offered elsewhere in the UK – and overseas. In a way, it was Jennifer's fault.

The European conferences were a revelation. The other men on the podium were so stylish and laid back, particularly my Danish and Dutch counterparts. I always thought I looked the business at work, suited and booted in my bespoke Gieves and Hawkes, but their example led me to conclude it was time to loosen up and try a new image, so I bought a wardrobe full of younger, trendier clothes and had an edgy haircut. I expected Jen to love my new look, but she appeared unimpressed, and I concluded she felt threatened. Her waistline was finally starting to thicken from the pregnancy, whilst I was looking fit and working out. No wonder she felt insecure.

Inevitably, the female delegates on the conference circuit noticed how good I looked. I admit I wasn't always a saint, while I was away, but you can hardly blame me. As a speaker, you're very visible, and women have a good excuse to approach you afterwards, to tell you how much they enjoyed your presentation. It's there for the taking, and chances are you're never going to see that woman again. She wants it to be a one-night gig, same as you.

Even so, I took precautions. I resolved only to conduct my extra-curricular activities overseas, as I didn't want to risk Jen finding out, even though it was highly unlikely any of these women would attempt to contact me. When Imogen next came to stay, she commented that my phone was always in my back pocket, just like it used to be when I was with her mother. Can you believe it? My own daughter, having a go at me and siding with my partner. I think it's known as the 'sisterhood'.

Talking of female solidarity, I checked Jen's browsing history one evening, as normal. She never deletes it and I find it useful to know what she has been up to online. On this particular occasion, I discovered Stella's website listed among the usual interior design and cookery sites. I found it amusing to think my partner was still insecure about my ex-wife, even after everything that had happened. With hindsight, I should have given more thought to Jen's motives, but at the time I was too busy to bother. It was also unwise to boast about how I had wrecked Stella's business. I misjudged the situation and thought – wrongly, as it turned out – that Jen would view my actions as proof of my loyalty to her. I believed it would make her feel less insecure to discover how much I hated my ex and still wanted revenge. For the same reason, I expected her to be pleased I had put a stop to Stella's new relationship. I imagined she would feel grateful I harboured no latent feelings for my ex-wife, but I was wrong. She wasn't remotely grateful, as I later found out.

With the benefit of hindsight, Jennifer is without doubt the most poisonous, ungrateful woman I have ever met. She puts even Stella in the shade. At the time, though, I still thought we were happy. The pregnancy was progressing well, and I had been offered a highly remunerative contract in Birmingham. The day rate was commensurate with my experience and the proposed duration was eighteen months, which would take my finances to another level. However, it was a tough gig and would mean long hours. I would be required to stay over in the city three nights a week, so I could put in the necessary effort and attend some evening engagements. I expected Jennifer to object to the long-term absence, but she was unexpectedly cool with it, so I rented a chic penthouse apartment and got to work.

At first we benefited from some time apart. It eased the tension between us, and we even enjoyed something of a second honeymoon, although of course we weren't married. I didn't play away too often, although I did sometimes feel the need for company in my Birmingham penthouse. I remained careful, though. I resolved I would never risk a local indiscretion and I stuck to it, with one exception. When I broke my self-imposed rule, I paid the price. That one small slip-up cost me everything.

This is how it happened. One of the wives on our dinner party circuit made her interest in me very clear. She was a highly successful lawyer, and her professional status was part of the attraction. She was a lot older than Jen, but incredibly hot. Clearly she was used to getting what she wanted, and I wasn't inclined to turn her down. We had already spent a few memorable afternoons in a country house hotel when she called me up one morning while I was working from home. A meeting had been cancelled, she had some time to spare and would like to pay me a visit. Jen was in her office in Manchester, so I agreed. How was I to know Jen would feel ill and come home early? She had never done that before.

Fortunately my lawyer friend had left by the time Jen arrived, so there was no unpleasant encounter. Even so, Jen picked up on something. She commented on the two coffee mugs on the kitchen counter and refused to accept my perfectly reasonable explanation that Steven, my financial advisor, had stopped by. To this day, I have no idea what made her doubt me, but women have a sixth sense for these things. I only wish I had not made coffee for that lawyer, afterwards. If she had left straight away, everything would have turned out differently.

Of course, I denied everything, and Jen had no proof, but even so, she overreacted massively. I put it down to her hormones. She marched into the bathroom and started packing up her cosmetics, to give the impression she was going to leave. I doubt she would ever have gone through with it, but nevertheless I was determined to stop her. She was the mother of my child, after all. I was still devoted to her.

I took hold of the cosmetics bag she had in her hand, to try and get her to stop packing and talk to me. Devastatingly, she chose that very moment to let go of the bag and lost her balance. She toppled backwards into the bathtub, and that minor accident caused her to lose the baby. I frantically called for an ambulance, which arrived just minutes later and conveyed us to hospital, where the staff did their best to save our son, but it was no good. We lost our little boy.

Afterwards, I was broken, but still I focused all my attention on Jennifer and her needs. I gently nursed her back to health, making sure she had the right food to aid her recovery and seeing she got plenty of rest, but she never once asked how I was feeling. It was all about her; my pain meant nothing, and she took my care for granted. Even when I bought her a beautiful remembrance bracelet, she didn't say 'thank you' or react in any way. I longed to return to Birmingham, so I could grieve and heal on my own. Before I left, though, I decided to try once more to get through to her. I bought a memorial tree for us to plant together in the garden, so we could share our grief. I carefully dug the hole, positioned the tree and tamped down the earth, while all the time she just stared into the middle distance, not saying a word. Afterwards, as we stood side by side, she never even took my hand, despite all the effort I had made to comfort her.

Suddenly it was all too much. The resentment I felt at having my grief ignored boiled over into a wave of rage, but I didn't lash out. I just told her, very quietly, that I blamed her for the loss of our baby. Now I know that's a cruel thing to say, and I could excuse myself by insisting I was overcome by anger and didn't mean it, but I'm too honest for that. The truth is, I did blame Jennifer. If she hadn't pretended to leave, we would still have our baby, and our relationship. It was all her fault.

After that, I couldn't return to Birmingham quickly enough. Even though my clients had been sympathetic and supportive, they were glad to have me back, as the programme had fallen behind schedule without me there to direct it. So I immersed myself in work and tried to forget what had happened. At night, I usually chose my own company. Often I would sit alone in a bar, drinking wine and watching the city lights dance in the coal-black waters of the canal outside. That's what I was doing on the night everything changed.

As I turned away from the window and reached for my wallet to buy myself another drink, I spotted a tall man walking towards my table. Smartly dressed in a camel coat, unbuttoned to reveal a sharp suit, there was something about him which reminded me of an old-style matinée idol. He seemed to belong in a different age. To my surprise, he greeted me by name, then introduced himself as Giles. I smiled politely while I wracked my brains, trying to recall how we knew each other and where we had last met. As I'm sure you appreciate, I meet a lot of new people and can't be expected to remember them all. Did this Giles work for my current client, or had he perhaps heard me speak at a conference? Perhaps we had met at a corporate event, or on a previous assignment? Turns out none of these explanations was correct.

Giles got straight to the point. He revealed he had been commissioned by a former associate, whom he wouldn't name, to threaten and intimidate me. Then he told me to put my wallet away and offered to buy me a drink. He said I would need it. Naturally I thought he was a lunatic and was about to make my escape while he was at the bar, but something made me stop and hear him out. After all, if he knew my name, it was likely he had more information about me, so I decided I had better find out what was on his mind. I reached for my phone and switched on the voice memo function, figuring it wouldn't hurt to keep a record of the conversation, however bizarre it turned out to be. Moments later Giles returned with a large glass of Merlot for me, and a Scotch for him. He shrugged off his camel coat, folded it carefully onto the bench seat opposite me, then sat down beside it.

'You probably think me deranged, Alex. I would, in your place.'

'The thought had occurred to me, but I'm trying to keep an open mind. Please explain why you've been asked to threaten me, Giles, and by whom.'

'As I said before, I decline to name the person who approached me. However, I will tell you who put him up to it.'

'Go on...'

'It was your ex-wife. Apparently she and your current partner both want you out of their lives, but they think you might need some encouragement to go quietly, as it were. Apparently you haven't played nice with these two ladies.'

'Is that so, Giles? Let me tell you, the opposite is true. In fact, allow me to show you what my ex-wife did to me.'

So I did. Giles took a long look.

'I see. So I would be right in saying that relations between you and your ex are not exactly cordial.'

'Correct.'

'Which, I imagine, is why she sought help from someone like me. She intends to make sure you do not try and take revenge.'

'What d'you mean, "someone like me"? Who are you, anyway?'

'Like you, Alex, I am a successful businessman. The head of a network of profitable enterprises run by men who can make sure you stay away from these ladies forever. Men you do not want to cross.'

'A criminal network, in other words.'

'I'd prefer it if you didn't refer to it in that way.'

'Tough. Just tell me how my ex-wife – and my partner – got involved with this associate of yours. Neither of them has any criminal connections. They lead affluent, sheltered lives...'

'That's as may be. I can't answer that question and I'd appreciate it if you would stop using the word "criminal". It makes my operation sound like a blunt instrument, when in reality it's much more subtle. If that weren't the case, I wouldn't be here speaking to you.'

'What are you talking about?'

'A lesser man would either have refused the assignment or done as instructed and moved on.'

'So why are you here?'

'I have researched your background, Alex, and I think we can help each other. We're two very successful men with a lot in common.'

'I need another drink, Giles. When I come back from the bar, I want you to tell me what is going on. Agreed?'

'Absolutely. A large Lagavulin, if you would be so kind.'

As I waited for the drinks, I stuck my hands in my pockets, trying in vain to stop them from shaking. Despite the old-fashioned courtesy, I could tell Giles wasn't bluffing. I had never encountered anyone like him before. I felt as though I had stepped into a parallel universe where the rules were subtly different, and I didn't understand them, but it wasn't fear which was making my hands shake. It was anger. I couldn't believe Stella and Jen had conspired against me. Clearly they thought they were cleverer than me, but I would prove them wrong.

'Thank you, Alex. Cheers. Now while I drink this fine whisky, let me tell you about this associate of mine. He is essentially a weak man who, for various reasons, thinks I am in his debt and can be controlled. He is wrong about that, but I need a way of bringing him to heel. Meanwhile, you are in a similar position. These two ladies think they can get you to run off with your tail between your legs, but I don't believe you're that sort of man.'

'Indeed not. I won't allow myself to be intimidated by anyone, especially not by them.'

'That's what I thought, and I believe them to be less ruthless than you, which gives you the advantage. My associate had clearly received instructions from your two ladies that you should not come to any physical harm.'

'That's big of them. I always knew they had a caring side.'

'Exactly; and we can both use it to our mutual advantage.'

'How?'

'Unlike us, my associate is prone to feelings of guilt. If he were to think we had eliminated you, as it were, I would have him permanently under my control, as he would be devastated by what he had done, and I would be able to prove he instigated the encounter. Like you, I recorded our conversation.'

Giles stared pointedly at my phone.

'It's fine, Alex. I don't blame you for taking precautions. I can easily dispose of your phone if we do not reach an agreement, but I anticipate we will. You see, you stand to benefit, just like I do. Think about it. If your two ladies think they got more than they bargained for, and believe they're jointly responsible for your death, they will keep their heads down forever. In my experience, guilt and fear do powerful things to nice people, while you and I are immune to it, which gives us the upper hand.'

'I see, I think. Taking the long view, if they thought I was gone forever, it would give me the element of surprise...'

'Precisely. You would be able to exact revenge, at a time of your choosing.'

'Tell me what you've got in mind.'

'Gladly. We have identified a location for the supposedly non-violent encounter requested by my associate. Not far from here is a flight of locks called Farmer's Bridge. You know the locks well, as you walk past them every day on your way to and from work. It's not the most direct route, but I can see you like to stay in shape, so I guess you want to boost your daily step count. Anyway, as you know, the towpath is generally deserted after dark. You have probably also noticed a block of flats halfway down, on the opposite side of the road. The top floor apartments have a partial view of one of the locks and would provide an excellent vantage point from where our associate can observe proceedings.'

So I've clearly been under observation for some time. A bead of sweat traces its way down my back, but I tell myself to stay cool and keep my voice steady.

'I imagine he requires proof that you've kept your promise.'

'Indeed he does; and we want him to witness what's going on. So we will conduct the encounter in such a way that it begins as agreed, but soon spirals out of control. What our associate will see, through his night vision goggles, is you refusing to co-operate, fighting back and getting stabbed repeatedly. He will then watch in horror as your body and belongings are disposed of in the lock, where they immediately sink without trace.'

'And how, precisely, will you make this happen, whilst I remain unharmed? The last part is quite important to me, as I'm sure you can appreciate.'

'We will use a dummy, dressed like you but riddled with holes, plus a laptop bag similar to the one you have with you tonight. After the charade is complete, my colleagues will depart swiftly, and you will remain concealed until our horrified associate has left his vantage point and departed the scene. You will then be free to go forth and live the rest of your life in peace and freedom.'

'Giles, I've got a lot of questions, plus some major concerns.'

'We'll need to work on the detail, I admit. That's just an outline, Alex. Let's discuss your major concerns first. Might as well get them out of the way.'

'OK. If I go through with this, I stand to lose out on a lot of money. I'm contracted for over a year on my current assignment, which represents a huge sum which I will fail to earn if I go missing.'

'Money first, Alex. I see where your priorities are, and I can relate, but like I said before, I've done my research. I know you're a very wealthy man. Your ex-wife and your current partner have no idea how rich you are, do they? Nest eggs have been squirrelled away without their knowledge. You know you can afford to do this – and pay me a reasonable fee for making it happen.'

'There's always the risk they'll track me down...'

'Come on, Alex. How likely are they to come looking for you when they know you're dead and believe they were responsible? They'll be torn apart by guilt, and by the fear of being found out. Perhaps a part of them will feel relieved to be shot of you, but they will even feel guilty about that. What they won't be doing is playing detective.'

'If you get it right, I imagine they might respond like that...'

'What do you mean, "if you get it right"? My men do not make mistakes, Alex. They're professionals, who successfully undertake far more complex tasks than this.'

'Then what about my children? I have two grown-up children, as I'm sure you found out from your extensive research. What am I supposed to tell them?'

'That's your call, Alex, but personally I'd leave it to your ex-wife. Let her explain why you're out of the picture. I'm sure she will think of something; she appears quite resourceful. Later, when you return, you will be able to expose her as a liar and a charlatan. You can tell them how she put you in mortal danger from a gang of dangerous and ruthless men. My hunch is they won't want much to do with Mummy after that. Sure, they'll have some short-term pain, but as you said, they're grown-ups. You can make it up to them afterwards. Make a fresh start.'

Suddenly I feel exhausted. A fresh start sounds perfect. Like some businesses I have worked with, my life has gone toxic, and drastic action is my only option.

'So I suppose your name isn't Giles?'

'What do you think? My name is of no consequence, Alex, and neither are the names of my colleagues, some of whom you will meet. After this is over, you'll never see any of us again.'

'What if I say no?'

'Then you will find you can't make such a clean break, but I don't know why we are even having this conversation. You have already made up your mind, Alex. I can tell.'

'You're wrong, Giles. I'm not on board yet. I need a lot more detail first.'

'Fair enough. I suppose I can't expect a man of your calibre to be a pushover. Look, here's what we'll do. I'll set up a follow-on meeting and bring with me the colleagues I propose to involve. The location will be more intimate than this; I'll book a private dining room in another pub near here, so we can talk freely, and we'll go through everything with a fine toothcomb. How does that sound?'

I picked up my phone, switched off the recording and entered the agreed date in my diary. Then Giles stood up and placed his elegant camel coat around his shoulders, as though he was about to sashay down the catwalk in Milan. He left abruptly, without another word.

19 GAME ON

After my split from Stella, I vowed never again to mix love and money, and I'm glad I stuck to it. The mortgage on the Wilmslow house was in my name only, and Jennifer and I had separate bank accounts. The arrangement suited her, as it allowed her to maintain her delusions of independence, but it was even more beneficial to me. It meant she never found out about the substantial cash reserves I had kept hidden from Stella – and from the divorce lawyers. I imagine you don't approve but trust me when I tell you anyone else in my position would have done the same thing.

Most of this wealth was lodged in offshore bank accounts and was managed on my behalf by a small number of highly experienced and very creative financial advisors, whose existence I concealed from Jennifer. The only advisor she knew about was Steven, my local accountant. Unlike the others, he played with a straight bat, which suited my purposes perfectly.

After my meeting with Giles, I contacted Steven and told him I was planning to relocate, but Jennifer would remain in the Wilmslow house for the time being. When she was ready to move out, she would be in touch to hand over the keys. Once she had done so, Steven was to sell the property and contents, pay off the outstanding mortgage and transfer the balance into one of my offshore accounts. I emphasised the importance of confidentiality, but I really needn't have bothered. Steven is a man of impeccable integrity and wouldn't dream of discussing my financial affairs with anyone, not even my partner.

A week later I reconvened with Giles in the private dining room. This time, he was accompanied by two colleagues; a human tank with a buzzcut, improbably named Sebastian, plus a wiry, weasel-faced individual called Barnaby. I wondered if their choice of posh pseudonyms, so at odds with their lifestyles and personas, was some kind of in-joke, but I decided not to ask.

Giles explained that the location for what he pretentiously called 'the intervention' had been chosen not only because it was on my daily commute, but also due to the locks being closed for repairs over the winter. Had they been open, the items they planned to jettison would probably soon have been discovered by boaters when they drained the lock to descend or ascend the flight. As it was, they would remain submerged until the repairs were carried out, by which time the 'intervention' would be ancient history. Giles pointed out that, although there would be nothing to link the items in the lock with any of us, you couldn't be too careful.

The chosen lock was in an unusual location, tucked away under an office block, alongside its underground car park. The concrete canopy over the lock, formed by the ground floor of the building, was supported by two huge pillars, which would be used to our advantage. As discussed at the previous meeting, the building opposite provided a perfect vantage point from which the associate could observe the tableau unfolding. Giles had procured access to one of the top floor flats for the evening and Sebastian would provide the associate with the access code for the front door of the building and arrange for the door of the flat to be left unlocked. However, the double-glazed windows would all remain locked, and the window keys would be removed from the premises.

My instructions were to supply Giles with garments similar to those I normally wore on a working day in winter: a heavy woollen overcoat, sports jacket, tailored trousers and a white shirt. I was also asked to provide them with a laptop bag which resembled my own. I decided to buy a new bag, empty my current leather rucksack and give them that instead. It had seen better days and I had spotted a superb Tumi backpack in Harvey Nichols the previous day. It wouldn't leave me enough change from a grand to buy a bottle of champagne at the cocktail bar, but price wasn't an issue. Then, all I had to do was walk home as normal on the appointed night and wait for Sebastian and Barnaby to intercept me beside the lock.

Initially there would be a verbal altercation between myself and the two men, which the associate would be able to see, but not hear, as the double-glazed windows would be locked. I would shout back, attempt to side-step my assailants and apparently refuse to co-operate. Things would escalate rapidly, illustrated by lots of threatening body language and an eventual tussle, during which I would be dragged behind one of the concrete pillars. Then things would turn extremely nasty. Our spectator would be treated to the gruesome, albeit partially obscured sight of me being stabbed repeatedly and manhandled into the lock by Barnaby and Sebastian, who would toss my laptop bag in after me. Once they were sure body and bag had sunk without trace, they would promptly leave the scene. All I then had to do was remain behind the pillar for at least half an hour, to allow the associate enough time to panic, decide what to do, leave the apartment building and disappear into the night.

'Are you sure he'll just run away, Giles?'

'Trust me, Alex – I know this guy. He will charge out of that apartment block like a headless chicken, then one of two things will happen. Either he will simply run off, or he might try and take a closer look at the scene, but he won't be able to get beyond the railings on the other side of the road. They're too high to climb and there's no gate nearby.'

'Hang on. What if he decides to try and find his way onto the towpath, so he can take a proper look? He could discover me...'

'It's highly unlikely he'll do that, Alex, but I've arranged for cover at all the local access points, just in case. He won't get near you, I promise. Not that he'll even try. He'll be devastated by what he has just witnessed; after all, he will have set in train the events which led to someone's death. We'll have him precisely where we want him, and you'll have your freedom. You'll never hear from us again and no one will come looking for you.'

'What about when the lock gets repaired, and the body is discovered?'

'All the repair crew will find is a shop dummy full of holes and a laptop bag full of bricks. They find much worse in the canals, including real bodies.'

Sebastian fixed me with a malevolent gaze, to ensure the last point wasn't lost on me. He wanted me to know he didn't always restrict himself to mannequins, and I received the message loud and clear.

'My hunch,' continued Giles, 'is that the repair crew will just throw both items in the skip, but even if they do suspect foul play, there will be nothing to link it to us.'

Over the next few weeks I thought a lot about how I wanted the rest of my life to play out, and I made plans. By the time the day of the 'intervention' arrived, I was nervous, but even keener to break free of the past and make a fresh start. I was supposed to be at a business dinner that night, but I predicted the client would not report me missing for a single no-show. Once they had failed to reach me on my mobile, they would conclude I was either sick, or had got the date wrong, although there was no precedent for the latter. I don't make schoolboy errors like that. Whatever conclusion they reached, I imagined they would complain briefly, then get back to their guests. It was only when I failed to show up for work the next day that they would consider reporting me missing, but by then I would be long gone.

I bought the car off Gumtree for less than the cost of my new laptop bag. The owner wasn't the type to ask questions; all he wanted was cash in hand. I drove the ramshackle vehicle back to the Jewellery Quarter and packed it up, ready for our one journey together – to a tiny regional airport you've probably never used, unless you happen to live near it. From there I would fly to Amsterdam, then on to Dubai. I would leave the English winter behind, along with the other aspects of my life for which I had no further use.

On the last day of my old life I was very busy, with back-to-back meetings and fires to fight, so I didn't have time to dwell on what awaited me after I left the office. It was only when I pushed through the revolving doors of the client's office for the final time and felt the shock of the frigid night air that it hit me. For an instant I was tempted to run, but then I thought of the freedom which would shortly be mine, squared my shoulders and began my commute home.

Once I left the bars and restaurants behind, the towpath was almost deserted. In front of the National Indoor Arena a young woman scuttled past me, her face mostly hidden behind a voluminous scarf. After that I didn't see a soul. I normally used the torch app on my phone to light my way downhill, along the towpath beside the locks, but tonight I relied on the ambient light and kept to the left-hand side, away from the still, black water. Then I focused on walking confidently, with a firm tread and a sure step.

As I approached the chosen lock, with its concrete canopy, the place was deserted. No one stepped out from behind the pillars as agreed, to intercept and intimidate me. It appeared that Giles had abandoned our plan. I forced myself to keep walking purposefully on, thinking it would be unwise to let the associate, watching from his top floor flat, see me hesitate. If he was even there. My brain scrolled rapidly through a range of options, all of which led to the same conclusion. I realised I had been conned and a wave of anger surged through me. Then I heard footsteps behind me and before I could turn around, I was grabbed around the neck and thrown brutally onto the concrete towpath. My right elbow took the impact, my bag fell from my hands and the pain blurred my vision for an instant. When it cleared, I rolled clumsily onto my back and looked up into the sneering face of Sebastian.

'That wasn't supposed to happen, Sebastian! You were meant to step out from behind the pillar!'

'Yeah well – it wouldn't have been a surprise, then, would it? And I don't have any confidence in your acting skills, mate. We've got to make this look real, haven't we?'

I struggled to my feet. These days I rarely notice Stella's handiwork and am completely accustomed to my prosthesis, but at that moment I could have used two fully functional legs. Nevertheless, rage helped propel me upright. Furious, I ignored the pain and threw myself at Sebastian. I lashed out wildly with my fists and he blocked me effortlessly, every time. Then he laughed.

'You're energetic, mate, I'll give you that, but you can't fight to save your life. You remind me of those two daft gits in that film the wife made me watch. "Bridget Jones", that's the one. Right – enough messing about. Time to get serious. Try and punch me – properly, this time.'

I gave it my best shot. I like to think I can handle myself, despite my disability, but Sebastian is a professional, so I feel no shame in recounting how he swatted my blows away like flies, moving closer each time, until he was right in my face. Then he jabbed his finger into my chest.

'Pick up your man bag, mate – and try to look defeated. Shouldn't be too hard.'

Even though I knew it wasn't for real, I was shaking with anger as I lifted up my laptop bag, clutched it defensively against my chest and obediently bowed my head.

'Good, Alex. You look like a dog that's been whipped, but I reckon you need to get a second wind, as it were. We need to show our friend at the window that you're down, but not out. Come on, office boy. Have another go. Try and sidestep me, like we agreed.'

I did as he said, but once again was easily rebuffed. Sebastian planted himself in my path, grabbed the lapels of my overcoat and yelled in my face.

'Right, chum – here we go. We're done with the foreplay. When I let go of your coat, you clout me with that bag of yours and I'll go down like a sack of spuds. When I get back up, you'll get your one and only chance to have a real pop at me. One punch – that's all you get. After that, my mate Barnaby joins the proceedings, then it's game over.'

I swung my laptop bag with as much force as I could muster. I was no longer acting, which I'm sure was Sebastian's intention. The bag connected squarely with the side of his head and down he went. I don't think he was acting either. His enraged roar sounded real enough, and as he sprung to his feet I realised the gloves were off, but I stood firm and delivered a solid left hook. Sebastian staggered backwards, towards the lock, but managed to stay upright. At that point instinct took over and I surged forward, trying to press home my advantage, but Sebastian was right. I only got one punch.

I never saw Sebastian's wingman step from behind the pillar. I didn't realise Barnaby was in play until he grabbed me from behind in a standing headlock and forced a gag into my mouth. I fought back for real; frustration and nascent fear made the experience savagely realistic. This scenario was not proceeding according to plan. Then the realisation struck me. The mannequin was a ruse, and I was the intended victim. My legs gave way from the shock, Barnaby's wiry arms caught me as I fell, and I kicked and struggled in vain as the two of them dragged me behind the pillar. The knife in Sebastian's hand flashed like a silver fish as he raised his arm backwards in a wide arc, then stabbed repeatedly with a downward motion. I thought the blade caught me, just once, but I later discovered I was wrong. I must have imagined it.

'That ought to do it.'

Sebastian slid the knife into the inside pocket of his coat, then he and Barnaby picked up the mannequin at either end. Either man could easily have dragged it across the ground, but it was essential to give the impression of strenuous effort and they did the job well. Laboriously they hefted the corpse into the lock, where it sank instantly. Next Sebastian picked up my old laptop bag and slung it in with a splash. A genuine effort was required this time; there must have been a lot of bricks in there. Finally, without a word, they walked calmly away in opposite directions; Sebastian uphill and Barnaby downhill, in the same direction as I was headed.

Behind the pillar, I pressed my body against the damp roughness of the concrete. Now the violence was over, the pain in my right elbow clamoured for attention, but I fought the urge to move. I didn't even allow myself the luxury of a shiver, although the cold crept in through the sole of my foot and the icy mist which had settled on the canal plastered my hair damply against my skull. The cars on the ring road were a muted soundtrack from another world.

Suddenly, I heard a different noise. It was sharper, more urgent – and nearer. A door had slammed in the apartment block opposite. Fast footsteps headed in my direction, then stopped. I held my breath and listened to the other man breathing. The sound was ragged and uneven, more like a series of gulping sobs. The footsteps sounded again, but this time they had no purpose. I pictured the lone figure, pacing up and down in front of the railings like a zoo animal, desperate and directionless. I knew then that I was safe. Giles had been right. This was a man in turmoil, who posed no threat. He had lost and I had won. I knew he would leave, sooner or later. All I had to do was wait.

I didn't have to wait long. Soon after, the footsteps retreated up the hill, back towards the National Indoor Arena where I had encountered the girl with the scarf, what seemed like years earlier. It was a long time before I could summon the courage to detach myself from the cold concrete and abandon my hiding place. When I eventually picked up my laptop bag and stepped out onto the deserted towpath, my icy legs would no longer co-operate. The purposeful gait I had adopted on the way down the towpath was no longer an option. Chilled and fearful, all I could do was scuttle away.

It's difficult to recall the cold now, as I relax on a hotel terrace overlooking Jumeirah Beach, enjoying a cocktail and a hookah pipe. The sun and heat have rendered the physical sensations of that night much less vivid, but I will never forget I didn't cover myself in glory. I could have invented a different version of events, but I promised to be truthful with you, and in any case I don't trouble myself with regret over my supposed failings or mistakes. Like guilt, regret is a waste of time, and I have far better ways to spend my new life.

When I first arrived in Dubai, I took my time and made sure I got acquainted with the right people. This patient approach paid off; gradually I acquired some lucrative business interests and established myself in the ex-pat community. I moved out of my hotel into a luxury apartment near the beach and bought a convertible sports car. These days I water-ski, drive over to Jebel Ali and journey into the desert. I enjoy bottomless brunch on a Friday, always with the option of unlimited alcohol. Sometimes, I'll segue straight from brunch to a casual hook-up with an ex-pat girl looking for a good time, with no strings attached. I work on my tan. I enjoy my life.

I bide my time.

20 REPAYMENT PLAN

So here we are again. As you know, Sergeant Dave Langley paid me a visit, so I figured I should tell you what happened next, to me and my brother. Don't imagine we just walked off into the sunset. You know us too well to expect a happy ending like that.

Let me take you back to my visit from Dave, the rozzer and superfan. After he told me about the drowned shop dummy, the laptop bag and the loyalty card, I cried. Did they tell you that? If anyone had predicted I'd bawl my eyes out in front of a rozzer one day, I'd have said they were barking, but it's true. Sure, none of that stuff that went down was my fault, but even so I was obviously glad I hadn't played a part in someone's death – not even a lowlife like Alex. Dave caught me out, that was all. He obviously thought the tears were out of character, and couldn't understand the reason for the waterworks, but I made up some crap about hormones and the change, and he backed right off. That kind of talk always freaks out guys like Dave.

After he left, I fancied talking it over with Dan, who luckily was in the studio when Dave dropped by, but obviously I couldn't. I hadn't told him anything about what happened that night, so I had to keep my mouth shut. No point in him finding out now; not when it was all sorted. I decided that from now on I'd have an open and honest relationship with Dan. He's different from all the others, so it feels wrong to keep secrets from him. Wish me luck.

I reckoned the best thing to do was go and see my brother on his boat and tell him the whole story in person. We hadn't really been in contact – not surprising, given everything that had gone down – and I wasn't sure if he'd pick up, so I texted him.

Me: Bro – I need to see you. Be on your boat tomorrow lunchtime. Don't bring Holly or Stevie.

Nathan: I'm not up for a social call, Nan. Sorry.

Me: I get that, but you need to hear this. Don't want to discuss over the phone. Nothing to worry about...

Nathan: I don't worry any more, sis. There's no point. The worst has already happened. OK – I give in. I'll be there.

Then I walked down to the studio, which is hidden in a forgotten corner of the marina. Ron and Joyce keep a bunch of chickens down there, and those birds are pretty much feral. I dodged my way between them and climbed in via the prow of the boat. As I entered the studio, Dan turned around and beamed. He's always so pleased to see me.

'Nan! I'm glad you showed up. I need you to re-record some vocals for me.'

'Sure. Dan, I'm going over to visit my brother tomorrow.'

'Good call. It's about time you two patched things up.'

'Yeah, well – I hope we can.'

'Just be patient with him, Nan – and try not to get wound up. D'you want to borrow my car?'

'Only if you're sure. I haven't driven in a long while. I'm worried I might prang the thing.'

'Course you won't. It'll all come back to you. Just wait and see.'

'OK, then. Thanks.'

'No problem. Right, have you got time to record these vocals?'

'Sure. Let me get a glass of water, then I'm good to go.'

It took us the rest of the day, and most of the evening, to get the vocals just right, which was cool with me. When I'm in the recording studio, I can't think about anything else, but later on in bed, as Dan snored away, I replayed what Dave Langley had said and told myself it was for real. After all, I had seen the photographic evidence, which proved that Alex faked his own death, with the help of those drug dealing snakes, and was out there somewhere. Still, I couldn't silence the small voice in my head which played in a loop, like one of Dan's chord sequences he lays down in the studio. Over and over again, it asked me:

'Are you sure?'

I didn't get much sleep that night. Next morning, I just wanted to head on out of there, which isn't like me. I'm not normally a morning person. Dan usually leaves me and my bad temper behind, but that morning he obviously reckoned I couldn't make the short journey to Foxton without breakfast. I let him make me coffee and toast, then told him to sod off to the studio and fed my toast to the ducks. After that I grabbed his car keys and left.

I had lots of time, which was just as well, as I was right about my driving. Dan was dead wrong when he predicted it would 'all come back' to me. As I drove across the car park, I crunched the gears and mangled the clutch like you wouldn't believe. Dan's car hopped out of the marina entrance like a boxing kangaroo, narrowly missing a van coming past in the opposite direction. Palms sweating, I weaved my way towards the Leicester Ring Road. Even for experienced drivers, this circuit is a form of torture, designed by sadistic town planners, but for someone like me, who doesn't dare look at the road signs in case they kill a pedestrian, it was a nightmare. I must have gone round the bloody loop at least three times and I was losing the will to live. I don't reckon I would ever have escaped, except I got lucky and spotted a fancy van with 'Foxton Flowers' on the side, so I followed it, hoping it was heading back to base. It was a smart move; before long I was on the A6 heading in the right direction, so I relaxed and followed the daffs and dahlias all the way to my destination.

I parked up near the canal basin. I was sure there was another car park closer to Nathan's boat, but I didn't trust myself to find it. Besides, I was strung out after the drive, so I figured a walk along the canal towpath, up the hill past the locks and out into the countryside, would help me get my head together before I faced my brother.

By the time I reached the top lock, I was knackered. I'm not the fittest, as I've told you before. I took time out to get my breath back and pretended to admire the view; fifty miles of patchwork fields to the north and a jaunty queue of narrowboats to the south. The lock keeper opened the gate for a solo boater, and I helped the guy on his downward journey to the next lock. I realised the next time I walked past here, my brother would be in a better place and able to get on with his life. Once I'd recovered from my uphill climb, I carried on down the towpath and left Foxton behind.

The walk was longer than I expected; at least two miles. I don't do long walks; I should have made the effort and parked closer. By the time I spotted Festina Lente, moored up alongside a farmer's field on the other side of the canal, I was gasping for a cold beer. Just as well I was driving and couldn't drink. I needed to keep a clear head for my conversation with Nathan.

My brother must have been looking out for me. As I approached, he leaned out of the side hatch.

'Over the bridge, Nancy – then through the farmyard.'

I figured that with my luck, I'd get mauled by some farm animal before I even had a chance to talk to Nathan. I picked my way through the cow pats, keeping an eye out for the beasts that had deposited them on the concrete, but they must have been shut away in a barn or a field, as I made it through the yard and onto the boat in one piece.

My brother had been painting. A fancy water can was drying on his workbench and he was cleaning his paintbrush with white spirit as I climbed in through the side hatch. He didn't stop when he saw me; Nathan has always been manic about his brushes and it meant he didn't have to look me in the face.

'If this is about that business at Farmer's Bridge, Nancy, I don't want to hear it. It's in the past, as far as I'm concerned. There's nothing we can do to change things, so there's no point in talking about it.'

'You're wrong, bro. Just listen. When Alex went missing, the police looked into it, but they drew a blank.'

'That's something, I suppose.'

'The thing is, they recently got some new information, so they've reopened the investigation.'

'Is that supposed to make me feel better?'

'It is. Let me explain. DS Langley, one of the rozzers who interviewed me, back when I was helping Stella, came to see me again. He told me his boss, the woman who was leading that original investigation, is working in Birmingham. On a temporary basis, like. When the cops there checked their records they picked up on her connection to Alex and asked for advice about his disappearance.'

'So the police are all joined up, for a change. This just gets better and better. I'm going to end up back inside, Nan. I can feel it.'

'No, you're not. Anyway, the Farmer's Bridge flight was shut for repairs, like it often is in winter.'

'Yeah – I know. I saw the sign, when I was over there.'

'OK. So, the Canal and River Trust drained one of the locks to repair the brickwork – and guess what they found?'

'What?'

'A shop dummy, dressed in business clothes and punched full of holes.'

'Man or woman?'

'Man.'

'And you know this – how?'

'DS Langley showed me the photographs. He said they just got lucky. One of the Canal and River Trust volunteers used to be a rozzer himself, so he stopped the others from chucking it in the skip and called it in to his old mates down at police headquarters.'

'OK. Some poor sod's business went tits-up, so he decided to fake his own death in order to claim on the insurance money. What's that got to do with me?'

'I'd have thought the same, bro – except they found something else down there.'

'What did they find?'

'A fancy laptop bag, which had seen a lot of wear and tear. The thing was empty – apart from the bricks someone had used to weigh it down. It had tons of pockets, and they had all been cleared out – apart from one small item.'

'What was it?'

'One of those frequent flyer loyalty cards. It was a silver one; I reckon its owner had been upgraded to gold, on account of his being a master of the universe, so he just shoved the silver one in a pocket and forgot about it. Want to know whose name was on the card?'

'Dunno. Surprise me.'

'I thought you'd show a bit more enthusiasm, bro. The name on the card was Alex Pitulski.'

Nathan dropped his perfectly clean paintbrush into a jam jar with the others. He wiped his hands on a grubby old tea towel, then sat down opposite me and looked at me properly for the first time.

'I remember what Alex was wearing on the night. He had a long overcoat on, as it was the middle of winter and freezing cold – and he was carrying a laptop bag. I remember thinking it looked quite heavy – but not like it was full of bricks.'

'Well it wouldn't do, would it – 'cos there was a similar bag, containing said bricks, hidden away behind those concrete pillars, ready to be used in an exclusive performance for an audience of one.'

'So what you're saying is they set me up, Nan. They made it look as though the whole thing had spun out of control and they had stabbed Alex to death, when in reality he must have been hiding behind the pillar when they chucked the dummy and his old laptop bag into the lock.'

'Correct.'

'And he was supposed to empty the bag beforehand, so there would be nothing that could be used to identify him...'

'Or use a new bag – except he wouldn't do, would he? A guy like Alex would see it as a good opportunity to upgrade his fancy man bag and chuck the old one...'

'Except he screwed up and left behind an incriminating piece of evidence.'

'Yep. Dude's not as bright as he thinks he is.'

Nathan leaned back and rested his head against Festina Lente's wooden panelling. He closed his eyes and sighed deeply. When he opened them again, they were bright with tears.

'So I'm not responsible for Alex's death.'

'No, Nathan. No one died, so you can stop feeling guilty...'

'...and start feeling stupid for having been completely outmanoeuvred.'

'That's one way of putting it. You were duped, good and proper – but I bet you'd rather feel stupid than guilty.'

'Too right. Thanks, sis – for coming over to see me like this. I don't think it would have sunk in, if you'd just told me over the phone.'

'You probably wouldn't have answered the phone in the first place. You haven't been doing – not lately.'

'True. Sorry, sis – for blaming you.'

'Not a problem. Let's move on.'

'Good idea. I'll make a start. Fancy a cup of tea?'

'Yeah – put the kettle on.'

While the kettle was boiling, I rolled a couple of cigarettes for us and speculated on the gang's motives.

'So I guess the boss Giles did his homework, figured Alex was worth a bit of cash and decided to have a little chat with him. I reckon he offered Alex the chance to disappear and make a fresh start – for a big fat fee. They were in it together – that's my take on it.'

'I'm sure you're right, Nan – but I guarantee it's not the full story.'

'How d'you mean?'

'Giles wouldn't go to all that trouble, just to make some cash. He's got plenty of other sources of income.'

'So why did he bother, then?'

'Isn't it obvious? He saw a perfect opportunity to get back at me, for refusing to play ball when I encountered Sebastian at Fradley Junction, then for trying to get him to do what I wanted by helping those two women get rid of Alex. My worst mistake was threatening him with Ray. I'm sure that's when Giles decided he had to do something about me. I reckon he had it all figured out, even before I left that gin bar where we met.'

'Had what figured out?'

'Giles knows me, Nan. He can read me like a book, and he knows the best way to keep me quiet is through guilt. He understands that if I think I've caused someone's death, albeit unintentionally, I'll blame myself, slink away and never surface again. There'll be no more requests or threats. And that's just how it happened. It would all have worked perfectly, if Alex hadn't slipped up.'

'But he did – so now you know.'

'Unless the shop dummy and the laptop bag are unconnected.'

I decided not to share my doubts from last night. 'Get real, bro. You saw them both get chucked in the lock. You know they're connected! Don't try and snatch defeat from the jaws of victory. Go back to Holly and Stevie – and enjoy the rest of your life.'

Nathan placed two mugs of tea on the workbench. Then he came and sat on the sofa next to me.

'Give me a hug, sis.'

'What's brought this on? We don't do hugs.'

'I know. Call it my way of saying sorry – for what I'm about to do.'

'What are you on about?'

'I can't just leave it, Nancy. The fact is – Alex will resurface at some stage and the whole thing will kick off again...'

'Sure, but you don't need to get involved – and I won't, either. Stella and Jennifer can look after themselves from now on, and you've got Holly and Stevie to think about.'

'I know, but I have to make a stand – and not because of Alex. Don't you see? If I don't, I'll live the rest of my life wondering when Giles and his mates will come calling.'

'They won't, bro. I'm sure they'll leave you alone from now on.'

'Are you really sure, Nancy? Come on. You know what these people are like.'

Nathan was right. The awkward sod.

'Nan, you've always lived life head-on. It's me who's been passive and weak – and look where it got me. There's only one way to earn my freedom and enjoy the rest of my life, and that's to take them on. That means no more lies. I'm going home now to tell Holly the full story about my trip to Birmingham last winter. I told her I was going to catch up with some old friends, but she deserves to know the truth. Maybe she'll leave me, or perhaps she won't, but at least I won't feel guilty anymore about lying to her.'

I hadn't been expecting this. I thought my brother would just be dead relieved by my news, then get on with his life, but instead the guilt-ridden hermit had been replaced by a fearless avenger. I wasn't sure which was worse. 'Let me come with you. I'll tell Holly it was my fault; that it was me who asked you to contact Giles. She can take it out on me. I deserve it.'

'Thanks, sis. That might help a little. Drink your tea. Let's go.'

So we locked up Festina Lente, crossed the farmyard and the red-brick bridge, then followed the towpath back to Foxton. When we reached the canal basin and the two pubs overlooking the water, the lunchtime shift was in full swing, so I suggested we stop for a beer before confronting Holly. I reckoned I could have one and still drive, but Nathan was having none of it, so on we went.

Holly was working from home, hunched over her laptop at the dining table. She looked up and smiled when she saw Nathan, but she stopped smiling the moment she spotted me and twigged something must be up. She flipped her laptop shut and took a seat on the sofa. My brother sat next to her and held her hand while he explained the real reason for his trip to Birmingham over the winter. While he was talking, she pulled her hand away.

'I always thought you had told me everything, Nathan. Ever since that night when I drove you back from Stratford and you confessed how you'd been to prison twice. I could tell it scared you to open up like that, and I admired your courage and honesty. That was when I decided to risk trusting you. It was tough for me to make that decision, after everything I'd been through with Stevie's dad, but I always thought it was the right call – until a few months ago. I've known for ages something wasn't right, but I couldn't put my finger on it. Now I see why. Turns out it was the wrong call, after all.'

I didn't give my brother a chance to reply. Instead I jumped in with both feet. I'm not big on blaming myself, but I figured in this case needs must. I said it was all my fault as it was me who had asked Nathan to help out. It was no use, though. Holly just turned to Nathan and said:

'You could have said no.'

It's impossible to challenge the logic of people like Holly, who occupy the moral high ground, but Nathan did his best. He insisted he was going to turn his life around and make Holly proud by putting Giles and his villains behind bars and 'living authentically'. I wouldn't have resorted to psychobabble, but that's my brother for you. Then he told Holly he loved her, and would give anything if she'd stick by him, but he could understand if she preferred to walk away. After all, she had Stevie to think of. I could tell he was sincere, and I'm sure Holly could too, but still she wasn't impressed.

'Good of you to mention Stevie, Nathan. Whatever I do, she's going to get hurt. She loves you like a father, and she's not going to understand why you've left – just like her real father did. Like you promised you never would. What am I supposed to tell her?'

'Don't tell her anything, Holly! Just let me stay. We can work through this together. I love you both, so much. I promise you I'll never lie to you again. I'm going to put things right – just watch me. Please, Holly. Give me another chance.'

For a few minutes Holly said nothing. She just sat and stared at her feet. A few tears plopped onto her woollen slipper socks, but when Nathan tried to move closer she raised her hand to warn him off. When she finally spoke, her voice was very quiet, but the message was clear.

'Go back to your boat, Nathan – and take your sister with you.'

After that, we didn't hang about. My brother shoved a few things into a small bag, then we were out of there. As we walked back along the towpath, towards the car park where I had parked Dan's car, my brother sobbed and clutched my arm.

'I don't get it, bro. You didn't have to torpedo your entire life...'

'I did, Nan. You know I did.'

I couldn't leave him alone. Not in that state. Also, if I'm being honest, I realised I'd have a lot of explaining to do when I got back to Allenby. If my brother had decided to go all truthful on me, it meant I had to come clean with Dan. If nothing else, I didn't want Nathan to have to lie to Dan next time he saw him. I knew there was a chance I could end up getting dumped like my brother, although Dan's different from Holly. He hasn't always been an angel, so he doesn't see the world in black and white. I hoped he would forgive me, but I knew it would be a tough conversation and I wasn't in a hurry to have it.

When we reached the canal basin, I called Dan and told him I'd be staying the night on my brother's boat as we had a few things left to discuss. In his sexy Irish accent, Dan told me how chuffed he was that Nathan and I were talking properly again, and to take all the time I needed.

'A word of advice, Nan.'

'What's that?'

'Don't get too pissed – either of you. I know what you two are like. Trust me – it won't help.'

'Thanks, Oprah. See you tomorrow.'

Nice try, Dan, but you could have saved your breath.

Nathan and I stood side by side, staring at the two pubs overlooking the canal basin. Both were almost empty, as the lunchtime crowd had long since cleared out and it was too early for punters sneaking a cheeky after-work beer. Our preferred option was the low-key boozer to our right, but Nathan reminded me this was the pub where he had first met Holly, on that night when her online date failed to show up. That one was out, then. The other pub, larger and much fancier, was the tourists' favourite. It wasn't our style, but we had no choice, so we stumbled over the swing bridge, arm in arm. I installed Nathan at a window seat, then headed straight for the bar and ordered pints plus whisky chasers. Then we talked.

'So you're going to take a stand against Giles and his crew. Explain to me how you plan to do this.'

'Simple, Nan. I'm going to go back to Birmingham and find this police officer you told me about. The one who headed up the original investigation. I'll tell her everything I know. Help her take them on.'

'Are you mad, or has someone body-snatched my brother? Think back to when we were growing up, Nathan. Nothing good ever came from talking to the rozzers. Anyone who did ended up in a whole heap of bother.'

'I know, but I've got to try. I can't fight these guys on my own; there are too many of them and Giles is way smarter than me. But I'm done keeping my head down and living my life in fear. It looks as though it's already cost me my relationship...'

'It might do the same for me.'

'I hope not, Nancy. Dan's good for you, and I don't want you to lose him, but if you do, we'll still have each other.'

I had to smile. 'Who'd have thought it, bro? You, me and a bunch of rozzers against the world?'

'I know. To be honest, I don't fancy our chances. I reckon Giles and his mates can run rings around the cops.'

'I agree, but seeing as you're determined to take them on, the officer you need to track down is called Dawn Burrows. Now get the beers in.'

Nathan brought us more beer and whisky, then we settled in for the evening and matched each other, drink for drink. Once we were done talking, we just sat and watched through the window as the twilight turned the canal water from muddy grey to charcoal black. The locks shut for the night and the few remaining spaces around the canal basin were soon filled with moored narrowboats. Some were a pristine labour of love for their proud owners. Others were shabby, with peeling paint and hulls pitted and scarred from countless collisions. One boat in particular caught my eye. It was a working boat, a bit like the one on which Nathan and I grew up. The owner was leaning against the tiller, smoking a roll-up and wearing the traditional billowing white shirt, woollen waistcoat and jaunty neckerchief, just like Nathan used to.

My brother nudged me.

'Looking at that working boat?'

'I am.'

'Brings back memories, doesn't it?'

'Yeah. Not all of them good.'

'Seen its name?'

'*Nemesis*. What about it?'

'I reckon it's a sign.'

'What are you on about?'

'Nemesis - the goddess of revenge. The celestial being responsible for divine retribution. There aren't many boats with that name. Funny we should see one now. That's why I think it's a good omen.'

My brother has always been the whimsical type; especially after a few drinks. I'm more down to earth. One thing's for sure – I'm not that optimistic. Not these days.

'Let's see, Nathan, shall we? Let's see.'

EPILOGUE

21 SCREW YOUR COURAGE

The walk from the station was not long enough. All too soon I found myself standing across the road from my destination. Opposite me was a concrete office block, with a big blue badge front and centre, above the main entrance. I looked around me, thankful that the pavement on both sides of the road was empty. Even so, I was acutely conscious of how conspicuous I was and knew I couldn't afford to hang around. I didn't want to be here, but now that I was, I had two choices. Either cross the road very soon, and walk through the door into that building, or give up.

I had spent the train journey questioning my choice of clothing. Nancy had advised me not to wear my one and only suit; the one I wore both times in court, when I was sentenced. She thought it would create bad vibes and make me approach this challenge with the wrong mindset, when what I needed was an attitude adjustment. This time round, I was on the side of the law, for better or worse, and I needed to act like it. So we decided I should dress to blend in. I needed to avoid looking like a boater and make like an average Joe who walks the streets of any city. On went my best jeans, a clean white T-shirt and the black leather jacket I bought with the money earned from my canal art. When I was ready, I called Nancy in. She looked me up and down, hands on hips.

'What d'you think, Nan?'

My sister smiled. 'The girls'll love it.'

'That's hardly the point.'

'You never know. It could help. You sure you want to do this, bro?'

'No, but I'm going to. I've told you all the reasons why.'

'Indeed you have. Plenty of times. OK then – get out of here, or you'll miss your train.'

Now that I was at my journey's end, trying desperately to summon up the courage to walk through that door, I realised that my concerns about clothing had been an irrelevant distraction. The only thing that mattered right now was the decision which confronted me. I knew that once I went in, there was no going back. I would unleash a chain of events I couldn't control. It was impossible to foresee the outcome and highly likely I wouldn't survive long enough to know how things ended. Undoubtedly it would be simpler – and safer – to keep my secrets to myself and live an uneasy, uneventful life.

I wiped my clammy palms on my jeans and turned away. I knew a quiet bar nearby. I'd have a few drinks, then catch the train home and tell my sister I'd reconsidered. I was sure she'd be mightily relieved.

It was all Shakespeare's fault.

As I began retracing my steps, Holly's face sprung to mind. As I'm sure you can imagine, she's never far from my thoughts, and I recalled the time we saw the Scottish play together in Stratford-upon-Avon, on the day she finally decided to trust me. Then I remembered what Lady Macbeth said to her husband, up there on stage, when she wanted him to man up. About courage and all that. Screwing it to the sticking place. I realise the blood-soaked duo are unlikely mentors, and things didn't end well for them, but nevertheless they reminded me that sometimes in life, you have to be courageous, even though courage usually comes with a side order of fear. As you know, I've struggled to make the right choices in the past – or any choices at all, in fact – but it was time for me to take control. So I changed my mind, turned around and walked through the door underneath that big blue badge.

I asked to speak to Detective Inspector Dawn Burrows. My voice quaked slightly as I answered the first, and easiest, of the many questions I would face.

'Yes. It is urgent.'

ABOUT THE AUTHOR

Felicity Radcliffe divides her time between a small rural village, where she lives with her husband and dog, and a narrowboat on England's beautiful canals. Broken Lock is her third novel; the sequel to Union Clues and the second in the Grand Union series.

MORE FREE STUFF...

Hello - thank you so much for reading Broken Lock. As with Union Clues, I'd love to know what you thought of it. I'm already working on the final instalment in the Grand Union trilogy, so your feedback would be very helpful. It might even influence the fates of my characters...

Please email me at **felicityradcliffebooks@gmail.com** to start our conversation. Alternatively, you can contact me via Facebook, Twitter or Instagram. Writing is a solitary process and I do get quite lonely at times, so it would be great to hear from you.

If you join my mailing list, I'll share a whole load of free stuff with you. I regularly send out short stories and poems, and I'll make sure you get a copy of each one. Most of my short stories are unrelated to the canals, as are many of my poems. However, I do have a long-term ambition to cover the entire canal network in poetry, and some of my poems revisit the locations in Union Clues and Broken Lock.

If you have enjoyed reading this book, please tell your friends and ask them to contact me. It makes my day when someone tells me that a friend recommended they read my books. It's also nice when I get reviews on Amazon, Goodreads and Bookbub, so please do leave me a review for Broken Lock. Whatever rating you choose to give, I value your opinion.

I'm looking forward to hearing from you. Thanks again for choosing Broken Lock.

Felicity Radcliffe
June 2021

Printed in Great Britain
by Amazon

26601349R00135